It's a gorgeous ride with a hell of a final shock

Star Magazine

'A fast paced story with a most unexpected twist'

Image Magazine

D0281217

Juliet Ashton

The Woman at Number 24

SIMON &
SCHUSTER

London · New York · Sydney · Toronto · New Delhi

A CBS COMPANY

First published in Great Britain by Simon & Schuster UK Ltd, 2017
A CBS COMPANY

3 5 7 9 10 8 6 4 2

Simon & Schuster UK Ltd
1st Floor
222 Gray's Inn Road
London WC1X 8HB

Simon & Schuster Australia, Sydney
Simon & Schuster India, New Delhi

www.simonandschuster.co.uk
www.simonandschuster.com.au
www.simonandschuster.co.in

A CIP catalogue record for this book
is available from the British Library

Paperback ISBN: 978-1-4711-5889-6
eBook ISBN: 978-1-4711-5890-2

Typeset in the UK by M Rules
Printed and bound by CPI Group (UK) Ltd, Croydon, CR0 4YY

This book is for Michael and Alison Anderson,
with my love and awe

The Woman at Number 24

Sarah's flat
A

Leo and Helena
B

Jane and Tom
C

Mavis
E

Lisa and Una
D

Prologue

ᗅONFUᗅIUᗺ FᗅKEᗅWᗅᖻ
Notting Hill, W11

This calendar is FREE to valued customers!
Friday 15th January, 2016

**BETTER TO LIGHT A CANDLE THAN
CURSE THE DARKNESS**

Sarah tried to leave straight after the registry office ceremony, but Leo wouldn't hear of it. He persuaded her to wait for the speeches back at the flat, then insisted she stay for the cutting of the cake. 'We'll have a boogie later,' he'd laughed as the music began.

No boogie had been had. Leo offered only scraps; a consolation prize that underlined what Sarah had lost. When she finally slipped away, Leo was engrossed in his bride. He didn't notice her leave, and nobody else tried to stop her; mostly they marvelled that she was there at all.

Out on the landing the bass banged in Sarah's ears as she eased off her shoes and rubbed her complaining toes. It was time to go home. Bed was all she wanted. Her chaste bed, no longer rumpled by the long legs of her man.

At least I don't need to call an Uber.

A flight of stairs was all that separated the wedding party in Flat B from Sarah's nest at the top of number twenty-four Merrion Road. The elegantly winding stairway sat like a spine at the centre of the house, the flats fanning out from it, one on each storey, except for the basement where heartless developers had crammed in two dwellings.

The bannister, polished smooth by two hundred years of use, was cool beneath Sarah's hands. The ascent seemed longer than usual, as if extra stairs had been stealthily added. She climbed with the careful weariness of an invalid, despite looking the picture of health in her tightly fitted, especially bought red dress. The bouquet in her hand drooped, splashing petals on the floor.

Had the bride thrown it directly at her? Sarah had had no option but to catch the flesh-coloured roses that flew at her face. There were shouts of 'You'll be next!' as the bridegroom gave her a complicated look. Sarah had been careful to look ecstatic; she'd acted her part well, but now the mask ate into her face and her bed beckoned from the top of the house.

'About time, missy!' A small spry figure of unguessable age barred the door to Sarah's flat.

'Hello, Mavis,' sighed Sarah.

'What are you all done up for? Don't tell me you went to the wedding?' Mavis was aghast, but delighted too, like a rubbernecker slowing to pass a road accident.

'Did you want something?' Sarah halted, fearing her legs

might not reboot. She felt as though she'd aged three decades on the stairs, the day's anguish eating into her bones and putting her on a par with her elderly neighbour.

'I've been knocking and knocking.' In her dusty dress Mavis was petulant, taking Sarah's absence personally. 'I had to sign for this letter while you were gallivanting.' She thrust an envelope at Sarah, in much the same way as the bride had propelled the posy. 'I do have a life of my own, you know.' Mavis's accent was from another age, imperious and entitled. 'I'm not a servant.'

'Thank you.' Sarah didn't ask why Mavis hadn't simply pushed it under the door. Past experience had taught her never to rise to the bait; Mavis drew nourishment from arguments, and right now Sarah needed peace.

'Aren't you going to open it?'

'Well, no.' Sarah almost laughed at such naked nosiness. 'I've had a long day, Mavis.'

'No need to snap, dear,' snapped Mavis. She stepped closer, peering into Sarah's eyes, which were carefully made up, their grey enhanced and their lashes lengthened.

The maquillage, the formal outfit, the new pashmina that kept slipping off Sarah's shoulders, were armour; she flinched as the wrinkled little woman's preternaturally bright eyes bored through her shield.

'You've been crying.' Mavis didn't ask why. Perhaps because it was obvious.

'Mavis!' A voice, clear high and bright, sounded from below.

3

'Keep your hair on!' shouted Mavis. She growled at Sarah: 'Bloody family. They think they own you.'

Inquisitive, Sarah leant over the bannister as Mavis plodded downwards.

Far below, a pale oval shone in the dark of the hallway. It was a woman's upturned face, austere and direct, whose eyes met Sarah's briefly before their owner stepped back into the shadows.

She was old, that much was clear even at such a distance, but she was beautiful in a timeless way, like a goddess from pagan times, whose gaze could save or destroy. She was familiar . . .

Recognition landed, and Sarah stirred with the almost sexual excitement that fame generates. 'Mavis! Isn't that—?'

'I'll tell you who that is, dear,' said Mavis, feet slapping on each step. 'None of your business. That's who that is.'

Fragile from the day's events, Sarah craved gentleness and comfort, proof that there was kindness in the world. Mavis was the opposite of what she needed so Sarah said nothing in response to the trademark rudeness and let herself into her own four walls.

Flat A was dark. The muted whoops and cheers bleeding up through the floorboards underlined its stale loneliness. Sarah imagined Leo down there, beneath her bare feet, showing off his new bride, agreeing that, yes, he truly was a lucky dog.

Peeling off the dress, Sarah exhaled gratefully. If the statistics were right and 42 per cent of modern marriages ended in divorce, she surely wasn't the first woman to attend her ex-husband's wedding. Sarah didn't feel modern; she felt like a child left at home on her own. She shook her lacquered hair, and confetti rained down around her.

With the lights off, the flat passed as normal. Darkness camouflaged the holes gouged in the walls and the wallpaper that peeled like leprous skin. The disarray accused Sarah, reminding her how behind she was with the plan to refurbish, sell up, and move on. It wasn't her plan. It was Leo's. *I agreed*, she reminded herself. A countdown ticked constantly beneath all her conversations, beneath every film she watched or book she tried to read. It was ominous, growing louder as it raced towards her deadline. August. Sarah had until the end of August to renovate the flat.

The moonlight glanced off the cheap glossy paper of the calendar tacked to the wall. The staff at Confucius, a Chinese takeaway near enough to trot to in slippers, had handed over the calendar with reverence; Sarah had felt mildly embarrassed at being one of their best customers. She reached out and tore off the top page, glad to see the back of a date that had lain in wait for her.

Littered with paint cans and stepladders, the bedroom felt abandoned, as if Sarah had moved out with Leo.

'But I'm still here!' said Sarah, defiantly tugging on her towelling dressing gown and pulling its soft collar to her chin. When she switched on her lamp, the room remained obstinately dark. She thought of the Post-it note reminding her to buy bulbs lying somewhere in the rubble. Finding a candle under the kitchen sink, she remembered the quote on the calendar and agreed that, yes, it *was* better to light a candle than curse the darkness. She climbed into bed, the walls wobbling around her in the flickering light.

In the candle's chivalrous glow, she couldn't see the half-sanded floorboards or the drooping curtain pole. On the bedside table, it prettily illuminated the Registered letter that Mavis had given her. Wondering what could be so important that it needed a signature, Sarah ripped it open.

The folded page was brittle, as befits a letter from a ghost.

Chapter One

The removals van and the hearse jammed the narrow street, both drivers refusing to give way. This was a busy day for number twenty-four; one couple moving in, another occupant very much moving out.

Double-fronted, strictly symmetrical, the Georgian house shimmered in summer's arms. Painted a pale blue, it belonged on a whimsical lane by the sea, not a traffic-choked side street in Notting Hill. The façade had seen better days.

Haven't we all? thought Sarah, staring down at the stand-off from her top-floor window. Hopefully, Mavis was still indoors, unaware that her sister's coffin was involved in a road-rage incident. Even the corpse's celebrity status couldn't protect it from this final indignity.

The only black jacket in Sarah's wardrobe was too wintry to wear. Forecasters promised – or threatened – ever higher temperatures as summer hit its stride. Number twenty-four, a veteran of every season, withstood the heat with insouciance, standing tall and still in the heavy air.

'You'll do.' Sarah snatched a navy sundress from the clothes rail she'd bought as a temporary alternative to a wardrobe two years ago. The last funeral Sarah had attended was her father's, and she recalled her mother's defiantly white coat. Sarah had been in black, the colour of crows and bad dreams. She'd avoided it ever since.

Adjusting a borrowed black hat in the pitted mirror propped against the pitted wall, Sarah tucked up her brownish blondish hair and pronounced herself ready. Confucius was worrying himself over nothing; the birds of sadness would never dare nest in such an untidy up-do. Sarah's childhood had knocked any physical vanity out of her. Today of all days it seemed disrespectful to fuss over her appearance.

One hand on the balustrade, Sarah picked her way downstairs in heels that were probably too high for such a solemn occasion. She hurried past Flat B, its glossy front door leaking classical music. Down at street level, the scuffed door to Flat C was wedged open by a pile of boxes. Bulky new furniture stood around like tongue-tied guests in the sitting room Sarah knew so well.

Framed prints, bold and colourful, were stacked against a shipwrecked sofa. A framed wedding photograph was at the forefront. In *de rigueur* black and white, the house's new couple smiled out at Sarah, having so much honest-to-goodness fun they were slightly out of focus.

Lovebirds.

Sarah hated how her lip curled but was powerless to stop it. The glowing pair weren't to know that Sarah's relationship with Flat C's previous tenant had helped kill her marriage. Smith had taken off in a black cab six months ago, but Sarah still managed to forget some days, to expect the familiar tread on the stair and the raucous laugh in the small hours.

The letter sent by Smith had arrived with exquisite timing, salvaging the black, bleak day of Leo's wedding. Sarah had it with her now; it went everywhere with her, even gate-crashing a funeral.

Pausing at the front door, as if at the border of a foreign land, Sarah's fingers delved in her handbag and found the letter.

There was no salutation, no signing off, just a few scrawled lines on a page torn from a diary. Sarah had committed every word to memory, like a poem from her schooldays.

If I can't see you then I have to write to you! I have no news, no nothing except some advice which you must take to heart. Promise? Be yourself, because, my sweet Sarah, you are more than good enough. And always find the beauty in everybody, because that's the magic formula to make everything A-OK.

He didn't sign it 'Love from' because he didn't have to.

The magic formula was trickier than it sounded. Finding the beauty in people could be mistaken for schmaltz, but Sarah noted that it was 'everybody'. Not just the beauty in the people she liked – that was easy – but the beauty in curmudgeons and trolls.

Speaking of which . . . alone at the kerb, Mavis was all in black, her moth-eaten winter stockings cocking a snook at the warm weather. She constituted Sarah's biggest challenge yet to invoking the magic formula.

As Sarah edged into the old lady's line of vision, Mavis's headscarf turned a fraction. No eye contact, of course: a little thing like death wouldn't change Mavis. But even an infamous harridan shouldn't go to a funeral alone, so Sarah took Mavis's loud sniff as an invitation to join her laying her only sister, the celebrated novelist Zelda Bennison CBE, in the earth.

Alongside the others at the graveside in black linen and swooping hats, Mavis looked like a charlady in her chain-store coat and face brutally bare. In accordance with Zelda's wishes, only a handful of mourners were present, each of them in deep shock. When Death visits, the reactions are the same, whether his victims are chic and moneyed, like Zelda's friends, or downright Dickensian, like Zelda's sister.

According to articles in the broadsheets, the novelist told nobody about the diagnosis of fast-acting motor neurone disease, not even Ramon, her husband of two years. Zelda had arrived to visit her sister at number twenty-four and never gone home, passing quietly away in the basement a few months later. Sarah had seen Zelda coming and going for the first few weeks, but after that Zelda kept indoors as her health deteriorated.

Aloof from the others, Mavis stared into the grave. The small slice of face visible beneath her scarf looked not grief-stricken but angry, as if she wanted to claw up the fresh mud and give Zelda a good telling-off.

On the far side of the mound of earth, a handsome dark-skinned man who pulsed with charisma dabbed at his eyes. 'That's the husband,' whispered a woman behind Sarah. The widower was thirty something years his wife's junior. From the *tsk*, Sarah deduced she wasn't the only one unconvinced by the eye dabbing.

Mavis was in a bleak world of her own as the coffin was lowered. She took no notice of the elegant assemblage, and hadn't greeted her brother-in-law. Edging forward, Sarah stood shoulder to shoulder with the bristling woman, even though Mavis's body language screamed *Keep away!* Sarah didn't need her qualifications in psychology to diagnose Mavis. Sarah was an expert in loss; she knew what it looked like close up.

The letter backed her up silently from the depths of her bag, urging her to see past the hostility to the humanity.

At the end of the short ceremony the small party turned as one. Sarah took Mavis's arm on the hard, uneven ground. Mavis shook her off and picked her way, head down, through the gravestones.

When they arrived at number twenty-four the mourners tailed Mavis up the stone steps, across the black and white chequered floor of the communal hall, and down a short flight of stairs to the gloomy basement level. Sarah saw the door of Flat D open a crack, then slam; a quiet civil war raged between the subterranean neighbours.

As if to underline how very alive they were, the handful of people murmured about a good cup of tea or a stiff drink. As Mavis searched for her key, a powerful communal hunger overtook them all – an affirmation on a macabre day.

With quiet optimism, Sarah anticipated a vol-au-vent, a retro classic which had lost its cachet apart from, she hoped, at funeral teas.

The widower had disappeared without a word. The guest who'd tutted said to whoever was listening, 'At least Ramon had the decency not to take over the funeral.'

'I should have been with Zelda when she died,' said another mourner, a small woman with a querulous face. 'We should *all* have been there. Why did she keep her illness secret? Why choose to die *here*?'

A rumble of agreement ran through the group, who

all seemed surprised to find themselves in such humble surroundings.

'She came home to her family,' said Sarah, hoping Mavis was too engrossed in undoing the six locks on her door to hear the exchange. 'It's only natural.'

Which made Sarah unnatural. She couldn't imagine a situation so dire that she'd flee to her one remaining family member.

Another woman stage-whispered, 'Accidental overdose, my eye. The Zelda I know . . .' She faltered, recovered. 'The Zelda I *knew* was fastidious. She did nothing by accident.'

Mavis let herself into her dark flat, closing the door behind her with a surly *clunk*. Sarah looked uncertainly at the others, who looked uncertainly back.

The great Zelda Bennison's funeral was over.

Chapter Two

Cinema-goers the world over feel as if they know Notting Hill. The place has a distinct sense of self. Dotted with trees despite the exhaust fumes, it's a borough of extremes: poverty and wealth; Cool Britannia and unemployment; carnival and riot.

The imposing houses built for olde-worlde society families fell into disrepair over the centuries, their grand salons carved into bedsits. After waiting patiently for the tide of gentrification to turn and snatch them back from renting singletons, their dazzling façades were now restored. But turn a corner and you were in the concrete tundra of a housing estate, or a mews that once housed horses but now housed advertising executives happy to forgo a garden for a W11 postcode.

14

Notting Hill catered for all tastes and pockets; within minutes of Sarah's front door she could buy – if she wanted to – vintage fashion, mind mind-altering drugs, and Pringles. Perfectly embodying this split personality, number twenty-four was a magnificent example of Regency architecture, but the glorious blue of its exterior was in need of a touch-up, and the windows reflected the differing fortunes of the residents.

Sarah's own windows were painted shut. Flat B's tasteful double glazing glittered in the sunshine, bespoke blinds standing to attention. Another floor down, Flat C's frames were rotten; Smith hadn't prioritised home improvements.

Pacing her sitting room, Sarah's arms were clasped about herself. It was unusual to be home from work at this time of the day; the flat seemed startled by her. Needing distraction, she noticed the 'Welcome' card she'd bought and went in search of a pen.

Her writing was shaky. She paused, took a deep breath and started again. The events of the morning had rattled her to her core. She'd dashed out of her office as if she was being chased by wolves, ignoring her supervisor's shouts. Now unanswered calls from Keeley stacked up accusingly on her phone.

Sarah licked the flap of the envelope and stole down two flights, passing from lino and the smell of Cup-a-Soup on her own landing, to carpet and a melange of fig and ylang-ylang outside Flat B. Her steps slowed as she reached the ground floor.

Flat C had been out of bounds since Smith's departure. Sarah dreaded seeing the familiar flat altered; another small proof that, despite the letter in Sarah's bag, Smith was gone for good.

The door stood open, the brass 'C' wonky. A diminutive woman, her back to Sarah, hands on hips, gave orders to somebody out of sight. 'No, no, not there, *there*.' Thanks to the mail on the communal table, Sarah knew that this bossy child-sized person was one half of Mr and Mrs T. Royce.

'Hello!' Sarah knocked needlessly on the open door, taking in the sitting room, its familiar kitsch wallpaper already obliterated by white emulsion.

The woman wheeled round, a smile already curving across an elvish face, her eyes wide at the sight of her visitor. 'Come in, come in!' She ushered Sarah into the chaos of packing cases. 'Christ, this mess. Sorry. We're still upside down.'

'I'm Sarah, from ...' Sarah pointed upwards.

'Heaven?'

'Top flat.' Sarah smiled; the cheer was infectious, and the power of the morning's crisis faded a little. She held out the card. 'To say, you know, welcome.'

'Oh, wow.' The woman put the card to her chest. The red of her closely cropped hair was nearer to ketchup than titian. 'Aren't you lovely? I'm Jane, by the way. Oh, and this is ...' She gestured at a tall man almost buckling under a box of books. 'Oh God, I've forgotten your name.' Jane apologised with an exaggerated gurn and turned to Sarah. 'But of course you two know each other. He's Mr Flat B.'

'Yes, yes, we know each other.' Sarah returned Leo's nod, both of them flushed, his hair wilted with sweat.

'Are you finished with me, Jane?' Leo was hopeful, mopping his brow. The burgeoning paunch beneath his shirt didn't suggest physical stamina, and he seemed grateful when she set him free.

'I nabbed him, poor thing, when he was whistling his way up the path.' Jane put her arm through Sarah's, drawing her in, chatty and intimate. 'He *loved* me bossing him about. Something about that wifelet of his tells me who wears the designer trousers in *that* relationship. He's attractive, if you like that sort of tall, public-school, corduroy-trousers thing, which I don't. I'm a one-man woman, me. When you meet my husband you'll see why.'

Without preliminaries, Jane parachuted into Sarah's life. As a woman who weighed up pros and cons before committing to a toaster, Sarah enjoyed the heady speed of it.

'Here. Make yourself useful.' Jane handed Sarah an armful of hardbacks. 'Stick those on the shelves. Any order. Doesn't matter.'

New shelving covered a wall which Smith had plastered with cheap prints of Matisse and Hockney, alongside a fading Photo-Me strip: Sarah and Smith entwined, giggling, a bit tipsy.

Sarah held up a paperback. 'You a fan?' *Sword of Lightning* was a Chief Inspector Shackleton mystery. Even people who'd never read any of the fourteen Shackleton books were aware of Zelda Bennison, thanks to the TV series.

'I've read everything Zelda Bennison wrote. Absolute favourite writer in the world. She died last week.' Jane's smile melted. 'Very sad. Motor neurone disease. She kept it secret from everybody. A real class act. Her mind was going and the poor woman took too many tablets. It's horrible to think she must have suffered and, you know, fallen apart before she finally went.'

'That funeral, yesterday? That was Zelda Bennison.'

Jane couldn't readily process that, so Sarah enlarged.

'Zelda Bennison was Mavis's sister. Mavis is—'

'—the old bat in the basement?' Jane put her hands to her face. 'Zelda Bennison was her sister? But Mavis is . . .'

'Horrible.' There was no other word for it. Mavis tried hard to be horrible; she was good at it.

'Did you meet Zelda?' The idea excited Jane. 'Apparently she was amazing.'

Hating to disappoint, Sarah explained that she'd glimpsed Zelda a handful of times. Like a well-dressed spectre, the writer had flitted through the hall, exquisite and ageless – the polar opposite of her sister. 'She stopped appearing. I guess that's when things got bad.' Mavis had rushed in and out, harried, anxious. Her devotion had surprised Sarah.

'Were they close?'

'According to Mavis, Zelda abandoned her the moment she found success. There was bad blood between them.'

Sarah regretted not asking to meet the writer and tell her how much she admired her work; dying was nobody's idea of fun, but dying in Mavis's basement must have been gruesome.

'Sounds like they kissed and made up at the end.' The thought seemed to placate Jane. 'I must ask Mavis about her sister.'

'Seriously, I wouldn't.' Sarah smiled at Jane's gung-ho; it was the gung-ho of people who petted psychopathic chihuahuas despite the owners' warnings.

'I heard her having a screaming row with some man down in her flat. Must be a boyfriend or something.'

The notion of Mavis having a boyfriend was beyond comedy. 'Was it a sweary, nasty argument? Did he call her a scrawny old bird?'

'Yeah. I almost intervened.'

'That's Peck, her cockatoo. Named after his favourite hobby.' The bird's gothic cage dominated Mavis's hallway. 'He's a lot louder and even more vindictive since Zelda passed away.'

'Just you watch. Me and Mavis will be buddies before you can say—' Jane's face lit up as she looked beyond Sarah. 'Tom!'

Turning, Sarah took in the tall man at the door, holding aloft a carrier bag like the Olympic flame. So the 'T' stood for Tom.

'Sarah, you'll stay for chips?' asked Jane. 'Nobody in their right mind says no to a chip.'

'Um . . .' Sarah was tempted. The conversation had already picked her chin from the floor; chips would chase the fiasco at work even further away.

'And mushy peas,' said Tom. 'Plus the finest pickled onions.' He smiled and Sarah beamed her acceptance; they were good at smiling, these Royces. Sarah could see why Jane was a one-man woman; Tom was straight-up and wholesome. Broad-shouldered, with what Sarah thought of as a noble head, waving chestnut hair backing off his forehead, tawny eyes amused. She sensed he was aware of his height and width; Tom wasn't the sort of clueless berk who'd clomp along the street behind a woman on a dark night. Tom would cross the road.

Sarah wondered how she was gleaning all this information from one short exchange about chips.

'Sit. Sit.' Jane flapped her hands, righting the sofa. 'No plates. They taste better out of the paper.'

The peculiar picnic was cosy. With Jane at the helm, conversation bounced up, down, all around, taking in the fact that Tom had upholstered the very sofa Sarah sat on.

'I'm impressed.' Sarah blew on a chip. She'd never met a man who knew what piping was, never mind actually piped. Interrogated in a friendly way, Sarah told them she'd lived at number twenty-four for two years, that her flat was similar in layout to theirs but without the inconvenience of being near the front door. She remembered Smith's rueful joke about buying a doorman's uniform.

'Finding this place was a once in a lifetime deal.' Jane

named a figure that would terrify an out-of-towner but sounded like a bargain to Londoners trapped in the capital's crazy housing market. 'We've got such plans for this flat.'

Each improvement would bump Smith further into the past.

Tom said, 'Don't worry. There won't be too much kerfuffle.'

'I don't mind a bit of kerfuffle.' Sarah liked that word, and she liked Tom for using it. 'Besides, I have plans too. I'm moving out.'

'No!' Jane was wounded, as if they'd known each other years instead of minutes. 'But you've got the attic space. Sloping ceilings and the best view in the house, I bet.'

I'll miss the view, thought Sarah. She smiled, showing all her teeth, hoping it convinced. 'Time to move on.' The countdown tick-tocked beneath her words. A patchwork of botched DIY, the flat wasn't the home she'd envisaged. Since Smith, she barely interacted with her neighbours, racing upstairs to put her key in the lock each evening.

The clock was heartless. It didn't care that Sarah would be homeless; sure, she could find four walls and a roof, but if home is the place that when you go there they have to let you in, then Sarah had nowhere. She imagined her mother's face if she turned up with her suitcases and almost laughed. 'The flat goes up for sale in August.'

'Reconsider,' said Jane. 'You'd be mad to move out of this gem. Just look at these cornices.' She waved a pickled onion at the ceiling. 'And the wide floorboards.' She moaned low. 'And the *original marble fireplace*, for God's sake!'

'Jane's in property,' explained Tom. 'That's why she gets orgasmic about skirting boards.'

'I source houses for rich idiots who are too bone idle to look themselves.'

'I hope you don't put it that way on your website.' The comment earned Sarah a *We like her* glance between her hosts.

'The official term is property search consultant,' said Jane. She paused as if something had just occurred to her. 'I could help you find a new flat. For free, obviously.'

'Oh, no need,' said Sarah hurriedly. 'Honestly. It's fine.'

'I get first dibs on loads of properties before they even go on the market. I'd haggle for you as well. Aren't I brilliant at haggling, Tom?'

'She is,' said Tom reluctantly. 'She saves people a ton of money.'

'What are you after?' Jane was keen-eyed. 'One-bedder? Two? Are you fussed about outside sp—'

'Seriously,' said Sarah. 'It's all under control.' It was like discussing who to marry next before your current partner was dead; *I'm a one-flat woman*.

'OK, if you're sure,' said Jane, slightly puzzled at this refusal of her expertise. 'I've just nabbed a new client. Bags of dosh. Wants a country pile in Suffolk, so I'll be tootling all over East Anglia this summer.'

'Sounds like fun.'

'Why not come with me?'

Tom made a noise in his throat. 'Sarah might have a life of her own and a job and stuff.'

'I could be an axe murderer for all you know.' Sarah admired Jane's emotional recklessness.

'We kind of have to be friends don't we,' said Jane, 'living in the same house?'

It hadn't worked that way up to now, but Sarah found herself laughing and agreeing. When Jane asked if number twenty-four was a friendly place, she said nothing for a moment and Tom butted in.

'There's your answer!'

'It's a typical London set-up.' Sarah defended the house's honour. 'We don't get involved.'

'But you talk to Mavis.' Idealistic Jane tried to disprove Sarah's theory.

'Mavis more or less talks *at* me.'

'What about the other tenants?' Jane screwed up her chip paper, greedy for nourishment of a different kind. 'What's the gossip?'

'Jane . . .' There was a gentle warning in Tom's voice. 'Let's move in before you start inserting yourself into everybody's lives, yeah?'

'Shut up.' Jane combined fondness and irritation so expertly that Sarah envied the Royces their ease, their understanding, the self-confidence of a happy marriage.

'I'm not good at gossip.'

'Rubbish.' Jane was a Labrador; playful but apt to mow

you down. 'Everybody's good at gossip. Flat B. That smoothie Leo and the super-sexy wife. What's the deal there?'

'Only married for six months,' said Sarah. 'He's an antiques dealer, owns that big emporium round the corner, the Old Church, and she's an interior designer. Match made in heaven. Helena Moysova. You might have heard of her.'

'I could find that out from their CVs.' Jane was disappointed.

'See? Told you. Bad at gossip.'

Tom, who'd dipped out of the room, reappeared with a hammer. 'Jane'll soon train you up.'

Sarah thought idly: *He suits hammers.*

'Nitty-gritty, please,' said Jane. 'The husband seems a bit of a one, if you ask me.'

Sarah agreed that yes, Leo was a bit of a one, and was relieved when Jane moved on to the basement.

'Who lives opposite mad Mavis? Youngish woman with a little girl. I smell sadness there.'

Rooting noisily in a box of nails, Tom said, 'I think you'll find that smell is damp.'

'That's Lisa. She works part-time as a carer for the elderly.' Sarah spilled what few beans she had; Lisa had been living with a guy called Graham, who'd moved out under a cloud of bad feeling after a string of very loud arguments.

'Poor woman.' Jane shook her head at the cruelty of life in general and men in particular. 'How's Lisa coping?'

Sarah couldn't say.

'I'll invite her up for a glass of rosé,' said Jane. 'We'll set the world to rights. I can babysit that little cutie if she ever wants to go out and drown her sorrows.' Jane's approach to her neighbours was highly un-London. 'What's her little girl called?'

It struck Sarah as shameful that she didn't know that either. She passed the child several times a week, always touched by the little one's self-possession and grazed knees. 'They keep themselves to themselves.' Sarah resorted to the hackneyed phrase trotted out by neighbours whenever there's a massacre in a suburban road.

As the child of a single mother, Sarah should have been empathetic. Unless that was the very reason she avoided them.

'And you?' asked Jane, her foxy face intent. 'What do you do, Sarah?'

'I'm a psychologist.' Sarah smiled at how much that impressed Jane. 'A child psychologist, to be precise.'

'A useful person.' Tom approved.

'Have you seen St Chad's? It's a big clinic a few roads away. We deal with CAMHs, mostly: children and adolescents mental health services. It's an NHS service for children from local schools and children's homes.'

'Must be satisfying.' Tom sounded envious.

'It is.' Sarah felt the truth of that simple statement. 'It really is.' Or was, up until that morning. 'But we're underfunded. Understaffed. All the classic gripes. We do our best.'

'I *knew* you were one of the good guys,' said Jane.

'Note how she takes the credit for your career,' said Tom.

Ignoring him, Jane asked the question Sarah dreaded. 'And your love life?'

'You don't have to answer that,' said Tom.

'My love life's missing, presumed dead.'

'I don't believe you. With all that hair and that lovely face?' Jane was as biased as the most indulgent grandma. 'Men go mad for women with a gap between their front teeth.'

'Hardly.' Sarah was being disingenuous: on their first date Leo had told her he couldn't stop staring at her mouth.

'Plus those come-to-bed eyes.'

Sarah's eyes were indeed heavy-lidded, but they hadn't invited anybody to bed for quite some time.

'If I was a man,' said Jane, 'I'd fall for you on the spot. Tom? Wouldn't you?'

'If I was a man, you mean?' Tom winked at Sarah, giving her the courage to say it out loud.

'I'm divorced.' It came out calmly enough, but inside, sirens blared as Sarah acknowledged Jane's crestfallen, wish-I-hadn't-asked sympathy. 'Still a bit raw, really.'

'How long?' asked Jane, sombre now.

'Six months.' Sarah could have told them to the minute. 'In fact,' she went on, 'it's quite a funny story.'

The Royces drew nearer, but neither of them laughed as Sarah told them how Leo had begun his affair with Helena almost as soon as the younger woman moved into the flat below them. 'I found out. We argued. I thought we'd get back on track. But no. He divorced me to be with her.' Sarah left out Smith for the time being; Smith wasn't the issue. 'Right after the decree nisi, they got married and now my ex-husband lives in the flat below me with his new wife.'

Jane said, eventually, 'I don't think that's funny at all'.'

'Me neither,' admitted Sarah.

Chapter Three

On the other side of the glass, a small girl with a closed face refused to answer the questions put to her by the matronly woman sitting opposite.

'Talk, please, Nadia,' whispered Sarah. She could see her colleague and little Nadia but they couldn't see her. The two-way mirror made a voyeur of her.

Nadia – or Child R as she was known to the courts – had the translucent look of a trampled daisy. Sarah had worked with her for a month, slowly gaining her trust. There'd been a breakthrough of sorts, but working with children was a marathon, not a sprint. The notes Sarah had made, now on the matronly woman's clipboard, outlined a careful plan to help Nadia deal with the abuse she'd suffered.

Sarah didn't turn at the sound of the door opening.

'This isn't good for you,' said a voice with a West Indian swing to it. 'Come on, you. Out.'

'How *is* Nadia? After Friday, I mean?' Sarah followed Keeley to the kitchenette where a valiant kettle boiled all day long. St Chad's clinic ran on tea.

'As you know, Nadia isn't your case any more, so I can't comment.' Keeley looked away, fussing with the mugs. 'We picked up the pieces, OK?'

'Pieces I broke.'

'Don't do that sullen thing, Sarah.' Keeley's fuse was short; she was overworked. 'You had a little wobble.' She softened. Theirs was a strong working relationship. As manager of the clinic, she supervised Sarah, sitting in on her sessions once a month, a reliable sounding board. 'We all burn out. You get back on the bike and—'

'It's more than that.' Sarah screwed up her face.

'Tell me about what really happened on Friday.' When Keeley had finally got through to Sarah, she'd admonished her for shutting her out. Sarah had heard the beads in Keeley's hair hiss as Keeley shook with anger. She'd given Sarah Monday off to gather herself. 'So ... talk.'

In the chaotic cubbyhole that was Keeley's office, Sarah moved files off an office chair and sat down. 'I was in the consulting suite with Nadia. She was moody, picking her nails. Nadia always starts off like that, but I've worked out little ruses to relax her. There was this stupid joke I wanted to tell her. And ...'

'And?' prompted Keeley, her voice gentle.

Sarah had thought of little else over the weekend. She closed her eyes and tried to make Keeley understand. 'I couldn't do it. I had no idea what to do next. I looked at Nadia and it was like one of those dreams where you're in charge of an aeroplane and you don't know what all the controls are for. So I ran away.' Sarah was ashamed of that. She'd left Nadia sitting on the leatherette chair as she wrenched the door open and dashed down the pastel corridor. The receptionist had stood up, called her name, but Sarah kept going.

Nadia had said nothing; at seven she was already accustomed to adults letting her down. For a second, Sarah had hesitated before the revolving doors and contemplated going back to wrap Nadia in her arms and take her home. *Best not share that with Keeley.*

'I often feel like running away.'

Sarah ignored that; Keeley would never desert St Chad's. 'It was as if Nadia was on one riverbank and I was on the other. I could see her but I couldn't reach her. I couldn't help her. If I can't help, then what use am I?'

'Nadia's been reassigned.'

Sarah hated that word. It sounded as if Nadia had been tidied away. It was time to confess. 'I can't connect any more, Keeley.' She saw her supervisor shift from one buttock to another, uneasy. 'I've known it for a while. There's a black hole in the centre of me and it's eating my ability to reach out to the children.'

As she often did, Keeley surprised Sarah with a question that felt irrelevant. 'How's the work on the flat going?'

'Fine,' lied Sarah.

'It must be getting near your deadline. End of an era.'

'I suppose.'

'Does that worry you?'

'A little.' Sarah's heart now beat to the rhythm of the countdown, each tick louder than the last.

Compassionate but knife-sharp, Keeley subjected Sarah to one of her stares. 'Let's go through your recent history.'

'Do we have to?'

'I'm the boss, so yeah, we do.' Keeley recited the significant events as if revising for a history exam. 'In the past year, your husband has had an affair, the whole Smith thing came to a terrible end, Leo divorced you, then remarried, and now he lives under your nose with Helena. Or, as we like to call her, That Bitch.' She shrugged. 'I'd be worried if you *didn't* wobble, to be honest.'

'Stop calling it a wobble.' Sarah loved Keeley for trying so hard, but facts had to be faced. She thudded her fist against her chest. 'I don't feel it *here*. There's a blank inside me. I'm not the same as I was.'

'Bullshit,' said Keeley with feeling.

'My heart's not in it. It's like I'm reading a textbook. We work with *children*, Keeley. They have the purest, simplest connection of all. How can I ask them to rely on me?' Sarah was crying, much to her surprise. 'How can I help them?'

Handing her a tissue, Keeley said, 'I hear what you're building up to, and no, I won't accept your resignation.'

Wiping her nose, Sarah said, 'You have to. I spent ages on the letter.'

'You shouldn't make major decisions in this state of mind.'

'I'm a danger to the children.'

'Lord help us!' Keeley laughed a rollicking laugh. 'Shut up, you drama queen.' She was all bustle, keen to get on. Standing, stacking papers, she said, 'I'm going to let you take a back seat. You know I haven't had time to interview a replacement since what's-her-name let us down.' The clinic had – or should have – two people on the front desk, but the new girl had failed to turn up for work one morning and was never heard of again. 'Take over her job. Just for a while.' Keeley put on her glasses and looked sternly over them at Sarah. 'While you recuperate.' She closed her eyes and shook her head as Sarah tried to protest. The beads in her hair clacked, and settled again. 'Don't argue. If you've really lost your mojo then I'll have to accept your resignation. The children are my priority. But try this first. We need you, Sarah.'

June stretched like a cat, the evenings longer, the air more sweet. As Sarah dawdled down Merrion Road after work, she heard a vacuum cleaner roaring inside Flat C. On the floor above, Leo's blinds were down. The front door was opening and two figures emerged into the light. On the kerb, a parcel delivery guy squinted up at the house.

'Can't get a reply from Flat E,' he said, foisting a package onto Sarah.

'But—' said Sarah to his disappearing back. The man didn't know that he'd condemned her to another conversation with Mavis.

The figures leaving the house firmed up in the hard blast of the sun. 'Hi Lisa!' sang Sarah, doing Jane proud. She bent towards the little girl, whose round brown eyes were set in a moon face with a blob of nose in the centre. 'I don't know your name,' she smiled.

'That's Una.' Lisa looked down at the girl with a static face. Dark, spare and sharp-featured, she lived in a perpetual huff.

Accustomed to reading people, Sarah found Lisa's refusal to meet her eye unnerving. 'Where are you off to, Una?'

The therapeutic tone of voice, carefully shaved of excitable top notes or low notes of emotion, came easily.

The big eyes held Sarah's as Una fidgeted with a button on her shirred dress.

'Save your breath,' said Lisa. 'She's given up talking, this one.'

'Really?' Sarah was careful not to overreact, not to show Lisa that she'd hit a nerve.

'Yes, *really*.' Lisa's lips were thin, her tone uptight.

Sarah thought fast.

It would be madness to get involved. The parallels were too stark. Empathising with the child of a single mother was one thing, but now Una's placid face stared back like a snapshot of Sarah's past. A past she'd been glad to leave behind.

'Could you help her?' said Lisa suddenly. 'You know, professionally. I heard you're a child whatsit, aren't you?'

'I am indeed a child whatsit.' It was too close to home, in so many ways. 'Lisa, I can't really, it's a bit—'

Lisa's scuffed face, accustomed to knock-backs, lost its light. 'Forget I asked.'

'Hang on.' Sarah felt herself fracture; she couldn't let a child slip through the net. 'Of course I can help.'

'*Thank you*,' mouthed Lisa, blinking, grateful.

'Take this card.' Sarah rummaged through the slurry of receipts and wrappers in her bag.

Lisa grabbed it, greedily scanning the details.

'Tell him I sent you. He's one of the best.'

Lisa dropped her eyes. 'I thought you'd . . . OK. Ta.'

'Call him!' Sarah repeated as Lisa tugged Una down the path. She watched them both until they were lost from sight, knowing the little face would remain with her all evening. At St Chad's, when Sarah despaired of making a difference, Keeley reminded her 'we can't save everybody'. She told herself that Una would be OK. Things would work out. *I was OK,* thought Sarah. *Eventually.*

She could have left Mavis's parcel on the hall table, but her weapons-grade conscience forced her downstairs. From within Flat E, Peck made hoarse threats. 'And you, mate,' muttered Sarah, jumping back as the door flew open. Half expecting to see a man-sized cockatoo, she was relieved that it was only Mavis.

'What are you up to?'

'Nothing. Just . . .' Sarah held out the package.

'That was kind of you,' said Mavis.

Taken aback by Mavis's civility, Sarah was as mute as Una.

'Was there anything else?'

The tiny blue eyes were so vivid, so quick, that Sarah found herself staring, seeing for the first time the ruins of beauty in Mavis's face.

Behind his owner, Peck bobbed indignantly on his perch, his own eyes – two suspicious raisins – also fixed on Sarah. 'Fool,' he cried, fanning out the immaculate white feathers on his head. 'Scrawny cow.'

'How *are* you, Mavis?' Sarah had to ask. This woman, however crotchety, had just lost her sister.

'How,' replied Mavis, 'do you think I am?'

'I think you're feeling low. There may be shock. Many people feel anger, or even guilt.'

'Guilt?' Mavis spat the word. 'Why guilt?'

'It's only natural,' said Sarah. 'When my father died—'

'My situation's nothing like that.' Quivering, furious, Mavis stepped back, the dark fog of her flat lapping at her outline.

'Of course not, no.' Wrong-footed, Sarah regretted throwing Mavis a lifebelt; the old bat had thrown it back, and tried to concuss her with it. 'I'm sorry, I—'

The door was half closed, but those blazing eyes were still on Sarah's. There was anger there, without a doubt, but Sarah perceived something else. The letter piped up again and despite Sarah's misgivings she applied the magic formula. Mavis was, first and foremost, lonely. 'Look, it's silly you being on your own down here and me on my own up there, so why don't I make us both something to eat and we can—'

The door slammed so resoundingly that the brass letter 'E' fell off and bounced on the stained carpet.

'Leopards. Spots,' said Sarah to herself as she took the stairs.

The official term for Flat A was 'work in progress', but a more honest description was 'Ground Zero'.

It had been a sound notion to knock through from the sitting room to the cell-sized third bedroom, but now the hole gaped like a wound. Ragged squares of paint colours – aqua, coral, and a daring red – framed the gap.

The bare bones of Sarah's home were classic, with the original windows and all-important 'flow' that interiors magazines drool over. The kitchen had the window seat she'd dreamed about as a child. In theory, the second bedroom doubled as a dressing room, which sounded luxurious but which was in reality a camp bed and a clothes rail.

Her own bedroom, the 'master', was strenuously simple, a respite from the anarchy of the other rooms. Just a bed with a silk cover the colour of pistachios. A muslin square tacked over the window softened the sunshine to golden talc.

Their plan had been to flip it.

'How have you never heard that term before?' Leo had been in love with Sarah back then, and found her ignorance enchanting. 'It means we buy a neglected flat in a good area.

We set a strict budget and refurbish it quickly with all the current must-haves. Let's say, a dressing room, an en suite, a range cooker. Then – bam! – we sell. In and out. Big profit. Move on and do it again. Soon we'll have enough to buy that dream house of yours.'

Before Leo, the dream house had been just that, a dream. With him, it felt achievable. It would have a garden, and open fires. It would be full of cushions and books. Sarah didn't want a mansion; she wanted a home.

Instead, she was marooned in a failed flip, staring at a workload that had been ambitious for two. For one it was daunting. Sarah changed into the baggy overalls she wore every evening. She put her hands on her hips and said, 'Right!' out loud.

Then she said, 'Yeah!'

After that she said, 'Let's go!'

Long menus had the same effect on Sarah. Faced with too much choice she could never decide between an omelette and a full roast dinner. There was so much to do in the flat she was paralysed.

It didn't help that she was a novice. She'd relied on Leo to know about things like grouting, or spirit levels. She had two spirit levels and used one of them as a paperweight.

The deadline was set in stone. It had to be met. It was now mid-June, and by the end of August the flat had to be a clean, blank canvas for the next owner. Both a whip and a carrot, the deadline merely added to the paralysis.

It'll be good to move on, Sarah told herself, picking idly through a toolbox, looking for sandpaper. The sitting-room door needed to be painted, which meant it first had to be sanded down; every project involved at least two or three steps, she'd discovered. *Moving on, the healthy thing to do.*

A new home, probably a new job. It was the thought of a new man that revealed the flaws in her optimism. Sarah had one foot in her marriage; everything had happened so fast she'd been left spinning while everybody else got used to the new order. She was still Leo's, even if he was no longer hers.

Sarah bought a lottery ticket every week, hoping to win enough to buy Leo's half of the property. The lottery had so far yielded nothing, and Sarah had no obligingly frail rich aunts who might die and leave her a fortune.

She applied the rectangle of sandpaper to the panelled door. It was easy at first, swiping it over the wood, but soon her fingers were sanded too, and the repetitive movement put a strain on her arm. The rhythm and the *sssh-sssh* hypnotised her. Her mind wandered.

A creature of habit, Sarah's mind always wandered to the same place. Hours had been lost to standing with a tool in her hand, staring into space.

Sarah had tried to hate Leo. Hatred was the sensible option, but Sarah couldn't think of him as the *real* Leo. The new model was so different to the one she'd met seven years ago it must be suffering a malfunction.

The real Leo had been the first man to properly excite Sarah. There'd been school boyfriends she'd tolerated, enduring football-based chat in order to get to the snogging part of the evening. In her twenties there'd been handsome man-boys who'd left her cold when their lips locked. But worldly Leo – older, raffish, wicked – had put a match to Sarah's desire.

They met amongst old things. Sarah had wandered into a Denmark Hill bric-a-brac shop, whiling away her lunch break from the Maudsley hospital. Leo, sizing up a rival's stock, eyeballed her as she mooched.

The untidy, upper-class, flamboyantly haired guy hadn't piqued her interest until he leaned across and said, 'Do you know what that is you're looking at?'

'Of course.' Sarah hastily scanned the label. 'It's a commode.' Up close, his grape-green eyes were naughty, as if he'd heard a joke he wasn't yet ready to share.

'And you know what a commode is?'

'It's, um, a chair.' Living in a forest of Ikea, Sarah had little interest in antiques. The throne-like chair was ugly; that she *did* know.

'Not quite.' Leo lifted the hinged seat to reveal a chamber pot. 'It's a discreet bog.'

'Handy,' grimaced Sarah.

'I'm Leo,' said Leo.

'I'm not,' said Sarah.

She played hard to get. For a whole hour. By the time he walked her back to the antiseptic maelstrom of the Maudsley, Sarah had decided that this Leo guy wasn't gangly but rakish, that he didn't look like an aristocratic tramp but had been manufactured in some celestial factory just for her.

Every time they met – in theatres and galleries, rather than the usual pubs and clubs – Sarah's blood fizzed in her veins like the good champagne he introduced her to. He was, she decided, amazing, with the superpower to make everything around him equally amazing.

Including me. Sarah felt amazing. And powerful, and sexual. As if she mattered.

For Sarah, love equalled Leo. The two words were even spelled alike; just jumble up the letters and excise that spiky 'V'.

Theirs was a short courtship. The language Leo used was extravagant; she'd 'entranced' and 'possessed' him. He wanted to meet her parents; like a suitor of old, he had a special question to ask her father.

Sarah was stung into silence. Hadn't he listened? She was certain she'd told Leo about her father's death, precisely because it wasn't something she spoke about readily. Not the whole story, not yet, but she was sure she'd told him the bare bones … Sarah ironed out this bump in their smooth road by blaming her memory.

'Brace yourself,' she warned as they pulled up outside her mother's house.

Leo needed a whisky after they left. 'I see what you mean, darling. She's …'

'Isn't she just?'

That was the moment to tell him about what her mother had done, about the consequences Sarah had suffered, but she missed her chance. Leo was already yammering on about

40

this incredible little bistro, where he would kiss her in a dark corner and give her an extra-special present. By midnight, Sarah was wearing an emerald ring and doodling 'Sarah Lynch-Harrison' on a napkin.

The age difference didn't matter. If anything, she relished it, the psychologist in her ignoring the words 'Father Figure' picked out in neon lettering. Sarah grew up in Leo's arms.

Her mother's approval of Leo felt like a jinx, but while it lasted Sarah had beaten the curse, repeated throughout her childhood: *You're just like your father!*

A diehard daddy's girl, Sarah had lived through the carnage her dad left behind when he moved out of the family home. She loved her father with the fierceness of a daughter, but she didn't want to be the person her mother described. Sarah was loyal and steady; these were the qualities she valued in others.

A suspicion flared early on, that Leo preferred the beginnings of things, but he was sexy, he was loving, and he would protect her from her mother. After six years of marriage – and a slight, inevitable dulling of passion – Leo began an affair with Helena.

'Why?' sobbed Sarah when she found a sext on his phone.

'You've changed,' shouted Leo. 'You're never here, Sarah! When I get back from the Old Church, you're either at that bloody clinic or downstairs doing God knows what with . . .' He hadn't needed to supply the name. They'd both known he was talking about Smith.

By that time, Leo and Helena had been sleeping together

for three months. Once the first shock had subsided, the aftershocks delivered more nasty surprises. It was a terrible blow to her confidence, not only as a woman but as a psychologist: Sarah wondered bleakly how on earth she could expect to connect with troubled children when she hadn't even noticed the man she knew best in the world was being unfaithful to her.

The sandpaper was idle in Sarah's hand. Confucius was right again; it was bloody hard work standing still. These excursions into the past exhausted her, but her mind circled the endless conundrum: how does such a bond dissolve? Her marriage had been strong and vigorous, like an oak. But even oaks topple, and this one had crushed Flat A.

With sarcastic timing, the sound of a popping cork ricocheted up from the flat below.

Sarah froze at the sound of footsteps thundering up the stairs. She threw down the sandpaper and pushed at her hair, rearranging her features as Leo banged on the door.

Framed in the doorway, Leo was too real for Sarah to take in. They'd passed on the stairs, pretended not to see each other in the street, but they hadn't spoken since his wedding day.

'Leo,' she said, hoping it sounded indifferent, knowing it sounded excited.

'Isn't it time,' said Leo, his head on one side, his face pleated into a poignant smile, 'we kissed and made up?'

It was so close to the storyboard of her nightly dreams that Sarah was lost for words.

Stepping into view, Helena said, 'He's right. Have a glass of fizzy-pops.' She brandished a bottle. 'Friends?' she said, her lipstick too glossy, her voice too sickly.

'I've gone off champagne,' managed Sarah.

'Are you demurring, Lynch?' Leo looked directly at her; this hadn't happened since Helena happened.

It was a rush, like a shot of tequila. He was playful, sunny. Leo had never looked so tall, so rumpled and earthy. She missed him with every lonely inch of her neglected body.

'Because,' Leo went on, 'when you demur, I pooh-pooh.' He barged in and the flat was suddenly alive and sparkling. Helena followed, dragging Sarah by the hand.

Up close, Helena was unlikely. Nobody could stroll around amongst mere mortals with skin that creamy, décolletage that mountainous, hair that sleek. Clothes, however minimal, seemed extraneous: she was designed to be naked, her tanned, polished, waxed and buffed body as smoothly perfect as a doll's. This happy friendliness was not her usual style; before the affair, Helena had ignored Sarah. After it, she'd ignored her even harder. 'The things I'd do with this place!' She looked around, a firework in a coal mine, at the mess. 'You know my apartment's doubled in price?'

Sarah thought she must be imagining it, but no, Leo was smirking at her over his wife's head. They used to laugh about their pretentious new neighbour, wincing when she called her flat an 'apartment'.

Accepting the booze she didn't want, Sarah's fingers

touched Leo's as he handed her a glass. She wondered if he noticed. 'What are we celebrating?'

'Life,' said Leo, with a collaborative look at Helena that sliced through Sarah like cheese wire. 'It's too short to waste on bad feeling. We all said things we regret. Can we put it behind us?'

Sarah felt railroaded – Leo was downsizing their divorce to a tiff – but she also felt flattered. Yes, that fluttery feeling in her chest was elation that Leo had noticed her again. That he'd been moved enough by memories of their relationship to mount the stairs and make a speech. 'Why not?' She raised her glass awkwardly.

'You angel,' said Leo.

Sarah knew his every look. He was admiring her. It was a long time since Sarah had been admired.

It was clear that Helena was oblivious to the ley lines that ran between the exes. Swinging her hair – she did this often enough for it to count as a hobby – she'd reached the end of her attention span. 'So, buddy.' She clicked her fingers at Leo. 'Let's grab a cab and get to town.' She turned towards Sarah. 'We're having supper at Claridge's.'

'Ooh,' said Sarah dutifully.

Leo's eyes opened wide and the boyish happiness of his expression threw Sarah down a time tunnel. When he woke up in their bed with that expression on his face it meant that by lunchtime they'd be on a ferry to France, or at the top of the Shard, or making love under a tree beside an ignored picnic. 'Come with us, darling!'

'I'm hardly dressed for it.' Sarah looked down at her overalls.

'You used to love surprises,' he said sadly, as if she was dead.

Helena said nothing, but she didn't have to; the daggers that flew from her eyes did all the talking.

'No? Fine.' Leo gave in, crestfallen. He was optimum Leo today, bubbling over with wicked fun, hair flopping, big hands never still. 'Then at least, please, just for me, will you girls get together for a coffee at some point?'

The 'girls' shuffled their feet and made small, negative noises, but Leo was a steamroller. Throwing an arm around each of them, he pulled them together like nervy cats. 'My two favourite women in the world should be chums.'

Close up, Helena's perfume made Sarah want to sneeze.

'Come on!' Leo shook them both, his hand a branding iron on Sarah's shoulder. It was so long since he'd laid hands on her. 'Why not meet for a coffee and a moan about me?'

Bridling, Sarah was insulted that Helena also bridled. It was, after all, Helena who'd stolen Sarah's man, not the other way around. A perverse impulse made Sarah say, 'I could do any day this week.'

'This week's no good for me,' said Helena, with that slight trace of accent Sarah had never pinned down. 'I'm so busy.' She fluttered her hands: 'Busy, busy, busy!'

'I'm not busy at all,' said Sarah, opting out of the one-upwomanship.

'I dunno,' said Helena reluctantly. 'Next Thursday?'

'That's a date!' Leo, at least, was happy.

'Listen, baby, we really should get going.' Helena's mood, always mercurial, had turned. The coo was an order.

'Dash down to the flat and fetch your bag, angel, and I'll meet you on the steps.'

Sarah had dreamed of being alone with Leo, but now she was shy of the man she'd shared a bed with for seven years. She recalled how they'd nod off spooning, but always wake up face to face.

As if sensing she needed space, Leo stepped away from Sarah. Gently he said, 'I'm sorry about the solicitor's letter. That was . . .'

It was cowardly, but Sarah had let Leo off the hook by blaming Helena for the ultimatum. 'You should have just come up and talked about it.'

'But we weren't talking. The wedding seemed to change everything.'

'Well, duh,' said Sarah.

On headed notepaper, Leo's lawyer had informed Sarah that his client had been 'most patient', but wasn't prepared to wait any longer for the jointly owned marital home to be liquidated. In stilted legal language it recapped what Sarah knew only too well.

At the time of the break-up, Leo had wanted to sell up right away. Sarah had asked for time to acclimatise. When that was up, she talked Leo into agreeing that the flat would sell for far more if she finished all the improvements they'd started together. Leo had given her until the decree nisi, coming up with half the mortgage each month.

To assuage his guilt, Sarah had thought. At the wedding she told Leo she still needed time. 'I'll pay the whole mortgage from now on,' she'd promised.

'Our client,' said the letter, 'insists that you have the flat ready for sale by 31st August this year. If you do not meet this target date, then Mr Harrison will arrange for the property to be professionally refurbished.'

Sarah asked, 'Would you really send in builders if I'm not finished?'

'What else can I do? It's been a year. I need my investment back.'

Me too, thought Sarah, although it wasn't the money she needed. It was the time, the happiness, the love. 'We always said we'd do this place ourselves.'

'A lot's changed since then.' Leo was disappointed in Sarah, like a kindly headmaster with her report in his hand. 'It shouldn't take this long.' He shook his head. 'Helena would've flipped the place by now.'

'She does it for a living.' Sarah was impressed; Leo had found a new way to hurt her. Being compared to the woman who's usurped your throne is never fun. 'I'm doing it on my own, remember.'

'Get a man in,' said Leo.

'I'm skint.' Paying twice as much mortgage saw to that. Sarah's savings were vanishing. 'Besides, I don't want my last few weeks at Merrion Road spoiled by whistling workmen.'

'One of us has to go, Sarah. You do see that, don't you?'

When she was thinking straight, Sarah saw it perfectly. 'I suppose it *is* a bit seventies sitcom.'

'You can't expect Helena to move out. That flat's her showcase.'

The assumption that Sarah should defer to Helena made her head swim. Had he forgotten how they'd laughed at the pretentious captions when Helena's jewel-box restoration of Flat B – all concealed doors and silk rugs – was featured in their local magazine? 'Does Helena still have that oh-so-wittily lopsided chandelier?'

Leo didn't recognise the quote. 'The crazy thing is . . .' He lowered his voice. 'I'll miss you like crazy.'

Sarah didn't know what to say, so she said nothing.

'Listen.' Leo swallowed. 'Let me help.'

'How?'

'Prepping. Painting. Tearing down those cabinets you hate. Whatever you need.'

'Thanks but no thanks, Leo.' It was so hard not to call him 'darling'.

'You need to finish the flat for the sake of up here.' Leo tapped her head lightly, something he'd done when they were married. It had irritated her then, but now it was the most loving touch she'd felt in an age. 'I feel responsible. After all, I kind of left you in the lurch.'

'Kind of?'

Leo had moved closer. His nearness had a narcotic effect. Sarah felt her gates clang open, her heart unfold. 'Let me. It would help me too. Because, well, you're not the only one hurting. Let me make it up to you a little. Let me ...' His green eyes, always mesmeric, were near. Too near, some might say. One of the ones who might say that was Sarah. 'Let me be close to you for a couple of hours now and then. Please.'

The front door, left open by Helena, delivered Mavis to them, her dirty white hair a chrysanthemum about her disapproving face. 'Hmm. Am I interrupting something?'

'No,' said Sarah and Leo in unison, the spell broken.

'Claridge's beckons.' Leo backed away. 'How about tomorrow? About seven?'

'No, I'll be ...'

'You'll be here, darling.' Leo was pressing down on a smile. 'And so shall I. Deal?'

Sarah looked about her at the wasteland of paint pots and dust sheets. 'Deal.'

Mavis watched Sarah as Leo left. 'That's the face of a woman who's made a pact with the devil.'

'Bit dramatic,' laughed Sarah.

'Not at all. I know what I'm talking about.'

'Can I help you, Mavis?' Sarah needed her out of there, so she could reflect on the deal. And regret. And cancel.

'Dinner, dear.' Mavis was querulous, like an angry bird that had flown in and would surely break a window and poo on the curtains before it flew out again. 'You invited me, remember?'

Sarah played for time, looking blank, wondering what

had possessed her to invite Mavis into her home. 'Um . . . but . . .' Sarah couldn't find a polite way to say *you shut the door in my face!*

Mavis had ironed one of her terrible dresses, a nylon number patterned with chevrons. She turned, with the slow mechanics of the elderly. 'You've forgotten. I'll go,' she said.

'No, hang on.' Sarah reached out, took Mavis's elbow, bony beneath the flammable sleeve. It was a long climb from the basement to the eaves, and an even longer climb down from the high horse that Mavis rode everywhere. 'Dinner. Great idea.'

The massive handbag clutched to Mavis's chest contained a bottle of wine which she brusquely handed over, as if being mugged. 'Are you decorating?'

'Trying to!' Sarah visualised the inside of her fridge as she swiftly improvised a table in the sitting room. Since the departure of Leo's mahogany dining set she'd taken her meals on the sofa. 'Let's open the wine!' Sarah glanced at the label. 'Bloody hell,' she said.

'Is it all right?' The voice was uncertain, Mavis reining in her customary growl.

'It's very much all right.' Even to Sarah's uneducated eyes, this was a choice wine, a bottle Leo might order when showing off. 'Are you sure . . . ?'

'Please, Sarah, open it if you wish. Just leave it if not.' Mavis coughed and held a handkerchief – a proper, embroidered one, of the kind only seen in period dramas – to her lips. Staying the right side of rude was evidently a strain for her.

The contents of the fridge were just as Sarah feared. As Confucius might put it, she who lives on takeaways has only odds and sods in the fridge.

A dejected lump of Red Leicester; an onion past its prime; a lonely egg. She hovered, letting the fridge chill her perspiring face.

Mavis was beside her, small as a child. 'Let's see . . .' She reached in. 'Welsh rarebit.' Closing the fridge door, she said, 'Sit,' with a regal edge that brooked no disobedience.

As Sarah sat in the window seat, Mavis cast about for a grater, and transformed the lurid orange cheese into a pile of shavings. 'This is how my grandmother made it.' Her arthritic hands moved surely.

'Family recipes are best.' Sarah's own mother had passed down only the phone number for the local curry house. Leo had loved Sarah's apple pie; the memory of their pastry initials entwined reminded her that she hadn't cooked a decent meal since he left. 'Did your sister like your Welsh rarebit?'

The kitchen seemed to clench, as if the cupboards and crockery sensed the darkening of Mavis's mood. For such a tiny person, she had a huge effect. Sarah quailed, gulping at her wine. This is what came of inviting predators to dinner.

'You should know,' said Mavis, without pausing in the massacre of the onion, 'that I don't wish, care, *want* . . .' Her head wobbled, its white mass of burst mattress hair shivering as she struggled for the right word. 'Look, child, never ask me about Zelda.'

51

'I'm sorry.'

'My sister's dead. Gone.'

'I'm clumsy sometimes, Mavis.'

'Yes.' Mavis cracked an egg. 'You are.' She threw the shell into the bin.

Because Sarah was humane, she took a deep breath and started again; because Sarah was scared of Mavis, she chose her words carefully. 'That's a funky way to separate the yolk from the white.' Leaning over from the window seat, she set down a glass of wine for the chef. 'I get it all over the worktop.'

'You can freeze that white.' Mavis put the little bowl aside. 'It'll come in handy for meringues.'

'You've got me mixed up with somebody who makes meringues,' smiled Sarah.

'I haven't made them myself for a while.' Mavis mixed the cheese and onion and egg with a practised twirl of her wrist.

It intrigued Sarah that at some point in her past, Mavis had been moved to make meringues. Surely *that* was a speck of beauty? Only there if you looked hard. A woman who made meringues couldn't be all bad.

There was something different about Mavis. Sarah tried to pin it down. It wasn't something extra, it was something missing.

Smoke.

The permanent nicotine fog that hugged Mavis as close as a lover was absent. 'Have you given up smoking, Mavis? That can't have been easy.' Mavis chain-smoked, lighting one cigarette from the stub of the last one.

'I didn't like to smoke around Zelda while she was ill. I don't feel the need to take it up again.'

Mavis was cut off again, those shutters down. The question had been too personal. Sarah tried, 'Peck's a character, isn't he?'

'He's a very demanding lodger.' Mavis seasoned the mixture, then grappled with the grill. It was an old-fashioned eye-level model; Leo had gone into raptures over the bulky white 1960s cooker: now he lived with a kitchen so minimal it looked like a mortuary. 'His feathers are falling out. Stress, according to the vet. I'm not sure what a cockatoo has to be stressed about.'

'It's not like he needs to fill in a tax return.'

'Quite.' *Quaite.* This was the longest Sarah had ever listened to Mavis; the old lady's pronunciation was quaint around the edges. 'Peck's tablets are more expensive than caviar. Foil?'

Puzzled for a moment, Sarah caught up and pointed. 'Second drawer down.'

'I do wish he wasn't so foul-mouthed,' said the woman who'd taught Peck the naughty words in the first place. 'This bread's past its best.' Mavis chiselled out the jade dots, her hands free of rings, the knuckles red, the palms chafed.

'Sorry about the rough-and-ready kitchen.' Sarah watched Mavis tussle with the grill pan, half rising, unsure whether help would be welcomed or met with a rap on the knuckles. 'My to-do list is longer than the bible.'

'It's no worse than my own home.' Mavis glanced about her, seeming to like what she saw. Perhaps, like Sarah, she saw past the damp and the discoloured patches and the copper pipes that snaked across the kitchen walls. 'So much light.' She raised her face to the window, as if sunbathing. 'Sometimes I feel like a mole down in the basement.'

'Sometimes I feel like an eagle up here.' Sarah felt her way, conscious that Mavis's good humour was brittle.

'Eagles mate for life,' said Mavis. 'Where's your eagle partner?'

As if a scorpion had lifted its tail, Sarah gasped. 'You know where he is, Mavis.'

Mavis frowned as she nudged one of the rarebits under the gas jet. 'Yet he visits, apparently.'

'That was the first time Leo's set foot up here since he remarried.' Sarah wondered why she was defending herself. 'He wants to be friends.' She blurted it out, trying it for size.

'Does he indeed?' Mavis looked sideways at Sarah as they waited for the cheese to bubble. 'You, of course, aren't foolish enough to believe such a thing is possible?' When Sarah didn't answer, Mavis said, 'A broken heart isn't a good compass, Sarah.'

'The cheese,' said Sarah. 'It's burning.'

Mavis seemed to ponder the obvious change of subject before acquiescing and dishing up the Welsh rarebit. As they enjoyed the sublime changes wrought on the humble ingredients, Mavis quizzed Sarah about her work.

Sarah saw through the ruse: if Mavis was asking questions,

she wasn't answering them. Mavis had never been remotely interested in Sarah – or anyone – before.

'What made you want to be a child psychologist?'

The only person who knew about the spark that lit Sarah's ambition – Smith – wasn't in a position to tell anybody. Not even Leo knew. Her mother knew, of course, because she'd been there.

The sanitised version Sarah gave Mavis was the truth, but not the whole truth. 'Children are vulnerable. They need advocates to speak for them. They need to be listened to. If you can help somebody at a young age, you make a change that stays with them for life.'

Satisfied with that, Mavis continued with her interrogation. They weren't probing questions, just the sort people swapped at bus stops. Sarah intuited that Mavis was fighting her own remote nature, like a turtle slowly poking its head out to test the air. 'Do you enjoy painting and decorating?'

'I hate it. Look around you, Mavis. I'll never get on top of this.'

Mavis sat forward, the hair on the mole in her chin catching the sunlight as she said, 'My sister . . .' she paused. 'Zelda wrote books, as you may know, and she told me once that each one felt like an impossible task but they always came together in the end.' She laid down her cutlery demurely, like a debutante, albeit one with red-raw fingers. 'I've broken my own rule.'

'Rules,' said Sarah, 'are made to be broken'. She was glad to hear Mavis mention her sister without a sneer.

'Some of them,' conceded Mavis, with a sketch of a smile, as if she was new to smiling and didn't want to run before she could walk.

'Nothing for afters, I'm afraid, unless you like very old ice cream.'

'Put it in a pretty dish and we won't know the difference.'

The pretty dishes hadn't been used for some time. 'Did you ever marry, Mavis?' asked Sarah, as she set down spoons. Her answer was a look of such shock that Sarah wondered if she had, by mistake, asked Mavis if she'd ever robbed a bank. 'That's personal, I'm sorry, I shouldn't—'

'It's quite all right,' said Mavis. *Quaite all raite.* Her tone made it clear it was far from all right. She didn't answer the question.

They ate the aged raspberry ripple in silence. The wine had erased the edges of Sarah's judgement. Bereavement may have blunted Mavis's aggression, but it couldn't turn a lifelong recluse into a chatterbox.

After a firm 'No' to coffee, Mavis said, 'Thank you, this has been lovely,' as if reciting poetry in another language. 'Next time,' said Mavis, gripping the bannister on her way downstairs, 'I'll do three courses.'

Next time? 'Oh, yes, um, lovely.'

Tidying away the debris of the modest meal, Sarah wondered if she'd made a friend. A scary friend.

Chapter Four

If you like people, a view of the backs of houses is a thousand times more fascinating than a television, and Sarah liked people; they interested her and they moved her and occasionally they scared the bejesus out of her. She was what's called a people person; that's why she was good at her job.

Why I used to be good at my job, thought Sarah, ploughing through her lunchtime sandwich and staring out from her kitchen window.

Since Leo moved out, Sarah had felt isolated. She didn't trust as readily. She couldn't blame Leo, but that didn't stop her doing exactly that when she woke up yet again at 3 a.m. alone in the big bed they'd chosen together. As a child psychologist, she led her small patients through their thought processes, but now her own were gnarled and twisted, like the wisteria that clambered over number twenty-four.

As a married person, one half of the Harrisons, she'd looked forward; alone, she harked backwards. Her childhood stalked her. Sarah shook herself, stood up, dumped the disappointing egg mayonnaise in the bin.

It was the second day in a row she'd come home at lunchtime to work on the flat. It was better than facing St Chad's kitchenette, knowing her colleagues were wondering why she was sitting at the reception desk instead of dealing with her clients.

The senior receptionist had asked no questions, patiently showing Sarah the ropes of the telephone system and the signing-in book, but their rapport was patchy; Sarah, usually one of the clinical staff, was suddenly on the receptionist's side of the fence. There could be no in-jokes about the therapists or rolled eyes behind Keeley's back.

Sarah drifted back to the sitting room and pulled on her overalls. With the half hour available to her she could undercoat the door she'd sanded. Another small job ticked, the flat pushed into its future.

It was a dangerous pastime, but sometimes Sarah imagined the old sitting room superimposed over this one.

There were still dimples in the carpet where the glass coffee table had stood. Intriguing objects used to just turn up: items Leo acquired for the Old Church but couldn't bear to sell. A chinoiserie vase had stood behind the mother-of-pearl frame that still stood on the mantelpiece, displaying a photo of her father, dashing and elusive in a colour-saturated snap from the seventies. She had his nose; according to her mother he'd also passed on other, less positive attributes.

Sarah visualised the pale Swedish grandfather clock that had stood sentry between the windows. She'd given it to Leo, along with the rest of the furniture, in a fit of self-righteous martyrdom when they were dividing their possessions.

To her horror he'd simply *accepted* them; she'd meant him to be dazzled by her selflessness and fall back in love with her.

Before Leo, Sarah had thought of antiques as 'old stuff'. He'd shown her how to penetrate the layers of neglect with a laser eye. He knew a piece's history, appreciated the knocks it had taken, and relished its patina. With Leo, Sarah had felt as understood as one of his artefacts; she felt beautiful. Even when pale and suffering with her reliably punctual period woes, she could rely on Leo to tuck her into bed and look after her. Without him watching her through love-tinted lenses could Sarah ever consider herself beautiful again?

A knock on the door and Tom filled the frame.

'I've been sent to fetch you.' The combat shorts that reached almost to his knees were perversely sexy despite their boy-scout vibe. 'She Who Must Be Obeyed wants you in the garden.' Tom smiled, that carefree smile that suggested there was nothing hidden, nothing untoward, even when he added, 'And so do I, obviously.'

A shout from the garden brought them both to the window. Jane evidently didn't trust Tom to carry out his errand. 'It's too sunny to be indoors!' she yelled, legs akimbo in denim cut-offs. 'Get yourself down here, madam!'

Sarah trotted down behind Tom, noticing his outdoorsy tan; a colour picked up on the move, not on a beach towel. Taking the back door, they crossed a narrow concrete strip that opened up into steps to the lawn. Windows from the basement flats looked out onto this unprepossessing strip of yard, and at one of them sat Una.

The window was open, and the child sat in the shade, her eyelids half closed, like a basking kitten.

'Hello there.' Sarah paused, one foot on the steps.

No response, just a widening of the eyes, like pansies opening.

'Would you like to come out into the sunshine?'

Una was snatched away, and the window was empty.

The sun pressed down on the lawn like a lid. Sarah regretted her overalls.

Jane said, 'Why is the garden so neglected? People *kill* to have outdoor space in Notting Hill!' She threw out her arms, encompassing the rectangle of lawn and its borders of tangled flower beds. 'There's even a shed! Every media moron wants a shed! A tidy garden adds thousands to a house's asking price.'

Tom, pulling on serious-looking gloves and picking up long-handled shears, said, 'It's nice for its own sake, Janey. Not everything's about property values.'

As Jane dragged deckchairs out from behind the shed, Sarah said, 'Nobody's ever taken the garden in hand. I'm too lazy to come all the way down. Helena created a wow-factor roof terrace on top of your kitchen extension. Lisa and Una stay inside all the time. And Mavis ... well, she's just Mavis.' Accepting an ice-cold can and marvelling at how thoroughly Jane took control of her surroundings, Sarah added, 'Lisa *used* to come out here before Graham left. He and Una planted sunflowers in that corner.' Straggling weeds marked the spot.

'So many break-ups.' Jane folded her arms, and gazed at Tom, who was engaged in hand-to-hand combat with the ivy that strangled every plant that dared to show its face. 'My marriage is for keeps. We're two peas in a pod.'

Sarah drank greedily; she wasn't so optimistic about marriage.

Jane lowered herself gingerly into a distressed deckchair. 'I can never get comfy in these things,' she giggled, her knees under her chin. When her bottom went through the striped fabric, the tearing noise sounded like an epic fart.

They all roared. Like a workout for the soul, the laughter sent blood coursing through Sarah. She hadn't honked like that in an age. The sun, no longer oppressive, felt like a caress. All it took to transform the tatty grass into a pleasure garden was the addition of two playful people.

'That's quite a laugh you've got there, Sarah.' Tom pulled in his chin.

'Like a goose being molested,' Sarah quoted Leo.

'Ha!' Tom let out a bark.

'And Tom's a Labrador being molested,' suggested Jane, sitting on an upturned crate.

'Watch out, Sarah. Jane'll take you over.' Tom put on his sunglasses and squatted to gather up clippings. 'Jane's always full on about people she likes.'

She likes me. That was a leg-up for Sarah's limping ego. 'I'll cope,' she smiled.

'Say no now and again. Keeps her on her toes.'

Jane said, as if she'd had a brilliant idea, 'What's your favourite colour?'

'What is this?' scoffed Tom, straightening up. 'A boy band interview?'

'You can tell a lot about a person from their favourite colour.'

'You can tell more by just talking to them, surely,' Tom added. 'Behind these dark glasses I'm rolling my eyes. Just so you know.'

'Turquoise,' said Sarah.

'Calm. Cool. Tranquil. But mysterious.' Jane's eyes flashed.

'My favourite colour,' said Tom, 'is bright red, the colour your forehead's going to be, Jane, unless you pop indoors for some sunscreen.' He turned to Sarah. 'Why can't she remember this stuff herself?'

'Because,' said Jane, springing up, 'I have *you* to remember for me. I'll winkle out Lisa and Una while I'm indoors.'

'Good luck,' said Sarah with feeling.

'Tom, tell Sarah about what you do,' called Jane as she went, unable to relinquish control of the scenario even when absent. 'He does a vital job, Sarah. More indispensable than your nurse or your fireman.'

'Shut up,' said Tom.

Sarah envied their easy, disrespectful rapport.

I used to tease Leo like that. She thought for a moment, realising that he'd hated it.

'I work mainly in Soho,' said Tom.

'Soho?' Sarah raised her eyebrows, thinking of seedy strip joints, and doorbells that promised 'Busty Blonde 3rd Floor'.

'Yes, Soho, I'm a prostitute,' deadpanned Tom. 'Soho's changed, you know. The strippers are outnumbered by advertising agencies. I'm a voice-over artist.'

'A what?'

'I do voice-overs. You know, on ads.' Tom returned to the ivy, booming out, 'Wake up with Kellogg's.'

'That's you on the commercial?' Sarah gaped, delighted. 'Do another one!'

Obligingly, Tom scrolled through his greatest hits. For Pampers nappies he was playful; building societies needed him at his most reassuring. 'I've just done Guinness. And Always Ultra.' He turned to say, 'With wings. Can't help thinking I was miscast in that one. Do you want to hear my sexy?'

'Um, OK.'

'Paco Rabanne. For men.'

'That's almost *too* sexy.'

'I have to be careful with it. In case women faint. In real life, I'm an actor. A failed actor. The voice gets plenty of work, but nobody wants my body, Sarah.'

Hoping she wasn't blushing, Sarah made a *pish!* noise.

Tom was a grower. At first glance he was well put together, nothing wrong with him, but not memorable. Spend a little while in his company and internal lights came on. His eyes, always narrowed, were kind and intelligent. His wide mouth, full in repose, opened out guilelessly when he was amused. Which was often. And his forearms were strong, with a rope of vein that ... Sarah pulled herself up sharply. It was safer not to eulogise married men's forearms.

'Acting's unpredictable. Hard to make a living. Before I fell into voiceovers, I had loads of jobs on the side, all sorts of strange skills.'

'Hence your ability to upholster a sofa.'

'Exactly.' Tom paused in his battle against nature to smile at her, chuffed that she'd remembered.

It was safe to find Tom attractive. Welded to Jane, the man was unattainable, like a film star. Since the divorce Sarah had a deep respect for couples who went the distance, glued together by mortgages and supermarket shopping and hoovering under the bed and, most importantly, plain old love.

Quite apart from his transparent decency, no man married to Jane would dare stray. *Perhaps,* thought Sarah, *I should have been more possessive of Leo.*

Tom and Jane weren't to know it, but they gave Sarah hope that there were happy endings out there.

'We need more chairs!' shouted Jane, leading Una by the hand, Lisa tailing them. Jane winked at Sarah, and Sarah was warmed by being part of something, a partner in kindly crime. 'Lisa has an hour before she goes to work.'

More chairs were found – Jane had a talent for it – and Lisa settled Una at her feet as if the child was a handbag. Una had no inclination to wander. She was a watcher, her round eyes travelling slowly over each of the adults.

'I've got to go to one of my old dears at half two and give her a bed bath,' said Lisa complacently. 'She's a bit forgetful. She doesn't keep herself, you know, *nice*.'

'My grandma has a carer,' said Jane. 'She's a saint. I don't know how you do it, Lisa.'

'Where does Una go while you work?' Sarah wondered how Lisa managed to hold down a job.

'My dad takes her. He's a bit unreliable, though. It's a nightmare some days. We just rock it and roll it.' Lisa shrugged; she was accustomed to hard graft and lack of help.

That struck Sarah as wrong.

'Oi, Sarah,' said Lisa, chattily. 'Jane and Tom are better neighbours than that Smith, aren't they?' A hand flew to her mouth. 'Oh shit, sorry, mate.'

'S'OK.' Flustered, Sarah grinned away the awkwardness. 'Smith wasn't everybody's cup of tea.'

'But you and – sorry.' Lisa's eyes fluttered everywhere but at Sarah. Her brown hair was pulled into a topknot so tight her eyes were slanted.

'Smith?' Jane was inquisitive. 'What was wrong with this Smith?'

'Let's drop the subject,' suggested Tom, crossing to the shed and giving the rusty padlock a tentative rattle. 'I think Sarah and Smith were close.'

'Smith *was* a bit of a mess,' said Sarah. 'But we just clicked.'

The other residents at number twenty-four had been immune to Smith's charms. Whimsical, extrovert, with a tendency to roll home in the small hours and leave the front door ajar, Smith played country music at stadium levels, and evaded paying Flat C's share of the communal charges.

'Remember the tattoo?' Lisa rolled her eyes. 'Elvis riding My Little Pony. Nutter.'

'Leo didn't like Smith,' remembered Sarah. 'The tattoo didn't help.'

'Or he didn't like *you* liking Smith.' Jane's head was back, her eyes shut, a pagan offering to the sun goddess.

'Very perceptive,' said Sarah.

'Not really. You can tell Leo's one of those macho types.' Jane beat her chest. 'Woman! *My* woman! Woman like *me* best!'

'It was Smith's smoking in the communal hall that got my back up,' said Lisa. 'I had a right go about it.'

'One time,' said Sarah, 'Smith was locked out and Helena's swanky dinner guests had to step over this snoring bundle on the doorstep.' Sarah had forgotten how much Smith made her laugh; there hadn't been much laughter towards the end. Lisa's comments were only one side of a complicated story.

'I saw through the bad behaviour. Smith was good to me when Leo buggered off; let me talk.' Sarah tapered off. She'd bored Smith, she must have done, but there was no murmur of complaint. 'Smith asked a lot but always managed to give back, despite the eccentricity.' Surprised at the tears clotting her voice, Sarah said, 'We all have something beautiful in us.' She started slightly; the letter was up in her flat. She didn't like being this far from her lucky charm.

'From anybody else,' said Jane, leaning over to rub Sarah's arm, 'that'd make me vom. But from you . . .' She smiled, slapped a bug on her shin. 'I can take it.'

By the shed, Tom glugged some water, his Adam's apple bobbing.

Changing the subject, Sarah said, 'That shed's never been opened in the two years I've lived here.'

'I've been here since Una was born,' said Lisa. 'The shed was already a dump then. Full of rats, probably,' she added, with some satisfaction.

'Or, if we're really lucky, a dead body,' said Tom. He yanked at the padlock and it gave easily, sending him careering back into the pile of ivy he'd just swept up.

Jane's laughter set them all off; Tom's attempts to stagger to his feet made them laugh harder. The harsh bang of a window closing silenced them all like a gunshot.

'That'll be Mavis,' said Lisa. 'She hates people enjoying themselves.'

'She came to mine for dinner,' announced Sarah to general amazement.

'Mavis *eats*?' said Lisa.

'I assumed she drank the blood of young maidens,' said Tom, upright again, dignity restored. In a way.

'I feel like Mavis is waving from out at sea,' said Sarah. 'She wants to be rescued.'

'If she wants to be rescued,' said Jane, 'she should stop putting on that old-fashioned accent.'

'Do you think she puts it on?' asked Sarah.

'Since when did people who live in poky flats and wear the same filthy apron every day talk like a duchess?'

The new improved Mavis #2 needed a champion. 'I see something in her,' said Sarah.

'Something beautiful?' Tom smiled directly at her.

'Something 'orrible,' muttered Lisa, just as Mavis appeared and said a loud, 'Good afternoon, everybody.'

Sarah jumped up, vacating her deckchair. 'Sit! Sit!' she said, into what was visible of Mavis's face between the immense sunhat and the buttoned polyester collar.

Tom waved a gloved hand. 'I'm Tom, the newbie. We haven't met properly.'

Sitting on the grass, at Una's level, Sarah listened as Tom tried heroically to engage his new neighbour in conversation.

'Great weather, isn't it?'

Nothing.

'You've lived here for some time, I hear?'

Nothing.

'I bet this house has a few tales to tell.'

Nothing.

'Remember,' said Lisa, leaning down to her daughter and enunciating carefully as if the child was foreign, 'when Daddy and you planted sunflowers?'

Una stared at the dry stumps. Tom looked too; when he realised Sarah was watching him, he pulled a sad face.

'She doesn't talk,' said Lisa.

In her chair, Mavis quickened, but said nothing.

'Not a dicky bird,' Lisa went on, bafflement and disappointment and something akin to anger underpinning her words. 'She just stopped one day. Worst thing is, I can't get any info out of her.'

'Info?' queried Sarah, locking eyes with Una, reading a great many things there, but unsure how much of it she was projecting. It was hard to look at Una without the whoosh of time travel in her ears.

'Information about Graham.' Una wrinkled her nose. 'I'm sure he's got a new bird, but Una can't tell me nothing when she gets back from his place. Drives me mad.' Lisa didn't seem to notice the concerned looks passing between the other adults.

Except for Mavis, who studied the patchy lawn around her feet, as silent as Una.

As if incanting a spell, as if the others weren't there, Lisa said dreamily, 'I reckon he left me for that tart, but he just says I'm mad.' This pebble was rubbed flat from being turned over and over in Lisa's mind. 'I'm not mad. I know what I know.'

Sarah wanted to smooth out Lisa's forehead with her hands. She was stuck in a similar loop, asking unanswerable questions about her own failed relationship.

When Jane went for a fresh supply of cold drinks, she took Una with her, showering her with the questions adults ask little ones: 'What's your favourite book? How old are you?'

That wouldn't help, Sarah knew. Little Una needed to swim about in her silence until she chose to talk. Direct queries only made her self-conscious.

The shed gave up its treasures. An old hoe. A stringless tennis racquet. A leaning tower of flowerpots. The women watched Tom work, all sinking into a blissful sun-baked torpor. Bees zipped by, purposeful busybodies, and the drone of the main road felt far away.

'Dahlias,' said Mavis abruptly, jolting sleepy Lisa awake. Mavis coughed, as if her voice was dusty. 'Dahlias would go nicely in that bed there.'

'They would,' agreed Tom. His nose was sunburned, just starting to glow in a prettily radioactive way. He winked at Sarah when Mavis looked down once again.

Is he flirting with me? Sarah was canny enough to recognise that she only suspected Tom of flirting because of her reaction to his wink. Like a scientist observing a lab rat, she noted the leap in her pulse. It was a relief to welcome back her libido, missing in action since the divorce. She could practise on Tom, knowing there was no pressure.

The man's innate decency was, ironically, one of the reasons she found him attractive. Even if Tom noticed her tiny – very tiny, vanishingly small – crush, he'd never act on it.

'An actual rose!' Tom reached into the undergrowth and plucked a straggly pink bud, its petals edged with the brown of decay. 'M'lady, for you.' He bowed and handed it to Sarah, just as Jane reappeared with her bounty of Coca Cola and Sprite.

'Watch out, Sarah,' she laughed, handing out the icily perspiring tins. 'You're just Tom's type.'

Flushed, Sarah held her can to her cheek. Guilt pounced, but she batted it away. Jane was joking, as usual, with the self-assurance of a woman who is soundly, roundly loved. She looked at her watch. It was almost time to speed walk back to St Chad's.

Una stayed on her feet, orbiting the adults. With Mavis in their midst, conversation was stilted. Jane pulled a helpless face at Sarah; tension emanated from the older woman, the heavy air shot through with prickly discomfort.

'Sarah, couldn't *you* help Una?' said Tom as he wiped the cracked window of the shed. 'Isn't that your line of work?'

'It's not that simple. I can't just lend a hand. There are procedures.'

Lisa slumped, her hopes raised and dashed in double quick time.

'Besides, there are personal reasons ...' Sarah, embarrassed, had everybody's attention. 'If you identify too closely with a patient, it can be problematical.'

'What personal rea—' began Jane, before Tom stopped her.

'NYB, Janey.'

'Not your business.' Jane translated for Sarah. 'I'll worm it out of you later,' she stage-whispered.

Perhaps it would be good to talk. Sarah could already imagine the partisan support, the hugs. It would be good to be hugged.

Turning to Mavis, Sarah roped her into the conversation. 'Jane's house-hunting in Suffolk for a client.'

'He's filthy rich, Mavis,' said Jane. 'No taste. Reckons he's looking for something medieval, but he'll cover it in leopard skin and stick a hot tub in the cellar.'

Mavis's shoulders lifted, but her face gave nothing away, as if there was a law against laughter. 'I'm very fond of Southwold, on the Suffolk coast,' she said.

'Yes!' Jane was thrilled, as if she'd won a prize. 'An old-fashioned pier and candy-coloured beach huts!'

'I went there once,' said Sarah, recalling an anniversary weekend. 'There's a lovely old hotel, what was it . . .'

'The Swan,' said Mavis.

Mavis by the sea required a leap of imagination. She was a creature of dank kitchens and dim back rooms. 'I didn't realise you ever leave London,' said Sarah. Mavis was part of the fabric of number twenty-four; no day was complete without one of her black looks.

'I, well . . .' Mavis responded to this throwaway question by clamping her teeth together.

'I didn't mean . . .' Sarah coughed. Talking to Mavis was like kissing a wasp.

'Hey, Una!' Jane stopped the child on one of her circuits. 'I've guessed your favourite colour. Is it bogey green?'

'Cunning, ve-ry cunning,' said Tom.

'Too direct,' whispered Sarah.

'Breaks my heart to see Una like this, it really does.' Jane sighed and rubbed Lisa's hand; Lisa enjoyed the attention. Turning, Jane said, 'And I keep meaning to say something to you, Mavis.'

'Yes, dear?' Mavis looked up, all attention.

'I'm so sorry about your sister.'

Sarah bounced, trying to catch Jane's attention, to semaphore 'Stop!' as Mavis accepted the sympathy with a stiff incline of her head.

'I'm Zelda Bennison's biggest fan,' said Jane. 'I've read every single book she wrote.'

'I haven't ready any of them,' said Mavis.

'Oh.' Jane did her best to smother her shock. 'Not even—'

'Maybe Una's silent because,' interrupted Mavis, her straw hat shading her features, 'she realises it's not necessary to talk *all* the time.'

As Mavis tried to pull herself to her feet, Jane's mouth was a shocked 'O'.

Mavis flinched from the arm Sarah held out. 'I'm perfectly all right.'

Watching Mavis retreat from the electric brightness of the garden, Sarah said to Jane, 'You touched a nerve.'

'Oh, yeah, it's *my* fault,' said Jane. 'How dare I praise her sister. What a cow I am. Honestly, Sarah, once an old bag,

73

always an old bag. That woman isn't who you think she is. There's no lovely old dame trying to get out. Probably just another, even worse old dame.'

'She's trying.' A ghost hovered by Mavis: the woman she wanted to be.

'She ignored me,' said Tom.

Sarah mewed her agreement. 'Mavis is like a problem toddler who doesn't play well with other kids.'

'It's simpler than that,' said Jane. 'She's horrible.'

Before Sarah could disagree, a raucous 'Hello!' made them all look up. Leo waved from the roof terrace, an oasis of potted palms and rattan recliners and Diptyque candles. 'Still on for tonight, darling?'

'Yes, OK.' Sarah had half expected Leo to forget his promise; feeling Jane's eyes on her, she realised she'd hoped to keep it secret.

When Leo disappeared indoors, Jane asked suspiciously, 'Still on for what exactly?' The explanation left Jane puzzled. 'You said you barely talk to Leo. Are you sure you want his help? You look anxious.'

Sarah's tummy, alive with butterflies, seemed to believe she was a virgin anticipating her first date. 'Leo and I are cool,' she said, feeling anything but; a forest fire swept upwards from her toes as she backed away over the grass. 'Even Helena and I are cool.'

'Rubbish,' said Lisa. 'I couldn't be matey with the woman who nicked my bloke.'

'No, honestly, it's . . .'

'Cool?' Jane was sardonic. 'Let *us* help if you need it. Sod stupid old Leo.'

Tom, from within the shed, called, 'Yeah, don't fall for it. You'll thank us later.'

Sarah saw how Lisa sat stock-still and listened, delighted, to the conversation. 'Guys, you're being very melodramatic.' Warmed by their concern, Sarah also wanted to brush them away, to gag the commonsensical uproar. 'It's just two people doing a bit of wallpaper scraping.'

'Hmm.' Tom emerged with a rake, looking wry. 'Why is Leo still in this house? I couldn't live in the same house as my ex-wife.'

'You don't have an ex-wife.' Jane was tart.

'Not yet,' laughed Tom, withdrawing.

As Sarah tiptoed away, Jane said, 'You could sell that flat as is, Sarah. Notting Hill properties get snapped up whatever state they're in. The truth is, you can't face moving, can you? You're putting it off. That's why you refused my help. You can't leave Leo behind.' She raised her voice as Sarah let herself in through the back door. 'I'm right, aren't I?'

'Sorry,' called Sarah. 'Can't hear you!'

Sarah typed and answered phones and soothed anxious parents' nerves. Keeley whisked past her reception desk a couple of times; Sarah felt her eye on her. And then it was time to go home.

Then it was seven o'clock.

Then Leo was there. In her flat. *Our flat*, Sarah corrected herself.

Leo wandered the rooms with his hands in his pockets, thoroughly at home.

'This is new.' He ran his hands over the butcher's block in the kitchen.

'I've always wanted one.' Sarah fiddled with the kettle. She used to sleep with Leo every night, but now she wondered what to say to him. 'You always vetoed it.'

'Bet you paid over the odds.' Leo slapped the butcher's block. 'Still, it's your kitchen now, darling.'

Leo's sense of entitlement had always charmed Sarah. It was part and parcel of his toff wardrobe of blazers and cords and a fondness for nursery desserts; Leo was anybody's for a Spotted Dick. Sarah, who needed a welcome before making herself at home, felt confident in the long shadow he cast.

Shouts drifted up from the darkening garden. Mischief was being made with a hose. Life was unfurling down there, in the previously barren earth. Its tentacles reached almost, but not quite, to the top flat, where time seemed to have turned on its heel and gone backwards.

'What colour are you going with on the walls?' Leo called into the kitchen as he made himself at home, feet up, on the sofa. He didn't even feign picking up a tool.

'White. To optimise the space.'

'How bloody boring. What did we choose?' asked Leo, sitting forward as Sarah emerged with a coffee made precisely to his tastes. Another redundant skill. 'Was it Farrow and Ball Incarnadine?'

'Yeah.' Sarah had privately thought it too gloomy.

'Shame ...' Leo was subdued. 'It would have looked amazing.'

Sarah's life was cluttered with would haves.

Leo patted the cushion beside him, but Sarah needed to pace, to keep on the move.

'Where are you looking?' he said.

Sarah looked puzzled, so Leo spelled it out. 'Where are you moving to? Notting Hill? Further afield?'

'I'm not sure. I haven't narrowed it down yet.' Sarah had yet to look in an estate agent window.

'Don't go too far, darling.' Leo scattered mixed messages like a trail of breadcrumbs.

Sarah walked to the window, digesting this, arms wrapped around herself as if strait-jacketed. She didn't quite trust herself around Leo. Whether she'd kiss him or break his nose she wasn't sure, but it was imperative to keep some open water between them.

Since he left, Sarah felt like one of the pale marks on the walls where his paintings had hung. There was no musky maleness to untidy her life. She missed Leo's thighs and his hands and the dark spread of his stubble.

He saved me. Sarah made no apologies for the colourful imagery; Leo had reached through a thicket of thorns and saved her. Her childhood had amounted to a PhD in self-reliance; she'd grown up to be staunchly independent, with a career that she adored (that her mother damned as 'dull, dull, dull!') and hadn't even known she needed rescuing until Leo did just that.

During their marriage Sarah had relaxed and let Leo take the reins. 'A man like Leo,' her mother had drawled, 'needs to be in charge.' Taking her mother's advice regarding relationships was, in retrospect, self-sabotage.

Sarah had naively believed they were together 'forever'. Now she felt cowed by his presence, even though she could map every freckle on his body. 'Don't go too far, says the man who moved out the minute I discovered his affair.'

Leo flopped back as if fatally wounded. 'Oof. You got me. I deserved that.'

'Yeah, you did.'

Leo let out a shocked 'Ha!' He bit his lip and looked her up and down, making Sarah wish she hadn't slipped into her overalls. 'All I'm saying, darling, is that it's a tricky decision to make while you're a wee bit fragile. Don't do anything rash. I care about you, Sarah.' The weather on his face changed. 'Very much.' He sat forward, earnest.

Unable to compute that Leo might still care, Sarah simply ignored it. 'If I *am* a wee bit fragile,' she said, 'whose fault is that?'

'Can't you lay down your sword for a minute?'

The sword was heavy, but it was glued to Sarah's hand. She'd been dignified throughout their divorce; now she wondered why she hadn't filed her teeth into points and pounded on their front door. The peaceful handover had been Sarah's last gift to Leo, and he hadn't even noticed. 'It all happened so damn fast, Leo. Last June, you told me about Helena.' To hell with polite language. Sarah rephrased it. 'Or rather, last June you confessed to shagging Helena.' She enjoyed Leo's groan. 'On the *same day*,' she stressed, 'you moved out and set a divorce in motion. It was a hit-and-run.'

'I should have been more sensitive.' Leo looked pained. 'I'm sorry, darling.'

Just like that. He said sorry at last. The room hummed with the power of the word. Leo, who never admitted fault, be it using the last of the milk or ruining his first wife's life, hung his head. Still smiling, of course; he hadn't *completely* changed.

'Thank you.' Sorries and thank yous were sacred talismans, charged with power to heal. Sarah used them both liberally, a direct rebuke to her mother's refusal to use them at all. 'I needed to hear that.'

'Excellent!' Leo clapped his hands, pleased with himself, as if he'd not only healed their rift, but solved Third-World hunger in the process.

'We're not quite finished.' This sadistic side to Sarah was new. 'So, as I said, you start the divorce, and the decree nisi arrived in January.' The document had exploded like a nail bomb in Sarah's heart. 'Within a fortnight, Helena was Mr Leo Harrison. A *fortnight*, Leo.'

'Surely the faster we went, the less pain for you?'

'Aw.' Sarah was all innocence. 'You did it for *me*?'

'Things have worked out, haven't they?' Leo fidgeted. This wasn't going how he planned.

'Have they?' In theory, sharing a house was civilised, modern; in actuality, Sarah's nose was daily rubbed in the happiness Leo had found without her.

She and Leo had been everything to each other. He'd never got along with her friends. 'The noise, darling, when you all get together and shriek!' Sarah had pointed out his sexism, but bit by tiny bit she'd shifted position, until she saw less and less of those strong women. Texts and emails crossed in the ether: 'It's been ages!'; 'Must get together!' Even the strongest thread has its breaking point. She'd buried herself in marriage; for all she knew, those friends had needed her desperately. As much as she wanted to, Sarah couldn't turn up now, needy and weepy.

Phoning her mother had been out of the question; why invite an up-to-date list of her shortcomings? Her father would have helped, but Death leaves no forwarding address. Sarah could piece together what he'd say from her patchwork of memories. Even if he was, as her mother insisted, a hound, he'd have been on Sarah's side. She blocked her ears to another of her mother's mantras: 'You wouldn't hero-worship him if he was still alive, believe me.'

Back in the here and now – Sarah had become proficient at slipping back and forth through slits in time – she handed Leo a wallpaper stripper.

He looked at it blankly. 'So we're actually . . . ?'

'What else are you here for?'

He didn't answer for a moment. Cogs seemed to whirr

inside his head. At last he accepted the stripper, chewing at the inside of his cheek.

Attacking the hall wallpaper side by side felt like the reprise of an old song. They'd spent hours on such tasks before the split. Almost touching, Sarah and Leo lapsed into personalities they'd shed last summer. He teased her. She reacted. He laughed. She pushed him.

The bare shape on the wall grew. Sarah shied away from examining the frisson she felt in the enclosed space, preferring to simply enjoy it for a few selfish minutes.

She hadn't appreciated the beauty of the everyday when they were together: there was a lesson in that, an exhortation to live in the moment. When Sarah was finally over Leo, she'd try and apply it.

Or, she thought, *when we get back together.*

That was the first sighting of the comet in her sky. Flashy and boiling with sparks, it drowned out what Leo was saying, and he had to repeat himself.

'I said working in this bloody hall in this bloody heat is like being in bloody prison.' Leo leaned back, pushing away the curls that flopped over his forehead.

'What are you in for?' Sarah, excited by the daring of her own subconscious, persevered with the faded greens and greys of the stubborn pre-war wallpaper. 'Murder?'

'I got life for strangling a cockatoo in cold blood.' Leo mimed this very act. 'That bird's a bastard. I swear it sits by the window and waits for me to come along. It told me it was sick of the sight of me this morning.'

81

'Peck has issues.'

'So has his owner.'

'Don't.' Sarah recalled the times they'd both mocked Mavis. 'She's changed.'

'Don't pretend to like that nightmare of a woman. You used to impersonate her for me.'

Guiltily, Sarah remembered her party piece. 'I didn't know her then. She's tricky, prickly, but she's trying. I think.'

Bored of Mavis, Leo asked, 'What are *you* in jail for?'

'Me? I'm innocent,' said Sarah piously.

'They all say that.'

Sarah was far from innocent; she was spending time with Leo under false pretences. She didn't want his help with the wallpaper; she wanted him near her.

He was, she thought, *my husband first.*

As a mitigating circumstance it was feeble. 'I might book a few days in Rome next month,' lied Sarah.

'Ah, Roma,' said Leo, as she'd known he would. He turned to Sarah. 'The Hotel Raphael.'

'Our room was all white.' Like the sheer drapes around their honeymoon four-poster, Sarah had been light as a breeze, made of nothing, with Leo's eyes on her. Presumably the same home movie played in his head; their slow lovemaking in the violet Roman dusk. Lust sanctified. Their skin scorched and tender.

'The church bells,' said Leo.

She'd lain in his arms, listening to them toll in the dark. 'Do you remember the amazing sunsets?'

'I remember it all,' said Leo.

'Me too.'

'Mostly I remember the never-ending conversation.' Leo leant back on the past. 'We talked about everything, didn't we? I knew if you were having your dreadful period pains, if your mother had picked a fight with you, if you needed a hot chocolate to put you right again.'

'Even married people don't discuss *everything*.'

'*We* did.' The look of uncertainty was rare for Leo. 'Didn't we? Name one thing we didn't talk about.'

'Helena,' said Sarah. 'Or more, specifically, you and Helena having se—'

'Well, obviously we didn't discuss *that*.' Leo punched her gently on the arm. 'Smith!' he yelped, like a bright boy with the answer to Teacher's question. 'We never discussed your *friend*, did we?'

Stung, Sarah found she had nothing to say. His callousness surprised her. Leo had been jealous of Smith, but surely even he could understand Sarah's pain at not being allowed a proper farewell? She took the wallpaper tool out of his hand. She felt him go still, waiting for whatever move she chose to make next. 'Does Helena know you're here?'

'Of course,' he said jauntily. He laughed. 'Of course not.'

'I just heard your front door. She's home.'

'Shit.' Leo looked at his watch. 'Right. Better dash. It's been real,' he laughed, kissing her hurriedly, fraternally, on the cheek.

As Leo let himself out, Sarah was freshly annihilated, as if he'd abandoned her all over again.

Chapter Five

ᏟᎤᏁᏑᏟᎥᎤᏕ ᎰᎯᏦᎬᎯᎳᎯᏏ
Notting Hill, W11

This calendar is FREE to valued customers!
Tuesday 21st June, 2016

DO NOT REMOVE A FLY FROM YOUR FRIEND'S FOREHEAD WITH A HATCHET

It was too new to be a tradition, but all traditions have to start somewhere; as they sifted, side by side, through the flyers and bills on the post table, Mavis had said to Sarah, 'Tuesday already, Sarah. My turn to cook tonight.'

One of Sarah's new roles at St. Chads was to take lunch orders and collect them from a nearby sandwich bar; some of her workmates couldn't overcome their awkwardness at asking the longest serving counsellor for a filled wrap. Sarah enjoyed doing it; not only did the guys in the sandwich shop flirt with her – and, it had to be said, every other female customer – but *everybody* at St Chad's was glad to see her when she went round distributing the baguettes. Food is a basic, wonderful way to communicate.

Perhaps not *all* food. The prospect of dinner down in Flat

E didn't excite: Sarah had never seen anything but the finest ready meals in Mavis's shopping bag.

Nodding at the parents and carers as they arrived with children, calling their designated therapist, manning the signing-in book – all of these tasks gave Sarah pleasure. The simple rhythm of the day was soothing. Sitting back, tapping her teeth with a pencil and looking out at the tree planted by a local councillor on St Chad's forecourt, Sarah felt a sense of peace that had been lacking for some time.

Her duties were straightforward. There was no grey area. It was important work, and it needed to be carefully done, but if she made a mistake all that happened was that a client waited an extra five minutes or the accounts department didn't get their sandwiches.

Nobody tried to harm themselves, or sobbed, or was sent home to a dangerous adult. While the blank inside her remained, Sarah couldn't work directly with children.

She greeted the little ones kindly, put them at ease, but she forbade herself to wonder about their cases. Only when her own ex-clients turned up, surprised and delighted to see her out front, did her resolve falter. Then she'd watch their backs recede as they walked down the corridor, each walk so idiosyncratic, each one of them carrying a burden. Trained to help, she also had a deep *need* to help; her feet felt nailed to the reception carpet as she fought the urge to follow 'her' children.

*

The hall wallpaper was gone. The woodwork was glossy white. A corner of her domain had become sellable. At seven, Sarah lay down her brush, civilised her appearance and set off on her three-minute journey to her dinner date.

Wondering which Mavis would greet her – Dr Jekyll or Miss Hyde – Sarah didn't recognise the click-clack of Helena's heels coming up the stairs until it was too late to turn back.

The cartoonish flash of teeth from Helena was empty. During the divorce Sarah had demonised her rival as a scheming she-wolf. Since then, she'd downsized the insults, in an effort to downsize her own anger, which was, of course, far more corrosive to Sarah than it was to Helena.

Bringing up the rear, like the Duke of Edinburgh escorting the Queen, Leo shouted, 'Darling! Hello!' as they passed.

'Hello yourself.' Leo had visited twice more; Sarah knew something Helena didn't know. The reversal was sweet.

As Mavis's door swung open, a sixth sense made Sarah look up. Way above her, Leo leaned over the bannisters and blew her a kiss. Sarah reached out to catch it – this was an old habit; its revival filled her chest with helium – but a small hand got there before her.

'Come in.' Mavis pretended to stow the kiss in a pocket of her baggy pinafore dress.

'You stupid old cow!' roared Peck.

'Forgive my lodger,' said Mavis wearily.

'Cow! Cow! Cow!'

Sarah caught his eye, the frosty white feathers on the cockatoo's head fanned out into an impressive crest. 'Fool,' he croaked, claws rattling as he staggered about the floor of his cage.

'What does Peck eat?' Sarah wouldn't have been surprised to hear 'souls', but the answer was fresh fruit and vegetables. His spotless wrought-iron mansion was far more homely than the narrow hallway piled high with newspapers that gave way to a square room so dark it could have been a mine. The wet velvet smell of mould clung to everything, the spores dancing down Sarah's throat.

'Make yourself at home, dear,' said Mavis, without irony. Sarah noted that pretentious 'deeah' again, and thought of Mavis's sister, a wealthy powerful woman. The difference in the siblings' situations had been profound; it was astonishing that Zelda Bennison chose to die in Flat E.

Disappearing to the kitchen, Mavis left Sarah on a chair with a ripped seat at a Formica dining table.

'Shut up! Shut up!' screeched Peck.

'I hope you like fish,' called Mavis.

'Stupid tart!' said Peck.

'Love it!' Sarah girded her loins.

'Stupid fathead!' bellowed Peck, bringing to mind another coarse voice. Sarah's mother used to welcome her daughter home from school with: 'You could look pleased to see me! How come your father's such an idol when it's me that puts up with your miserable gob day after day?'

Mavis interrupted Sarah's mother. 'Eat up, dear.'

On a Pyrex plate sat a glistening slab of coral-coloured salmon, surrounded by a salad of asparagus and watercress, with baby potatoes nesting in the leaves.

'This smells amazing.' Sarah hoped her surprise didn't tip over from 'appreciative' to 'rude'. 'Is that ginger?'

'And soy, plus a kiss of garlic.' Mavis, her naked, corrugated face wry, asked, 'Why, dear, what were you expecting?'

'Nothing, no, it's great.' Sarah, flustered, tried a mouthful and then another and the ambrosial dish was all gone.

'More?'

Sarah liked that word. 'Please!'

Dessert of poached pear was sparse but ladylike.

'It makes a change to be cooked for,' said Sarah.

'I used to love being in the kitchen, but now . . .' Mavis's face twitched and she collected the plates, moving arthritically towards the kitchen. Instinct warned Sarah not to leap up with offers of help.

Aid isn't always welcome. Sarah recalled helping Smith into the cab to the airport. Smith's irritation at needing support had curdled their goodbye. There'd been the same suppressed sigh whenever Sarah tried to help with making the bed or putting away groceries. Sarah remembered the firm 'No!', the burning eyes.

A snapshot flashed into her mind, a fragment of memory. A bright day. A taxi pulling away. The back of Smith's head. Sarah's desire to race after the vehicle like a dog. Neither of them knew that the credits were rolling over their movie, that they'd never see each other again.

Standing, Sarah shredded her fingers. Six months was the blink of an eye. The past was an anteroom into which she stepped far too often; she was summoned back by Mavis calling from the kitchenette.

'Do you have room for a glass of dessert wine?'

'I always have room, Mavis.' Sarah had never tried dessert wine, shying away from its twee connotations, and her first sip was cloyingly sweet. The second was honeyed, and she got with the programme, savouring its slow warmth.

'You're sad,' said Mavis, with the same peremptory tone she'd once used to say 'You've put on weight,' when Sarah passed her in new jeans.

'I am, a bit.' This honesty was new: hiding her emotions was a tic engrained in Sarah's childhood, when any hint of melancholy would provoke a tirade about ingratitude and you-don't-know-what-I-go-through-for-you. 'I've been thinking about people who've gone.'

Mavis held up her glass in a silent toast.

'Mavis, I'm sorry. That was insensitive.'

'Not in the least. We all share the sadness of loss. Unless we never love. And that would be an even greater loss.'

A little late, Mavis's heart had been jump-started. Why had she chosen to hide her compassion until Zelda's death? Something dark must have happened to the young Mavis to make her bury herself in the basement of number twenty-four. Sarah said, 'I was thinking about Smith.' How much Mavis knew, Sarah wasn't sure.

'Smith?' Mavis looked confused.

'Smith.' Mavis's confusion confused Sarah. 'My friend in Flat C. Before the Royces.'

'Yes, yes, Smith. No need to talk to me like a child.'

Sarah's professional expertise was with patients at the other end of life, but she identified Mavis's gruff assertion as typical of a dementia sufferer. She wondered how long they'd been happening, these lapses, when facts dropped out of view and Mavis had to grapple for clues about things she should know.

'Smith. Flat C.' Mavis nodded as if everybody in the world knew of the famous Smith in Flat C. 'You and he were friends.'

'He?' Sarah leant forwards, as if there were eavesdroppers who might notice Mavis's blunder. There was only Peck grouching to himself, the sound warped and tantalising, like an argument heard through a wall. 'Mavis, Smith was a "she".'

'Of course.' Mavis's laugh was unconvincing. She tapped her glass with a gnarled nail. 'Blame this,' she said. 'I remember Smith. Flamboyant girl. Carried a guitar everywhere. But not awfully good at it.'

'That's her.'

'Do you remember,' asked Sarah casually, 'that day she and I were staggering through the hall with that statue and you were *furious* with us?'

'Of course.' Mavis coughed self-consciously.

You don't remember at all.

The statue, an armless Roman beauty, had been

languishing outside a garden gate with a note saying "Please take me!" taped to her flaking bosom. Smith, who could never resist a freebie, begged Sarah to help her cart it home.

A big girl, the statue was heavy: more than once they almost dropped her. Laughing so hard at the absurdity of carrying a naked woman through Notting Hill didn't help. First Smith got the giggles, then Sarah was infected, and they'd have to stop and rest until the laughter died down, only for it to start up again when they caught each other's eye.

Mavis – ever alert in those days to sounds of human enjoyment – scurried up from the basement as they groaned their way across the scruffy hall. 'Don't drop that!' she'd barked. 'You'll scuff the floor.'

'Yes,' whispered Smith to Sarah as they hunched over their cement hostage. 'Mustn't scuff this beautiful floor.'

'What's that, madam?' Mavis had been imperious. 'Speak up!'

Letting the statue down gratefully, Smith had caught her breath and said, 'Mavis, this beautiful lady looked so lonely we just *had* to bring her home. Don't you think she's pretty?'

'Load of old tat,' grumbled Mavis.

Smith had never reflected Mavis's bad temper back at her. Sarah only realised this now; *Smith always spoke to her politely, calmly.*

'I like her, Mavis, and she'll make a nice quiet flatmate.'

'She's filthy,' Mavis had persisted.

'None of us'd look our best if we were left outside and

91

forgotten about.' Smith had managed to find Mavis amusing. Sarah remembered wishing the old lady would leave them to it.

Now, in the Smith-less present – *I really miss those breezy high spirits* – Mavis said, 'Do you want this kiss I caught?' Mavis blinked artlessly as she reached into her pocket. 'Or shall I throw it in the bin?'

The idea of Leo's kiss – even a make-believe one – in with fish scales and pear peel made Sarah frown.

'Sarah, you must be aware that Leo has only lent you this kiss.'

'You can't borrow love, Mavis.'

'Hmm, love.' Mavis's woolly eyebrows met. 'Peculiar, wispy beast. It lands. It stays. It scampers off.'

'Have you ever—' began Sarah.

'Sad about that little girl, Una. Do you think there's hope for her speaking again?'

'Definitely.'

'The child cowers from me. I snarled at her, before . . .' Mavis sounded small. 'I've burned a lot of bridges.'

'They can be rebuilt.' Busy hammering her own rickety bridge to the past, Sarah wanted to believe this. 'Look at me and Leo.'

'I'd rather not,' said Mavis, the old model reaching out a claw from beneath the new plumage. 'How complicated we make our lives. Everybody in this house has a unique set of circumstances, their own complexities. And the house next door will be just the same. And the one the far side of that.'

'Do you include yourself in that analysis?' Time to push a little at Mavis's cast-iron borders.

'If you mean, am I human, absolutely.'

'I meant, have you made your life complicated, Mavis?' Sarah thought of the schism between the Bennison sisters, the socialite writer and the bad-tempered mole.

'I wish ...' Mavis felt her way, taking bite-sized pieces. 'I wish ... I hadn't ... I mean, I wish ... my sister ...' She stopped. 'You tricked me into talking about Zelda.'

'Sorry.' *Not sorry.*

'The answer's yes, I've made a spectacular mess of my life. My sister's death ...'

'Is none of my business.' Sarah touched Mavis's fingers.

Pulling her hand away as if Sarah was red-hot, Mavis said, 'It *is* your business, because you've shown me kindness. All these years living here, pushing people away, makes it difficult to surface.' Mavis mimed swimming upwards, her white hair thrown back, her face troubled and yearning. Sitting back in her chair, she said, 'You're a lifesaver, Sarah.'

'What if we're pulling each other back to shore?'

'Saving each other's lives, you mean?'

'This house – well, I don't need to tell *you* this, you've lived here longer than me – but this house is changing. I'd run up to my flat, lock the door and it was like the rest of number twenty-four didn't exist, apart from Smith. I nodded at Lisa, ignored Helena, and, frankly, I kept out of your way.'

Mavis closed her eyes, accepting it.

'Now the house is waking up. Shaking itself. I'm waking up, too, and you're part of that.' The evening had been fun. More fun than dinner with an elderly sourpuss had any right to be.

'I have so much to atone for.'

'Stop dragging around your past, Mavis.' Sarah didn't know what had happened to make Mavis so cynical, but she knew what had brought her to her senses. 'Zelda's death was a crossroads, wasn't it?'

'It changed everything.'

'Death steals the wrong people.' Sarah thought of her father's face, frozen in time on her mantelpiece. Crazy that she'd never know what kind of old man he'd make.

'This time it certainly did,' said Mavis.

'You nursed Zelda until the very end. She must have been so grateful to have a sister like you.'

Mavis went so quiet that the room seemed to close down around them. Even Peck stopped grumbling. 'You'd be surprised what Zelda might have to say about me. And my nursing skills.'

'Survivor guilt. You did your best.'

'It was she who banished me, you know. My sister never loved me or anybody else.'

Staying very still, Sarah listened. It was a skill she called on daily in her job. She listened not only with her ears, but with her brain and, crucially, her heart.

'I couldn't help loving Zelda, even though she told people

I'd forsaken her. The truth is, when she died I should have died with her.'

'I for one am thankful you're still here.' Sarah meant it. 'Let's swim to shore together, Mavis.'

The words rustling like dead leaves, Mavis said, 'I'd only drag you down. I ...' Mavis took a breath, started again. 'There are aspects of ...' Something was tunnelling its way out of her. 'If you knew all about me, Sarah, you'd run for the door.'

'Get lost, bum face!' hollered Peck.

'For once,' said Mavis, 'he's right. I mustn't keep you.'

They were on the verge of a meaningful breakthrough, a possible end to Mavis's self-imposed exile in the belly of number twenty-four. 'You were about to tell me something.'

'Nothing interesting, I assure you.' The atmosphere lost its poignancy. They were just two women in a dingy room.

'What if,' said Sarah impulsively as they reached the front door, 'I was to help you sort out the flat? Or maybe style your hair? You'd look wonderful with it all swept up—' The hand she reached out was slapped away.

'Excuse me? I need a haircut? The flat needs *sorting out*?' Mavis held the phrase between two fingers as if it was dirty.

Peck whistled low.

'That came out all wrong.' Sarah backed away. 'Thanks for the lovely food.'

'Perhaps you could show me how to cook it better?'

'Bugger orf!' yelled Peck.

Chapter Six

Pembridge Road was a row of eccentrically disordered shops, the antithesis of the bland British high street, so it was perfect for an individual who wanted to lose themselves in trivia, to pull together their scattered fibres. That Wednesday lunchtime it was perfect for Sarah, who'd awarded herself time off from scraping and painting and breaking her nails.

The colours and fabrics in the window of Retro Woman were sensory passports to another time. Even though the shell-pink slip had been sewn long before Sarah was born, it sparked nostalgia in her, as did the narrow satin shoes and the moulting boas. The colours were faded, subtle, difficult to pin down; were those suede gloves pinky beige or beigey pink?

The price tags were clear enough. Notting Hill re-packaged the olden days at very modern prices.

Spending time with Leo gave Sarah a hangover. An urge to rush about and clear the air of its charged atmosphere. All they'd done the evening before, after Sarah's dinner with Mavis, was smooth Polyfilla over the dents in the sitting-room wall, but Sarah felt like a fallen woman.

The snatched half-hours were a mixed blessing. Leo incited a tingle of excitement and guilt, plus dismay; after all, his help made it more likely she'd meet the deadline. At the end of August Sarah would run out of road.

Jane had begun showing her listings. Airy maisonettes. A spacious doer-upper. A shoebox with a bed that came down from the wall. None of them looked like home.

'Look!' said a woman to Sarah's left, in the sing-song voice adults use with children. 'Pretty!' Lisa was pointing to a rainbow-coloured dress but Unà ignored her, her earnest face tilted towards Sarah. 'Oh. You,' said Lisa, noticing her neighbour.

'Hello!' Sarah compensated for the woman's blank rude-ness. 'And hello you.' She bent down to Una.

'No point. She doesn't—'

'You told me.' Perpetually reiterating Una's muteness over her head underlined it. 'Maybe, just maybe, if I point at the lovely bits and pieces in this window, Una will smile when I get to her favourite.'

'I'm telling you, no point,' repeated Lisa.

'The bag. The shoes.' Sarah wondered which of the

window's bounty would appeal to a child. 'The red shoes with the polka dot bow.'

A smile, small but boisterous, couldn't be contained.

'A-ha!' said Sarah.

'Bloody hell.' Lisa gawped. 'How'd you manage that?'

Her rule about not discussing children in their earshot was one Sarah never broke. 'The garden's looking better, isn't it?'

'Yeah,' said Lisa.

'Yeah,' said Sarah. The two women had much in common, both of them making the best of abandonment, but they had no conversation at all. Lisa was as barricaded in as her little girl. 'So, anyway.' Sarah backed away, shoulders hunched, a cheerily faux *goodbye!* grin pasted on her face. 'Gotta dash.'

The rooms were naked, echoing.

'There's something special about empty houses.' Sarah spun in the middle of the floorboards, arms flung out, taking in the enormous salon. 'All that potential. And history.' The bare space awoke memories of her father showing her around his bachelor pad, calling it 'our flat' to soften the blow of his leaving. She could almost, not quite, feel how small her hand seemed in his; the knowledge of him, physically, came and went, like stuttering Wi-Fi.

'It's the smell of plaster and paint that does it for me.' Jane sniffed the air. She'd turned up, tooting the horn, in St Chad's car park at the end of Sarah's working day, begging for company as she checked out a couple of grand properties.

'If I didn't do this for a living I'd have to break in and wander around empty houses at night.'

'D'you think your clients will like this?' Sarah crossed to the tall window. 'They'd be crazy not to. Stucco exterior: tick. Cantilevered staircase: tick. Original elm floors: tick. Plus a space-age kitchen that would spark sexual fantasies in all right-thinking women.' The house was waiting, already haunted by its future inhabitants. 'I'd love to live here.'

'Maybe. But you're not the wife of a Russian billionaire who has three hundred pairs of shoes to accommodate.'

Sarah had eight pairs of shoes, all past their prime, only six of which fitted her. She peeked through a doorway which led onto another doorway. The house unfolded neatly, the way life should but rarely does. The emptiness begged to be filled: Sarah felt the same. A thought she usually held at bay stole through her defences: *will I ever live in a house with a man to call my own and children around my feet?*

'Plus she doesn't do stairs, and I can't see where to put a lift.' Jane made a *tsk* noise with her tongue and scribbled on a clipboard. Work-Jane was subtly different to home-Jane: twinkle intact, but sharp with it. Attractive in the literal sense of the word, she was a blurred point of activity in any room, a colourful scrawl lit from within.

The basement was no subterranean Mavis-style lair: it had been dug out and transformed into a swimming pool. Empty of water, its pearly tiles glistened. Jane ran a hand along the walls. 'Patchy finishing.' Disappointed, she made a note on her clipboard. 'Leo scuttled off pretty quick when I nipped up to yours last night.'

'He didn't scuttle.'

Jane peered at the lighting panel. 'It was a classic scuttle. As if I'd caught you doing something naughty.'

'Nothing naughty about D.I.Y.' Sarah turned away. Anything she did with Leo, no matter how chaste, could be classified as 'naughty', simply because she'd begun to day-dream about the ex-Mrs Harrison becoming the third Mrs Harrison. The current Mrs Harrison might have something to say about this fantasy; Helena wouldn't go down without a fight.

Locking up the vast front door, Jane wouldn't drop the subject. 'Leo's face was a picture. He's after you, Sarah.'

'He left me, remember? I'm the one he *doesn't* want, to paraphrase Olivia Newton-John.'

'Perhaps cheating turns him on.' Jane led the way to her car out in the mews. 'Hop in, missus, and stop blushing.'

'I'm not blushing.' Sarah buckled up and pulled down the mirror on the sun visor. 'Oh.' She was the colour of the tomatoes that sprouted as and when the fancy took them on her windowsill.

'What do you, *did* you see in Leo, exactly?' The car rolled out through electric gates that delivered them from the ease of wealth to the noise of the street.

'He's . . .' Sarah didn't understand the question. Surely every woman fancied Leo? Wasn't he catnip, with his wry face and his just-fallen-out-of-somebody's-bed allure?

'I get the upper-class thing, although I prefer a bit of rough myself.' Jane leaned forward, pushing through the traffic. 'But the paunch and the cigar habit . . . Leo looks as if he'd conk out if he had to run a hundred yards. Whereas you . . .' Jane sighed. 'You think Leo's the prize, but it's you, you fool.'

'Leo and me, it's complicated.' Sarah held on to the seat belt as they found a stretch of clear road and the car barrelled along as if they were making a getaway.

'Nothing's complicated.' Jane peered over the steering wheel as she zipped through some lights. 'We all know when we're being reckless. We just don't acknowledge it. Before I got married my love life was a soap opera. I chose the wrong guy, over and over, like somebody who keeps ordering the same dish on the menu, thinking this time it'll taste better. But,' said Jane philosophically, as she cut up a lorry on a roundabout, 'eggs Benedict is always eggs Benedict. And I *hate* eggs Benedict.'

'Then you met Mr Right?'

'I *grabbed* Mr Right. Poor sod had no choice in the matter. My days of eggs Benedict are over.' Jane's smile needed an extra face to do it justice. 'Oh, Sarah, it was so perfect. I knew immediately. I almost scared him off. I was all—' She took her hands off the wheel and waved them maniacally, screaming for extra effect. 'In the end, he gave in. As I tell him every day, it's the best decision he ever made.'

'You give me hope.'

'Why do you need hope?' Jane was warmly scornful.

'You could jump out of this car and nab a bloke before you reached the end of the road.'

'What if I don't want this hypothetical bloke?' In any way that truly mattered, Sarah was still married.

'Then you go on to the next one. And so on and so forth,' said Jane loftily, 'until you find the one that floats your boat, rings your bell, et cetera, et cetera. Then you snog off into the sunset and settle down and have babies and all that shit.' They idled at a red light. 'If you want babies, that is. Not everybody does.'

'Leo and I never got round to it. I wanted to establish myself at St Chad's. Perhaps I should have ...' Sarah blew out her cheeks. 'I thought we had all the time in the world.'

Jane darted concerned looks at Sarah.

'It feels like a door slammed. The idea of having a child with somebody else ...' Sarah shuddered. She couldn't even picture herself naked with A.N.Other, as if her body was jointly owned by herself and Leo in the same way as Flat A. 'Maybe I should have let nature take its course. I would have coped, somehow, with work and a child. And now I'd have something to love.' *Something of Leo's.*

'You have me!' Jane beeped the horn at a jaywalker. Her eye caught something and she rolled down her window. 'Oi! Yes you! Hop in.' Settling back, she said, 'You don't mind a hitchhiker, do you?'

Tom stood on the far pavement, raising a broad palm in greeting. As he watched the cars for a break in their ranks, Sarah said, 'How about you, Jane? Are babies on the agenda?'

Tom saw his chance and took it, sprinting towards them.

'Depends. There are ... oh, it's boring, but my womb's a bit uncooperative. Dull medical shizzle.'

'I see.' Sarah regretted asking so blithely.

Tom swung into the back seat, slinging his rucksack ahead of him and bringing the mercury scent of the street.

'And besides,' said Jane, 'you need to have sex to make babies and *that* doesn't happen very often.'

Glancing behind her, Sarah checked whether Tom had heard.

Pulling on his seat belt, shimmying into a comfortable position, he laughed 'What?' when he saw Sarah's stricken face. He looked out of the window, and Sarah found his profile in the driver's mirror, studying him without his knowledge as Jane chattered.

The feelings Tom invoked weren't entirely new but they'd been absent for so long that Sarah had to dust them off and examine them a little more closely before deciding exactly what they were.

Not exactly desire. But not *not* desire, either.

She noticed details. How his nose looked daintily broken. The stubble that broke through on his chin. The clever straightness of his eyebrows. Like a virus, it raged through her, this not *not* desire, this *interest*.

'Are we headed home?' asked Tom.

'We're going for ice cream.'

'Why?'

Jane was scandalised. 'Surely you mean why not?'

With Tom and Jane jousting about which radio station to listen to, Sarah felt as if they were all off on a jaunt, like normal people. In Sarah's new regime, 'other' people went on holiday; she hadn't slept a night away from her peeling, creaking flat since the great upheavals began.

'Sarah's been at it again,' said Jane.

From the back, Tom asked what 'it' was, but guessed before anybody answered. 'Why do you hang out with Leo? I don't get it.'

'She loves him,' said Jane, matter-of-fact. 'Even after what he did. Don't you, Sarah?'

'Don't put her on the spot, Janey.' Tom leaned forward and ruffled Sarah's hair.

She almost burst into tears at the touch. Having held herself aloof for months, Tom's brotherly gesture breached her firewall. 'Whether I love Leo isn't the point,' she said. 'It's a step forward. I can't stay angry with him for the rest of my life.'

'Why not?' Jane tapped the steering wheel, winking at a cyclist beside them. 'Chop off his balls and sauté them. He deserves it. Doesn't he, Tom?'

'I don't know enough about the situation to—'

'Oh, do shut up,' said Jane. 'You should hear him go on about Leo when you're not here.'

'I don't!'

'He does. He thinks the guy's mad, giving you up for that overdressed slapper. Look, Sarah, I'm not judging you. If you want to grapple Leo back from Helena, fair play.' She ignored Sarah's splutterings. 'But you'll break your own heart again if it doesn't work. Even if it does work, you'll feel like crap, because you, lady, are not cut out to be a mistress. You're one of nature's goody-goodies.'

Goody-goody was unsexy. Goody-goody was the polar opposite of red-hot Helena. But the signs were all there: Sarah was a Waitrose card holder, a picker up of litter, and could be relied on to say 'Bless you' after a sneeze. 'I've never done anything really *wrong*,' admitted Sarah. So wary of proving her mother's prophecy right – *Just like your father!* – she had an exaggerated conscience. The letter, each word revered as holy scripture, exhorted her to be herself, but Sarah's instincts and her needs were at war. 'Even though Leo and I don't even touch each other it feels wrong.'

'Because it is!' Jane wouldn't let her off the hook. 'He's somebody else's husband now.'

'We're all moving on, like adults. Helena and I are having a coffee tomorrow.'

Consternation broke out in the car.

'You what?' Jane went cockney with horror. 'She nicked your man! Why have coffee with her?'

'I want to, I . . .' Sarah ran out of steam; she couldn't sell such a lie.

From the back seat, Tom asked, 'Whose idea was it?'

The silence was silver-tongued.

'Leo's,' said the Royces in unison.

'He didn't realise what he was asking of me.' They didn't

understand Leo. He was broad strokes, loud noises, but he meant well.

'Either he didn't realise,' said Tom, 'or he didn't care. Either's bad.'

The growl of the handbrake put a full stop to the subject. 'The ice creams are on you, Tom.'

'As usual.' Tom nipped out and held the door for Sarah. 'Funky shoes,' he said, pointing. 'New?'

'Yes.' Sarah tapped the polka dot bows together. 'My stylist chose them.'

Chapter Seven

As Sarah pieced herself together to meet Helena, she allowed herself to admit how keenly she dreaded it.

Trousers? Dress? Hair up, down, back, messy? She cursed Leo for marrying a woman whose style was eulogised in gossip columns.

Opting out of a competition she couldn't win, Sarah pulled on her jeans and took the letter's advice: 'be yourself because you're more than good enough'.

Just the way Sarah was that morning included a stain on her tee and a constellation of heat bumps on her collarbone, but Sarah was more or less at peace with herself. She was a woman-shaped woman, dressed for the sunshine, and sporting the same smudged eyeliner she'd learned to apply in the school loos.

London perspired beyond St Chad's revolving doors, the cracks in the pavements dry as ash. There was a scenic route to the main road, passing white mansions and bijou cottages, but Sarah opted for the other way to save time. She'd lumped her morning and afternoon tea break together, but that only gave her forty minutes. All life is a matter of choosing the various roads that diverge in the woods, and today Sarah chose the tarmac path through a housing estate.

Low-rise, it had probably been a model development before British weather got hold of the concrete facings. British teenagers hadn't done it any favours either; graffiti informed Sarah that 'Annette is a slag' and Manchester United were 'king'. It was a village of sorts, and she sensed a community spirit beneath the dispirited raw materials; the small flats looked cosy.

A baseball cap caught her eye. Or rather, the face beneath it. Graham looked cheesed off, his default setting, as he waited for somebody to catch up with him on a first-floor glass walkway, most of its glass cracked or absent.

A dark-haired woman, skinny, eager, jogged after him.

He had a type; the new girlfriend looked like a younger Lisa.

Laden with shopping, they stopped by one of the doors and scrabbled for keys. Graham glanced down and caught Sarah's eye.

She waved, but didn't break step. When Graham came to the edge of the balcony and called her name she suppressed a sigh. He was a soul Hoover, ever ready to sour the atmosphere.

'You found me out, then,' he called down to her, a raggedy Romeo to her reluctant Juliet.

Sarah shielded her eyes, squinting up. 'How'd you mean?'

'Yeah, yeah, so I'm living with my bird. Big deal.'

Sarah held up her hands. 'Sorry. What?'

'Don't tell her.' Graham jabbed his finger. 'Lisa'll go apeshit.'

'Why would I . . .' The quickest way to end this surreal conversation was to acquiesce. 'Sure. No problem.'

'I mean it.' Graham shook off the appeasing hand of the child woman.

Feeling she'd indulged Graham's paranoia enough, Sarah hurried on. Fear of Lisa's wrath was understandable; his ex had an uninhibited vocabulary and uncanny aim with a shoe.

The encounter gnawed at Sarah as she left the estate and crossed an invisible border into the land of delicatessens and frozen yoghurt purveyors and art galleries which sold ugly prints for more than Graham would earn this year.

In the window seat of the organic farm shop cafe, Helena sat among carrier bags as if styled for a shoot. For Helena, being herself involved layers of make-up that made her face look nude, and a bandeau dress that, along with the dramatic sweep of glossy dark hair and polished olive skin, made Sarah think of business-class flights and white beaches.

Before Helena noticed her, Sarah paused. She looked down at herself, wildly fearful that there'd be clues on her person to what she'd done the night before.

There were no fingerprints on her skin; she and Leo hadn't made contact. The radio burbling in the background, they'd manhandled the furniture out of the spare room and ripped up the hated carpet. Leo had tackled the more tenacious areas, 'to save your hands'. Even so, she'd scratched her finger and he'd commiserated. One cup of tea later and he'd been on his way. It had been chaste, impeccable.

So why do I feel like a hooker?

Sarah and Leo were building something as they dismantled her flat. The rags of their rapport were being stitched back together; the pattern it made was pleasing to her eye.

Helena looked up and smiled, putting aside her magazine.

'Nice place,' said Sarah dutifully, taking the seat opposite her at the wooden table.

'I know,' agreed Helena, taking credit for the cafe's bright, spare interior. 'They know me here.'

'They don't know *me*.' Sarah had passed it by, wondering (a) how on earth a farm shop could stray so far from the sound of tractors and (b) how the food could be 'locally sourced': Notting Hill was short on actual hills.

'The latte is to die for,' said Helena.

'I might try a croissant.'

'They're organic,' said Helena. 'And artisanal.'

Sarah had no idea what that meant. 'They probably grind the flour in the basement using locally sourced stones.' Sarah motioned to the waitress. 'And they're baked by Booker Prize winning novelists.'

'I don't think so.' Helena looked both puzzled and pitying as if Sarah believed her own joke. She adjusted the neckline of her dress, which was doing its level best to deal with her breasts. All Helena's clothes were as tight as corsetry. 'I mean, it's probably made by, like, proper bakers.'

Realising that Helena had stayed home from school the day they covered irony, Sarah asked, 'Will you join me? In a croissant? Not *in* one, just . . .' There truly was no point making jokes around Helena.

'I'm cutting out, like, carbs.' Helena's exotic accent combined with West London Trustafarian tics was peculiar.

It was also alluring. Sarah, fastidiously fair, couldn't deny Helena's sex appeal. 'Carbs are the best bits.'

'My personal trainer would kill me.'

'He works for you, not the other way round.' Sarah didn't understand slavish devotion to personal trainers, high priests of the new order. 'A little of what you fancy does you good.'

'But it's never just a little.' Helena eyed the jam that arrived with the croissant. 'Is it?'

'Thankfully, no.' Sarah refused to be bowed. In the same way she scrolled past any hint of online body shaming bikini body nonsense, she refused to let puritans spoil her enjoyment of food. 'Have you noticed the changes to the garden?'

'It needs hard landscaping. Grey pebbles instead of the grass. Maybe a small water feature and some wind chimes. Very Zen. So soulful.'

'Hmm. Nothing soulful about sunbathing on pebbles.' Sarah spread butter – local, organic, possibly made from angels' breast milk – on a second croissant. It pained her to admit it, but the chic snack *did* taste better than standard coffee shop fare. As if the napkins and the pedigree of the waitress somehow elevated the food.

'That chap, what's his name, Tim, is really putting his back into it.'

The casual tone was what poker players call a tell: *So you fancy Tom, eh?* 'Tom, you mean.'

'Yes, him. Married to that mannish woman.'

'What makes you say Jane's mannish?'

'The hair. The walk. And oh dear, the clothes.' Helena flashed her eyes and the black flicks she drew so expertly on her upper lids lifted like claws.

'She's my friend, so . . .' Half an hour ago, Jane had raved over the phone, 'You're only meeting that rancid blow-up doll to please Leo. He walked out, Sarah! You don't owe him a thing!'

It had been tricky trying to explain without exposing the dubious heart of the matter: *I'm doing what Leo wants so he'll love me again.*

Technically, it was rude behaviour when Helena's head tilted like a meerkat as she surveyed the social scene of the farm shop, but Sarah welcomed the break from laboured conversation. They had little to say to one another; their only common ground was Leo, and Sarah still found it hard to hear his name on those plumped lips.

112

When the affair came to light, Sarah had asked, 'Do you love her?'

When Leo nodded, Sarah felt like a building left standing after everybody in it has died. Only the iron girders of pride held her up.

'I want to be with her.' Leo had had the decency to cry a little.

'Not with me?' Sarah whispered.

'No, my dearest darling,' he'd said sadly. 'Not with you.'

Contemplating the croissant crumbs on her plate as Helena mimed 'Call me!' at somebody, Sarah wondered why she'd behaved so graciously. She remembered her mother's operatic hysterics when her father left, while his face gave nothing away. Perhaps her mother was right: *I am more like him than her.*

'Is there something on my face?' Sarah wiped her mouth self-consciously as Helena scrutinised her. It was the way Leo looked at antique tables when working out whether they were the real thing or clever fakes.

'Your bones . . .' said Helena, thoughtfully, 'Not half bad, actually. A damson lip, a coral cheek and a teeny-tiny shot of Botox just here . . .' Helena leaned over to tap the bridge of Sarah's nose. 'Plus, of course, a decent cut and blow-dry, and you'd be cute.'

'Kittens are cute.' Sarah didn't share Helena's passion for the surface of things, but that didn't mean she was immune to her judgement. 'Next to you,' she said, forgetting to self-edit, 'I feel like an elephant. An elephant with bad dress sense.' It wasn't just that pneumatic Helena was smaller, it was that she was so securely bound, so professionally finished, all her gestures Geisha-neat. 'An elephant with a bad haircut. Let's not forget the bad haircut.'

'Silly.' Helena was playful: compliments stoked her fire. 'You only need to lose a stone or so.'

'I don't like diets. Food is food.' There were no bad guys and good guys in Sarah's fridge.

'Sweetie, detox for one month and you'll wave goodbye to that back fat.'

'I like my back fat.' This wasn't entirely true – Sarah hadn't known she even had back fat – but she stood, Canute-like, against the tide of self-hatred that washed over the children she treated. Seven-year year-olds who kneaded their own – gorgeous – tummies, saying 'Yuk', needed reinforcement that their cuddly young bodies were wonder-ful; instead popular culture set them up for lifelong warfare with their own skin. 'Is back fat even a thing?'

'Whatever, whatever.' Helena dismissed such Amish non-sense. 'Detoxing makes you feel fabulous.'

Everything was fabulous in Helena's world of gratuitous overstatement.

'It's only the toxins holding me together.'

'You'll thank me one day,' said Helena. 'Did you get my email about Mavis?'

'About Mavis?' Helena and Mavis – one perfumed, the other smelling of cockatoo – inhabited separate universes.

'I'm trying to bring the tenants together,' said Helena.

Surprised that the thaw in number twenty-four had reached as far as Helena, Sarah said, 'That's nice. We're already much more friendly than we used—'

'I mean,' interrupted Helena, 'we need to get together and bully Mavis to improve her flat.'

'Over my dead body will anybody bully Mavis.' Since the soured farewell after their last dinner, the old lady had been invisible. Trying to make friends with Mavis, whose skill was for making enemies, was a matter of one step forward, two steps back.

'Bullying is the wrong word. English is my second language. I mean "persuade". If Mavis was to develop her apartment—'

'Let me stop you right there,' said Sarah, amused despite herself. 'Mavis isn't the developing kind. She hasn't bought new curtains since God was a baby.'

'The basement is dragging down the value of the whole house.' Helena looked aggrieved; money was a religion with her. 'If Mavis modernises Flat E we'll all be in the money.'

'We *are* all in the money.' Notting Hill property appreciated at the speed of light. 'Remember Mavis has lived at number twenty-four . . . forever.'

'She'd be happy anywhere. As long as it was filthy.' Helena laid a reassuring hand on Sarah's. Her touch was cool, lizard-like. 'I'm just brainstorming for now, seeing who agrees with me.'

'I don't.'

'The Royces will see my point. She's in property, I believe.'

Yes, but she has a heart. 'Lisa'll get on board,' said Sarah. Lisa's dislike for Mavis had gone up a notch since a recent spectacular snub in the corner shop. Sarah saw it as another sign of possible dementia but Jane had pointed out it was entirely in character and more likely just Mavis being Mavis.

'Lisa's no use to me, she doesn't own her flat.'

'Apparently the landlord's a crook. Refuses to fix the boiler or repair the kitchen floor or—'

'Yeah, yeah.' Helena waved her hands, dismissing Lisa and her boring cracked floor. 'My point is, Lisa doesn't have a vested interest in the value of the house. Eventually,' said Helena gaily, 'my plan is to get rid of her, too.'

'This is starting to feel like genocide.'

'Just common sense.'

How Leo could have leapfrogged from her bed to Helena's baffled Sarah. The differences between the women went beyond the physical; their values were at odds. Sarah's perfect world would entail everybody raised to the same level, whereas Helena would airbrush the unsightly poor out of the picture.

A vivid memory flared in Sarah's mind of Leo, brandy balloon in hand, begging, 'Oh, do put a sock in it, Sarah darling! I do so hate your woman-of-the-people schtick!' He'd never understood why she bled on behalf of strangers, why she cried at the news and pledged money for famine victims. Now he was with a woman who'd never challenge his blinkered apathy.

'I'm toying with making changes to my apartment,' said Helena.

Flat B was an endless project. A new mural here. Some fresh gilding there. 'Surely there's nothing left to do.'

'Leo and I will need some extra space at some point.' Helena was coy with a capital 'c'.

'What for?' The answer shimmered just out of reach; masochistically Sarah reached for it.

'We'll need a nursery, silly.'

'Are you . . .'

Helena jumped, and laid a hand across her midriff. 'Oh my God, do I look fat?'

'You look like a leaf, Helena.'

Pacified, Helena said, 'Let's put it this way: we're trying.' She giggled suggestively. 'Trying hard!'

It wasn't malice. If Helena had popped that image into Sarah's head on purpose, Sarah could have simply hated her for it, but Helena wouldn't bother trying to make Sarah jealous; she barely noticed her. She'd embezzled Leo with little effort, and now she managed to forget that Sarah was Leo's ex-wife.

'What about you, Sarah? Is your biological clock ticking?'

Out and out cattiness would be preferable to this insulting amnesia. Rivalry would elevate Sarah to her proper position as Wounded Ex. 'If it is,' said Sarah, 'it's not ticking very loudly, 'cos I can't hear it.'

'How's your flat coming along? It's a lot of work for one person.'

'I've had some help recently.' Compulsively, Sarah outed Leo to his wife; if they all had their cards on the table, Sarah's conscience would clear. If Sarah was to turn the juggernaut of Leo's second marriage it must be done out in the open. 'Leo's been amazing.'

'Leo?' A tiny crease appeared between Helena's on-point brows. '*My* Leo?'

Sarah couldn't bring herself to say 'Your Leo'. 'He pulled up a carpet today and whisked it off to the dump for me.'

'Sarah, you know I don't understand your humour.'

'The other day he waxed a dresser.'

Helena stared hard, then threw back her head and showed off her long lovely throat to cackle so loudly she drew looks. 'Oh, that man of mine! What a clever old dog.' She recovered. 'He's a sly boots. The more Leo helps you, the quicker your flat gets finished and the quicker we get our hands on it. Confidentially, all gals together ...' Helena lowered her voice. 'I wanted to make you an offer right after the wedding, but Leo thought that might be inappropriate. You know what a softie he is.'

Winded, Sarah asked, 'Why would you want my flat?'

'We'd knock them together. Imagine it! A fabulous two-storey penthouse. They command a premium. Plenty of space for little ones ...' Helena winked and Sarah's stomach lurched. 'Don't tell Leo I told you this, but he's planning to make an offer through a third party. He knows how proud you are and he wants to make sure you ask the full price. He has the silly idea you might give him a discount. I told him not everybody's as soppy as he is.'

'Yeah. I mean, no.' Sarah was thrown.

'It's sentimental but he wants to set you up with a nice

pot of money. Says he hurt you and wants to make up for it.' Helena pulled a mock sad face and then laughed again. 'I said to him, oh don't you worry about Sarah. She'll meet somebody new and forget all about you.' She drummed her gel nails on the table. 'I wonder. Do I have a man for you?' Helena looked at the ceiling, as if an eligible bachelor might be entwined around the light fitting.

'I'm fine on my own, Helena.'

'That,' said Helena with a mew in her voice, 'sounds so, so sad.'

'It's perfectly possible to live without a man.' Sarah sharpened a little blade she rarely used. 'You did, after all, before you bumped into Leo.'

'That was different.' Helena, apparently, also carried a knife about her person. 'I'm not you, Sarah, am I?'

After a brief polite tussle about paying the bill, Sarah waited for Helena on the pavement as elaborate goodbyes were made to the manager. The organic croissant sat like gravel in her stomach, as painful to digest as Helena's casual shredding of her hopes.

Leo's motive wasn't romantic; it was practical.

And yet. That sounded too neat. As if Leo was a super-villain. Sarah knew him better than that. Her mother had been wrong; all men weren't the same. *I won't crucify Leo without evidence.*

'I have to be somewhere.' Helena appeared and offered her cheek. 'We must do this again. But not for a while. I'm snowed under.' Helena looked down and put her hand to her throat. 'Ooh no, no, no.' Biting her lip, she glared at Sarah's feet with something approaching repulsion. 'Those polka dot shoes *have* to go.'

Number twenty-four dwarfed Sarah as she dawdled up the parched path after work. She was more preoccupied than tired. She'd been distracted from her filing and tea-making and saying 'Hello, St Chad's, how can I help you?' by a mass of half-formed thoughts.

Helena was the gift that never stops giving. Her throw-away remarks had ignited a reappraisal of the past and the present.

When Sarah and Leo had said they'd 'get round' to having children, she'd assumed they had years ahead of them. Perhaps his 'respecting her career' was a sham – *what if he simply didn't want a child with me?* The ink was barely dry on Leo and Helena's marriage certificate and already they were 'trying hard'.

Letting herself into the house, Sarah wondered at her younger self's chutzpah. *As if babies just come when you whistle for them.*

The new regime had solidified. It was fruitless to wait for Leo to come to his senses, for this second marriage to disintegrate.

Babies were cement. Babies were superglue. If Helena fell pregnant, Leo would never leave. He was a cad, yes, but a cad with morals.

Lingering in the cool, shady hall, with the house alive

around her, a door closing somewhere, a television set burping out news, Sarah wondered why they'd never sat down and discussed when, how, *if* to start a family.

Was she mourning an intimacy that had never existed when she mourned the end of her marriage?

Cocooned in the hall, Sarah shivered despite the heat of the day. This sanctuary was threatened. It was a timeshare, not a home. In just – she counted on her fingers – in just nine weeks she'd have to relinquish her queenship up on the top floor.

In need of distraction and consolation, Sarah almost reached out to knock on the door of the ground-floor flat. For a moment she forgot that Smith wouldn't answer, that Smith was gone, that there'd be no automatic 'Come in!' and the pop of a cork and the sharing of some escapade.

Sarah laid her palm flat on the door. Jane had repainted it. It felt smooth and sleek. There'd never be a 'KEEP OUT BITCHES!' sign tacked to it again.

That sign had warned Sarah not to knock because Smith was entertaining a gentleman caller. Or 'shagging some poor bloke's brains out,' as she'd preferred to describe it. Smith had a different job each week, and each new job brought a brief new relationship. And a new 'KEEP OUT BITCHES!' sign.

Always cash-in-hand and casual, Smith's career covered waitressing, barmaiding, dog walking. Her stint as driver for a mobile puppet show had lasted longer than most. Sarah had wondered if her friend was doing something crazy like settling down, but Smith handed in her notice after a night of passion with her boss.

'He insisted on keeping Captain Cuckoo on his hand while we ... you know.'

'His puppet?' Sarah pulled a face she'd never pulled before at the mental image Smith conjured up. 'Jesus!'

'And he talked in Captain Cuckoo's voice.' Smith was shaking now, with laughter and remembered revulsion. She imitated her suitor despite Sarah's pleas. 'Do you like that? Captain Cuckoo wants you to—'

'Stop! Yuk!'

Sarah smiled sadly and laid her forehead against the door. Another memory popped up. That very same man, the puppeteer, turned up on the step a few months ago, asking if Smith was in. He'd looked sad to hear she'd gone, and Sarah wondered if perhaps this man, despite the fetish, might have had been a potential 'keeper'.

'So *you're* the amazing Sarah,' he'd smiled. 'Smith went on about you all the time.'

'Did she?' Sarah had laughed.

'God, yeah. Sarah this. Sarah that. No offence, but I got sick of the sound of your name.'

Sarah closed her eyes, back in the here and now, leaning against the door. It had been reassuring to hear from a stranger that Smith had treasured her, that the to and fro of their friendship had been as vital to Smith as it was to Sarah.

Straightening up, she knocked. Jane wasn't Smith but

she was special, too. No reply. Perhaps she was out in the garden, with her uncomplicated enthusiasm and open arms. Maybe Tom was there, too. And that would also be good, although it was good in a slightly different way. A way Sarah dare not examine.

Over the years, extensions and new windows had erupted from the back of the house as flats were carved into its original grandeur, leaving scars on the bricks and mortar. The building's imperfection made it benevolent, or so Sarah now fantasised, as it stared down on her pale arms and dangerously rosy forehead: Sarah was not a natural sun-worshipper. She tended to fricassee.

Anaesthetised by the heat, the rampant shrubs were static. There was no Jane, but there was a sweating Tom, toiling up and down the patchy grass with a lawnmower. Leaves and dust were trapped in his hair, and a bitchy rose brush had scratched his shoulders. He called a greeting over the whine of the mower as Sarah took a deckchair.

Spotting Mavis's wan face at an open basement window, Sarah waved. Mavis waved back. She didn't slam shut the worm-eaten frame. Perhaps Sarah had been forgiven for her *faux pas*.

Tom pointed to a cooler in the grass. The beer, not Sarah's usual tipple, tasted foreign and refreshing, like their new friendship. Being around Tom was informal, simple; a relief after her coffee with Helena.

Tom's loyalty to Jane raised the bar for mankind. The fact that Tom was tall, virile, and as deliciously wantable as a freshly baked – and sexy – cake was a detail that Sarah could acknowledge, because fancying him was a harmless hobby. Like crochet.

'Shall I put some trellis up the side of the shed?' Tom paused near her with the mower.

'How do you know how to do that stuff?' Accustomed to living in her head, Sarah had excessive admiration for people who were good with their hands.

'I just figure it out.' Tom seemed surprised by the question.

'Nice to see practical work getting done. It reminds me that not everything's virtual reality.'

'Sitting at a screen all day would send me crazy.' Tom wiped his brow with his forearm, flattening his hair. He looked about twelve, and Sarah saw the boy he'd been, all conkers and scabby knees and home-made go-carts. 'If you build something it's *there*.' He gestured squarely with his hands. 'You can touch it.'

'We all need something solid,' agreed Sarah, keenly aware that Tom and Jane had built something together. Once, she'd been able to touch the four walls of her own relationship, but now she was . . . Sarah shied away from bleak metaphors of deserts or tundras. Leo was still nearby; she could touch him if she so wished. *I even have his wife's permission.*

Tom glanced at his watch and, ludicrously, Sarah felt quashed.

'You off?'

'A voice-over at seven. It's an emergency, last-minute

thing. I don't have to go yet. Before you ask, it's for toilet cleaner. "But, Tom," you say, "toilet cleaners can't talk!" I, madam, am the Robert De Niro of toilet-cleaner acting and you too will believe that bleach can speak.' Tom bowed low, then sprang back up, as an angry yell sounded across the garden.

'Lisa,' murmured Sarah, darting a look at the open windows of Flat D.

Graham yelled next. 'Just look at her! Look at the kid!'

As Sarah cringed, Tom said, 'The kid has a name,' his body tense.

'Lisa, you've messed with that child's head!'

'It wasn't me who walked out on her!'

'Why would I stay here and listen to your bullshit?'

'You're ruining your daughter's life! You and that slag!'

'If Una lived with me she'd fucking talk!'

Tom stopped pretending to work and stood, arms hanging. 'Can't they do that somewhere Una can't hear?'

'This is their business, Tom,' warned Sarah as he flexed his fingers. She looked over at Mavis's window, but it had closed.

'Aren't troubled children your territory?'

'I can't help Una, Tom.'

'But she's only a few yards away.' Tom flung out an arm. 'It couldn't be closer to home.'

'That's the point. Una's too close, in all senses of the word.'

'I didn't mean to pressurise you. It's just hard listening to that.'

'You didn't.' He had. A little. Sarah understood and forgave; funny how often those two impulses arrived hand in hand. 'I can't help Una, much as I'd like to.'

Not all the past could be packaged as nostalgically as Retro Woman's window display; the child was a clouded looking glass, one that Sarah had avoided looking in for years.

'I've had enough. I'm going home,' shouted Graham.

Sarah imagined him carrying his pent-up anger back to the expressionless young girl she'd seen with him. She sat up abruptly. *I get it.*

'Er, bye then!' called Tom as she sprinted for the back door. Sarah didn't hear him; she was making up for lost time.

Lisa opened her door a slither, and said sulkily, 'I know, it got a bit out of hand, won't happen again,' and was closing it when Sarah asked to come in. 'If you want.' Lisa watched her visitor sceptically, as if Sarah might pull a gun. 'S'cuse the mess.'

A leatherette sofa sat alone in the featureless magnolia square of a sitting room. A teddy bear lolled, paws in the air; this, possibly, constituted the 'mess'.

'It's so cool down here.' Sarah was glad of the respite.

'Damp in winter, cool in summer. Swings and roundabouts.'

A blurred stain crept like fog across the ceiling. Lisa, ever touchy, followed Sarah's gaze and snapped, 'Lovely, innit?'

'Your landlord should—'

'Yes, he *should*,' interrupted Lisa. 'But he doesn't, so . . . Did you want something? I'm only just in from three home visits on the trot and then that sod was waiting to do my head in.'

Una appeared, a stampede of one, drawing to a breathless halt when she saw a visitor. She looked down at Sarah's feet and her mouth fell open.

'Yup,' said Sarah. 'You liked them so much I *had* to buy them.'

Sarah slipped off the polka dot shoes and Una stepped into them, her chubby feet only half filling them. Her face sweaty with happiness, she lurched off to her room.

Yah boo sucks, Helena, thought Sarah. *My style guru approves, even if you don't.*

The view from the bay window was bisected by the raised lawn, reducing Tom to a pair of feet. If it wasn't for the waiting-room decor and the damp, Lisa's flat would be cosy. 'Can we talk about Una?'

Lisa bristled with Keep Out! signs, arms folded over her blue nylon uniform.

'Tell me how it is, Lisa.'

Something in Lisa gave way; perhaps sympathy was rare in her neck of the woods. 'It's bad,' she said.

That seemed to be all she had to give. Sarah waited. She had inside information on little Una: some of it decades old; some brand new.

'School's, y'know, difficult.' Lisa's head bobbed, her face's unhappiness brutally laid bare by her dragged-back hair.

'They were helpful at first, but teachers are busy, you know?' Lisa began to pace. 'I thought it was a phase, but now it's like Una's just that kid who doesn't talk. The teachers work around her. Her little bestie and her, they used to collect sweet wrappers together … *sweet wrappers.*' Lisa almost crumpled at such endearing silliness. 'The girl moved on to another friend. One who talks back. So Una only has me, just me, and I'm …' Lisa raised her arms at her sides and then let them fall.

Sarah took a moment before she spoke. Lisa was fragile, and when Sarah thought of Una, she saw her tiny and silent, marooned in a desert, standing in her sandals, her hair tidily brushed, miles from civilisation.

That's me I'm seeing.

'Lisa, you're strong. You're holding everything together. You're doing your best.'

Lisa turned away, as if Sarah had slapped her. As if sympathy was dangerous.

'You've been the lynchpin, but now you need a hand.'

Lisa's face was belligerent.

'I can help you.'

'Don't tell me to ring some doctor I don't know,' said Lisa. 'I threw away that stupid card you gave me.'

'Me, I'll help. If you'll let me. This is what I do for a living and I'll do it for you and for Una.' She read Lisa's expression and put her mind at rest. 'For free. Just between us.' She hesitated. 'As friends.'

Chapter Eight

Not a morning person, Sarah went over her groggy features with a cotton wool pad and brushed her teeth on automatic pilot. Officially 'bad in the morning', the thought of her little clients waiting for her used to prise her out of the house.

Now the children waited, but not for Sarah.

The intercom buzzed. 'Sarah, dear,' said Mavis. 'There's a large package for you.'

A few nights before, Sarah had been sucked into the supernova of eBay and now here was her reward for beating all the other bidders.

At the bottom of the stairs stood Mavis, demure in another of her collection of threadbare dresses, her wiry hair pinned up anyhow. 'Good morning,' she said civilly, carefully.

'Talking to me again?'

'Of course.' Mavis wasn't playful; she was grave, and Sarah regretted being breezy. Mavis was turning round her own juggernaut; rejoining the human race was a massive undertaking for an older woman with her record. She stood beside a huge unwieldy shape, smothered in thick plastic. 'It looks like an old-fashioned chair,' said Mavis. 'Rather grand.'

'And much too big!' Sarah circled her purchase. 'Jesus, it pongs,' she said, and Mavis winced her agreement. A strong musty smell escaped the wrappings.

Footsteps – plodding but heavy, like an approaching bear – announced Leo. 'Ladies.' He tipped an imaginary hat at them both.

The tilt of his head, the gleeful private joke that simmered between him and Sarah, the greed in his eye – Leo didn't have the acting skills to pretend he had feelings for Sarah just for the sake of getting his hands on Flat A.

She felt lighter. If the letter was right – and Sarah believed in its wisdom the way some people believe in the bible – then perhaps the beauty in Leo was this uncomplicated love he had for Sarah. Even when he shouldn't. Even when he was married to somebody else.

Always drawn to furniture, Leo laid his hands on the wrapped chair. 'Old, darling, or repro?' He peered through the cloudy plastic.

The front door opened, and Tom appeared, backlit with a halo of sunshine: St Tom of Notting Hill. 'Morning all,' he puffed, bending over, hands on knees.

'It's too hot to go running,' said Mavis reprovingly.

'I have to keep in shape, Mavis.' Tom stood and stretched, exuding a warm male scent of exertion and health. 'For my job.'

As Sarah endeavoured not to look at Tom's chest as it rose and fell under his tight camouflage fabric running top, she felt Leo staring at her. Perhaps he felt the contrast as keenly as Sarah did, of the younger man exuding well-being, and the older one with the marks of the pillow still on his face. 'Why do you need to keep in shape,' he asked, jocular, 'for doing funny voices?'

'I'm not just a voice-over, I'm an actor,' said Tom. 'This yours, Sarah?' Tom nodded at the chair.

'Yes, but ...' Sarah suddenly hated the chair. 'I thought ...' She felt their eyes upon her and had to confess. 'Laugh as much as you like, but I thought I'd bought a doll's house chair.'

They did laugh; Mavis reluctantly, Leo at full throttle.

'You still play with doll's houses?' asked Tom.

'I do. With the children I treat.' *Used to treat.* 'Rearranging tiny tables and beds can help them open up about their home life.'

'Plus ...' Tom put his face close to hers, examining her. 'You love it.'

'Guilty as charged.' In a doll's house, people could be scooped up and set down. No fuss. No divorce. All cosy and hygienic and pain-free. 'Most grown women miss their dolls, deep down.'

'I bet you were a cute kid.'

That veered perilously near to one of those giveaways women recognise, the ones that say 'I like you'.

Her confusion was contagious. Tom stammered, 'But then all kids are cute.'

Leo said, 'Not a word a child psychologist uses, eh, Sarah? *Cute*.' He stood at her shoulder, Teacher's Pet.

'Are you two strong chaps going to carry this upstairs, or do Sarah and I have to do it?' Mavis flexed a puny arm.

'I'll do it,' said Leo. 'On my own.'

'Your back . . .' cautioned Sarah. He'd once spent a week in bed after bending to pick up an olive that fell out of his Martini.

'Let me,' said Tom.

'You're not needed,' said Leo.

Tom's expression glitched.

'Why not do it together?' suggested Sarah.

Leo and Tom confronted each other over the chair, the hallway crackling with their antipathy. Sarah was the root of their rivalry; Leo had a proprietary she–was–mine–once–mate reaction to a male on his territory, and Tom was acting out his disapproval of Leo's behaviour.

She liked it more than she should have done.

'Left side up a bit, old man,' said Tom.

'Careful you don't break a nail, Meryl Streep,' said Leo.

'Back up, back up!'

'You're dropping it!'

Sarah followed the chair on its cumbersome journey

towards the top of the house. Leo huffed, Tom groaned, and both believed they were doing the lion's share of the work.

'If you'd just—' gasped Tom.

'Why can't you bloody—' grunted Leo.

Outside Flat A, the air foggy with testosterone, Sarah thanked them both.

'No problem.' Tom tried to look as if he wasn't out of breath. 'I'm off to look on eBay myself. Jane and I need a cheapie stand-in until some fancy armchair she's ordered turns up.'

'Have this!' said Sarah. 'It smells a bit, but it's free.'

'What a sales pitch. Are you sure?' Tom looked at Sarah closer, making her wonder if he stared at everybody that way; some people's faces are built to flirt.

'I'm sure.' Bodies are their own bosses; while Sarah's mind rebuked Tom for straying over a line, her body buzzed with the static of sexual attraction. There was little point to her body's insistence; as if wrapped in crime scene tape, Tom was firmly off-limits. Marriage vows were sacred to a woman whose own echoed pointlessly.

Leo watched Tom heave the chair downstairs, arms folded, no intention of helping this time. Turning to Sarah, he said, 'I can give you an hour at lunchtime, darling.'

'That's big of you.'

Sailing past her into the flat, Leo didn't register her tone. 'Did you pick up the paint?'

It would be simple to step into the familiar dance; Leo

calling the tune and Sarah waltzing, always backwards, always in step. 'How do you mean you can give me an hour?' A throb beat in Sarah's temple.

'I meant, um . . .' Leo shook his head. 'What do you think I meant, silly? I meant we'll have an hour while Helena's at Pilates.'

Sarah sensed Leo working out his next move, as if this was a game of chess. *Does he feel this as keenly as I do?* It was dangerous to be the only one playing for high stakes. 'We don't need to sneak around any more.'

'Sneaking? Let's not call it that. But, believe me, Helena wouldn't understand.'

'Helena understands perfectly. I told her.'

'You . . . ? Right. O . . . K . . .' Leo's sangfroid slipped. 'Why on earth did you do that, darling?' He seemed genuinely intrigued and a little disappointed but not in the least annoyed.

'Didn't Helena mention our conversation?'

'Not a dicky bird.' Leo looked at the floor. Schoolboyish body language was a refuge of his when cornered.

Sarah took a deep breath. Despite witnessing at close hand her mother's disastrous love life, Sarah had followed her advice about Leo. She'd let him believe he was 'in charge', which meant Sarah had never stood up to him, even when he began to peel away from her. The weekends away 'for work' had gone unchallenged; his explanation about the perfume on his skin had been accepted. It was time to assert herself. 'Helena reckons you're only helping me to get me out of here quicker. Then you'll buy the flat pretending to be somebody else and turn the top two floors into a penthouse.' She didn't mention the nursery. She couldn't.

'I'm *terribly* underhand, aren't I?' said Leo. 'Come on, darling, see the funny side. Am I that Machiavellian? That's a bloody long game to play.' Leo leaned against the wall, amused. 'Am I or am I not the most impatient, laziest slob you've ever met? That's an exact quote, by the way. From a certain Ms Sarah Lynch.'

'What's that got to do with the price of fish?' Sarah knew Leo's modus operandi. The genial 'who-me?' The softening-up of his accuser. The finale where she ended up apologising. 'I'm not one of your customers, Leo. You can't soft-soap me.'

'Anybody who comes to the Old Church takes away satisfaction as part of the package.'

He was wounded. Leo was proud of the emporium. Sarah was framing the word 'Sorry' when she realised he'd almost managed to invade the moral high ground. 'Are you or you not planning to buy this flat, Leo?'

'Look, darling, I'm here with you because this is where I want to be. I don't scheme and plot. I'm a pleasure baby, not bloody Napoleon.'

Put like that it was funny. Sarah wanted to see the joke; if she laid down her cudgel they'd have a carefree lunch hour painting together, the radio playing, memories being disinterred and polished. Then, after he left, she could spend a further hour staring into space at St Chad's reception desk as she analysed the declaration he'd just made about wanting to be there. *With me.*

As if her mother was standing in the room with them, Sarah heard her shriek, exasperated, 'For god's sake let him win!'

'But, Leo,' began Sarah.

His shoulders sank. 'But *what*? Darling, we have so little time. Is it yes or no?'

Sarah wavered. Was Helena playing her? The manipulative monster she described would hardly wait a whole year, paying half the mortgage for most of that time. Leo had been patient. '*But*,' she repeated, unable to let it go, 'how can I believe you when you lied to me before about Helena?'

'Jesus,' muttered Leo, irritation gaining the upper hand over good humour.

'Be honest with me, Leo. Are you shooing me out of the house so your wife can fill my flat with murals and ... and ... and ...'

'Radiator covers,' suggested Leo. 'She likes those.'

'Don't make me laugh when I'm telling you off!'

'Sorry, Miss. Look, think about it, silly. Why would Helena let you refurbish the flat and *then* buy it? She goes through a property like Attila the Hun. She strips buildings back to the beams and starts again.'

'She said she wanted to make an offer right after the divorce but you said it was inappropriate.'

'She's teasing you. Helena wouldn't back off because of a little thing like feelings.' Leo pushed away from the wall, agitated. 'Isn't it enough that I'm here, that you're here, that this is . . .' Leo searched for the *bon mot* until he spat, 'fun?'

'It's not much fun right now.'

'And whose fault is that?'

That was one of Leo's catchphrases. 'No, no, no,' said Sarah. 'You don't get to blame me. You pinned the end of our marriage on me, when it was *you* who bludgeoned it to death.'

'Your running off to Smith every five minutes didn't exactly help matters.'

'Did you ever, once, try and understand about Smith? Was that too much to ask?'

His blather muted, Leo groused, 'Oh God, *this* again. If you want, we can, you know, *talk* about Smith.' Leo was diffident, as if offering a kidney he hoped nobody needed. 'If you like.'

'I do like.' Sarah noted how his face dropped. 'Why didn't you cut me some slack after Smith's diagnosis?'

'Smith was S.E.P., darling. Somebody else's problem.'

Illness frightened Leo. He believed even depression to be contagious. While Sarah was preoccupied with hospital waiting rooms and blood tests, Leo had turned towards the light pulsing from Helena, a floor below. Bright, healthy, *alive*.

'Smith was my friend, so she was my problem. What about me? I was your wife. Was I S.E.P.?'

The hinge of her marriage, the day so much changed, had started ordinarily enough. Sarah let herself into Smith's flat – the key was always under the mat – and pulled the sitting-room curtains.

'Christ, even by your standards this place is a mess.' Tidying around Smith, who was under a blanket on the sofa, Sarah suggested a shower and dangled the promise of a bacon butty. 'Come on, Smithy. Up and at 'em. You've had hangovers before.'

That's when she noticed that Smith was crying, knuckling her eyes as if trying to gouge them out.

Smith never cried. The hard knocks she alluded to but never properly explained had cured her, she said, of crying. Now the backdated tears arrived all at once.

'Shush, no, shush.' Alarmed, Sarah sat beside her friend, smoothing back hair which, that week, was pastel blue.

'I haven't got a hangover,' hiccupped Smith.

She looked wild, her eyes pressed into her pale face like drawing pins. Sarah couldn't persuade her from the foetus position. 'You're scaring me,' she said. She felt on the brink of something, some new place she wouldn't much like. 'What's happened?'

'I saw a specialist. Yesterday. I didn't want to worry you.'

'You're worrying me now.' Sarah was startled by the volcano of feeling.

'I have a brain tumour,' said Smith, hands over her eyes.

'We'll get a second opinion,' said Sarah automatically, fending it off, desperate to shove the words away. 'This stuff is misdiagnosed all the time.'

'This was the third opinion. It's real, Sarah. I have a brain tumour.' Smith wound her dry lips around the proper term. 'It's called an astrocytoma.'

They sat side by side, immobilised. The room shimmered, like a stage set waiting to be struck. Smith lived in flux, the furniture constantly changing, the colour scheme morphing as she switched the blankets she flung around. All was cheap and disposable; an air of impermanence surrounded the slip of a girl with a different hairstyle for each day of the week and a conviction that striped tights went with everything.

There was no point suggesting that a lone ranger like Smith involve her family. There was no 'home' for Smith apart from the fort she'd built with other people's cast-offs. Even her hold on Flat A was tenuous, sublet from 'this guy I had a thing with, not a big thing, just a, you know, *thing*,' while he mooched around India.

Sarah had often wondered how she'd lose Smith – there was something mercurial about her – but she'd never dreamt it would be like this. 'Lean on me, OK?' She took Smith's limp hand. 'Until you're better again.'

'Nah,' Smith said. 'There won't be any getting better.'

Sarah returned her attention to Leo, to the present. 'There's no need to talk.' She heard him exhale, relieved. 'We both know what happened with Smith. I was engrossed in St Chad's and then I threw myself into looking after Smith. You were neglected.' As if Leo was a puppy or a new baby.

'True, I was neglected.' Leo sounded saddened, but also glad that Sarah appreciated how very hard it had been for him. 'But that's no excuse. I never said I was a good man, darling.'

The disrespect Sarah had repressed throughout their marriage surged through her. Why did Leo always accept his own shortcomings? Why hadn't he rolled up his Savile Row sleeves and mucked in for once? It had been, literally, a matter of life and death. What's more, Leo's affair had started a full two months before Smith's diagnosis. 'You could have helped instead of turning away.'

'If it had been anybody other than Smith . . .'

'What? She didn't *deserve* kindness?' Smith's loveless upbringing would have KO'ed silver-spoon Leo. 'She did what she had to do to get by.'

'Christ, you sound like bloody Peck, parroting what Smith said about herself. She was a taker, and you were a giver. She used you up, darling. There was nothing left for me.'

'Do you ever listen to yourself? Where's your heart, Leo?'

'It used to be here.' Leo looked around as if sizing up the flat. 'Not any more.' He stared Sarah in the face. 'Not any more, darling.'

'Why did I marry a man who uses endearments as weapons?' Sarah stalked to the door and held it open with a flourish. 'Thanks for all your help, *darling*.'

'You're throwing me out?' Leo fluttered between disgust and laughter, unable to alight on either. When the door remained obstinately open and Sarah didn't speak, he passed her and she closed the door firmly behind him.

Chapter Nine

℃ONFUℂIUS FAKEAWAY
Notting Hill, W11

This calendar is FREE to valued customers!
Saturday 25th June, 2016

THERE IS ONLY ONE PRETTY CHILD IN THE WORLD, AND EVERY MOTHER HAS IT

'Snap!' Sarah pointed first at her own dungarees and then at Una's dungarees.

Una looked up at her severely, tiny mouth set in a pout. 'You don't seem to think so, but I assure you I *am* funny,' said Sarah. 'We'll be about an hour,' she told Lisa, adding a reassuring, 'We won't go far, just the garden for now.' The woman looked apprehensive, as if she was handing over a hostage.

'Up we go.' Sarah led Una up the three steps from the yard to the lawn. Once an emblem of neglect, the garden, primped and tidied, was now a bright star, dragging the residents into its gravity. 'There's Tom!'

'Una!' crooned Tom, pleased to see her.

The child looked to Sarah for approval and dashed to Tom, who kneeled down to greet her.

Giving in to an impulse she should have ignored, Sarah glanced up at the roof terrace. Leo liked to linger there over a coffee before setting off for the Old Church, which opened later on Saturdays. Rewarded with a view of his disappearing back, Sarah knew he'd gone inside to avoid her. She turned to Tom. 'What are you all ponced up for?'

'Audition.' The crumpled pale linen suit had a hint of the roaring twenties about it, bringing out the chestnut in Tom's hair and accentuating his rower's shoulders. 'And by ponced up I assume you mean stunningly handsome, yeah?'

This glamour was a revelation, as if Tom kept an alternative, seductive self in a drawer. He sent a razor-sharp charge through Sarah, who covered up her quickened breathing with a question. 'What's the role? A biggie?'

'A huge-ie. The Beeb are adapting *Vile Bodies* by Evelyn Waugh.'

'I did it for A-level.' The outfit made sense now; Waugh's Bright Young Things of the nineteen twenties lounged around in linen when they weren't shimmying in tuxedos. 'Which part are you up for?'

'Adam Fenwick-Symes.' Tom pulled in his chin. 'Yeah, I know,' he said, as Sarah's eyes widened. 'The lead. I won't get it. Will I, Una?'

Sarah would have to let Tom in on the golden rule: no questions! 'I bet you a tenner you get it.'

'Never has your money been so safe,' laughed Tom. 'It must be a mistake, I hardly ever get a crack at a telly gig, and if I do, it's always "Best Friend of Hero" never actual

"Hero". My last audition went so badly I had an out-of-body experience.'

'If Jane was here she'd spank you for that attitude.'

'Well she's not, so . . . ?'

'I'm not going to spank you, Tom. Where *is* Jane?' Even though Tom's flirting was harmless, Sarah felt the need to draw a firm line in the sand; one extra-marital imbroglio was plenty.

'On her way back from Suffolk. The client's being, apparently, a total utter freaking dickhead.'

'That's our Janey,' said Sarah. 'What's Una so interested in over there?' She saw them then, their flamboyant radiant heads on sturdy stalks. 'You planted sunflowers to replace the ones that died.'

'Una can help me look after them. If she likes.'

The child liked, that was clear. Tom was already a hero in this garden; Una was smitten. She wandered ahead of Tom and Sarah, making a slow tour. They travelled at Una's pace, allowing her time to peer closely at minutiae.

'She's very into ants,' said Tom. 'Is this . . . are we in a *session*?'

'Yes.' Sarah kept her voice low; those little bat ears of Una's picked up more than adults realised. 'It'll feel like play. The key is for Una to relax, for us to interact gently. Una needs a safe space with no pressure to talk. A place where, if she decides to say something, she won't be judged.'

Una examined every flower, every fallen leaf, every miscreant mushroom that pushed through the grass.

'I saw Graham the other day. It's obvious he's already living with the new woman in his life . . .' Sarah left the dots for Tom to join.

It took a moment. 'I see. We know that Lisa interrogates Una after she visits Graham . . .'

'And Una knows that Lisa will kick off if she tells her about the cohabitation.'

'Long word,' said Tom. 'Impressive.' He looked tenderly at Una. 'Poor kid. She shut up rather than make matters worse. That's a lot of responsibility for a six-year-old.'

Sarah was impressed. Thoughtful, kind Tom *got it*.

'Are you OK?' asked Tom abruptly. 'The weather in your eyes has changed. As if something's on your mind.'

Sarah fibbed into that honest, open, concerned face; she couldn't admit to being tied up in knots about Leo. 'I'm fine.'

Her fractious goodbye to Leo squatted in her mind like a toad. They'd been getting somewhere and she'd shattered their momentum.

With hindsight – that useless, late-to-the-party false friend – Sarah saw the simple truth, Leo wasn't hustling her out of the flat. The second Mrs Harrison had felt her crown wobble and swiped a manicured paw; Helena was better at guerrilla tactics than Sarah. There was more than one way to fight a war, however: Sarah would win back Leo fair and square with the eco-friendly power of love, not the dark arts of the boudoir and the cheap thrill of secrecy.

An excited noise, not exactly speech, came from Una. She

was crouched over a small dark shape which moved with a feeble, jagged action.

'A hedgehog!' said Tom, incredulous.

'It's tiny,' said Sarah.

Una, bent double, shaking with delight, tailed the creature as it stumbled away. It was as if one of her toys had come to life.

'Must be a baby.' Tom didn't sound entranced. He sounded worried. 'I don't like the way it's walking.'

Meandering, staggering, the miniature beastie seemed drunk. Its snout rose and twirled, and it made a piping, impossibly high sound.

'It's distressed,' said Tom under his breath. Una hovered over the hedgehog, vibrating to the noise it made, full of joy.

'I'm googling it,' said Tom, reaching for his phone.

Una darted out a dimpled hand to the hedgehog whose paws were held so high it was frogmarching.

'Careful!' Sarah hovered, expecting tears. Those quills were like razors.

Una was gentle, scooping up the hedgehog, bringing its snout to her nose. It was miniature, like her; she understood it.

The animal curled inwards in Una's hand, closing over itself and showing only its prickles. Una's breath was hot and sweet upon it and it tentatively opened up, showing its pinky brown face, then its forelegs. Then its hind legs folded out and it lay there, legs akimbo, in its thorny onesie.

Una blew it a kiss. Sarah wondered if it had fleas.

'Why's it making that noise?' she asked Tom, who was reading the small screen of his phone. The hedgehog warbled on, singing silvery high notes that were surprisingly loud.

'Hold on. I'm not quite an expert yet.' Tom scrolled down.

Pale spines fell like a quiff over the triangular face and over just the one shining dot of an eye. Sarah's heart creased at the shallow dent where the hedgehog's other eye should have been. 'You're like Mike Wazowski,' she told it.

'Who?' Tom was lost in the internet.

'Una probably knows who I mean,' said Sarah without looking at the girl. 'Mike Wazowski is the round one-eyed green monster in *Monsters Inc*. He's funny and sweet. Like this fella.' Sarah risked a question. 'Una, shall we call him Mike?'

Una seemed to fill up, her chest rising. Locking eyes with Sarah, she gave the faintest of nods.

It was historic, that nod.

'That's decided, then.' Sarah bent to the hedgehog's level, burying her delight. 'Hi there, Mikey!' The small triumph lit her up. Inside, a small engine that had lain idle and rusty let out a small growl. *We connected.*

'Mikey has problems.' Tom frowned. 'No hedgehog should be out in the open during the day, according to this website. I reckon from the look of him he's about three weeks old. Too young, apparently, to have left his mother.'

'Let's take Mikey back to his, um, is it a nest?'

'Yeah, that's the term.' Tom let out a huff of breath and placed his hand squarely on Una's head. The child quailed, but let it stay there. Touching Una so casually wasn't what Sarah would advise but the little girl permitted it. Tom was special to her. 'We can't, sadly, take Mikey home.' Tom angled his phone so Sarah could see the screen.

Handling a young hedgehog will result in transference of your scent onto the animal, resulting in the mother rejecting it or even eating it.

'Sounds like my mother,' murmured Sarah. She read on: *Orphans can be reared but it's time-consuming and success is not guaranteed. Far better to let nature take its course and leave the animal to its fate.*

'Put Mikey down, Una,' said Sarah gently. 'Let him get on with his day.' She was furious with herself for naming the animal.

Una held Mikey curled up against her chest, her face defiant. She was clearly ready to fight for him. Mikey regarded them with his one good eye, safe and possibly a tad smug.

'It's for the best,' said Sarah. How to explain to a six-year-old that shit happens, that cuddly animals perish, that the weak don't always find the help they need? Sarah knew Una had already glimpsed these truths.

The birdsong receded as Sarah and Una gazed at each other. The girl's eyes, unclouded by late nights or house wine or money worries, were clear as spring water. Sarah was engulfed by Una's stillness. The little girl's silence was dense and wide, as clean and weirdly impressive as snow.

The spell was only broken when Una's face crumpled and she began to sob.

'It's OK, it's OK.' Sarah crouched in front of Una. Empathising so deeply made such a crisis more likely, besides robbing Sarah of her authority and making it difficult to halt the tears. 'Una, sweetie . . .' She tried to hold the little girl, but Una wriggled, holding poor doomed Mikey to her chest. He let out a desolate cheep.

A basement window flew open and Lisa struggled through, throwing her leg over the sill. 'What the hell?' she shouted.

'I'm sorry, it's a hedgehog, we—' Sarah got no further.

'You're supposed to be helping!' Lisa scurried across the grass. 'Look at her! How can I go to work and leave her with Graham when she's in this state?'

'Everything's going fine. This is just a—'

'She's *crying.* C'mere, baby. Oh shit, what's that in her hand?'

'I'm trying to tell you; it's a hedgehog. Lisa, we're in this for the long term. It won't all be plain sailing.'

'Urgh! A hedgehog?' Lisa backed away, her face contorted. 'I was looking forward to an hour of peace and quiet, not . . .' Lisa was lost for words. 'Not *this*!'

'I'm not a childminder, Lisa.' Sarah's professionalism dropped over her shoulders like a cape. 'The aim isn't to give you a lie-down. The aim is to help Una.'

'Yeah, well . . .' Lisa's anger petered out. 'I don't like seeing her upset.'

'I know what'll cheer Una up,' said Tom. 'I'm going to look after Mikey and help him grow up strong and healthy. Una can help me if she likes. He'll soon be right as rain.'

Emerging from the house, Jane was twirling her car keys. With a wink at Sarah, she draped her arm around Lisa's shoulder with a casual informality that Sarah wouldn't have dared attempt. 'Lisa, love, you sound like you need some of Doctor Wine's special medicine. Up to mine for half an hour, yeah? We'll kick back while this lot get to know their hedgehog.'

Lisa looked so grateful it made Sarah want to cry. 'I'd love that,' she said meekly.

'Let's get started,' said Tom, leading Una to the shed. 'First we need a box for Mikey to sleep in.'

Her arm still comfortably over Lisa, Jane said, 'He'll make a wonderful father one day.'

'You hero-worship that man,' laughed Sarah, loving Jane's easy, inclusive pride in Tom.

'Sometimes. Other times I'd happily kill him with the nearest blunt object.'

When Jane spirited Lisa away, Tom went inside too, to source the various kit they'd need to keep Mikey alive. The animal himself was still in Una's cupped hands, where he fitted nicely. His new guardian couldn't tear her eyes away from him.

As Sarah knelt beside Una on the grass, savouring the shared moment, aware of the battering heat of the day, Mavis appeared.

First her head, then her dreadful dress, as she climbed the steps with a tray of clinking glasses. 'Cold lemonade!' she said, cheerfully; her good humour had a wary edge, as if she was acting a part at gunpoint.

'You lifesaver!' Sarah stood and Una scrambled to her feet, wobbling a little because both her hands were still around Mikey.

'Is that a hedgehog?' Mavis bent to see, then straightened up with visible effort as Una stepped deliberately behind Sarah.

'She's feeling shy today,' said Sarah, as Una pressed into the back of her legs, her face buried in the denim of her dungarees.

'It's come to this,' said Mavis in a low, desperate voice. 'A child is frightened of accepting lemonade from me.'

'Those bridges you burned,' said Sarah, calmly, gravely, 'can all be rebuilt, remember?' She was taken aback by the level of Una's agitation, and by the level of Mavis's regret. It would be unhelpful to point out that Mavis had gone to great lengths to alienate everybody in number twenty-four, but it would be true. 'Here's what you do. You leave the tray with me, and you go and sit in that plastic chair over there, in the shade. Una will stop noticing you, start taking you for granted, and that's the first step to making friends with her.'

Doing as she was told, Mavis settled beneath the cherry tree in the corner, whose blossom had dropped and rotted some time ago. The speckled shadows turned drab little Mavis into an artwork.

Crediting Mavis for the lemonade that Una wolfed down – 'She's a kind lady, isn't she?' – Sarah had a one-sided conversation with the top of the child's head. 'I've got a story for you and Mikey. Once upon a time. No, hang on, that's lame.'

A snuffly giggle encouraged Sarah. 'This story's all true, by the way. There was once a little girl. She's all grown up now, but this happened when she was a bit older than you. About nine.' That was, Sarah knew, an impossibly sophisticated age to a six-year-old. 'Like you, she was an only child, which was fab when everybody got along, but when her mum and dad argued, it was less fun. In fact, it was no fun at all. When her parents yelled, the little girl watched and listened and felt very afraid and a bit lonely.'

Una sat very still, listening politely. *No,* thought Sarah, *more than that.* Una, with her close-up focus on the little things, knew that this ordinary story was important.

'One day,' said Sarah, 'the little girl's worst fears came true. Her dad went to live somewhere else. She begged him to stay, but he went anyway. The little girl knew her dad still loved her, but it was horrible seeing her mum so sad. Sometimes it all got a bit much for mum and she shouted at the little girl. When you love somebody you try to understand them, and the little girl did her best, but she felt weird when her mum was mean to her.'

Una's straw found the last of the lemonade and gurgled like a drain.

'The little girl made a discovery. The thing that upset

her mum the most was when the little girl talked about the fun she had at her dad's house. Her mum reacted as if the girl had done something naughty, but she was a good girl. Like you. Like me. In fact, she secretly believed that if she was as good as she could possibly be, then her parents might get back together. If I could, I'd tell that little girl a very important fact; it's *never* your fault if your mum and dad break up. You are not to blame. Perhaps one day, Una, you'll tell her for me.'

Una was listening so hard she trembled; Mikey, now quiet and comfortable in her lap, was an anchor.

'The little girl had a plan. If talking made her mum unhappy, the best thing to do was zip up her mouth and keep all the dangerous words inside her.'

Words can be weaponised. Sarah heard her own mother's voice, riffing on a favourite tune of Sarah's childhood: 'You're a bad seed. Your father and I were fine before you came along!'

Photographs existed of Sarah's mother: younger, ecstatic, holding a brand new Sarah to her cheek. Sarah never opened the album; the happiness trapped between the pages was extinct.

'Soon, people stopped expecting the girl to talk and she felt safe in her new quiet world. Until one day, she wasn't happy any more. She wanted to speak, to say something, anything, but it felt as if everybody would turn and look and point. She worried that she'd left it too late. But, Una, it's never too late. You own your voice. Say what you want, when you want.'

Una's gaze was a straight arrow from one broken soul to another. Sarah ruffled Una's hair and thought what a formidable, brilliant woman this little girl would become.

'Right.' Tom bustled across the lawn in his linen suit. 'I've got all Mikey's gear. Let's get him settled into the shed so I can go and mess up this audition.'

Officially, Mikey was a hoglet, explained Tom, as Una shredded newspaper for lining the cardboard box.

Mikey was weighed on the kitchen scales, then Tom oversaw Una placing a hot-water bottle on top of the paper, then a folded towel. 'It's one of Jane's best. Don't tell her, for God's sake.'

After Tom checked the creature for ticks – 'Clean as a whistle!' – Una ceremoniously bedded Mikey down in his new home. The hoglet was tentative at first, probing the towel with spindly paws before lying down.

Lactose-free milk, which Tom had, astonishingly, found in the corner shop, was offered to Mikey from a plastic dropper. Again Jane's, last used when she had an eye infection. Again, a secret. Finally, sated, the cosseted hedgehog fell asleep.

'He snores!' laughed Sarah.

Mavis had tiptoed into the shed, like a tardy shepherd come to worship a hoglet Jesus. Una stepped away from her, venerating Mikey from Sarah's other side, but this was a less dramatic reaction than previously. Sarah and Mavis shared a look; another small step for mankind, another giant leap for Mavis.

When Graham arrived to pick up his daughter for her weekly sleepover, the child didn't want to leave Mikey's bedside.

'Una!' Graham stuck out his hand.

The tone was better suited to training a dog, but Sarah held her tongue. She wasn't there to criticise, just to help. 'Our first session was very illuminating, Graham. You have a lovely little girl.'

'Yeah, I know.' Graham's lean face was dark. 'Don't tell me about my own daughter. I'm not buying into this crap.'

It had been a fortnight since Sarah had stepped down from her vocation, but the carefully level voice she used for tricky parents was second nature. 'I believe I can help Una to express herself, given time. And your support. You and Lisa are the most important people in Una's life.'

'Like I said, I *know*.' Graham was in no mood to be mollified. 'Come *on*,' he said impatiently to Una.

'Daddy's waiting!' sang Lisa with a withering undercurrent that nobody could miss, not least a six-year-old who hung on her every word.

Sarah waved as Graham marched Una away, forcing her little feet to pedal super-fast. There was no goodbye, no soft word for Lisa.

The droop of Lisa's shoulders no longer seemed churlish; it was eloquent of hopes dashed, of love lost. Sarah risked a hand on the small of Lisa's back and a sympathetic smile.

Surprised, Lisa blinked and strode away. Sarah, who knew how it felt when ordinary dreams collapse inwards, watched her go. A touch on her arm reminded her of Tom's presence.

'The hot-water bottle has to be changed every four hours. Can you take care of it while I'm out?'

'Sure. And Tom? This hedgehog . . .' Sarah folded her arms. 'It's dangerous to make promises to children you can't keep.'

'Or adults, for that matter,' said Tom.

'True.' Sarah glanced up at the terrace. It was empty.

'Don't worry about Mikey. I keep my promises.' Tom cocked an eyebrow. 'Believe me?'

'I guess I'll have to.'

Chapter Ten

The UK had finally coughed up one of those long, drowsily hot summers that all Brits think they remember from childhood. Sarah was drawn to the reception's plate-glass wall, cursing the stuttering air conditioning that made no difference to St Chad's sultry microclimate.

'I'm melting,' she complained to Keeley at the end of the day, when her boss came to flick through the appointments diary Sarah now kept for her.

'The interview rooms are nice and cool.'

'Cheers.'

'How long will this last?' Keeley's braids were wound together on top of her head, making her a foot taller. She was imperious, stapling Sarah to her swivel chair with a glower. 'You're the most overqualified receptionist in the world.'

'I, it's, I—' Sarah couldn't drag together a sentence. She'd settled into her new persona and was comfortable with its lack of responsibility. There was a pride to be taken in doing the many small tasks well; she knew she could deliver excellent tea, deal sympathetically with stressed parents on the phone, tick appointments off one by one as the clients arrived. None of it felt beyond her. How to explain to fierce, righteous Keeley that for the first time in a long time Sarah had stopped feeling as if she was treading water in the open ocean?

'You keep quoting that letter of yours yet you ignore its advice,' said Keeley. 'You're good enough the way you are, sure, but the real you is a child psychologist, Sarah. We need you.' It must have been a stressful day because she added, 'If that means anything.' She turned at the sound of a tap on the revolving doors. 'Looks like you're finished for the day,' she said, picking up an armful of case notes and heading for her office. Slowly. Keeley was built for comfort, not speed.

Sarah waved at Jane and pressed the switchboard to answerphone. She felt wounded, as if Keeley had lifted a scorpion tail from beneath her floor-length dress and lashed her with it. The sting tore through the tissue of Sarah's denial; she couldn't stay indefinitely at St Chad's as receptionist. Her days there was were numbered, just like her days at number twenty-four.

Keeley wouldn't stay angry; Sarah knew that. *I hope I know that,* she thought, as she stooped to pick up her bag. The rot went deep: Sarah was still on that opposite riverbank, wondering about the people on the other side, people she used to know well. How could a woman who hadn't noticed her husband falling out of love trust herself to counsel children?

'Fancy a stroll?' said Jane when Sarah emerged. Then, 'What's happened?'

'Nuffink. Honest!' Sarah laughed when Jane pursed her lips and they idled through the curving backstreets of Notting Hill, Jane pushing her bike, its wheels making a lazy *tchat-tchat-tchat* as they shared a punnet of obscenely ripe strawberries.

'You've got juice on your chin.' Jane's shorts were shorter than Sarah's; they verged on indecent. 'I saw a cracking flat today. Kitchen-diner. Shared garden. Needs a bit of TLC but the price is just stupid.'

'Nope.'

'Nope what?'

'Nope, I don't want to go and view it.'

'It's a bargain. Not far away and—'

'I'm not ready.' Looking at flats would be like adultery. It would be an admission that she was leaving number twenty-four. Sarah knew that she was in denial, but she liked it there; it didn't make her want to cry, for one thing.

'I don't want you to move, you know that, but I'm getting scared you'll end up sleeping on someone's floor.' Jane sounded anxious. 'Please let me set up a couple of viewings. No pressure.'

'How did Tom's audition go?'

Jane tutted at the clunky change of subject. 'No way of knowing. According to him, it couldn't have gone worse unless he'd actually murdered the director, but Tom always thinks he's flunked auditions. He's confident about his voice-overs, but he refuses to see that as an actual talent.'

'He's a complex boy.'

'Try living with him,' said Jane. 'There's this girl chasing him. Camilla, she's called. Some actress, they meet now and then on the voice circuit. Always texting him, suggesting a cocktail. Poor bloke's scared of his phone.'

'She's got a cheek.'

Jane shrugged. 'Tom's a good-looking bloke.'

'Doesn't it annoy you?'

'Nah.' Jane laughed, snaffling the last strawberry as they ambled past a cobbled mews peppered with geraniums and olive trees and sports cars. 'She's barking up the wrong tree, poor cow.'

'Let's be honest, your husband wouldn't dare cheat on you, would he?' The idea was laughable.

'God, no! I'd kill him,' said Jane. 'And her. And then I'd bring him back to life and kill him again.' She stopped dead. 'We're here!'

'Where's here?' Apparently, they hadn't been moseying aimlessly; Jane had been leading them to a small edifice of old brick with two oversized arched windows either side of a stone porch.

'That antique place.' Jane pointed at the pleasingly plain building. 'It's shut every time I drive past.'

'The owner's a bit lackadaisical about opening times,' said Sarah.

Leo emerged from the cool of the interior to fuss with the dusty books displayed in a wheelbarrow beside the sign that read: 'The Old Church Antiques Emporium – Browsers Welcome!' When he looked up and saw the women on the opposite pavement, it seemed that this welcome didn't extend as far as Sarah.

'You mean . . . ?' Jane, who'd heard about the squabble, bit her lip. 'Shit, I forgot this is Leo's place, let's just . . .'

It was too late to sidle off. Leo revamped his face and waved them over. 'Greetings,' he said, just like the proprietor of an eccentrically charming emporium should. 'Looking for something in particular?'

'Bedside tables,' said Jane, leaning her bike against a Victorian chimney pot.

'Mismatched? Or a pair?'

'Either.'

The women followed Leo inside, and the sun was swallowed up by the high-raftered church, where the air smelled of wax and wood.

Sarah hung back. It was peculiar to be a visitor in a place she'd regarded as her territory. She used to turn up with a deli lunch and they'd eat it sitting in an old pew or a repurposed cart or metal bed – whatever Leo was trying to flog at the time. She'd help him haul pieces around, the legs squeaking on the parquet floor, debating where to hang the signs the Old Church was famed for. Glancing at the current stock, she particularly coveted an old tin 7Up advertisement.

Leo's charm, the easy patter of the salesman, wasn't working on Jane, who barely looked at the tables he showed her. Sarah knew the charm wasn't hollow, that Leo loved every piece that went through his hands.

The phrase struck her as eerily apt. Was she just another piece that went through his hands? The antiques that Leo stroked and admired were forgotten as soon as they were sold. Sarah's self-esteem was a drunkard since the divorce, reeling this way and that; now she shored it up by reminding herself that she had more patina than Helena.

'S'cuse me, Leo.' Jane put her trilling phone to her ear and had a short conversation. 'OK, yes, sure, bye.' She found Sarah in the doorway. 'Bums. Gotta dash. This client thinks he owns me.' She made a polite, frosty goodbye to Leo, and put her arm through Sarah's.

'Actually,' said Leo, 'I've got a little something you might find interesting, Sarah.' There was an appeal in his face. Humbled, not his usual blustering self, Leo moved Sarah, in a deep place where very few people penetrated.

This was a fork in the road. She could go forwards or back.

'You go.' Sarah smiled at the face Jane pulled. With a tut that echoed in the cavernous space, Jane left them to it.

'I didn't think you'd . . .' Leo was chastened, wary.

'I didn't think *you'd* . . .'

They both laughed.

'Look at us,' said Leo. 'Lost for words.'

'I'm sorry. Well, not sorry,' began Sarah, who wanted to both apologise and reiterate her gripe; the trouble was, she hated to see Leo squirm. She hadn't turned off the love like a tap when he moved out.

'I know what you mean; I'm sorry and not sorry too.' Leo edged closer, stealing around an inlaid harpsichord, trailing his fingers along its polished surface. 'What I meant to say the other day, and it came out all wrong, is that Helena's talking bollocks. She was miffed about our assignations so she put a spin on them that simply isn't true.'

Sarah moved away as Leo made ground, noting that he hadn't thrown in a 'darling' yet.

'Cross my heart, Sarah, I just want you to be happy again.'

'To make yourself feel better?'

'Partly. But mainly because you deserve happiness.'

Marriage had made Sarah happy. As had the flat. 'Selling up,' she admitted, in a small voice, 'is breaking my heart, Leo.'

Leo didn't have anything to say. He skirted a dresser populated with a Festival of Britain dinner service, and Sarah took a step backwards. He noticed, and looked wounded. 'Am I that bad?'

Backing towards the entrance, towards the glowing outdoors, Sarah said, 'It's not because you're *bad*, Leo. It's because we were good.'

The honesty shocked Leo. 'We were, weren't we, darling?' he said.

A-ha! thought Sarah. *We have a 'darling'!* 'All past tense.' Sarah was at the porch, her shape outlined by dazzling sunshine.

'Helena and I . . .' Leo looked at the tiles on the floor, the Grade II listed ones he wasn't allowed to remove and sell. 'It's good, yes, even great at times, but . . .'

'But?' Sarah hated herself for that prompt. She pleaded in her own defence that Helena had so much. *And I have so little.* A crumb might sustain her for months.

Leo approached her and this time Sarah didn't move away. '*But*, Leo?'

Closer, he said, 'But she's not you.'

Leo was close enough to touch. Sarah was unable to back off or move in.

Leo said, 'You're amazing, Sarah.'

'So amazing that you left me.'

'I didn't go far.'

'True.' Sarah gulped. 'I wish you'd gone further.'

'Truth is, I couldn't.' Leo leaned past Sarah's shoulder and pushed the emporium door.

The noise reverberated in the church. Their faces were close. Sarah turned and twisted the huge old key in the lock.

Leo took a hank of her hair in his fingers. 'Sarah.'

It was neither a question nor a rebuke. It was her name, and it was Leo saying it. Time contracted, folded in on itself and she fell into him.

Later she'd remember that they were equal partners. Nobody was taken advantage of. Both consenting adults knew exactly what they were doing.

Their mouths met, her head back. The fit was as sexily unequal as she remembered. She felt dainty against his bulk.

Sarah pulled back to attack the buttons on his shirt, ravenous. They tottered together, crashing into a glass-fronted cupboard which lurched on its painted legs. As Leo greedily trailed his mouth over her forehead, kissing her hair, Sarah tugged at his belt.

Hardly any clothes were removed. The bare essentials were undone, or pulled aside. Staggering, they lay down on a vintage kilim.

The first time was hurried and rough, little more than a blur. They lay flat on their backs, staring up at the hammered beams far above them.

'Wow.' Leo's chest rose and fell.

'We should get divorced more often,' said Sarah. The flippancy surprised her. Sex had liberated her spirit. It had brought them close. Intimacy had washed their slate clean.

Leo gasped with delight and shock and then, despite their lack of breath, laughter rolled over them. Sarah hooted, knees up against her chest. She was as light as a feather, as old as the hills: she was loved.

Then Leo turned to her, purposeful, his lips, foreign and familiar, were on hers and this time it was slow, and Sarah cried as they moved together.

*

Infamously able to sleep anywhere, Leo was silent beside her on the rug.

The hectic noise, the whispers, the feel of soft bodies, hard bodies, had all receded and the Old Church was its stately self again. A dog barked outside. Pipes gurgled. Sarah's stomach grumbled.

She wondered how they would be with each other now. The rightness of it receded. Doubt sneaked around her like a serpent. Sarah's exposed breasts seemed improper. She inched her knickers up past her hips.

Like a B-movie Dracula, Leo shot up. 'Bloody hell, darling!'

'Yeah,' agreed Sarah. 'Bloody hell.'

They giggled, coyly, until Leo reached out and pulled her face towards his, crushing her lips and knocking the breath out of her all over again. Their foreheads touching, he whispered, 'It's best if you leave first. We can't get home at the same time.'

Disassociating her lips from Leo's, Sarah felt like a hit-and-run victim, until she realised Leo's actions didn't match his words. He stared, as if committing her to memory.

'You are *sublime*,' he whispered.

Suddenly gallant, he turned his back as they dressed. Sarah heard Leo do up buttons and drag up a zip as her body sparkled. She was radioactive.

Clothes back on, knees wobbly, Sarah felt musky, primal, not at all ready for the sunny streets of Notting Hill.

*

Back at number twenty-four, Sarah sat perfectly still in a patch of sunlight that lay across the floorboards like a rug. She heard the street door close and listened to Leo's feet on the stairs. Then the door to Flat B opened and shut and he called, 'Wifey, I'm home!'

That was how he used to greet Sarah. She shut her eyes to it, squeezing them tight, forcing away the feeling of being replaced, as if she was a toy, by a newer version.

The downside would have its moment, but for now Sarah held on to the euphoria. Love did indeed turn this wise woman into a fool. No shower. She preserved Leo's invisible handprints on her body, at her throat. She wandered about the flat, her thoughts like chiffon hanging in pretty rags.

Leo wanted her. He still needed her. The sly story about buying Flat A was a red herring; Helena was *jealous*.

After months of beige celibacy, the technicolour sensuality of lovemaking had shaken Sarah. She was in love with herself. Her toes were in love with the floor. Her fingers were in love with the cup of mint tea she held.

A shout from the now twilit garden drew her to the window. Tom was threatening Jane with the watering can; Jane fled, prettily, crazily.

They looked so fresh in their summery whites, playing a blameless game. An invisible barrier divided them from Sarah. The Royces were married and she was a mistress; they were the heroes of their own story but Sarah was the villain of somebody else's.

Chapter Eleven

Sarah was something she'd sworn she'd never be: an adulterer.

Her own family had been blown to smithereens by infidelity, the parts finally reassembling to make a Frankenstein version of the original Lynches.

As a child she'd believed that her mother drove her father to have an affair; Sarah absolved her perfect daddy. Now, as Sarah finally accepted the truth of her mother's insult – 'You're just like him!' – she realised it had been his choice.

She'd made a similar choice, fully aware of the deadly wake left by her little boat as she chug-chug-chugged into Leo's arms.

Jane had called her a goody-goody. *And now here I am, having an affair with my own husband.*

*

Jane caught up with Sarah as she left for work. 'I'll walk you part of the way.' Jane was en route to the tube station. 'Yet another meeting with this damned Suffolk guy. He's narrowed the search area down to Southwold, but I can't make him understand that there's nothing on the market that's big enough.' She was smartly dressed; this was Work Jane. 'I won't ask you if you've thought about a new flat, what you can afford, square footage. I've given up on you.'

'Good,' said Sarah, who didn't believe a word of it.

'I've got a mad day ahead and so has Tom. He has a second audition for *Vile Bodies*. So tonight we're going to drink ourselves stupid. I know you never leave Notting Hill but if you pack your passport and a sarnie for the journey you could join us in Covent Garden later.'

'Tonight's Mavis night.' Sarah had already planned dinner; Mavis set the bar high.

'There are easier ways to give to charity,' said Jane, 'than sitting through dinner with our resident witch.'

I look forward all week to my meal with Mavis. 'Witch was often another name for the wisest old woman in the village.'

'It was also the name for a witch.' Jane was rooting in the large satchel she always carried. 'Old ladies eat early. We're not meeting until nine. Come after you've kissed Mavis goodnight.'

'Can't,' said Sarah. 'I'm meeting Keeley, my supervisor, for a glass of wine.'

'To chat about your job?' Jane winced. She knew about Sarah's predicament.

'Yeah.' Sarah nodded as Jane swallowed the lie. It was ugly to bend trust out of shape.

'Did you and Leo kiss and make up after I left the Old Church?'

That was so near the mark that Jane jumped; she'd certainly kissed most of him. 'What? No. Well, yes. We're talking again, and before you start, Jane, it's better when Leo and I are friends.' She almost coughed at that whitewash of a word.

As they parted, Jane found what she was looking for in her satchel. 'Reading matter for your coffee break. A *Sunday Times* magazine I kept from two years ago.' Walking backwards, she said, 'It explains Mavis's accent. Those Bennison birds grew up in luxury.'

A cloud hung over St Chad's despite the battering sunshine. The police had been called when a man with a history of domestic abuse had barged in, demanding to take his eight-year-old son home. There'd been whispers of a knife that had proved to be untrue, but the whole building was jittery.

None more so than Keeley, who'd been to a budget meeting with her superiors; from the look on her face as she stalked the corridors it hadn't gone well. Sarah kept out of her way at lunchtime, tucking herself into a corner of the staffroom with an indifferent salad and the *Sunday Times* magazine.

Zelda Bennison: a life in writing

'I believe in love, all kinds of love,' the prolific novelist tells Jodie Leskovac on the publication of her thirty-eighth book *Tell Me What to Do*.

The five-storey house in one of London's smartest streets is the perfect backdrop for Zelda Bennison CBE. Like her surroundings, she is tastefully put together and doesn't show her age; it's incredible that the woman pouring us both a bracing Scotch is seventy years old.

'No surgery, I assure you.' The author wrinkles her nose distastefully. 'I wash my face with soap and water and I live cleanly.' She lifts her glass. 'Bar the occasional indiscretion.'

Her study is tidy and organised, her writing materials neatly laid out on an antique desk. Tantalisingly, the computer is dark and the notepads are face down. Like all Bennison fans I'm keen for titbits about the next book.

'It's about love.' Bennison's hair should probably be white by now, but it's tinted a cashmere blonde, cut to hang crisply above her shoulders, which are neat in a sharply tailored dress the colour of the autumn leaves in the private garden square beyond the window. 'All my books are about love.'

'Even the murders?' I venture.

'Especially the murders. One must feel very strongly about another person in order to expend so much energy killing them. What's that if it isn't love?'

The topic seems timely, as Bennison is a newly-wed.

'Yes, my darling Ramon.' Bennison's austerely attractive face softens as we look at a framed photograph of the actor Ramon Kaur that adorns her desk. 'Call him a toy boy and I'll never buy *The Times* again,' she warns over the rim of her tumbler.

The three-decade age gap is 'simply a number. We respect each other. It's rather beautiful after the pain of the recent past.' The sudden death of Bennison's first husband, publisher Charles Mulqueeny, ended forty-five years of marriage. Photographs of the pair show a dashing, well-matched couple, both handsome, both undaunted by impending old age. She won't discuss her bereavement beyond saying, 'It tests one.'

Such reserve is unusual. Despite her aristocratic bearing, Bennison is open with journalists, laying out the facts of her life with honesty and humour. On being childless, she tells me, 'I dislike the term. I'm not childless, that implies a lack. Charles and I chose to live a life dedicated to work, to each other, to travel. We were family. It was more than sufficient.' She pauses and glances down at her hands, a glittering ring on each finger. 'I do so loathe talking about him, and not to him.'

A childhood in Plymouth, the daughter of a successful businessman – 'He imported iron. Dull but profitable.' – and a titled, socially prominent mother, Bennison grew up 'utterly ignorant of what it means to be loved'. Her parents, who appear in her 1998 autobiographical essay for this newspaper, were distant, outsourcing their childcare to an ever-changing squad of nannies and housekeepers. She wrote in that piece about growing up with 'a madwoman in the attic'.

Bennison places the cold glass against her temple. 'My maternal grandmother suffered from something I now know is called frontotemporal dementia. It's rather like Alzheimer's. My parents were ashamed, and now I'm ashamed of *them*. My poor granny was locked away on the top floor, and discussed in whispers. We could hear her sobbing. She had no idea where she was, or who we were. Some love would have helped; it always does. But no. Mother and Dad swore us to secrecy. My sister Mavis takes after her, apparently. Mother would say, "One day you'll go the same way." Not particularly helpful, don't you agree?'

Her mother's parenting style has been a rich source of inspiration, notably for the mother in *Mantled in Mist*, and the unforgettable anti-heroine, Marianne, in *The Mustard Seed*. Before, Bennison has referred to her as a 'cold statue, lovely but alien', and today she remembers, 'Mother cringed when our little hands came near her frocks, and Dad referred to us both as the pests, as in "Doo put the pests to bed so we can relax."' Her sister, claims Zelda, 'fought back, tiny fists pummelling, demanding love from them both. I scribbled my stories, and dreamed of the day I could leave their comfortable, cold house.'

When I ask about Mavis, Bennison's only sibling, she asks wryly, 'The ghost sister? That's what journalists call her. Not I.'

Is she still alive, this spectral figure who turns up in so many of Zelda's books, including the best-selling *Climbing Rose*?

'As far as I know. There was contact, sporadically, but

now ...' For the first time, this sure-footed woman falters. Words are her slaves, but she looks flustered trying to explain. 'Mavis and I are very different. I tried to keep the connection taut. Neither of us attended our parents' funerals, which sounds cruel, but it would have been hypocritical. I found love with Charles and that made me receptive, helped me recognise friends. But Mavis chose a solitary path, keeping the world at bay. That world included me. She turns up in my novels because I dream about her, you see, and I write about the ethereal, lonely woman who visits me at night.'

Sometimes, I venture, you have the Mavis character bumped off.

'You're not the first reader to remark on that. It's not wish-fulfilment, I assure you. It serves the plot, that's all.'

And not even a teeniest part retribution for her sister's withdrawal?

'Perhaps a teeny-tiny part. But no more than that. If either of us was going to kill the other, I feel certain I'd be the victim, not the murderer.'

I don't believe her for one moment.

Tell Me What to Do is published by Simon & Schuster (£12.99)

Sarah fed Mavis a rice salad flecked with vegetable jewels, and a platter of cold meats.

'This bread's very good.' Mavis tore off a chunk. 'Did you make it?'

'God, no!' Sarah, jittery since The Old Church, giggled at the thought of herself doing such a thing. 'I'm no domestic goddess.' She paused in her mission to extract the red peppers from her rice, wondering as she did so why she'd added an ingredient she disliked to her own dish. 'Do *you* make bread?'

Mavis chewed for a moment, her eyes on her plate. 'Um, no,' she said finally and not very convincingly.

This reticence was typical. Their conversation eddied in pleasant circles until Mavis would close down, refusing to offer some commonplace detail. When Sarah asked, idly, if Mavis had ever been to Ireland, Mavis took an age to answer, finally offering a vague, 'I've been to lots of places.'

Mavis: international woman of mystery.

It was self-evident that Mavis had a life pre-number twenty-four, but until the recent glasnost, Sarah had imagined her as part of the building's fixtures and fittings, cursed to live in the basement forever.

Reading about the Bennison sisters' childhood had brought Mavis into focus. Young Mavis had been grown without love, like a neglected plant in a greenhouse.

Sarah remembered the part about Mavis fighting her parents, fists flying, desperate for a reaction. To be touched. To be valued. When Sarah had worked directly with children at the clinic, she'd met many, many little Mavises. Her heart contracted every time, and it did the same now, looking at the ex-child opposite her.

We're all just children at heart; a bit taller, that's all.

'Room for a little lemon syllabub?' Sarah had put down her paintbrushes in order to whip together cream and sugar and wine and lemon zest, and the result pleased her. As she brought the chilled glasses to the table, Mavis looked her up and down. 'You've dressed up for me, dear.' Mavis had, as usual, dressed very much down.

'Not really.' Sarah frowned, as if she applied careful eye-liner and pinned up her hair every night.

'I like the glittery blouse.'

'It's not really glittery.' Sarah looked down at the new, loose, definitely glittery top.

Mavis, puzzled, opted not to take it further and wielded her spoon like a scimitar over the dessert. 'Mmm, exquisite. You're too good to me, Sarah, dear.'

'It's nice to be civilised once in a while.' The improvised table was covered with a quality linen cloth, left behind by Leo. The glasses matched, the cutlery sparkled; Sarah had made an effort. 'Usually I sling something in the micro-wave.' She'd thrown away the Confucius cartons in the Great Tidy Up before Mavis arrived.

'Living on one's own,' said Mavis, 'it's easy to forget the niceties.' She laid down her spoon. 'Now,' she said. 'Leo.'

'What about him?' Mavis wasn't the only trickster at the table.

'Down in my dungeon I have little to do, but I hear and see a great deal, and most of all I *sense*.' Mavis leaned across the table, the collar of her nylon blouse flaccid in the heat. 'I worry about you, dear.'

'Why?' Sarah laughed.

'Because the hanky-panky with Leo can't end well.' Mavis's eyes, so disconcertingly bright in her grey complexion, impaled Sarah. 'You're fretful. He's shifty. Something's going on.'

'There's no point fibbing to you, is there, Mavis? Things have gone a little too far. I didn't mean to . . .' Sarah stopped herself: no adult can use that excuse. 'He was mine first. I know that's feeble, but surely I have *some* rights over him?'

Mavis shook her head of wiggy white hair. 'No, Sarah, you don't. You're bad at this, and you're up against a seasoned competitor in Helena. Do you really want to put Leo to the test? Could you bear it if he had to choose between you?'

'Yes.' Sarah nodded vehemently. 'Because then I'd know.' Sarah had decided to hope. She'd decided to trust. *I know Leo*, she thought. Inside out. Better than Helena knew him; Sarah felt guilty for ever believing Helena's silly fable.

There was love between Sarah and Leo; they could patch it up, make all the seams safe again. 'We have unfinished business, Mavis. Leo's as drawn to me as I am to him.'

Mavis's look said *I could say a lot more on the subject but for now I'll hold my peace.* Instead she said, 'When I worry about you, I'm also worrying about my own sad and sorry self, Sarah. I couldn't easily do without you now.'

'Snap,' said Sarah, surprised by how much she meant it.

Sarah was pushing forward on two major fronts, both of which would mean moving out. If she and Leo rekindled their marriage, they couldn't possibly live in the same house as Helena. If he spurned her again, Sarah would have to move out as planned. The countdown, which had been muffled since she and Leo made love, boomed in her ears. The walls around her, the floorboards beneath her – all were temporary.

Sarah walked Mavis home, down through the layers of the house, each door the seal on a secret or two, and noticed that Mavis was even thinner than usual. As if she was fading into the pre-war decor of Flat E.

'Bugger orf!' bellowed Peck as Sarah walked away.

The hotel cocktail bar felt like a place where only good things could happen. Shoes made no noise on the silk carpet. The reflections confronting Sarah in the mirrored walls were of her best blurred self. The staff – each of them movie-star handsome – whispered, as careful of her comfort as the most devoted nana.

Sarah felt herself relax in the golden lighting. Each surface was strokeable, the glassware exquisite, the seating plush. It wasn't somewhere she'd have chosen, but now that she was here Sarah let herself be seduced by Mayfair.

Sipping a Prosecco, she looked to her phone for company. A gossip page vomited Ramon Kaur's name immediately. 'Currently being comforted by a hot US reality star after the death of his much older wife.' Sarah's lip curled. As if 'much older' was all there was to say about a woman like Zelda Bennison. The great writer was fresh in her grave but her duck-lipped widower was already being 'comforted' by a woman half *his* age.

Love is a dance of changing partners. The music shifts. We whirl faster or slow down completely.

A man at the bar – about her age, tie undone – raised his glass to Sarah. She smiled back, then resolutely avoided his eye. All those bedrooms above their heads, all those room-service trays and satin bedspreads; hotel bars were on a knife-edge, places where things could turn sexual very fast. She stared into her drink and wondered if this had been a terrible idea.

The phone's beep made her jump. Sarah read the text sadly but without surprise.

> A thousand apologies, my dearest darling! I can't get away from the ball and chain! Have some champagne on me! xxxxx

Leo had wanted to meet at the Old Church again, or failing that, her flat. His intentions were clear. The sex had been nostalgic and exhilarating. It had been *too* powerful: Sarah couldn't do that again without some sort of promise, some flag of hope. She'd insisted they meet somewhere grown- up, public; saying yes to Claridge's, she'd been too blinded by the glamour for it to register that hotels are adulterers' playgrounds.

Sarah wanted Leo, but not just for panting interludes. Sex confused the issue; it was already established that Leo would do anything for an extra-marital bonk. Only love – the real, true, unvarnished thing – had the power to drag him back from the scented quicksands of Flat B.

She'd rehearsed a speech. Long, detailed, it could be condensed to this: 'no more sex until we're a couple again'. Beating Helena fair and square would make victory all the sweeter.

Dressed up with nowhere to go, Sarah ordered another Prosecco. All that awaited her at home was a blank wall; *I can paint just as well tipsy.* On a sudden caprice she typed a website name into her phone.

smithlifeline.co.uk's banner headline was still bright; Sarah half expected it to be covered in cobwebs, but nothing ages on the internet.

It made sense to close down the site, but just thinking that felt treacherous. On the virtual outcrop, Smith was still herself, sparkling and irreverent. The beaming, wonkily beautiful face at the top of the page grazed Sarah's heart. She traced the zigzag shapes in Smith's cropped hair, remembering how they'd shaved off her mane once the radiotherapy kicked in. They'd cried and giggled in the bathroom, holding up peroxide hanks, wondering if they could stuff cushions with it, eventually turning quiet as the buzzing clippers finished the job.

The content beneath the 'About' tab had been rejigged endlessly, Sarah and Smith sloshing wine over the keyboard as David Bowie belted out in the background. Finally they'd agreed on the vital few lines. Sarah still hated the double exclamation marks Smith insisted on.

Smith is my friend. She's loyal and funny and the best company, but you have to like getting into trouble!! I knew Smith was kind and honest, but I had no idea how brave she was until she was diagnosed with a grade 4 brain tumour, specifically an astrocytoma, just two months ago.

This disease is relentless. Smith's friends are facing the fact that she has about three years to live. We are determined to do all we can to extend her life (and her quality of life) and we're asking for YOUR donations to help.

Groundbreaking research by world renowned Dr Sebastian Vera in Santiago could be a lifeline for Smith. Dr Vera is a controversial but distinguished oncologist who is trialling a new and radical treatment called antineoplaston therapy, which you can read about here.

Sarah tutted: that link still didn't work.

We need your help!! It will cost £10k to send Smith to Chile – every penny counts!!

Head over to our 'Get involved' page to discover how YOU can be part of Smith's amazing journey!!

Number twenty-four hadn't rallied around. All Sarah got from Helena was a rolled eye. Mavis didn't even break step when Sarah tried to enlist her in the hall. Lisa and Graham were locked into their shoot-'em-up of a relationship.

The donation graphic inched up, heartbreakingly slow. Leo had given the first donation, but with the proviso that Sarah didn't talk about the campaign at the dinner table. 'It's Smith who's got cancer, darling. You can't have it for her.'

The breakthrough had involved baked beans.

How or why Sarah decided to bathe in beans was still hazy, but somehow she found herself in her own bath, up to her chin in Heinz's finest, giving a shaky thumbs up to a photographer from the local paper.

Perched on the loo, Smith had hunched over, breathless with laughter. Scurrying around buying up baked beans – it had taken almost two hundred tins – and then opening them all and tipping them in had exhausted her dwindling energy capital.

'Are you cold?' asked Smith as the photographer clicked away.

'Freezing!' Tomato sauce in Sarah's gusset was a new and wholly unwanted sensation. Leo had refused to kiss her for days afterwards: 'You smell like a cafe breakfast.'

Sarah clicked through to her blog post titled 'Beanz Meanz Smith!' and saw that she'd jokingly quoted Leo, even though the comment had hurt.

Money began to trickle in; Sarah and Smith watched the cartoon thermometer rise and rise. Locals carried out their own stunts, inspiring those farther afield. The website's chatty updates reached a small town in the States, an oil rig, a woman who used to teach Sarah in primary school. They opened their hearts and their purses, many of them motivated by their own brush with cancer. Some got in touch to say how much they appreciated the language Sarah used; she'd been careful not to describe Smith as 'battling' cancer. It was a disease, not a foe, and the brave didn't necessarily win.

All the while Smith changed. She grew smaller, paler, and retreated inside herself more and more. An inveterate partygoer, she stayed indoors. A lover of talk, she sat silent.

But she still found the vigour to be a friend. Sarah remembered a night when the dark sky had pressed down hard on the roof of number twenty-four, a night when she'd expected Leo home after work but he was nowhere to be seen and she couldn't face ringing his phone and hearing, yet again, the click as it switched to answer mode.

I knew, thought Sarah, amazed at how easy it had been to wrap herself in denial. *In my heart I knew he was having an affair.* Sarah stared up at the bar's gilded ceiling, reassembling her memories. There'd been other nights Leo had gone AWOL, but she'd suppressed thoughts of them. Because they didn't fit with the nostalgic PR her broken heart was spinning?

That night she'd flown downstairs to Smith. There'd been a break in the clouds over Flat C; Smith was feeling a little brighter, her energy levels on the rise. When she opened the door, she wore a bright scarf wrapped around her naked head, the tassels dangling around a face that popped with the artificial colour of lipstick and blusher. She was gaunt, but game; a flash of her old hale and hearty self showed in her eyes.

'What's up?' Smith had known immediately something was wrong.

'Doesn't matter. You're going out.' Too late, Sarah remembered that Smith had been looking forward to this evening for days on end. An old flame had reappeared, said he found her baldness 'sexy', and asked her out for a drink. Such events were rare in Smith's calendar as her body gave up on her.

'What,' repeated Smith firmly, 'is bloody well wrong?'

'Nothing. Well, just Leo. I can't get hold of him. Bit worried, that's all. In case he's ill or something.'

'Hmm.' Smith knew that Leo wasn't ill. She knew that Sarah knew he wasn't ill. They'd both been dancing around their suspicions, neither of them willing to be the first to say 'affair'. She shrugged off her jacket, a musty patchwork affair, and threw her keys onto the coffee table. 'This feels like a *The Good Wife* kinda night.'

The Good Wife was their go-to when they felt down; they'd been known to devour four episodes on the trot.

'You have a date.' Sarah picked up the jacket and held it like a maître d'. 'Come on. I know you like this guy.' She didn't say that Smith deserved some fun, because it might sound patronising and Smith was violently allergic to being patronised.

'You know what, I'd rather stay in.' Smith whipped off the scarf. Her scalp looked pale and vulnerable. The lipstick suddenly seemed wrong, and garish.

'No, absolutely not, come on.' Sarah had ruined Smith's last gasp at a social life.

'I'd rather,' said Smith, looking her in the eye, 'be with you. OK?'

Finally giving in, sinking to the sofa, Sarah's 'thank you'

made Smith roll her eyes. Sitting there, re-watching a familiar episode from season two, bitching mildly about the characters' hair and whitened teeth, Sarah had felt looked after. Cared about.

By unspoken agreement they didn't discuss Leo. When they heard him creep in at two a.m. Sarah had yawned and gone out to greet him, but not before Smith had taken her by the arm and whispered, 'Listen, you, this Sarah-shaped person, is fine, is sweet, is special. Do you hear me?' She'd pulled Sarah to her, her arms like chopsticks. 'You're not the problem. Remember that.' She'd pushed her away. 'Now skedaddle,' she'd smiled, obviously exhausted and ready for bed.

Leo had been fearful, penitent, afraid he'd gone too far. Sarah, too tired to probe, had accepted his cock and bull story. As she listened to him snore beside her, she thought of how he regarded Smith as a destructive, selfish person, with no notion that Smith was keeping her upright.

The last blog was titled 'Bon Voyage!!' Headscarf wound around her naked head, Smith beamed, cheek to cheek with Sarah in the back of a taxi. Sarah recalled the thrum of the idling engine and the taxi driver asking, 'Which terminal, ladies?'

'Don't say "terminal"!' There was no situation dark enough to blunt Smith's funny bone.

The second glass of Prosecco appeared on the table. Sarah looked up to say 'thank you'.

'This one's on me.' It was the tieless man from the bar.

His jacket was over his shoulder. His head was to one side. He smelled of spirits and his smile was wolfish.

Sarah sprang up.

'Whoa!' The stranger caught the toppling glass. 'I don't bite.'

'I have to . . . the loo.' Sarah pointed to the lobby, as if he might not know what a loo was.

'Hurry back.'

From the tone of his voice, he knew she was escaping. A doorman let her out and she sped down the street, her phone to her ear.

Jane was delighted. 'Get your arse over here! There'll be a negroni waiting.'

It wasn't far to Escapologist, a cocktail bar in Covent Garden that was darker than Claridge's, with leather chairs and tiled floors beneath an arched ceiling.

'Fancy meeting you here.' Tom rose from a low seat in the candlelit twilight.

Sarah laughed. She was uneasy; Tom was bathed in the blinding light of fidelity. He made her feel shoddy.

Tom bent forward to kiss her cheek, then seemed to think better of it. 'You look . . . nice, pretty, um, great.' Tom looked helpless. 'You're not an easy woman to compliment, Sarah.'

'I've scrubbed up, that's all.'

'See what I mean? Hard to compliment. You look *great*.' Tom maintained eye contact as they took their seats so that the compliment landed.

'Where's Jane?'

'She had to leave.'

'What? I spoke to her a few minutes ago.'

'She gets these migraines. Has she told you?'

'Yeah.' Sarah had seen Jane in the grip of a migraine. 'Poor thing!'

'It's been bubbling under all day, apparently, and then it suddenly kind of blossomed and she had to go. She said to say sorry.' Tom looked apologetic himself. 'So it's just me, I'm afraid.' He pushed a tumbler towards her. 'And this, of course.'

'You'll do,' smiled Sarah. The amber cocktail winked at her from its crystal glass. The room was womb-like, relaxing. The company was good. 'I just ran away from a man,' she laughed, and told her tale of the smooth operator at Claridge's.

'He's probably sitting there wondering if you've fallen down the toilet.'

'It was mean, wasn't it?'

'Nah.' Tom had little sympathy. 'He'll survive.'

'He seemed the type who does it all the time.' Sarah sipped her drink. It was bracing, to say the least. 'Once upon a time I would have sat and let him chat me up. I used to like adventures.'

'And now?'

'I was scared.'

'It's only what? Six months since your divorce. You're out of practice.' Tom raised his glass to her. 'I'm sure you have many more adventures ahead of you, Sarah.'

The famous quote from Ernest Hemingway, that drinking makes other people more interesting, didn't apply here. Tom interested Sarah hugely; it felt odd, even a little wrong, to be alone with him without his wife, her friend. *But he's also my friend,* she reminded herself. 'A night out feels like an adventure these days. The flat takes up all my time.'

'Is it rude if I say you don't get out enough?'

'Almost, but no.'

'You're finally getting over *him*, aren't you?'

'He has a name,' smiled Sarah. 'Yes, I'm getting over Leo.' No need to tell Tom she was getting over Leo by getting back with Leo. 'But, I've always been a homebody, even when I was young.'

'There's a difference between being at home and being imprisoned.' Tom flicked a look at her, as if to gauge her reaction. 'Stop me if I'm being an arse.'

'You're not in the least arse-ish.' Like Jane, Tom's bluntness sprang from a good place, somewhere near the heart. Sarah intuited that it was unusual for Tom to intervene like this; the thought warmed her.

He sat forward, startled. 'Hang on, aren't you on Mikey duty?'

'I swapped with Lisa.' A rota hung over the table in the communal hall. Mikey had the residents of twenty-four eating out of his tiny paws. His hot-water bottle was changed regularly, as was his shredded paper bedding. He'd put on a little weight, and was, Sarah felt, enjoying his new lifestyle.

'I hope she remembers to feed him.'

'For a professional carer, Lisa sometimes seems, well, *uncaring*,' said Sarah, 'but trust me, round about now she'll be serving the finest minced cat food to the young master.'

'Mikey has to get better. I made a promise.'

'And you never break your promises.'

'Never.'

'I believe you.'

The bar filled up. Every now and then, another drinker gave them a look, an easily translated glance that was best summed up as 'nice couple'. Perhaps it was the easy conversation or the body language as they tilted their frames towards each other.

Maybe, thought Sarah, her negroni to her lips, *it's the crackle of sexual attraction*. She hadn't realised it was mutual, but the hive mind of the Escapologist thought differently. Her wayward libido agreed, treacherously sending a frisson shooting through her whenever her foot touched Tom's by accident beneath the table.

Her conscience made amends by drawing Jane back into the circle. 'This feels peculiar without Jane.'

'Does it?' Tom looked mildly aggrieved. 'It's nice to get away from the non-stop personal comments, to be honest.'

'She has a right to make them,' smiled Sarah.

'Well, yes and no.' Tom looked quizzically at Sarah, as if he'd just realised something. 'Are you, does this ... would you rather not? Without Jane to chaperone us?'

'I love having Jane around, that's all.'

'Me too, but I'm allowed out without her.' Tom's phone, face up on the table, glowed and he jumped. 'Sorry,' he said, glancing at it. 'I'm really not one of those people who look at their phone all the time but I'm waiting to hear from my agent. One of the producers of *Vile Bodies* is in the States, and he's getting in touch at the end of their working day which is round about now.'

'Fingers crossed,' said Sarah, doing just that.

'And everything else. Legs. Eyes. The lot.' Tom leaned back and groaned. 'I promised I wouldn't let myself get all het up about this . . .' He sat forward, his face intense. 'I want to make a mark, you know? I don't want to die without *doing something.*'

'What does making a mark entail?'

'I'm not sure.' Tom laughed. 'My job's so trivial. In your line of work, you see the difference you make.'

Sarah had come across this misapprehension before. 'It's not a Michelle Pfeiffer film, where the gutsy lady gets through to the troubled young street punk and suddenly the kid's learning the violin and going to Harvard. It's slow and dispiriting at times, with a few steps back for every morsel of ground you win.'

'But you love it.'

'I used to.' Tom deserved a sincere reply. 'I'm trying to feel that way again, but falling back in love is tricky.'

Tom was surprised. 'I've seen you with Una. You care.'

That compliment meant more to Sarah than any amount

of ovations for her hair or her eyes or her 'curves'. 'Thank you.'

The phone beeped again. Tom moved his head and harrumphed. 'Jane making sure I'm looking after you.' He drained his glass and motioned to a waiter. 'Now you know what keeps me awake, what do *you* worry about?'

'All the usuals.'

'What're they?'

'Sickness. Poverty. Dying alone.' Sarah puffed out her cheeks. 'The fun stuff.'

'You won't die alone.' Tom seemed sure of this.

'I'd like that in writing, please.' Sarah tucked her feet under her chair. *Boundaries.*

The waiter hovered and Tom checked with Sarah whether she wanted another negroni or something different. 'Olives?' he asked. 'Are you hungry? Do you need some tap water on the side?'

'Jane'll be proud of you.' After years of playing both PA and au pair to Leo it was novel to feel looked after. Even the strongest, most independent woman can unbend now and then, let another adult take the strain. Sarah had been clenching her buttocks, and her mind, for months; she felt some of the tension dissolve. *No doubt it'll be patiently waiting when I get back to number twenty-four.* 'Where did you grow up, Tom?' She imagined him in a comfortable home, with comfortable parents; he was the product of happiness, she felt sure.

'Gloucestershire. Place called Fairford.'

'Sorry, never heard of it.'

'No reason why you should, unless you're into tea shops.'

'Actually, I am,' said Sarah. 'Heavily.'

'Teenage boys, as a rule, have zero interest in scones, so I got out the millisecond I could. Came to the smoke, as nobody ever actually calls it.'

'And found Jane?'

'Yup. In a *revolting* two-bedder over a minimart in Dalston. This was before the hipsters invaded.' Tom rubbed his nose. Hard. As if he wanted to rub it clean off his face. 'With you, all roads lead to Jane.'

'Not for you?' Sarah found herself listening hard to his answer. A dash of disrespect and this night out would turn sour.

'She's part of me,' said Tom.

The simplicity put Sarah's mind to rest.

Olives arrived. A couple had a row at the bar. The music got a little louder. At Tom and Sarah's table the conversation was fluid, easy, *ordinary* even.

But not dull. Sarah thought of Jane, at home in the dark with lights exploding in her head, willing herself better before the next day's trip to Southwold. A quaint town marooned in Suffolk's infamously flat landscape, Southwold wasn't dull, despite its lack of skyscrapers; *Tom and I are Southwold, in human form.*

Sarah loved Southwold.

It'd be effortless to love Tom, too, if he was free, if she was free. Another woman might have capitalised on her rapport with Tom – another woman like, ooh, Helena, for example – but Sarah dotted her i's and crossed her t's when it came to love.

Apart from that big fat affair-shaped situation I have going on with Leo, obviously.

'It's almost midnight.' Tom looked at his watch, eyebrows hoiked. 'Where did the night go?'

The bill arrived. 'Let me . . .' Sarah always paid her way.

'Shut up. And no.' Tom was firm.

A torrent of tourists still milled on the cobbles. Covent Garden felt like a scene from a movie, brightly lit, full of life, with the Victorian bones of the grand old buildings as a backdrop.

It was oddly date-like, Tom and Sarah leaning close together as they navigated the crowd. Sarah thought of Jane, wondered how she'd feel about somebody borrowing her husband in this way. Jane's fiery friendship was important to her; the minuscule redhead was a giant oak. Perfect for sheltering under, roots reaching far beneath her feet. How could a kook be so solid? Number twenty-four was – a little late – reaching out its arms; even Mavis was one of Sarah's posse now.

When Tom's phone let out its attention-seeking buzz, they both ducked into an arched doorway. Sarah listened as he said, 'Seriously? I mean, for real? Jesus. OK.' He put his phone in his pocket, his face blank.

'Bad news?'

'I got it.' Tom put his hands to his head. 'I got the part, Sarah. I got it.'

'Oh my God! Congratulations!' Sarah did a wee dance. 'You're going to make your mark, Tom.'

'We should celebrate.' Tom shook himself and grinned, waves of elation radiating from him. 'I know just how to do that.'

Tom's lips were full, bold, as they moved against Sarah's for a second or two at most. He spoke, his face so close it blocked out their surroundings. It was just them. 'We should do this again. What do you say?'

Tom didn't recognise Sarah's silence as horror. 'You. Me. A table covered with food. A bottle of something cold.' The silence persisted; Tom lost some of his confidence and his face moved away and the world crowded back in. 'Sarah? Say something.'

'And Jane? Is she invited on this picture-perfect date?'

'Jane *knows*. She's known I've felt . . . like this, since I met you.' Tom was halfway to angry as he said, 'Look, Jane and I do our own thing.'

Sarah wiped her lips and Tom took a step back. 'She doesn't need to know,' he said. 'If that's what bothering you.'

'Christ, you're . . .' Sarah backed away, as if Tom was infectious. 'Why would I want to have dinner with somebody like you, Tom?'

'Wait a minute.' Tom put up his hand. 'Time out, woman.'

'Do *not* call me woman.'

'OK, time out, crazy bitch,' said Tom. 'I got it wrong. Fine. I thought this was going somewhere. Let's walk away, yeah? Pretend this car crash never happened.'

'You need to think about why you do this.'

'When I need psychoanalysis I'll book you for an hour. Until then, back off. Now, much as I'd love to hang around for further character assassination, it's late.' Tom turned, with a terse wave of his hand that was more good riddance than goodbye.

Chapter Twelve

CONFUCIUS FAKEAWAY
Notting Hill, W11

This calendar is FREE to valued customers!
Sunday 24th July, 2016

**THERE IS NOTHING MORE VISIBLE
THAN THAT WHICH IS SECRET**

The sun persevered; confounding all the doubters who believed it favoured the other side of the Channel. July took up the baton from June, weeks unfolding in a bright haze.

All the windows in the house were open. No longer hermetically sealed boxes stacked on top of one another, number twenty-four felt like a doll's house, its back opened up for play.

From Sarah's kitchen she heard the ambient sounds of Notting Hill. The buses wheezing on the main road. The clatter of workmen excavating basements. Feuding R'n'B in the back gardens. She painted, hypnotised by the repetition of the brushstrokes.

The flat was beginning to look like somewhere a person could live: *not me*. Each sweep of the brush brought her closer to the deadline. Sarah was being dragged towards the end of August by summer's implacable forward motion.

She tried not to think about it, and thought of little else.

Down on the emerald lawn, Tom snoozed in a deckchair. These were his last few weeks of anonymity before the BBC publicity machine turned him into a star. A Mr Darcy. A Poldark.

Since the night in Covent Garden four weeks earlier, Sarah and Tom had stayed clear of each other. She listened for his footsteps on the stair before she ventured out, hanging back if she heard his voice in the hallway, grateful that he did the same.

One morning, thrown together at the post table by sarcastic fate, she'd said, 'If you're wondering why I'm avoiding you—'

'Nope,' Tom had said, shortly. 'I'm not wondering. It's fine by me.'

Anger had redoubled, inexhaustible. Four weeks had done nothing to dent the intensity of her outrage, both at what Tom had done and his lack of repentance. She was a liberal person, slow to condemn, quick to justify, but Tom had gone too far for any defence to be credible.

Tom's allure had always been difficult for Sarah to acknowledge; now she saw it as simply sexual. Tom was a good-looking guy; to admit she'd been drawn to his personality would mean she was a terrible judge of character. *Again*.

The attraction was only ever meant to be hypothetical;

he overstepped the mark. That vigilant conscience of hers muttered that she was no angel when it came to adultery, but Sarah had an answer for that: *Leo's different! He used to be mine, and might be mine again.*

At times Sarah grew hot worrying that Jane knew about the horrible kiss.

In truth, the kiss hadn't been horrible. When narrowed down to one mouth meeting another, Tom's lips had been almond-sweet.

I pulled away.

Sarah revisited her behaviour like an investigating police officer.

I did nothing wrong.

If that police officer dug deeper, Sarah looked less lily-white. She'd fancied Tom, despite her efforts not to, since they'd met. Had her body, her scent, her eyes betrayed her, and given Tom the confidence to make a move?

Male voices drifted up from the garden. Sarah peered down to see the two decorators from Lisa's flat lighting up cigarettes on the lawn.

Lisa was there, too, giggling, pushing back her fringe. Even from this distance, Sarah could make out her Cleopatra eyeliner.

You go, girl.

A short rap sounded at the door. A signature knock, she heard it most days, and Sarah knew who to expect when she opened the door.

'Darling!' Leo was out of breath. 'We haven't got long,

my sweet. Helena's gone for a massage.' He passed her, rushing to the bedroom. 'You know what I'm here for!'

Sarah handed him a paint roller. After Leo's no-show at Claridge's, Sarah had refused to meet outside number twenty-four. It felt risky and wrong, in a way that it couldn't possibly do inside Flat A. Inside *their* flat. She felt it embrace them, breathe easier, as the old status quo was restored. For an hour at a time.

It had taken a while to convince Leo that Sarah only wanted him there to paint and grout and varnish.

'You're not bloody serious?' Leo had been shocked the first time he climbed the stairs after their tryst in the Old Church. 'Darling, Helena won't be back for *hours*. We can swing from the sodding chandeliers if we feel like it!'

Sarah had reminded him that she didn't have any chandeliers. 'If you really want to help, stay. But if you're here for a quick leg-over, off you trot.' She'd been trembling, and hoped Leo couldn't see. 'I want you to stay, Leo. But for the right reasons.'

He'd stayed.

'I do loathe white walls,' he complained, as he moved the stepladder, dust sheets coiled around his feet like loyal dogs. 'No personality.'

'It's not supposed to have personality. It has to appeal to as many buyers as possible.' Sarah imagined these prospective buyers as an invading horde, with daggers between their teeth. 'Shut up and paint, Leo.'

He chuckled.

If my life was a play, thought Sarah, *it'd be a farce.*

Worse, if it was a film, it'd be a *Carry On.* Leo scampered up to Flat A whenever Helena turned her back; the rendezvous were secret again, even though they were chaste. Whiter than white. As white as the walls.

On his best behaviour, Leo did exactly as Sarah asked. He painted, he scraped, he varnished. Touch was confined to a hug on leaving; if that embrace lasted a fraction too long Sarah pulled away.

The wanting him hadn't diminished, but it was on her terms. A little distance from Leo had given her perspective. She hadn't noticed his selfishness when they were married; now it was undeniable. *If I let him turn me into a bit of slap and tickle on the side, he'll never leave Helena.*

It was obvious that Helena had played a clever game; Sarah took tips from the master. *Or should that be mistress?* Physical intimacy was ruled out, but emotional intimacy was a different matter.

'Your hair's getting very long.' Sarah eyed Leo as they stood side by side, claiming the wall, stroke by stroke. 'Are you going for the Greek god look?'

'Mock all you like.' Leo lifted his chin, his face imperious. 'I'm making the most of it before the bald patch takes over.'

'You don't have a – oh.' Sarah saw the coin-sized pink shape as Leo ducked to show it off. 'It's tiny,' she said encouragingly. This banal sign of ageing sent a chill through Sarah. There were many landmarks in Leo's future that she might not be privy to. They used to joke about her pushing him around the supermarket in a wheelchair; it was crazy to regret she'd never get to wipe his wrinkled bum, but Sarah managed it. 'Your dad's still got a wonderful head of hair at eighty.'

'My mother, though,' sighed Leo, 'was as bald as a coot.'

Sarah giggled and shoved him.

It was hard to imagine her successor being playful. Helena possibly emerged from the womb in high heels. In the old days, the Harrisons had satirised their neighbour for her haughtiness and her salon hair. Leo dubbed her decorating style 'Empress Josephine meets Miss Piggy', and they'd both smirked when Helena explained that the apartment was a showcase for her interiors brand.

'Do you remember how we used to hang over the bannisters watching Helena's guests arrive?' Sarah put a hand to the small of her back; she'd woken up with a gnawing tummy ache and it was getting worse. 'You'd nudge me when you spotted a celeb.'

'We almost got caught a couple of times,' said Leo.

'Speaking of celebs ...' Sarah had seen a well-known actress going into Flat B the evening before. 'What's she like? They say she's a—'

'Sarah, darling.' Leo held up one hand, like a magistrate. 'She's a mate. It wouldn't be fair to gossip about her.'

Leo was too chivalrous to dish the dirt on a soap actress, yet he'd jumped into Helena's bed (canopied, of course) without a thought for his wife on the floor above. 'Remember when ...' Sarah paused; so many of her sentences began that way with Leo. As if all they had left was the past. 'Remember when you saw Hugh Jackman in Tesco?' It might be timely to remind Leo of his old star-struck self. 'You were hysterical. I thought you'd been mugged.' She landed the killer blow. 'And it wasn't even him.'

'He really looked like Hugh Jackman.' Leo flexed his fingers and put down his brush, strolling over to the window. Leo was a stroller; nothing made him change speed; he would stroll out of a burning building.

Following him, Sarah persisted. 'He had a squint, Leo.'

'Funnily enough, Helena's remodelling Hugh Jackman's London place. We're having dinner with him next week.'

'Let me know if the food's from Tesco.'

Leo giggled, one of his burbling grunts that shook his shoulders. 'What is it, darling?' he asked as Sarah grimaced, bending forward slightly.

'Ouch.' Sarah held her tummy. 'I feel a bit ...' She grasped backwards for a chair and sat on it heavily. Her head swimming, she felt bile rise in her throat.

'Women's problems?' Leo sketched quotation marks in the air. 'You girls and your mysterious insides.'

'Don't.' Sarah grimaced as a pain shot through the centre of her.

'Only joking.'

'It's not funny.' Perspective had also shortened Sarah's patience with Leo's sexism. 'Our mysterious insides, as you call them, keep the human race going.'

'Yes, they do.' Leo was sorry. Comically so.

Sarah, the pain passing, had to laugh, and he laughed with her, until they were laughing just because they were laughing, the original joke forgotten. He was still her lighthouse, the beacon that meant home. Sarah still steered her little boat towards him.

'Admit it,' said Sarah, standing back to survey the finished job. 'The white looks good.'

'Never.' Leo wiped his hands on a rag, shaking his head.

He loved shadows and antiquity; Sarah loved him for being different to her. It would be so easy to sidle up to him, nudge her way into his arms.

The loud knock on the door startled her out of her what-if's. 'Una,' they said together. The little girl now laboriously climbed up her three flights to collect Sarah for their sessions; a small act of independence.

Sarah opened the door, surprised to see Una sitting on a huge, squashy wing chair.

'Bloody hell, that's very pink,' said Leo.

Upholstered in fuchsia velvet, trimmed with turquoise braid, fluorescent yellow buttons punched into its back, the chair was bright on the dim landing. Una bounced, giving it a clear six-year-old seal of approval.

'Where's it from?' Leo circled it.

'It's the one I bought on eBay. Tom must have reupholstered it.'

'Hmm.' Leo's mouth turned down. 'Not my cup of tea.'

Sarah allowed Una to lead her downstairs, shedding Leo outside his flat. On the bottom level, Una tapped at Mavis's door, and the old lady emerged as quickly as if her wide-fit sandals were oiled. Una had overcome her dislike; Mavis was a new favourite, and was always invited out to the garden during Una's therapy sessions. Mavis was aware of the immense honour conveyed on her.

This trust had been won, partly by bribery – Una's fondness for Nobbly Bobbly lollies was an easily exploited Achilles' heel – and partly because Mavis was patient and calm and desperately keen to be friends. Mavis, with her candyfloss hair and laddered tights, would never rival her sister for elegance, but Sarah wished Zelda was there to see how hard Mavis was working to overhaul her life. Perversely, Sarah felt as if she knew Zelda from what Mavis *didn't* say. The dead are present so long as anybody who loved them is still alive; just like Sarah's father would always be her companion, so Zelda was still a force in Mavis's second stab at living.

'Silly mare!' shrieked Peck as the trio invaded the lawn, the sun on their faces like a blessing.

Una dragged Sarah towards Tom: her hero, her champion, saviour of one-eyed hoglets. He stood up, eyes alight, arms open.

Tom had accepted he was part of Una's therapy. In a taut discussion, Sarah had explained how, for good or ill, they'd become a model of coupledom for Una. 'We can't disintegrate like her parents.'

'No problem.' Tom had been breezy, as if the showdown in Covent Garden had never happened.

In the present, in the sunny garden, Tom said, 'Today's the day, Una.'

The thriving hedgehog had outgrown his cardboard box. Robust, handsome – probably, it was hard to tell – Mikey's spines had darkened, leaving them white at the tip. He was groomed to perfection; his weekly bath was a spectacle, as he lay on his back revolving slowly in the suds, his face distracted and dreamy. (Or so Sarah chose to think; Mikey had just the one expression for all occasions.)

Tom had hammered and sawed and created a deluxe hedgehog new-build. Sarah had watched, unable to ask questions, as he built what amounted to a squat wooden crate. Mikey was ready to re-enter the garden, but there would be no roughing it. His new home boasted a sloping roof and a gangplank and wall-to-wall moss carpeting.

Slow on the uptake, and contrary to boot, Mikey turned his back when Tom set him down in front of the wooden house, ambling off in the wrong direction. With some encouragement and a stern look from Una, he finally tottered up the drawbridge.

'It's built on legs to keep him safe.' Tom pointed out the design features to Una and Mavis. Sarah, his demeanour suggested, just happened to be there and could listen if she wanted to. 'It's dry, cool, and he'll sleep there during the day. Do you like it?'

He'd forgotten the cardinal rule. Una ignored the question, but her pink excited face gave Tom his answer.

'It's a masterpiece.' Mavis ran her hands over the sanded

roof. 'Quite, quite perfect. Does this mean the rota is no more?'

'Yes,' laughed Tom. He bent down to Una. 'Let's leave him to settle in.' The maturing Mikey didn't appreciate being handled as much as he had in his youth. They set off on a tour of the garden, another part of the ritual Una insisted on. For somebody who never spoke, she was a stern taskmistress.

'Tom . . .' The name was cumbersome on Sarah's lips. 'Thank you.' She was awkward. He was awkward. She rushed on. 'For the chair.' She hadn't wanted it, she'd never sit in it, but she couldn't ignore it.

'No worries.' Tom waved her thanks away, as if a gift that had taken many hours to create was nothing at all.

The sunflowers swayed, magnificent. Tom and Una weeded them together, Sarah taking a seat beside Mavis on the deckchairs. Mavis closed her eyes, tilting her face to the sun.

What a shame, thought Sarah, *that the garden wasn't like this when Smith was ill.*

Sarah and Smith had been confined to quarters last summer, as the astrocytoma stole Smith's brain, cell by precious cell.

As it grew, so had the fund to send Smith to Dr Vera's clinic. Pound by pound, fitfully, the total increased. There would be weeks of inactivity and then some generous soul would send a three-figure sum. Finally, after months of banking, creating receipts, filling in paperwork, and adjudicating a meatball-eating competition, the target had been reached.

It was an anticlimax. No hurrahs, no ticker-tape parade, just the jagged realisation that it was crunch time. Dr Sebastian Vera's radical treatment might cure Smith, or merely prolong her life for a few extra listless months. It might make no difference whatsoever.

Sarah and Smith had stared at the total on the screen. They'd hugged, Smith's shoulder blades sticking out like knives. By then things were different between them.

Sarah had pretended to herself that she and Smith had been tight until Smith left for Chile.

A deadline helps to concentrate the mind. With only five weeks left in her sanctuary, Sarah confronted the truth, and the truth was this: by the time Smith drove away from number twenty-four, the friendship was stretched to translucency. Sarah had dismissed it as the inevitable narrowing of focus as Smith prepared for the intensive treatment; Smith joked that when Death stares you in the face it's only polite to stare back.

A gnarly suspicion had lurked for some time. *Perhaps, on some level, Smith resented my fundraising efforts, the way I threw myself into it.* If that were true, then Smith's behaviour on the last day made sense.

Four days after a strange, subdued Christmas – the two of them pulling a cracker in front of an *Only Fools and Horses* repeat – the air was cold, brittle.

Suitcases around her feet, the cab tooting its horn at the gate, Smith had said, tearfully, as if the words were ripped from her, 'You're my guardian angel, Sarah.'

'Save it for the departure gate.' Sarah had tugged on her jacket, double-checking that the passport and boarding card and pesos were all safely stowed in the plastic wallet she'd bought. She had bored Smith with the instructions to hand the bank transfer for the scarily large amount to Dr Vera as soon as she arrived. The fact that the clinic didn't accept payment until they'd assessed each patient had helped calm Sarah's fears about the possibility that this famous doctor – the man Smith pinned all her hopes on – was a sham.

'I don't want you to come to the airport.' Smith held Sarah's eyes. 'I feel . . . suffocated.' Her eyes were huge and hunted in her wasted face. 'Nobody can walk this last mile with me, Sarah. Do you understand?'

Sarah nodded. She did understand, on one level. On another, she felt shut out by the person whose illness had put such a strain on her marriage that it had snapped. Suddenly superfluous after months of a double act, Sarah kissed her friend and held her tight, her tears blotting the lapels of Smith's charity-shop coat. 'Don't forget to come home,' she managed.

'I'll email the minute I get there and I'll blog on the site.' Smith pursed her lips then blurted, 'Sarah, my landlord's selling the flat. I'm not coming back to number twenty-four.'

That sounded like a dare to the universe. 'Shush!' Sarah had laid a finger against Smith's lips, tinted scarlet as ever. 'You *are* coming back. You can stay at mine for as long as you like. Just get well, yeah? For me.'

One last snap in the back of the cab, and Sarah had gone back indoors. From the top window, Smith looked breakable, too small to be out on her own. Sarah dashed down the steps, reaching the kerb just as the cabbie indicated to pull out.

'Here!' She'd thrust an envelope through the open window. 'Take this. It'll help. Bring it home to me,' she said, with meaning.

The cab pulled away, Smith obscured by the sharp December sunlight glinting off the cab windows.

Smith knew how much the letter meant. It was all Sarah had left of her father. His words were a powerful talisman that would protect Smith; the responsibility of returning the letter to Sarah would drag her through her treatment and bring her home again.

Sarah had shivered as she went back inside. She felt two losses now: her friend and her father's letter. Both had sustained her. Both told her she was good enough at a time when she didn't feel that way.

There'd been a text from the departure gate, then a photo of an inedible in-flight meal, followed by a blurred video of the panelled reception area of Dr Vera's clinic.

The void left by Smith's departure allowed the soundtrack from Leo and Helena's flat to seep in; Sarah refreshed smith-lifeline.co.uk constantly over the next couple of days. Not your average holiday snaps, there were no sunsets, but there was a close-up of a cannula in a bone-white hand. 'Here goes nothing!' was Smith's caption. Image followed image:

the sterile cafeteria was followed by Smith lying back on starchy white sheets. She'd looked brave, even cheerful, but Sarah saw fear in her gaunt face.

Or did I project that onto her? Sarah second-guessed herself, revising history, realising how much of it she'd bent to suit herself.

There'd been a close-up of spare ribs above Smith's jaunty 'Guys, Chilean hospital food is NOTHING like NHS din-dins!!!!' Sarah had known that Smith would only manage half the hefty portion, but she hadn't known it was the last snap Smith would ever send.

New Year's Eve was an endurance test. The flat was quiet as fireworks boomed and house parties staggered into the small hours. When Sarah logged on the next day, hungry for news to start the new year, she read Dr Vera's stark one-liner.

'With regret, I must tell you that my patient Karen Smith passed away peacefully last night.'

Smith's death daubed a blood-red full stop to nine months of blogging and research and worry. It had no effect on the loving.

The funeral, announced on Smith's Facebook page, would be in her home town, up in the Midlands, 'family only'. Smith had often told Sarah, 'You're my family now!' but blood turned out to be thicker than water after all.

Sometimes when Sarah was assailed by memory, she fretted that the journey to Santiago had been too much for Smith. *Should I have discouraged her?*

Maybe Leo and her mother had been right. 'It's always

about *you*, really,' her mother used to sigh. 'You're as selfish as your father.'

In quick succession, Sarah had lost Leo, Smith, and her dad's letter.

But one of them had come back. Smith had kept the letter safe. She'd – unusually for Smith – thought ahead. Her family had respected her wishes in the end, and sent it to Sarah.

The return of the letter was a small event, but the smallest gestures can have huge repercussions. Sarah had pined for it, even though she knew it by heart. Her father's expressive handwriting, the impatient jagged edge where he'd torn the page from a diary, the folds, the ink blots, made it a charm stronger than any rabbit's foot. It was suffused with love. It breathed. It whispered.

Sarah had no legacy from her dad. Her mother had excised him like a gangrenous limb, refusing to look through his possessions after his death. Father and daughter had been forcibly estranged; Sarah's mother was a gatekeeper who used access to their child as a weapon.

The letter was the only heirloom, written days before he died – his last act of love. *Smith knew that*. The friendship had been strong, beneath the tension.

It was the last good deed Smith did for Sarah, but it wasn't the only one. The other residents had seen only the non-conformist side of Smith, but Sarah had been warmed by her generosity. There were times when Smith didn't want to play the fool, but she switched on that side of her to lift

Sarah out of a dark mood brought on by a setback with a child, or, increasingly towards the end, problems with Leo. Sarah had brought balance and structure to Smith's life, but it was only after Smith died that Sarah realised how much plain old good times Smith had brought to Sarah's.

Sarah closed her eyes, mimicking Mavis, but she wasn't sun-worshipping. She was remembering her friend, and wondering when she'd stop missing her so keenly. There was no schedule to bereavement; everybody follows their own grey star. It was what . . . coming up to seven months since Smith died. It felt like yesterday; it felt like a hundred years.

Two small cool hands were laid on Sarah's cheeks. She opened her eyes and looked into Una's grave eyes. The child was comforting her; Sarah took the hands and held them. 'I think somebody would like to look through my handbag.'

Una never tired of sifting through the lipsticks and pens and stray Polo mints, examining each of them like a scholar.

Above her head, Sarah talked in a low, smooth, monotonous voice. 'Secrets,' she said, as if wondering aloud. 'We all have secrets, Una. Sometimes we don't mention things because we know we'll get told off.'

'They're bad for the health,' said Mavis, her eyes still closed.

'Especially if other people ask us to keep their secrets for them.'

Una's hand paused for a millisecond over Sarah's purse. Sarah had hit a nerve; this was the slow nature of her medicine. Una kept Graham's secret for him, at the expense of her own peace of mind.

Una carefully set down all Sarah's cards on the grass. Her debit card. Her credit card. A loyalty card for a bookshop. A gift card that harboured twenty pounds to spend in a shop Sarah never visited. She sorted them sedately, following some mystical order, before putting them back in their slots. They meant nothing to Una beyond their colour; money and debt and the struggle to survive that consumed Lisa was meaningless to her.

Sarah envied her innocence. The drop in pay from St Chad's had bitten. She said casually, 'If one of my friends – you, for example, Una – shared a secret with me, maybe I could say "hang on, this isn't your secret at all" and throw it over my shoulder. It would have no power over my friend at all. She'd be set free.'

A shadow fell over Sarah and Una.

'Sounds simple,' said Tom.

'It is.' Sarah ignored him until he walked away. A surge of discomfort flowered in her belly, and she put a hand to it, happy that Una didn't notice. She frowned and did some arithmetic, the ancient sort that women do each month.

Chapter Thirteen

In a fug of cigarette smoke and Radio 1, the decorators had painted the downstairs hall a curd yellow, which helped to lift the Ghost Train vibe a little. Until, that is, Mavis opened her door and Sarah entered sunless Flat E to Peck's discouraging welcome.

'Ugly!' declared the bird, his barrel chest puffed out. 'Ugly old cow!'

'Nice to see you at lunchtime, for a change,' said Mavis.

As a receptionist, Sarah had one afternoon off a month. She'd felt guilty clocking off while St Chad's was still buzzing. Keeley had passed her with a nodded 'goodbye', holding a small boy by the hand. The child looked ready to cry and Keeley looked overworked; now that she kept the diary Sarah knew that Keeley had no space for another client.

Sarah's feet had slowed. She'd stood for a moment, feeling the pull exerted on her by the boy's face. By his need. She'd walked on; the children were the priority, and she couldn't offer him what he needed. There was still a pane of cold glass between her and the children who came to St Chad's.

Lunch was a roast chicken salad, as delicious and light as Sarah had come to expect. Mavis's personal rehabilitation inched forward, but there was no change in her surroundings. In a pinafore dress with its hem coming down, she was a chameleon perfectly in tune with her habitat; only Mavis's mind shone in this vault.

The light that came from Mavis only seemed to shine on Sarah; the rest of the house – apart from wise little Una – still thought of her as a vicious crone. Sarah felt chosen, which was nice; she also felt frustrated, which was not at all nice. She was a missionary, desperate to spread the word: *Praise the Lord! Mavis has a heart!*

'Will Leo be lending a hand today?' asked Mavis. When Sarah didn't answer, she went on, 'When there's already so much unavoidable pain in life, why are you sleepwalking into a firing range, dear?'

'It's not like that.' Sarah felt her tongue fork. There was a part of her that hoped it was exactly 'like that'; she was waiting for Leo to lift his head and realise his terrible mistake. 'I've made it clear there'll be no monkey business.'

'You can say "sex" in front of me.' Mavis lifted one unruly eyebrow. 'I may be ancient but I remember how it feels to want a man.'

Sarah enjoyed hearing that red blood beat in those vari-
cose veins. Perhaps Mavis carried around a broken heart
under her terrible clothes.

'Just because your liaisons aren't physical,' said Mavis,
'doesn't mean they're innocent. This is a cliché, but clichés
are clichés because they're true: if you play with fire, you
get burned.'

'What if,' said Sarah hesitantly, 'I don't mind getting
burned? If the pain proves I'm alive?'

Mavis gazed at Sarah's face, her eyes searchlights seeking
out all Sarah's raw truths. 'Oh my dear,' she said, and it was
enough.

Sarah felt comforted. So comforted she wanted to cry, so
instead, in true Sarah fashion, she changed the subject and
ploughed on. 'I'm getting somewhere with Una. I can sense
it.'

'Your job is as much about the heart as the head,' suggested Mavis, as Peck executed a perfect fart noise which
they ignored.

'I certainly know the drill for dealing with elective
mutism,' said Sarah darkly.

'The mute child you described to Una was you, yes?'

'Yes.' The focus was sharply back on Sarah. She wanted
to resist, to say *Let's talk about you,* but she found herself
describing the events of almost thirty summers ago, when
her parents had sprung apart like an overwound elastic band.

'Your mother,' said Mavis, after listening for a while,
'sounds like a difficult woman.'

'One way of putting it.' Sarah went further; Mavis deserved more than her stock supply of wry one-liners. 'My mother finds it hard to love.'

'That's more common than people think.'

Are we talking about you, now? Sarah remembered the *Sunday Times* article, and Zelda's take on this woman.

'Mum did, *does*, love me. I hope.' Sarah couldn't be certain; she'd set sail into adult life without this vital component in place.

'What about your father?' asked Mavis in a canny way, as if expecting the change that came over Sarah. The softening. The relief.

'Daddy adored me.' Sarah made a small 'O' with her mouth. 'I haven't called him that in years. Since he died. You'd have liked him.'

Mavis smiled at the compliment. 'What sort of man was he?'

'He was my saviour.' Sarah's vocabulary was rusty from underuse; she rarely discussed her summer of silence, when she'd had a ringside seat at her parents' brawls. She'd seen their separation coming and tried to fend it off by being extra good and avoiding the cracks in the pavement.

Somehow this powerful voodoo failed.

Peeking through the bannisters, she watched her father stand at the front door and blow her a kiss. He was crying. Dad *never* cried; Sarah felt the open-tread stairs shift beneath her bare feet.

After that, Sarah's mother had only one volume: too

loud. She threw her grievances around like Zeus flinging thunderbolts. They ricocheted off the walls around her small daughter, who was head down, playing with her dolls.

Crash! 'That bastard!' *Zap!* 'He doesn't care about us!' *Bang!* 'It was all fine until YOU!'

'According to Mum,' said Sarah, 'I didn't only spoil her figure when I was born. I ruined Mum and Dad's marriage. She'd grab me and say, "I know he loves you more than he loves me!" Sarah could feel her mother's breath hot on her face. 'Then she'd ask me . . .' Sarah shivered at the memory, wrapping her arms around her torso to reassure herself she was no longer nine and at her mother's mercy. 'She'd ask, "But you love *me* best, don't you?" When I stammered out yes, she'd call me a liar and send me to bed.'

'*Did* you love your father more?' asked Mavis.

'I didn't love either of them more. They just "were", like the weather. I preferred being with Dad, because he was kind and he gave me room to breathe, but I do love my mum.' Sarah stopped dead, looking at Mavis in amazement. 'I don't think I've ever said that before. Loving her has never been enough – to prove it, I wasn't allowed to love Dad. All the love in our house had to go in my mother's direction.'

'To blame you for alienating her husband is cruel.'

'It is, isn't it?' Like a jolt of adrenaline, the common sense was exhilarating. Perhaps her mother was wrong about the selfishness that Sarah had apparently inherited from her father; she still fretted about her real self bursting out, like an evil alter ego. 'Obviously having a baby changed things for Mum, but surely that's why people have them.'

'I couldn't tell you, dear.' Mavis shifted on her chair. 'It never happened for me.'

Sarah felt her stomach. It was tender and heavy, as if she'd eaten a bowling ball for dessert. 'I know Dad had affairs. So, Mavis, I do listen when you warn me of consequences.'

'Why did you stop talking?'

'The one bright spot was my weekly night at Dad's new place. I thought it was so modern and swish, but really he was living in a whitewashed box because he couldn't afford anything more. He let me stay up way past eight o'clock and we had McDonald's for dinner. Dad was making up for what happened the rest of the week. He *saw*.'

'What did he see?' Mavis's voice was low, like a hypnotist's.

'Mum was never what you'd call stable. She saw conspiracies everywhere, forever falling out with friends who let her down, according to her.' Sarah hesitated; self-pity wasn't a good colour on her. 'He saw what Mum did. That she took it out on me.'

When her father found a new partner — younger of course; her dad was a man, after all — Sarah liked her. 'She gave us space when I visited. She plaited my hair.' Sarah smiled at how easily children are pleased. 'When I got home, Mum would bombard me with questions. "Is she prettier than me, your father's whore? Can the slut cook?" I'd tell her no, she wasn't half as pretty. One time I slipped up and told Mum about the lovely shepherd's pie I'd eaten.' Sarah remembered the killer question, the stiletto knife that slid in so easily Sarah hadn't felt a thing. 'Mum asked me if I liked this new girlfriend and I said, chattily, "Yeah, she's great. We're friends."'

'Oh dear,' said Mavis.

'She broke every plate in the house. She packed a case for me. "Go and live with her if you love her so much!" The adult me can see that Mum was afraid, that she felt as if everything was being wrenched away from her ...'

'Your answers to her questions caused trouble so you stopped speaking.' Mavis sat back and contemplated that for a moment. 'Makes perfect sense. You needed some control, dear.'

'Exactly.' Sarah had luxuriated in the quiet while her mother thrashed about on the other side of it. 'I was dragged off to doctors, who prescribed vegetables and fresh air. Mum shouted, cajoled, cried.' For the first time it occurred to Sarah to feel sorry for her mother; *everything Lisa's going through, Mum went through too.*

That was sobering: in Sarah's memories her mother rarely emerged as a person. A force of nature, yes, or a freakish storm system. But not a woman, like any other.

Like me. In Lynch family mythology, Sarah wasn't allowed to resemble her mother; she was her egotistical father all over again. Proving that she wasn't narcissistic, that she was a builder not a destroyer, was one of the reasons she'd gone into a healing profession.

'What was the breakthrough?' prompted Mavis.

'A holiday.' Sarah slowed. 'Dad took me away, just me and him, to Spain. I still don't know how he got Mum to agree to it. Have you ever ...' Sarah remembered just in time Mavis's allergy to questions. 'Empty beaches. Campfires. Weird food. Dad laughing at my face when I tried calamari for the first time.' The fortnight was washed pink by sunsets and scented with coffee. Her father was relaxed in the snapshots her brain had stored. Looking ten years younger, his shirt unbuttoned, eyes dark in his tanned face. 'Dad didn't ask one single question. Not even what I wanted for breakfast. He kept up a commentary the whole time. Like background music. Silly thoughts, daft jokes.' She remembered drifting, eyes shut, on a lilo in the pool, bobbing, secure. 'Then, in a dusty backstreet, we were walking, he had my hand, and a tiny creature darted across our path. I said ...' She swallowed. 'Look, Daddy, a lizard.'

'Look, Daddy, a lizard,' repeated Mavis approvingly.

'He didn't miss a beat. Didn't mention it. He acted like it was totally normal when I chattered for the rest of the trip. We got home and Mum was amazed.'

'I can imagine.'

'Not just amazed, she was *annoyed*.' Sarah shook her head, still confounded decades later. 'As if she was angry because I'd recovered with him and not her. So she stopped me seeing him. There was a different excuse every time. She wouldn't pass the phone to me when he called, said I was "tired". So he wrote to me and luckily I got to the post before Mum that morning.' Sarah leaned sideways in her chair, reaching for her bag. 'This letter.' She handed it over, and Mavis read it aloud.

'If I can't see you then I have to write to you! I have no news, no nothing except some advice which you must take to heart. Promise? Be yourself, because, my sweet Sarah, you are more than good enough. And always find the beauty in everybody, because that's the magic formula to make everything A-OK.'

Folding the letter back into its original creases, Mavis said, 'He was contradicting your mother's cynical take on life. On *you*.'

'He absolved me. Said none of it was my fault. He saved me.'

Seeming to understand that Sarah needed to pause, Mavis rose and left her at the table as she cleared the tea things. Sarah's fingers moved over her father's words as if they were braille.

'Thank you,' called Sarah into the kitchenette. She rarely spoke about her maligned father, the *roué* who'd abandoned her and her mother, and she never got to paint him as a white knight. 'For listening and for being, well, *kind*.' Such an underrated commodity, one that Sarah valued highly. There was no reply. Sarah stole over to see Mavis standing at the worktop, her hands still tightly gripped around the tray, her eyes staring into the middle distance. 'Mavis?' she said softly.

Mavis continued to gaze at nothing, certainly not the wall outside the window.

'Mavis,' said Sarah, a little louder.

Mavis shrank, startled to find Sarah so close. 'I drifted away for a moment.' Mavis put the plates in the sink. 'I can feel you gawping at me, Sarah.'

They'd hit one of those hairpin corners again. Mavis was rigid, robotic.

Either courageous or foolhardy, or both, Sarah said, 'Mavis, if anything was wrong, if you were ... unwell, you could tell me.'

The memory lapses – asking if Sarah had a partner, forgetting that Smith was a woman, not recognising Lisa in the corner shop – meant little on their own, but together they made a pattern. Dementia had many guises and titles: frontotemporal dementia had blighted Mavis's grandmother. 'You can tell me anything. We're friends.'

'Friendship has its limits,' said Mavis. 'Let's not test ours.'

'Test me, go on,' laughed Sarah, careful not to push too hard in case she summoned up the old, evil Mavis. 'You once said there was something I didn't know about you, but we glossed over it.' This was marshy ground: when Mavis had hinted that Sarah would walk away if she knew all about her, it had ushered in a cold war. 'It sounded important.'

'Oh that.' Mavis batted the air with one hand. 'I have a peculiar sense of humour.'

'Mavis, it's a sin to lie.' Sarah thought she'd said it tongue-in-cheek but Mavis's reaction told her different.

Wrinkled cheeks flushed, Mavis said, 'I'm familiar with every one of my sins, thank you.'

'I know your bad bits, Mavis, and I still like you.' Sarah smiled. 'So there.'

'You're wrong. You don't know my *worst* bits.' Mavis refused to be light-hearted.

Trespassing on a roped-off area, Sarah said, 'Perhaps you buried them with Zelda. No, hear me out,' she begged, as Mavis pushed past her, back into the sitting room. 'Death tosses the ones left behind in the air, and we land with a bump somewhere new. It can make us bitter. It can make us fearful.' Sarah recognised herself in that description. 'Or it can bring out our inner sweetness. That's what happened with you. All is forgiven, Mavis.'

Stern self-control kept Mavis's tears at bay. 'You can't forgive what you don't know about.'

'Try me. Tell me about this scandal that can never be pardoned.'

Mavis wavered.

'I warn you, Mavis. Anything up to murder will be immediately forgiven.'

As Mavis put her face in her hands a loud banging at the front door spooked Peck into a stream of curses.

'Sarah! Are you in there?'

'Helena?' Sarah looked to Mavis for permission to answer her door but her neighbour still hid behind her fingers. Opening the door the width of a pizza portion, Sarah said, 'Yes?' as non-committal as she could.

'There you are!'

Heart hammering, palms slick, Sarah bowed her head. *I deserve this.* A small hand stole into hers: Mavis.

'What's this about?' Mavis asked imperiously. 'I want no trouble at my door, Mrs Harrison.'

'There's no trouble.' Helena didn't waste charm on Mavis, a pale smudge in Helena's colourful world. 'Sarah knows what this is about. Don't you?'

'Yes,' said Sarah, her chin up. Shaking, but up.

'I've been complaining about the leak since I moved in and now there's a big brown stain on my dressing-room ceiling.' Helena frowned. 'It's nothing to smile about! It's ruined my *trompe l'oeil*.'

'I'll get onto it. Promise.'

As the door closed, Sarah leaned back against it, recovering.

Mavis let out a meow of a yawn.

The moment to press her for an answer had passed.

The white walls made such a difference that Sarah wondered why she'd even considered red paint. Even though the new colour scheme was for somebody else's benefit, she felt renewed, as if she'd taken a long shower. It was partly thanks to the white-out and partly to Mavis; by listening she'd purged Sarah of some small poison.

Sarah circled the chair. *That* chair. The pink colossus. She ran her fingertips along the studded curves, resisting its velvety charisma.

Pulling and pushing, Sarah reorganised the room, setting the sideboard along one wall, and a leather and chrome sling chair just so by the window. She remembered Leo's sniffy, 'It's pure tat, darling' when she'd brought the modern piece home from a car boot sale. A patterned rug, long rolled up in a corner, stretched out on the newly varnished floorboards.

The room sat up, took notice, like a patient recovering from a long illness. No longer just a storage locker for ill-matched, miserable pieces, it looked inviting.

The most inviting item of all was Tom's chair, a pink blob of funky luxury. Rolling smoothly on new castors, it came to a halt by the sideboard.

It was delightful. As delightful as Tom had once seemed. *Can I separate the chair from my opinion of Tom?* Leaning on the back of it, stroking the sensuous pile, Sarah thought, *You're overthinking, you silly cow. Sit on the damn chair.*

Her bottom was a centimetre from the damn chair when she heard Jane's voice calling her name. Propelling herself away from the chair, Sarah rushed to the window, pink with guilt; for what, she wasn't sure.

Press-ganged into keeping Jane company while she upgraded her phone in the high-street showroom – 'Come on, it's cruel to make me do it on my own!' – Sarah stood to one side as Jane nodded along with the salesman's excruciating spiel.

Sarah enjoyed the demands Jane made on her. She'd missed the back and forth of female friendship; being needed was a privilege. Perhaps that was something Mavis only realised as Zelda lay dying. Sarah sensed that she could lean on the frail old lady; she was, as daytime talk shows say, 'there' for Sarah. Just as Sarah would be 'there' for Mavis, if necessary.

Some decisions make themselves: *I'll take up the slack as the dementia gets worse.*

'Right, that's done, thank the sweet Lord.' Jane fled the shop and the salesman, who looked about twelve in a suit three sizes too big for him. 'Fancy a glass of wine?' Jane clamped her lips together, rethinking. 'Hang on. No. Better not. I've got an actual date night tonight with my actual husband.' She hugged herself as if she'd won first prize in a raffle. 'I don't want to be squiffy.' She nudged Sarah. 'I might get some action for a change.'

'Enough information, thanks.' Sarah laughed, but inside she felt her stomach disappear down a plughole. The perfection of Jane's marriage was a mirage: her friend was shackled to a man who not only rarely made love to her, but sought his kicks elsewhere. All Jane's colour and vivacity and twenty-four carat kindness were squandered on a cut-price Casanova.

They parted on a corner, Jane, waving and giddy, off home to shower and pamper, Sarah headed for the supermarket. Trying to clear her head of Tom and Jane, she compiled a shopping list in her head as she walked.

Apples. Small bananas. Eggs, definitely eggs.

What kind of friend doesn't tell her mate that her partner made a pass at her?

Washing-up liquid. Sarah abandoned the list as a suspicion formed.

What if Jane knows all about Tom's little hobby?

Jane certainly had the self-discipline to blur the truth, to look the other way and pretend it wasn't so. Sarah didn't need her professional expertise to diagnose that attitude as unhealthy, but if it was Jane's choice then Sarah must proceed with caution. Such a belief system could only be dismantled with care.

Telling the truth seemed like the right thing to do, but it would mean losing Jane. Sarah went back to her shopping list, glad of its impartiality, and wondered if she had a lemon in the flat.

'Sarah!' Her name was shouted over the impudent honk of a car horn.

Turning, Sarah saw the un-cool, third-hand Ford Fiesta that sat outside their front door and, according to Leo, brought down the value of the house all on its own.

'Hop in.' Tom leaned over and opened the passenger door.

'I'm busy.' Sarah kept walking.

The car kept pace with her, passing white flat-faced houses. 'You were right. We should talk.'

'I'm not in a talking mood.'

'You're holding up the traffic.'

'No, *you're* holding up the traffic.'

Horns beeped their displeasure. Somebody shouted, 'Oi, mate!'

'Please.' Tom leaned over, steering with one stiff arm.

With misgivings, Sarah climbed into the stickily hot interior. 'For future reference, this is kerb-crawling.'

'I snatched my chance. I never see you except when we're with Una.' He looked uncomfortable. 'Did I embarrass you?'

Struck by his remorse, Sarah remembered just in time that Tom was an actor. 'Never mind,' she said. 'Where are we going?'

'I'm sick of all this sunshine.' Tom turned into a garage forecourt. 'Let's go find some rain.'

Tom wasn't to know that Sarah's favourite childhood treat was going to the car wash with her father in his lumbering Volvo. A personal, benign storm raged outside the car just as it had during Sarah's silent summer, when the sopping flap of the brushes had calmed the chaos in her head. 'I'm holding out an olive branch,' said Tom.

Wrong-footed, Sarah studied him. The masculine cast of Tom's face, so right for his role in *Vile Bodies*, was softened by uncertainty. *He's afraid of what I'll say next.* 'So the chair's a bribe?'

'In a way. But not in a bad way. I mean ...' Tom hit the steering wheel. 'Yes, the chair's a bribe, sod it, but I loved working on it and, actually, no it's not a bribe, it's a gift.' Head down, he turned to look at her. 'Do you like it?'

Unwilling to lie, Sarah admitted, 'It's gorgeous. The colour and the feel of it. It's changed the mood of the room.'

'Good. That dreary shrine to Leo just isn't *you*.'

'Don't, Tom.' The slavishly attentive brushes whirred over the windscreen, replacing the outside world with snowy suds. 'I keep worrying that Jane knows.'

'Knows what?'

'What do you think?' Sarah felt the olive branch wither.

'Oh, *us*.' Tom gave the word an ironic spin.

'What if she's guessed something happened?'

'Believe me, if Jane guessed, we'd both know about it.'

'She loves you.'

'And why not?' Tom shrugged, his rugged face amused. 'I'm highly lovable.'

A monsoon beat on the roof. 'Is that all you can say?'

Tom leaned back, as if taking a hard look at the strange life form in his car. 'Jane has to love me, doesn't she? That's the deal.'

'Jane keeps her blinkers on, but I see you. I see you only too well, Tom Royce. You're dangerous. You grab what you want, like a baby, with no thought for the consequences. You're conceited and selfish and you need to wake up and look around you. I'd kill for the love you have in your life. You don't deserve what you have.'

'What *is* your problem?'

Sarah wrenched the door open. 'You!' she yelled, stepping out into the artificial storm.

It was a damp walk home in the sunshine.

Chapter Fourteen

'Hey there, sexy!'

Sarah turned to see Keeley laughing, her braids in a topknot like a beaded handle to pick up the abundant woman. If you dared. 'You thought your luck was in.' She fell into step with Sarah and, getting down to business, said, 'How long have you been recepting now?'

Sarah counted on her fingers, using personal historical landmarks.

Four weeks since I rejected Tom in the car wash.

Eight weeks since Leo and I made love.

Nine days until the flat goes on the market.

'About ten weeks,' said Sarah.

'There's something you should know.' Keeley slowed, looking at the ground as she balanced her rucksack, her takeaway coffee, her phone and her discomfort. 'I'm advertising for a new receptionist. It's time, Sarah.'

'Oh.' Sarah blinked. 'OK.' She let Keeley go through the revolving door ahead of her. Her days were numbered at work as well as at home. Flat A was now a snug white palace, the floors varnished, the cracks filled. 'I understand.'

'Good, 'cos I don't.' Keeley swept down the narrow corridor that lay off the airy reception space. 'You should be doing what you're good at.' As she reached her office, she looked back and said, head down, eyes glittering up at Sarah, 'The children can't wait forever.'

Later, taking sandwich orders, Sarah went to the small pharmacy at the back of the building. 'What'll it be, Gan?' she asked, dusting off her best smile.

The pharmacist's crush on Sarah was St Chad's favourite open secret. After a stumbling slow dance at a leaving 'do' when Gan sprouted an extra pair of hands, Sarah tended to avoid him. Not today. Once she'd written down his precise order – 'cheese but not cheddar and no mayo although gherkins are good but it must be on wholemeal bread' – she asked for his help.

Gan swaggered slightly in his lab coat. 'Shoot,' he said.

'What can you tell me about a drug called Rilutek?'

Gan told her everything he knew.

'Thanks. I thought as much.' As she left, Sarah was too pre-occupied to notice Gan gazing after her, or hear the remark he made about her bottom to an uninterested colleague.

*

Sarah was turning over what Gan had told her as she stepped into her flat. She stopped, sniffing the air. The scent of her favourite, outrageously expensive bath foam curled around her. A trail of petals led from the doormat to where candle-light flickered from the bathroom.

Leo.

He'd always laughed at Sarah's habit of taking baths in even the hottest weather, snorting as she pulled the blinds and lit candles, blocking out a beautiful day to create her own sultry night-time.

'Leo?'

He stepped out of the candlelight. 'Your bath, m'lady.'

Putting down her bag, Sarah considered what to do. Without meeting his eye, she said, 'You kept your key.'

'Very naughty of me, but yes.'

Sarah went into the bathroom, forcing Leo to step out of her way. 'Is this a bath for two, by any chance?'

'It always used to be.' Leo leaned against the door frame.

He was full of tricks, her ex-old man. Sarah held his gaze, then pushed the door to, so he had to jump backwards. 'I bathe alone nowadays.' He was, she knew, a sucker for this kind of teasing.

The scrape of a chair being pulled up, then Leo asked, through the door, 'What has you so down, darling? I could see your little head drooping all the way up Merrion Road.'

They'd always chatted while Sarah bathed, although Leo used to perch on the closed loo seat with a glass of something red. Here was a reprise she could enjoy without guilt, surely? A solid door stood between them.

Eager to be in the water, Sarah shucked off her clothes. 'Can I tell you something, Leo? Something important?'

'Of course. This is us, remember.'

'Us,' she repeated, liking the soft sound as she lowered herself into the bubbles.

'Us,' repeated Leo breathily as if his mouth was to the crack of the door.

'I'm in a bit of a state about something.' Sarah shut her eyes and leaned back, her hair making mermaid shapes beneath the water. 'Mavis is dying.'

'Mavis who?'

'Leo! Our neighbour. From the basement!'

'Ah. Yes. Oh dear. That's sad.'

She told him about how she'd popped in to see Mavis on her way to work for an early morning cuppa; a new habit. 'Mavis had a terrible headache, and she sent me to her bathroom cupboard for painkillers. While I was looking, I saw a half-empty bottle of pills. It set alarm bells ringing; Mavis has never mentioned being on medication.' She paused. 'You still there?'

'All ears, darling. All ears.'

'I asked the pharmacist at St Chad's about them, and—'

'That guy has the hots for you, doesn't he?'

'What? That's not the point. The thing is . . .' Sarah didn't want to let the words escape. She imagined them taking shape in the steam, firming up, becoming irrevocable.

'Mavis has motor neurone disease. It's so cruel, Leo. That's what her sister had, so she knows exactly what to expect.'

'Poor woman.'

'She's dying, Leo. It won't be pretty.'

'Poor, poor thing. Terrible, isn't it?'

The symptoms had misled Sarah. It wasn't dementia that nibbled at Mavis's mental acuity; it was the early stages of motor neurone disease. 'I've made a decision.'

'Yes? Does it involve me and that bath?'

'I'm going to look after Mavis.'

'Oh God.' Leo groaned. 'It's bloody Smith all over again.'

The bath bubbles seemed to wilt a little. The candle guttered. That jokey, what-are-you-like response turned the water cold. 'Leo, look, it's been a long day. You'd better get back to Helena.' Sarah sank beneath the water. When she rose up, Leo was babbling, trying to undo the damage through the bathroom door.

'Darling, sorry, that was rude, it's obviously nothing like Smith. Let's start again. *Mavis.* Right.' He sounded puzzled. 'But ... exactly why is she your responsibility? Isn't she a dreadful old baggage?'

'She's my friend. She has no family. Mavis has nobody but me.'

'All the same, darling, there are systems in place. Nursing homes, hospitals—'

'Mavis is mine.'

'You can't save everybody, you old softie. Mavis'll be fine with the good old NHS.'

'Mavis will die knowing she's loved.' Sarah was wading through the big issues – life, love, death, duty – while Leo paddled in the shallow end. She sank again.

The water helped with the nausea and the pain in the small of her back. Sarah had to admire Mother Nature for her exquisite sense of the absurd. It was on the tip of her tongue to tell Leo – who better? – but his presence was making her feel not safe but besieged. 'Please, Leo, go.' Sarah wasn't willing to give him the benefit of the doubt this time. She was already nostalgic for ten minutes ago when she still believed him to be tender; when she believed he not only desired her but loved her. Love is blind; Sarah agreed with Confucius but only up to a point. *My sight's coming back.*

When Leo spoke he was arch. 'Want me to send Tom up to scrub your back?' He let Sarah exclaim for a moment or two. 'Darling, the entire postcode knows you have the hots for each other.'

'Rubbish!' snorted Sarah, sitting up, the bathroom no longer magical, just a tiled cell with a loo that didn't flush properly. All the bath gel in the world couldn't scent this situation. 'We don't—'

'You're fooling nobody by ignoring each other.' Leo was enjoying himself, she could tell. 'Tell the truth and shame the devil, Sarah. You fancy the pants off our little actor.'

Sarah could imagine his face. Leo was possessive; even, it would seem, of what he threw away. This was as much a fishing expedition as an accusation. *I'll refuse to play his game; I'll tell the truth.*

235

'You're right, Leo. I do fancy Tom. But it's purely a physical thing. I wouldn't touch him if you paid me.' Sarah knew Tom was toxic, but if her body wouldn't listen to her brain then she'd have to let it go its own foolish, pheromonal way. Apparently, lust was just as blind as love. 'Do you think Jane's noticed?'

'Ha!' Leo's delight bruised Sarah; he'd never known when to tread lightly. 'She'd be an idiot to miss it. And Jane's no idiot.' Leo was further away now, evidently loitering by the front door. 'I'm so jealous of the man I could strangle him, Sarah.'

His jealousy would have thrilled Sarah at one time, but now she saw it as useless posturing. Support was what she needed. Knees to her chest, Sarah had an epiphany in the bathwater. 'Leo!' she called and she heard him trip lightly – probably gleefully – back to the bathroom door. 'I'm not moving out. We're not selling up.'

The countdown stopped dead.

'Sarah, you promised.' Leo sounded panicky. 'We agreed the end of August. I've been patient. I've waited a whole year. Your time's up, darling.' He waited. He tutted when she said nothing. 'Sarah! Are you listening?'

Not really.

Leo receded as Sarah mapped out the next few months. Mavis would deteriorate, and die – that was a given. But she would die with love all around her. She would die cared for. 'Leo . . .' Sarah knew how it felt to have no one. She stood, water cascading down her body. Love is as much a decision as a feeling; Sarah loved Mavis and she'd see it through.

'Yes, darling?' Leo sounded hopeful, as if he thought Sarah might have come to her senses.

'Leave your key.'

There was a clang as something hit a small brass bowl. The flat door slammed.

Sarah was alone.

It could have been Sarah's imagination, but Jane seemed to jump when they ran into each other in the hall.

'Hi there stranger! Haven't seen you in a few days.' Just because Sarah was paranoid didn't mean she wasn't right: Leo's poison had done its work. 'How was the latest recce? You must know Suffolk like the back of your hand by now.'

'Suffolk was ... Suffolk.' Jane didn't meet Sarah's eye. 'The last few days have been interesting, though. In lots of ways.' Jane's brio was playing truant; she was a glass of champagne the morning after. 'Some good, some bad.'

'Bad? In what way?'

Jane took an audible deep breath. 'Would you tell me if—' She shut her eyes. 'Are we friends, Sarah? Really friends?'

'Absolutely.' Sarah waited.

'People are such shits. Why can't we all just play nicely?'

Sitting it out to see where it was going, Sarah discerned confusion, concern, but no anger.

'Listen, I'm worn out.' Jane headed for the stairs. 'But we should ... let's have a chat tomorrow evening, yeah?'

'About?'

Jane was gone.

Chapter Fifteen

ᴄᴏɴꜰᴜᴄɪᴜꜱ ꜰᴀᴋᴇᴀᴡᴀʏ
Notting Hill, W11

This calendar is FREE to valued customers!
Tuesday 23rd August, 2016

HE WHO STRIKES THE FIRST BLOW
LOSES THE ARGUMENT

The sunflowers nodded their heavy heads, and the grass grew a centimetre or two even as Sarah watched from a deckchair. Late August laid a heavy hand on the hot garden.

A small finger poked her in the side. Una held up Mikey for inspection. A spiny sphinx, the hedgehog saw everything with his one good eye but never commented or got involved. Sarah could learn a lot from him. 'You're getting fat, Mikey.'

Una smiled happily. Mikey's weight had been a source of worry throughout his recuperation. Now that he was living the high life as a hedgehog-about-town, his plumpness was often commented on approvingly. No body-shaming for Mikey.

The little girl flew back to Tom. That evening's session

was over; Lisa was often late coming out for Una. Sarah didn't mind. She had nothing else to do; work was finished on the flat, now a white uncluttered series of rooms.

Sheers hung at the windows, stock-still in the heat. The carpet that had been there when they moved in was gone, as were the dusty patterned rugs Leo had brought home from the Old Church; Sarah's toes hugged the floorboards when she drifted through her transfigured home.

There was space between the few items of furniture she'd chosen. There was ease and certainty. The hated deadline, now abandoned for Mavis's sake, had forced Sarah to concentrate. For so long she'd felt helpless, like a leaf blown about by the breeze. She resisted the breeze now; the leaf was in charge of its own destiny.

It was a bold, empowering feeling. The tragedy unfolding in the basement had shocked Sarah back to life. She was a lady-in-waiting no more; she was queen of Flat A. *And about time too,* she thought.

Avoiding Leo since she got home from work, Sarah knew she had to face him at some point. They had to talk money. Disentangling him from the flat would sting. Giving up the hanging-on-for-dear-life fantasy that Leo still loved her would take some doing; the hope was all that had kept Sarah going some days.

Tom laughed, saying, 'Careful, Una!'

Sarah knew where he was without watching him. She felt him move around the garden as if he gave off more heat than other mortals. Leo's assessment was only half right; Sarah couldn't help her gut attraction to Tom, but Tom had moved smoothly on. They only spoke over Una's head. The rest of the time they passed each other like ghosts, as if neither saw the other.

She risked a glance at him and saw him look over at the windows of Flat C. Sarah followed his line of sight to where Jane stood, half hidden by the new striped curtains Sarah had helped her hang, before stepping back and out of view. Sarah flinched; she'd soon find out what Jane needed to 'chat' about.

Clambering up the steps from the basement, Graham's body language semaphored extreme umbrage. Sarah stood, awkwardly finding her sandals with her bare feet in the grass, as he marched towards her.

With graceful speed, Tom inserted himself between Sarah and Graham, so that Graham had to lean around him to jab a nicotine-stained finger. 'This is getting out of hand. I don't pay you to play with hedgehogs, love!'

'You don't pay me at all, Graham.' *Plus I'm not your love.* Sarah took a step to stand shoulder to shoulder with Tom, her face the calm mask she'd worn for just this kind of confrontation at St Chad's. 'Why not say hello to Una?'

'Why not keep your nose out of my business?'

'Dude.' Tom inclined his head. 'Hey. Come on.'

'No kids of your own, love?' Graham wobbled his head mockingly. 'So you mess with other people's, is that it?'

'Hey.' Tom upped the ante, standing straighter, radiating strength. 'No need for that.'

Accustomed to parents blaming her for situations that had been years in the making, Sarah didn't take it personally. 'Graham, let's not discuss this in front of Una, eh?'

'No wonder your husband dumped you.' Graham took Una's hand and wrenched her over beside him.

'Enough!' Tom was angry.

'Tom, I can handle this,' said Sarah quietly.

'Why can't you just tell me what Una's problem is?' Graham was wild now, looking from one to the other as if they were keeping a secret from him. 'Is she mental?'

Tom shook his head in disbelief. 'Your little girl's right there,' he hissed.

'Tom.' Sarah took charge, even though it meant losing the reassuring bulk of his presence. 'If Graham agrees, could you take Una over to check on the sunflowers while he and I talk?' She looked to Graham, who nodded gracelessly.

Tom whisked Una into his arms with a flourish, the way she liked.

'See you in two ticks,' said Sarah to Una, composing herself to face Graham.

'I'm waiting,' said Graham sarcastically.

'Graham, we have to examine the family dynamic.'

'I'm not interested in your fancy phrases. What's wrong with my daughter?'

'This isn't an Una problem. It's a family problem.'

'I *knew* it!'

Sarah sensed Tom's ears prick up at the increase in volume.

'Graham, I'm not—'

'You're accusing me! Like it's *my* fault! Typical woman.'

'If you just listen—'

Graham grabbed Sarah's upper arm, hard. Hard enough to leave livid marks, it explained Lisa's penchant for sleeves.

'No, you listen!' Graham got no further because Tom had crossed the garden in two strides. He bundled Graham to the floor and pinned him there.

'Listen, idiot,' shouted Tom, leaning into Graham's face, invading his space the way Graham had invaded Sarah's. 'Don't annoy an actor 'cos at some point we all learn some moves. Sarah's trying to help.'

'But,' said Graham, wriggling.

'No buts.'

Una dashed to Sarah and threw her arms around her legs. Her two heroes were fighting.

'Your dad's a bit overexcited.' Sarah smoothed Una's tidy chestnut hair. 'It's going to be fine. Isn't it, Graham?'

'Yes,' snapped Graham, with the fury of the impotent. He leaped up, bristling, when Tom released him, trying to look as if he could have jumped up at any point.

'Let's go and find your mum, Una.' As Tom passed Sarah, he murmured, 'For God's sake don't annoy him. That's the sum total of my moves.'

After a few moments decompressing, Graham was calm enough to talk. His restless eyes were reminiscent of Peck's.

'As you know, Graham, I saw you go into the flat you share with your new girlfriend. That's none of my business.

You can live where you please. But Lisa doesn't know: am I right? OK. Have you specifically asked Una not to tell Lisa about your living arrangements? Right. In that case, Una has a secret. It's unhealthy for small children to keep secrets from a parent. You can double that when the secret's about the other parent. At the moment, Una feels responsible for your family's happiness.' She felt Graham move, as if to protest, but he said nothing. 'Obviously that's not true, but Una also believes in unicorns so we're not dealing with Stephen Hawking here.'

'This isn't my fault. Lisa's a bitch and I—'

'If it's not your fault, it's not Lisa's either.' Sarah could go schoolmarm when necessary. 'If you could try – just try, Graham – not to bad-mouth Lisa around Una, then maybe Una can start to relax. She desperately wants to believe that her mummy and daddy respect each other, that there's love there.'

'I did love Lisa,' said Graham.

'I know,' said Sarah. 'Una wants the family back together. That can't happen the way she wants it to, but you and Lisa *can* learn how to co-parent so that Una feels secure.'

'What do you mean, "learn"?'

'Don't worry. It doesn't entail going back to school. All it takes is a little consideration, thinking before you open your mouth, and placing Una front and centre. I know you can do that.'

'Of course I can,' said Graham. 'Una's my princess.'

'First of all . . . bring the secret into the open.'

There was a long silence filled only by hip-hop bleeding from a passing car out on Merrion Road. 'You mean, tell Lisa I'm living with Ruby?'

'Exactly that. It won't be fun, but it'll set Una free.' Sarah knew what she was talking about when she said, 'Little girls need to see their daddies doing the right thing or they grow up with warped ideas about men.' Hoping it had penetrated the heavily fortified area where Graham kept his feelings, Sarah said goodbye and started to clear up the pencils and drawing paper she and Una had used.

Now for Jane.

She felt rather than saw Tom come out of the house and cross the grass. She swallowed when he touched her arm.

'Be careful with Jane.' He was earnest, steady, his eyes on hers.

'What does that mean?' Sarah glared at Tom. *Another man expecting a woman to keep his secrets!*

'This has really thrown her,' said Tom. 'Just, you know, be careful,' he muttered, turning away as if he knew his words were wasted.

'No, Tom,' said Sarah to his back, hating how she could only relate to him in this spitty, sarcastic manner. '*You* be careful.'

Chapter Sixteen

ℂONFUℂIUS FAKEAWAY
Notting Hill, W11

This calendar is FREE to valued customers!
Thursday 25th August, 2016

**DISTANCE TESTS A HORSE'S STRENGTH,
TIME REVEALS A PERSON'S CHARACTER**

Notting Hill was gearing up for the annual madness of carnival. Barriers sprang up. Sound systems rose improbably high on street corners. Life sprang from the pavements. From Friday to Bank Holiday Monday, W11 would party.

In the calm before the storm of good times, Tom stood on the steps of number twenty-four, watching Sarah and Jane drive off, with his hands deep in the pockets of his jeans and his broad shoulders hunched.

'He's not a happy bunny,' said Jane.

'That's an understatement.' Sarah was still settling down in the passenger seat, playing with the seat belt and stowing Fruit Pastilles in the glove compartment. It was going to be a long journey.

'He keeps calling it "your cock-eyed road trip". Said we're a poor man's Thelma and Louise.'

Tom hadn't been protecting his own interests when he warned Sarah to be careful: the dreaded chat with Jane hadn't been about him. Relieved to the point of light-headedness at the time, Sarah now half wished the decision to tell Jane about the kiss had been taken out of her hands. It still weighed heavily on her thoughts, but the matter at hand was dark enough and thorny enough to require all her attention. 'Mavis is against it, too.' Sarah didn't describe Leo's reaction. His belly laughter had undermined the seriousness of the situation and she'd found herself, once again, pointing out that he'd missed the point. She'd come away exasperated; he'd refused to discuss the flat, saying airily there was nothing to talk about. She remembered him saying, with great good humour, 'We'll stick to the plan, darling. You'll thank me later. Although,' he'd added, 'we'll have to think of somewhere else to meet.'

Nothing dented his iron-clad confidence. Sarah had always found that amusing. The joke was wearing thin.

'How *is* number twenty-four's favourite witch?' Jane knew about the motor neurone disease.

'Too thin. Not sleeping enough. Disregard for personal grooming.'

'No change there, then. Was your boss cool about taking today off? I know you were worried about it.'

'Cool-ish.' Keeley had listened and put her hand to her mouth. She'd advised Sarah not to do it and then hugged her and sighed that, yes, of course she could take the time away from St Chad's. Being Keeley, she'd muttered something about how come Sarah could be so decisive when making a foolish decision, yet drag her feet when it came to restarting her career. 'She's nagging me about going back to my proper job.'

'Is that how you think of it? Your *proper* job?'

'Yes and no. It feels as if somebody else took the exams.'

'But you're doing so well with Una.'

'S'pose.' Sarah wasn't sure. Was it therapy or friendship? She knew better than to blur the boundaries.

'You know, getting a mortgage is tough enough without taking a hit in salary. God knows, I don't want you to leave number twenty-four, but . . .'

'I know. The sensible thing is to sell up and move on.'

'But doing the sensible thing,' smiled Jane, 'is no longer your style. Got it.' She mimed pulling a zip across her mouth.

Conversation, usually so bouncy and plentiful, lapsed. Sarah registered the looks Jane threw her as the car ate the road.

'You're OK?' said Jane as they turned onto the A12.

'Too late to turn back now. Besides, I love Southwold.'

Jane's 'That's my girl!' almost made Sarah cry; providence had given her this staunch friend, but had also provided her with a pin to prick Jane's bubble.

Southwold hadn't changed since Sarah's weekend there with Leo. The small town was a dream of an England past, its high street colourfully eclectic, and its eccentric bathing huts keeping watch over a murky sea. That Thursday it came complete with Hitchcockian theme music.

Jane locked the car. They both shilly-shallied, checking their bags for purses, locating their sunglasses, until Jane grasped Sarah's hand and said, 'We don't have to. If you can't face it.'

'We do have to.' Sarah drew strength from Jane's slender arm.

'In that case, it's just up here on the right.' Jane led the way out of the car park, past a row of shops so full of gee-gaws and what-have-yous that the stock dribbled out onto the pavement. 'Here goes nothing.' She pushed at the door of Dolly's Kitchen.

An aproned middle-aged woman was summoned by the tinkling of the bell. 'For two?' She laid laminated menus on a table by a mullioned window, although there was barely room among the fresh flowers, cruet set, and sugar sachets. 'Quiche is off,' she said, leaving them to it.

The menu was just a mass of squiggles to Sarah.

'If we've chosen the wrong day . . .' Jane drummed her fingers, craning her neck to peep past contented menopausal women ploughing through cream teas. 'Oh God. Here she comes.'

'What can I get you?' The waitress was chummy, her apron a strange match for her punky clothes. 'The quiche is . . .' She took in Sarah's face and gaped. 'Off,' she said eventually.

'Hello, Smith,' said Sarah.

*

The stones of Southwold's beach dug into Sarah's bottom as she and Smith, together again, sat staring out at the sea. A bird, wide-winged, swooped.

The cafe owner had allowed Smith to take her tea break there and then, her face concerned as they left. Evidently Smith had found herself another benefactress.

Sarah was determined not to speak first. She was afraid her anger would flood out and consume them both. A head of steam that had been building all morning threatened to blow.

Smith forced out a question. 'How, you know, how are you?'

'How am I?' Sarah was stupefied by the banality of Smith's line. 'How do you think I am?'

'If you just snap my head off we won't get anywhere.' Smith was sullen, as if Sarah had caught her stealing the last biscuit.

'What if I don't want to *get anywhere*?' Sarah mimicked her cruelly. 'What if I just want to . . .'

'Punch me?' suggested Smith. 'You can if you want. I deserve it.'

'You deserve worse than that.' Sarah felt anger bleed through her, like acid . She fought it. And wondered why she was fighting it. Smith deserved every syllable that queued on the tip of Sarah's tongue.

Smith put her head in her hands. Her shaved hair had grown back. Now dyed black, it was augmented with extensions and pulled into a ponytail. She had a new piercing in her nose. She'd put on weight; her arms were arm-shaped again.

Smith was a stranger. One of the undead.

The sea bounded in, then dragged itself back out. The spume fizzed just a few metres from their feet.

'I'm sure you've got a speech all ready,' said Smith miserably. 'Go on. I won't interrupt you.'

Sarah had plenty to say. She'd had forty-eight hours to prepare her sermon, taking care to strike the correct note of righteous anger, but now she abandoned it. It would be wretched and empty, just the way she felt.

Two days before, sitting opposite Jane at a kitchen table that still bore a John Lewis price tag, Sarah had listened to a tale of an egg and cress sandwich.

'I'd spent the morning crawling over a manor house, so I stopped at this place called Dolly's Kitchen for lunch.'

The waitress, a chatty girl who seemed too large and charismatic for her staid surroundings, had brought her a sandwich and a pot of tea. When she'd cleared the table, her sleeve had ridden up to reveal a tattoo of Elvis astride My Little Pony.

There couldn't be two of those in existence. 'Your dead friend,' Jane told Sarah, her eyes sad, 'is alive and well and serving cream teas in Suffolk.'

Sitting on the pebbles beside her dead friend, Sarah had only one real question. 'Why, Smith?'

'Because ... because ...' Smith's shoulders were around her ears. She'd always hated having to account for herself.

'Why'd you leave me?'

'Don't put it like that.' Smith scoured her eyes with her fists. More silence. This woman could teach Una a thing or two.

There was one basic mystery Sarah needed to clear up. 'Did you ... did you actually have cancer?'

A long sigh, from the very depths of Smith. 'No.'

Sarah exhaled, disillusioned all over again. This woman beside her disgusted her. 'How could you lie about something that affects so many people? I thought you needed help. I thought you ...' Sarah petered out, unable to articulate her scorn.

'Do you really want to know why?' Smith sounded weary.

'I really do.' Sarah stood. 'Let's walk.' Did Smith feel that this grumpy schoolgirl act did justice to their situation? *Where the hell is my apology?*

The path stayed loyally parallel to the sea, with high rustling grasses on one side and tumbledown chalets on the other. Southwold was a charming town, but Sarah would never return.

Smith cleared her throat. 'That morning you found me on the sofa and asked what was up, I *was* ill. I felt like I was dying.'

'What was really wrong, now that we know it wasn't an astrocytoma?'

'It was a hangover. Not from booze.' Smith hung her head and eyed Sarah from beneath her fringe, like a dog that's eaten its owner's favourite shoe. 'Cocaine. I had a real

251

problem a few years back. I never told you because, well . . . because. Thought I'd whipped it, but no. Coke's a persuasive playmate.'

'Impossible. I'd know if you had a drug problem.'

'I'd been clean for months on end, but the night before this random guy in a bar offered me a toot and, well, I was off. Your classic binge.' Smith looked away. 'So. Now you know. I'm a drug fiend.' She pulled an ironic face.

'Don't make out I'm Queen Victoria.' Sarah had always stepped around drugs, but she'd never pontificated about them. Leo had been partial to a few lines when they met. He'd given it up, claiming Sarah was the only stimulant he needed. 'You could've told me. I'd have thrown a blanket over you and brought you a sarnie when you were up to it. You know that.'

'You're very sure about what people know, Sarah.' Smith blinked, shook her head. 'I never kid myself I know what people are thinking.' She turned to her as they strolled at the deadly pace of two people going nowhere. 'Look, I'm not like you. I've been rejected since I was in the womb.' Smith's family was constantly at war. There'd been stints in children's homes. 'I never take anything for granted.'

'We talked about this. I thought I was helping you to trust.'

'You can't solve people. Well, you can't solve *me*. I'm too far gone. I always worried that one day you'd look at me and I'd see it in your eyes. To put it another way, I *wouldn't* see it in your eyes. Love. Friendship. Whatever you call it;

there'd come a day when I'd wear you out and you'd give up on me, just like everybody else.' With sour triumph, Smith said, 'And looky here! I was right.'

Her throat tight, her eyes full, Sarah shouted at last, the way she'd fantasised all the way down in Jane's car. 'That's not fair! We're here because you *dragged* us here. I'm not a saint. Do you expect me to just forgive you for faking your own death?'

'Seriously, you really thought I was dead?'

'Are you kidding?' Sarah was spluttering. Had Smith alleviated her guilt by assuming that Sarah saw through the game? 'I grieved for you.' She hesitated, unsure whether to show the extent of her pain. This woman was now an enemy of sorts. But it was true, so she said it. 'I'm *still* grieving for you.' The Smith Sarah knew *was* dead.

'Look, wring the details out of me if you like, but the bottom line is; it was a shit thing to do. But then, I *am* shit, Sarah.'

'No, you're not,' said Sarah before her brain caught up with her instincts. Even after all that had happened, Sarah couldn't allow anybody to say that about themselves.

Smith gawped at her. 'Don't be nice,' she said in a small voice. 'I can't do this if you're nice.'

She walked Sarah through the scam. None of it would have happened if Sarah had simply stayed away that morning. Smith had woken on the sofa feeling like, 'well, death'.

Shivering, retching, her body begging for chemical

intervention, Smith hated herself. 'I'd spent money I didn't have taking drugs with a shower of arseholes who wouldn't spit on me if I was dying. I didn't want to be me. I wanted to be normal. Like you.'

But I loved you because you weren't normal, thought Sarah.

'Then in you walked, all fresh from the shower. You actually smelled of fucking roses and there was me, squirming in my own sweat. You were nice to me. You looked worried. I couldn't tell you the truth. I couldn't run that risk. Shush, Sarah, I *know*, OK, you would've understood, I get it, but remember, I was off my head on class A's and paranoid as hell. I couldn't bear you thinking I was a skank. I needed you.'

Huh. 'You needed me so much you disappeared.'

'I know how it looks but . . .' Smith bit her thumbnail. It was short already, and it bled. 'I needed your approval to feel OK about myself. Bagging that flat on Merrion Road was a fluke, but it was the only decent base I've ever had. I never wanted to leave! I've always pissed people off. I make bad situations worse. But *you* liked me, so, well, I couldn't be all bad. Because you're so . . .' Smith scowled. 'I hate the word "nice" but you're nice, Sarah. Not sugary, not girly. Strong. Real. You were good to me.'

'It was easy to be good to you. That's what friends do.' It sounded hollow; Sarah felt hollow. 'I would never have turned my back on you.'

'Don't you understand?' Smith's voice rose. 'I couldn't believe that. I've never been wanted, Sarah.'

'You had a different guy every weekend!'

'You're the pscyho–wotsit. Does a happy woman drag home a tourist every Saturday night?'

'You called it . . .' Sarah faltered. 'You called it celebrating your sexuality.'

'I was pretending I was loved.' Smith seemed disappointed in Sarah.

Which is pretty bloody ironic. 'Whatever. Go on,' said Sarah, weary.

'It wasn't planned, this whole thing. When I said I was ill, the look on your face, the sympathy . . . it was more addictive than the coke. I upped the stakes. Said I had cancer.'

'This doesn't make sense. You had all the info at your fingertips, as if you'd researched it.' Smith had been convincing. *Although*, thought Sarah, *it's easier to be convincing when somebody trusts you.*

'While I lay there on the sofa, coming down, wanting to die, the telly kept me company. This documentary had been on, some medical thing.'

'About, let me guess, astrocytoma.'

'I just said the word. It leapt out of me. I was surprised, actually, how simple it was. You never challenged me.'

'Again, Smith, you sound as if it's *my* fault.'

'I don't mean to. But you . . . *believed* everything.' Smith had shaved her head, patchily, to mimic the side effects of chemotherapy. 'I went on the most drastic diet ever.' While Sarah waited in the hospital reception area, Smith had sat smoking in the grounds. Letters from doctors had been created on Smith's ropey laptop. 'You took them at face value.'

'Did it feel good making a fool of me?' asked Sarah, who'd surfed through anger and was now on a miserable plateau where nothing she heard would surprise her.

'Never. Not for one second. The situation ran away with me. There was no way to turn it round. No off switch. All the acting . . . it was so hard to remember to be weak all the time. Then you'd try to help me and it made me feel terrible. I could hardly look at you.'

'I felt you pull away,' said Sarah. 'I thought I was crowding you.'

'Nah. I couldn't stand the kindness. Remember how you helped me shave my head?' She looked pained. 'You said I looked fierce.'

'Being bald suited you.'

They shared a tentative laugh, Sarah cutting hers short. *I'm not here for a cosy chat.*

'Look, while I'm being honest, I have to say this: I liked the attention,' blurted Smith. 'Cancer was a magic charm. People wanted to help. Well, most people. That bird downstairs, Lisa, wasn't interested. And Mavis never changed.' Smith grudgingly admired the old lady's consistency. 'She gave me the same dirty looks.'

'Does Dr Vera exist?'

'The pictures of his clinic are a yoga retreat in Ibiza that I swiped off the internet. Don't *look* at me like that! Once the first fib took hold I was trapped. I went downhill, picking up speed, making up more and more outrageous stuff. It got easier and easier. The worst bit, well, *one* of the worst bits – there were loads of them – was when you started raising money. Do you remember I was against it?'

'Mmm.' Sarah recalled Smith's gaunt face. *It seemed like she was resigning to fate, giving up.* She'd refused to let Smith accept Death's offer to dance. She'd pushed. She'd nagged. She'd created the 'giving' page as a *fait accompli.* 'I thought I was doing the right thing,' she whispered.

'The money made me feel guilty. *More* guilty. I went to sleep feeling guilty and I woke up feeling guilty. When the donations started to mount up, I realised I'd have to actually go through with it. I'd have to, well, *die.*'

'I sat in a bath of baked beans for you.'

Smith laughed, then put her hand to her mouth as she realised she and Sarah weren't in harmony.

'It's not funny, Smith.'

'Sorry.'

'So, Christ, it's hard to get my head around this.' Sarah rubbed her temples. 'What did you do when you got to Chile?'

Smith looked blank. 'Eh?'

'You mean you didn't go to Chile?'

'Of course not.'

'But the ticket. I bought it online myself. And the taxi . . .' Sarah remembered how she felt, watching it go.

'The ticket just went to waste. The taxi took me to the station. I got the hell out of London.'

'You faked pictures of your hospital bed. And hospital food.' Sarah didn't try to hide her disdain. 'Hundreds of people commented on those snaps.'

'I didn't read the comments.'

Sarah felt ill. She put a hand to her stomach, telling it, *Not now!* 'Do you know how long it took me to return all those donations?'

'What?' Smith looked amazed. 'Why didn't you just, I dunno, give it to charity?'

'Because pensioners and children gave their money. I did it for *you*.' Sorting out the money had been a last act of love. Like her father's letter. 'I don't know you, Smith. You're a stranger. My Smith is the one I sat up late with, who was funny and who cared. Who helped me cope. Who made me laugh.'

'Both Smiths are me. See?' Smith was petulant. 'I knew you'd turn against me.'

'*What?*' Sarah shook with consternation. 'Nothing could spoil our friendship, Smith. I was your wingman. But, yes, I admit it, faking your death has got me a bit bloody peeved!'

'Peeved is a very you word,' said Smith.

Ignoring her, Sarah said, 'I'm still getting my head around this. So, if Dr Vera didn't exist . . .' Sarah could see him, solid and dark-haired, in a crisp white coat with glasses. 'That means you posted your own death notice?'

Smith nodded. 'That was freaky. Then I realised you'd expect a funeral.'

'You say that so calmly.'

258

'I thought you'd smell a rat when you heard the funeral was a family affair.'

'You're still not in touch with your folks?'

'God, no. You?'

'Nope. When did you get back from Chile?'

'Sarah,' Smith stared at her. 'I was never in Chile, remember?'

'Oh. Yeah.' *This must be how Mavis feels when the world turns too speedily for her liking.*

'By that time I was in a commune in Dorset. Terrible place. A funny thing happened though. I—' About to embark on a story, Smith thought the better of it. 'Another time,' she murmured.

There won't be another time. 'How'd you end up here?'

'It's far away from London.' The subtext was clear: far away from Sarah. 'I fancied the look of Suffolk on the map. Like a bum sticking out into the sea.'

There were questions queuing, but Sarah found she didn't need answers any more. She turned. 'Let's get you back to work.'

The cafe was animated, the eponymous Dolly run off her feet. Jane's face was a question mark as Sarah sat down opposite her, and Smith tied her apron with a determined double knot.

'Everything OK?' Jane checked out Sarah's face like an anxious mother.

'Why don't you go on ahead? I'll say goodbye and catch you up.' Everything had been said, and nothing had been said at all.

Jane paid up and left, looking back, her face intent.

When Sarah stepped out of Dolly's, Smith followed, holding the door ajar behind her. There was the smell of cookies in the air, the content fug of all-day tea-making.

Another leave-taking. Sarah was glad to know that Jane was waiting in the car. 'So, goodbye I guess,' she said gruffly.

'Want to know the worst part of it all?' asked Smith in an urgent whisper.

Sarah was puzzled; she hadn't realised that any of it was an ordeal for Smith. She thought of her as a schemer, a con-woman. *I assumed she half enjoyed it.*

'The worst part was when you handed me your dad's letter.'

Sarah's lips pressed hard together.

'I knew how precious it was to you. It was like you'd given me a slice of your heart. The responsibility was too much. I read it over and over. It made me cry.'

Sarah's words had run out.

'I don't agree with your dad, though.' Smith glanced over her shoulder as Dolly called her name. She spoke rapidly, edging back into the cafe. 'There isn't something beautiful in everybody.'

That was it. The missing piece of Smith that meant she was doomed to know the price of everything, but not the value. Sarah had often wondered, in the old days, why such a warm and lively woman had no other friends. This lack of belief in people was her fatal flaw. Sarah grabbed her arm and Smith looked her full in the face.

'I see something beautiful in *you*,' said Sarah. 'I always did.'

Smith tried to pull away, saying 'Just go, please,' but Sarah held on tight.

'It was beautiful of you to return the letter.' Sarah let go and the two women regarded each other with a fierce sadness. 'Thank you for that, at least,' said Sarah, and she turned away.

Chapter Seventeen

ꓛꓳꓠꓝꓴꓛꓲꓴꓢ ꓝꓐꓗꓰꓘꓪꓘꓰꓫ
Notting Hill, W11

This calendar is FREE to valued customers!
Monday 29th August, 2016

KISSING IS LIKE DRINKING SALTED WATER:
YOU DRINK AND YOUR THIRST INCREASES

Bank Holiday Monday was the final day of carnival, its crescendo and crowning glory. Music flowered everywhere, and number twenty-four felt festive, as if it was a sunny Christmas, with steel drums instead of carols.

The parade crawled, swinging its hips, along the map of west London, bombastically loud, then muffled, then surging back to riotous life as it turned a corner. Sarah's toes tapped as she brushed her teeth.

The end of August, only two days away, was a just date, no longer a deadline. It would be Sarah, not some stranger, who'd enjoy the new Nordic feel of Flat A. *If I can arrange a loan.* Another thought followed, hard on the heels of the first. *If I can reason with Leo.*

As it was a Bank Holiday, Sarah gave her troubling

thoughts about Smith the day off. They eddied in a circle, going nowhere. Discovering that Smith was alive had cut off Sarah's mourning at its root, but a different grief persisted.

At noon, music struck up not outside the house but within it. Helena's 'famous' carnival party kicked off, and Sarah fled the uproar to find sanctuary with Mavis. As she accepted a pleasingly cold glass of something, she said, 'If I hear one more artificial laugh from Helena's terrace I'll . . .'

'You'll what? Storm in and demand they stop enjoying themselves?' When Mavis was amused she looked utterly different; younger and less wrung out. This was one of her good days. 'Envy gives you wrinkles, Sarah.'

'Why not come to the carnival with me and Jane, Mavis?'

'Last year I . . .' Mavis passed a hand over her face. 'What did I . . . ?'

Last year, as every year, Mavis had glowered from the front step.

'Please come.'

'I don't think so, dear.'

'Please!' *It might be your last carnival.*

'I said, I don't think so.' The old Mavis peeped through the new shell. 'Kindly don't ask again.'

They sat down to risotto, a dish Sarah had never expected to emerge from the forlorn kitchenette. It was fragrant with herbs and studded with green asparagus arrows. 'This is *good*.'

'I like feeding you.' Bad Mavis had receded. 'You're so appreciative.'

They talked, and the talk ranged from the weather – still doggedly hot – to Una's new shoes to Smith. They could skim and they could go deep, before returning to trivia. This sprightly interaction never, of course, veered anywhere near Mavis's health, but Sarah knew the moment would come when she could say 'motor neurone disease' and start an entirely new conversation.

'Perhaps Smith has Munchausen's syndrome,' suggested Mavis.

Mavis's condition was capricious: she couldn't remember last year's carnival yet she plucked Munchausen's syndrome out of the air. 'No. Munchausen's is a psychological disorder. Smith just told an opportunistic lie and then had to run with it.'

'That young woman was not what she seemed.'

Neither am I. The journey to East Anglia had changed Sarah. Or rather, it had exposed a change that had already taken place. She could no longer hide behind the wretched yet oddly comfortable mask she'd worn for so long.

Smith had told Sarah something as they plodded back to Dolly's Kitchen. Just when Sarah assumed there could be no more grotesque surprises, she'd pulled one last humdinger out of the bag.

Mavis put down her fork. 'Leo made a pass at a dying woman?'

'Yup. As far as he knew, Smith was at death's door, so that was the moment to put his hand on her thigh and tell her he'd always fancied her. Somebody needs to throw a bucket of cold water over that man.'

Mavis placed a withered hand on Sarah's. 'I'm sorry, dear. That must have been hard to hear.'

'Don't be sorry. It was the key to my cage.' Sarah's feelings were a smorgasbord of hurt and relief and pure joy. She almost didn't recognise the joy, but that's what it was. 'Who could love a man who'd do that, Mavis? Not me, that's for sure.'

'You're . . . cured?'

'I was already cured, but I misdiagnosed myself. These feelings I have for Leo are residual. They're last year's fashions and they don't fit any more, but I've been pulling at the zips and settling the collars and pretending they look just fine.' Sarah was able to say it and mean it: 'I don't love Leo any more.'

Meeting the Royces, as arranged, on the front step, Sarah engineered the 'Ciao' she gave Tom so it was warm enough to satisfy Jane but left him in no doubt of her cold shoulder. His mouth maintained its usual wry line and his eyes creased with, if anything, extra amusement. As if he enjoyed subterfuge.

'Wait up.' Tom bounded back indoors. 'I forgot something.'

Hostility boiled within Sarah. How could he be so free and easy around her? She rubbed her lips as Jane danced on the spot. Her mouth burned since Tom's kiss.

She faced a fact she'd been avoiding. It was time to make a full confession, if only to herself.

I have feelings for Tom.

Beyond reason, shameful but undeniable. It wasn't just physical. It was something chemical, which managed to be poetic. Sarah and Tom resonated to the same note, as if they were a pair of tuning forks.

What's more, he feels it too.

Tom's taste for adultery wasn't enough to stop Sarah falling for him. Tom was her kryptonite; she was powerless in the face of her desire. All she could do was accept it, knowing it must never be consummated.

When Tom reappeared, Mavis was with him, clasping a handbag large enough to smuggle a child across a border. 'Would you mind awfully if I accompanied you? This young man made me an offer I couldn't refuse.'

'We'd love it.' Sarah steadfastly ignored the barbed look Jane sent her way. 'It'll be fine,' she whispered to Jane, taking Mavis's reed-thin arm.

Mavis welded herself to Sarah's side as they stepped into the human river flowing past number twenty-four. Carried upstream to Ladbroke Road, Sarah's blood jumped to the jittery rhythm as Notting Hill surrendered to carnival.

Except for Mavis, whose silver head was down.

'Do you like reggae, Mavis?' asked Sarah playfully over the music.

'It's soca, actually.' Tom corrected Sarah without looking at her. 'More Latin than reggae.'

Whatever it was, Mavis was immune, withstanding rather than enjoying the magic.

'If you like, we can go back.' Sarah was loath to swap this

explosion of colour and life for her stuffy flat, but Mavis was as tense as a hostage.

'No, no, it's charming.' The words fell like stones.

Jane's hips described a figure of eight as she gave herself over to the vibe, hands in the air. 'Sarah, dance with Tom!' she yelled. 'Tom!' She pushed him. 'Be a good boy. Dance with Sarah.'

'No, I can't—' Sarah gestured to Mavis.

'Me and Mavis can get acquainted while you and Tom get down with your bad selves.' Jane, mistress of the revels, transferred Mavis's clamped fingers to her own suntanned forearm, evidently believing she was sacrificing herself for Sarah's good. 'Have fun! That's an order!'

Sarah looked questioningly at Mavis, who'd lifted her head in something like fear, but Tom grabbed her hand and propelled her into the road, where the crowd devoured them.

Twirled by Tom, Sarah had no choice but to move. Sticking to her guns, she danced with her back to him, trying to pull off the impossible, to dance haughtily.

Hands grabbed her waist and Tom spun her neatly. She was facing him, and her hauteur dissolved. Keeping hold of one of her hands, Tom danced with more enthusiasm than style. He had rhythm, though; that wasn't lost on Sarah. The music, the ambience, the sun, all ganged up on her. She allowed herself to enjoy being near him, and gave in to the music. Somebody whooped: *it was me!*

Knees in the air, elbows dangerously zigzagging, Tom

was a happy health hazard. On the sidelines, Jane laughed and clapped. Sarah, mid-spin, sought out Mavis's face; she was smiling.

Danced out, Tom and Sarah staggered back to the others. When she realised she was leaning on him, Sarah pulled away. She could tell he felt her do it; she could tell he felt insulted.

The four of them meandered through the changing soundscape, rooting out change to buy pineapple kebabs and coconut water, eschewing the strange patties sold by a cheerful septuagenarian.

'Are we in danger of bumping into your secret lover?' Jane's question made Sarah jump, but she meant Leo.

'Don't worry. He hates street parties.' With no mention of selling the flat, Leo had been texting hopefully about 'popping upstairs' over the past two days, but the virus had worked its way out of Sarah's body. She and Leo had built something – again – and now Sarah had to tell him they'd been wasting their time. *I owe him a face-to-face.*

'Curried goat, Mavis?' There was a dare in Jane's question for the conservative old dame.

'I adore goat, but not today,' said Mavis, tucked in between the two women. 'I practically lived on it in Montego Bay.'

As they waited for Mavis outside the public toilets, Jane said, 'She's been to Jamaica?'

'Hidden depths,' said Sarah.

'Really well-hidden depths. While you were dancing – great

moves, by the way – we had a good old chat. She's ...' Jane puckered her nose, unwilling to admit she'd been wrong. 'She's interesting, dammit.'

'Told you. Mavis is a changed woman.'

'I wonder if she's fallen down the loo.' Jane was impatient to get on. 'Ah, here she is.'

Sauntering, snacking, the three women tailed Tom, who seemed content to clear the way for them. 'Your Tom's a striking chap,' said Mavis to Jane.

The admiring glances of passing women, clad in anything from jeans to bikinis to full-on feathered headdresses echoed Mavis's opinion. Although a non-flashy brand of male, Tom was a classic. Tall, broad, his colouring was next door to nondescript but the total effect was arresting. Tom was a slow burn.

Sarah touched her lips, where the slow burn had scorched her.

'He is, isn't he?' Jane sounded proud.

'Looks, of course, aren't everything.'

'You sound as if you know what you're talking about, Mavey.'

'Sadly, I do.' Mavis lifted her chin slightly.

Gesturing at Mavis, Jane said, 'This one has a few tales to tell.'

Fearful that Mavis might feel cornered and lash out, like a tabby showing its claws, Sarah said, 'A lady doesn't kiss and tell.'

'Only room for one storyteller in the Bennison family,

eh?' Jane blundered obliviously across landmines. 'God, I love your sister's books. The pace, the characters. We lost a special lady when she went.'

Mavis slowed.

'Oh look!' Sarah pointed at something, anything. 'There's a . . . band.'

Blithely, Jane went on. 'I admired Zelda Bennison as a woman. Not just a writer. She was a role model.'

Like a discarded doll, Mavis sank to the floor.

Crouching beside her, Sarah was in a forest of feet as merrymakers stepped over and around the prone woman, some bending, some gasping, others asking 'Oh my God, is she OK?'

The only answer was 'No'. Mavis was conscious, but fading. Sarah was incompetent with panic.

'Let's get you home, Mavis.' With gentle arms, Tom lifted Mavis as easily as if she really was a doll. 'You need a cup of strong tea and a sit-down.' Tom was calm, as if he scraped old ladies off the pavement every day.

Heart hammering, Sarah said, 'She should go to A and E.' What she'd come to think of as the Mavis Situation had nosedived.

'No hospital.' Mavis's voice was a rasp, her head lolling against Tom's chest.

'Why don't I get her home, make her comfy?' Tom lowered his voice over Mavis's head. 'A and E will be bedlam today, Sarah.'

Mavis collected herself enough to say, 'I know exactly

what's wrong with me. Casualty can't help. You girls stay out and enjoy yourselves. Please.'

Mavis put a lot into that 'please'.

'But I—' It went against the grain for Sarah to let Mavis go.

'She'll be fine.' Tom bore her away through the crowd.

Watching them go, Jane said, 'Mavis hasn't changed. Funny how she collapsed when I praised her sister. She was fine until then.'

'She wasn't. I could tell.'

'Your reformed Mavis has a guilty conscience. Bet you anything she nursed Zelda so she could get her hands on her money.'

They sat on the kerb, letting the carnival flow around them. 'You're wrong,' said Sarah. 'If she's suddenly a millionaire, what's she spending it on? She lives in squalor. Besides, the Mavis I know would never worry me by pretending to faint.'

'Wouldn't she?'

Sarah was so accustomed to biting her lip it had a groove in it. *It's you who needs a wake-up call about your nearest and dearest.* 'When I look at Mavis I see damage, iron self-control, boundless anxiety and a woman who's trying to conquer the frankly *horrible* personality that's blighted her life.' Sarah was following the advice in her father's letter yet again; it might lead her down some dead ends, but not this time. There was beauty in Mavis. 'Aren't we all just trying to communicate, when it comes down to it?'

'Good thing Tom was here.' Jane drained the last of a can of something fizzy. 'Old dears always love him.'

'Mavis is no cookie-cutter old dear!' Sarah stuck a toe in some murky water. 'What about *young* dears? Did Tom have masses of girlfriends in the old days?'

'How come you're so interested?'

Sarah reddened, but Jane was tickled rather than territorial. 'No reason.'

'Is there something you'd like to share with the class, Sarah?'

'Well . . .' Sarah blotted out the tumult around them, the choirs and the samba dancers and the tipsy limbo novices. Perhaps it was time to clear the air. If it lost Sarah a friend, then that was the price of doing the right thing. *Why*, she thought, *does the right thing always have to be the hardest thing?* 'Jane,' she began.

Jane's phone buzzed. 'Hold that thought!' Her face brightened as she read a text. 'My hubby!'

'Is he on his way back?'

'Yes!' Jane punched the air. 'He says he'll be here in three weeks' time.' She wiggled excitedly on the kerbstone.

'But he only went around the corner.'

'Cyprus is hardly around the corner.' Jane texted back, her fingers skipping over the keys.

'Cyprus?' Sarah was disoriented. 'Jane,' she said, 'Tom took Mavis back to number twenty-four.'

'Not Tom, silly.' Jane looked up from her phone. 'Jamie. My husband.'

It took a minute or two to untangle the crossed wires, and another few minutes for Jane to stop laughing.

'What? Tom? My . . . oh dear God. He's my brother, you idiot. Eurgh. Yuk. No. How come we've never had this conversation?'

'But we have.' Sarah's mind raced. 'Haven't we? Your surname . . .' She remembered her sleuthing at the hall table.

'Yeah, we're both Royce. I didn't change my name when I got married. Not that sort of bird. But there's never been any post to Mr and Mrs Royce. Your brain filled in that blank all on its own.'

'You have a framed picture of Tom and you getting married!'

'Obviously I *don't*. If you look at it properly you'll see it's me and Jamie.'

'Why is your husband in Cyprus?'

'I've seriously never told you Jamie's in the army?' Jane shook her head. 'I feel as if I've always known you, but obviously I've left out chunks of my life story.' She wiped her eyes, enjoying herself. 'Quite important chunks.'

Sarah was in free fall. 'So, let me get this straight, when you talked about Jamie, about being two peas in a pod, about him never being unfaithful . . .'

'You thought I was talking about Tom!'

The repercussions were too big to grasp all at once. Pedalling backwards, Sarah reassessed Tom. No longer devious, love rat Tom, he was instantly promoted to glorious, handsome, *decent* Tom. He'd been free and single and available, and he'd liked her enough to try and cross the drawbridge that Sarah pulled up after Leo left.

They'd been at cross-purposes since the first hello. What should have been simple and straightforward had been dragged out of shape by Sarah's talent for leaping to conclusions.

He's always wanted me. It was a revelation. *I've always wanted him.*

An unattached Tom was a different beast to a married Tom; Sarah recalled her behaviour, the names she'd called him. 'Jane, I've been a fool.' Something welled up inside Sarah, something shiny and strung about with fairy lights of hope.

'Tom's only living with me to keep me company until Jamie leaves the army next year. Then I'll find Tom somewhere fabulous of his own.'

'I said some terrible things to him.' Sarah wanted to scream with a mixture of embarrassment and elation. 'He thinks I'm crazy. He hates me.'

'Do shut up. Tom fancies you rotten.' Jane looked sceptical. 'How could you not notice?'

The crowd looked different. The music was louder. The sky was bluer than blue above her head. Sarah was supercharged with emotion, realisation thundering through every vein and sinew. Tom was available. More than that, he wanted her. A dream had come true, the way they hardly ever do, except in fairy stories. It could really happen, this longed-for love. She was halfway there already; one kiss would send her over the edge. *And I'm taking Tom with me!* Suddenly his head was visible above the crowd. Sarah stood up and tugged at her bra strap and cleared her throat as Tom came towards them. He was transfigured. As if light poured out of him. As if he was more real than the sepia drones around him.

Tom was no longer off limits.

He's mine.

Sarah ran to him, stopping just shy of his chest so he had to stop too. 'Um, yes?' he said uncertainly.

'Yes!' she repeated, without the bemused question mark. 'Yes, yes, yes, Tom! Yes! Bloody *yes*!' Reaching up, Sarah pressed her mouth, her lonely mouth, to Tom's.

Tom's lips remained passive. The lips of a statue. A statue who was staring at Sarah with an expression that see-sawed between astonishment and dismay.

Stepping back, Sarah saw in her peripheral vision that Tom's outstretched hand was in the grasp of a small woman. Blonde, appealing, her face a picture of perplexity.

'Timing,' said Tom, wiping his mouth – a gesture that struck at Sarah's heart – 'isn't your strong point.'

The woman let out a cry and yanked her fingers free, darting off through the mob.

'Camilla! Hold on!' Before Tom turned to chase her, he said, witheringly, 'Thanks a million, Sarah.'

'Who *is* that woman?' Sarah was wild-eyed.

'She's Camilla.' Jane put her arm around Sarah. 'The actress who's been chasing him. He finally slowed down and let her catch him.'

'When did they get together?'

'About, ooh, eight weeks ago. He only just told me about her this morning.'

Right after their tussle by the Thames. Sarah recalled the scene at the car wash and cringed at how she'd taken Tom's 'olive branch' for a pass: he was already seeing somebody else and was merely trying to patch things up with his screwball neighbour. 'Is it ... are they serious?' *Surely,* she thought, *eight weeks isn't long enough to fall in love.*

Jane looked as if she'd rather not have to answer. 'Tom,' she said, 'is always serious about women.'

Chapter Eighteen

CONFUCIUS FAKEAWAY
Notting Hill, W11

This calendar is FREE to valued customers!
Tuesday 30th August, 2016

THERE ARE THREE TRUTHS:
MY TRUTH, YOUR TRUTH
AND THE TRUTH

The note had been slipped under the door during the night.
Sarah recognised Leo's writing.

Darling! I feel as if there's a terrible cloud hanging over us. We must talk about the flat. Don't worry – we won't fall out about it. We couldn't, could we? We're us, after all. H is whisking me away for a Cotswolds mini-fucking-break. I'll race upstairs the moment I return. Please be there. It makes me happy to know you're waiting for me. L xxx

Yes, it'd be nice for you, thought Sarah, *but not so nice for the woman doing the waiting.* She tore the paper into tiny shreds.

Not with fury, but with the same satisfaction as finishing the ironing pile or clearing her email inbox. She was no longer Rapunzel, winding down her hair for Leo.

Because consciences don't atrophy overnight, Sarah knew she must face Leo, one on one. Not just to reiterate that she was staying put – Sarah was pinning her hopes on a meeting with a financial adviser later in the week – but to explain that she was opting out of their game of Grandma's Footsteps. It had gone too far. *We even made love . . .*

A one-night stand with your ex is more than the sum of its parts.

Outside, Notting Hill straightened its wig and withstood its hangover. A platoon of street cleaners had cleared the slurry of litter at dawn. There would be no more samba outside the corner shop until next August.

Number twenty-four was quiet as Sarah ran from the very top to the very bottom of the house to check on the Mavis Situation. Sarah knew how it feels to be neglected when you're poorly – her mother had believed all Sarah's child-hood illnesses to be attention-seeking charades – and so she let herself in to Flat E, armed with a newspaper, a bottle of elderflower pressé and one of Tom's sunflowers, ceremon-ially decapitated for the VIP patient.

'Such a gent,' Mavis was saying, as Sarah handed her the paper.

Surreptitiously, Sarah did a brief inventory of the invalid. Mavis's voice was firm and her movements brisk. As Sarah nipped to the bathroom, she heard Mavis say, 'So thought-ful, so kind.'

'Who is?' Sarah hurriedly counted the tablets in the blister pack. None had been taken since she'd found them a week ago. Mavis was ignoring medical advice, as if motor neurone disease might blow over, like a cold.

'Tom, of course,' said Mavis as Sarah returned and sat on the end of the bed. 'I know deep down he's a rotter, dear, but he was tender with me, even when Peck called him a bleeping bleepy bleep.'

'I have something to tell you about Tom.'

The tale of mistaken identity had to be recounted twice. Mavis simply didn't believe it the first time around. 'So the caddish behaviour wasn't caddish at all. He was simply asking you out.' Mavis couldn't find any humour in the story. She lay back, fidgeting. 'Can you still feel it?'

'Feel what?' Sarah sat on her hands to stop herself bulldozing through the clothes and shoes and tat on the floor, and the carrier bags bulging with more clothes and shoes and tat that huddled in the eternal dusk of Mavis's bedroom.

'The kiss, dear. Can you still feel Tom's kiss?'

'No! That was ages ago.' Sarah put her fingertips to her mouth. Her lips swelled.

'The best kisses linger forever.' Mavis closed her eyes. She looked eerie, almost dead, her white hair and her white skin barely making a dent in her once-white pillow. Sarah reached over to the wardrobe, surreptitiously tucking in the sleeve of a coat that peeked out. Her fingers lingered; cashmere. Checking that Mavis's eyes were still shut, Sarah leaned forward to investigate the cupboard's dark interior. Satin. Velvet the colour of raspberries. A Chanel-styled jacket. No, a *Chanel* jacket.

Blimey. Sarah sat back. 'Which kisses do you remember, Mavis?'

'We're not talking about me.' The eyes snapped open. 'We're talking about you and your complicated love life.'

'More like lack of love life.'

Mavis shook out her newspaper. 'Tish,' she said. 'A lovely hunk like Tom after you? You're about to embark on something wonderful.' She peered over the headlines. 'Or is there a fly in the ointment?'

'A fly with good hair that has been chasing Tom for months and has finally caught him.' If it wasn't for the mix-up, Sarah and Tom could be knee-deep in a relationship by now. 'I want to know him, Mavis. He intrigues me.' Tom was the box set she'd been waiting for, the long bath, the weekend break, the morning run.

'It's not just that he's handsome? Because he's really rather gorgeous. I didn't notice until yesterday.'

'Am I fickle, Mavis? I was waxing lyrical about Leo until recently.'

'Do these feelings for Tom come from the very core of you?' Mavis folded the paper and regarded her seriously, an aged child in her prim and proper nightdress. 'Or is he a passing fancy?'

'I don't know much,' said Sarah, 'but this I do know. I could make Tom happy, and if he cared about me, well, I'd smile for the rest of my life.' She sighed. 'I'd smile in my sleep.'

'But he *does* care about you, dear. The infamous kiss that was an evil kiss but is now revealed to be a romantic kiss . . .' Mavis drew breath. 'That tells us he finds you appealing.'

'No. It tells us he *did* find me appealing before I went nuclear at him.' Tom had been forthright about his attraction to Sarah; she'd smothered her response with the remnants of her need for Leo, and misplaced loyalty to Jane. 'He has a girlfriend now. I can wait.' She wouldn't wait for Leo, but Tom was different. 'I've had a lot of practice at that.'

'By which time you'll be with somebody else and so on and so forth.' Mavis raised a ragged eyebrow. 'You snooze you lose.'

'Get you with your cool and groovy sayings. You don't think I'm fickle, then?' That had been one of her mother's favourite put-downs about the father Sarah resembled.

'Far from it. I longed for you to see through old Leo the lion. Rather a scraggy mane and no use at the hunt, I imagine. I couldn't nudge you, though. One has to be patient with people.'

I'm certainly being patient with you, Mavis! Today, with Mavis recuperating, was not the time to confront her about her condition, to say: 'I know your big secret and it's going to be OK.' It would take sensitivity and persistence to discover why Mavis neglected to take her medication. Perhaps she wanted to follow Zelda. Sarah took a chance. 'Mavis, are you happy?'

Mavis answered without bluster. 'No, dear, I'm not. I've made foolish choices that I deeply regret. I have a liaison with darkness I can't avoid. Learn from me, dear. Don't let life have its way with you. Stay in the driving seat.'

'I hate to think of you unhappy.'

'*You* make me happy. I'm nearer to the final chapter than you, which means I've earned the right to speak my mind, so here goes.' Mavis fixed her with those animal-bright eyes. 'I love you, Sarah. So do me a favour, dear, and stop worrying about me, and get on with living your life.'

'Am I allowed to say I love you back?'

Mavis went back to the headlines. 'Just this once.'

After the long weekend, St Chad's had a sluggish air, as if everybody would rather be in bed. Sarah went about her duties automatically as the day dragged its feet around her.

She had a sense of displacement. The same feeling she had when she overdressed for a casual birthday do in a pub. Behind the reception desk she was uncomfortable, marooned, unsure of herself. She missed, she realised, the insulated calm of the therapy suites.

At about three o'clock, Nadia came through the revolving door with her key worker. 'Sarah!' said Nadia. 'Look.' She held up an ice lolly. 'It's orange-flavoured,' she added helpfully.

'Your favourite,' said Sarah, turning the book so the

middle-aged woman holding Nadia's other hand could sign them both in.

'Why aren't we friends any more?' asked Nadia evenly, licking the lolly.

'We are, we are,' said Sarah. 'But this is my job now. Out here.'

'You're the hello lady,' said Nadia.

'I am,' smiled Sarah.

'Aw,' said the other receptionist as Nadia walked away. 'Bless her.'

Sarah was made of fire. She wanted to leap up and run down the hallway, blazing. She wanted to catch up with Nadia, crouch beside her, *talk* to her. But Sarah simply touched an icon on the screen in front of her and said 'Good morning St Chad's' into her headpiece. She barely listened to the reply and possibly put the caller through to the wrong extension. Sarah couldn't care; her head was full of Nadia. And Shavonne. And Lily. And Conor. All the children she'd got to know who had wormed their way into her soul. *Only for me to drop out of their lives.*

There was a sacred aspect to St Chad's work. Not that Sarah saw herself as a high priestess – far from it – but there was something soulful and right about a building full of people working towards the emotional health and safety of vulnerable children.

It felt like shirking not to be involved when she was so highly qualified; sometimes Sarah wondered if she was kidding herself that it was fear that held her back.

The real reason, though, was simple. *I can't offer them what they need.* With Una it was as if she was talking to her younger self, but at the clinic it was different – Sarah wasn't the person she used to be.

Some of the changes were for the better; seeing Leo's faults in 3D was a major step forward. Some of them were disastrous, such as her misreading of the people around her.

Sarah had, in no particular order, revised the end of her marriage so it bore no resemblance to the truth; believed Smith's shambolic lies; overlooked the pearl that was Mavis; married off a brother and sister. Her confidence was riddled with bullet holes.

Keeley felt differently. 'You're as tough as old boots,' she'd said, cornering Sarah for yet another 'little chat' about her future by the microwave. Waiting for a bowl of soup to heat, she'd said, 'Look, girl, you recovered from Leo. You refused to give into temptation with a world-class hottie because of loyalty to your mate. You withstood a nightmare childhood. You're *exactly* what I need on my team. Use all that fear and sadness and longing and . . . and . . .' Keeley had waved her arms, '*shit* to help our clients.'

Sarah had assumed that a switch would flick in her head when it was time to return to her 'real' work, but when she looked at Nadia she felt only her own need. There was no answering swell of confidence or wisdom. Maybe it wasn't a matter of 'when' but 'if'.

Maybe, Confucius, that's my *truth*.

*

The organic farm shop's delights were passed over in favour of the greasy spoon three doors down. With Jane about to depart for Suffolk again, a debriefing was necessary.

'Still can't get my head around it.' Jane took up her bacon butty. 'Me and Tom married. It makes my toes curl. I have to stop thinking about it in case I go into a terminal cringe and actually die of *yuk*.'

'I feel so stupid. Lisa knew you were brother and sister. And Leo; he knew.' Sarah realised she'd misjudged his nonchalance about whether Jane had noticed the attraction; he'd rightly assumed that a sibling wouldn't be jealous. 'I misled Mavis, who's had to listen to me bang on about how guilty I felt. All this is your fault,' she said. 'Brothers and sisters don't normally live together at your age.'

'You make us sound like fairground freaks. Tom was sick of house-sharing and it made sense for him to move in with me and help fix the place up. I get miserable without Jamie. Nobody to snap at in the mornings. Nobody to snuggle up to when EastEnders comes on. Oh, sorry . . .'

'Don't be silly.' Sarah hated being the poster girl for the sad 'n' lonely. 'You're allowed to miss your husband, Jane. The amazing, sexy, funny Jamie.'

'You're going to love him.' Jane drummed her feet. 'He's going to love you! I can't wait for you to meet.' This was her forte; pushing people together whether they liked it or not.

Thankfully, we like it just fine. 'Remember when you said you rarely have sex?' Sarah stirred sweetener into tea strong enough for a mouse to trot across. 'I thought that meant your marriage was in trouble.'

'It's only 'cos the British Army keeps us apart, the bastards. I mean, never mind protecting the realm, what about my nookie? Believe me, if Jamie were here all the time we'd—'

'Stop! You're the queen of oversharing.' Sarah was about to make a joke along the lines of married people never having sex, when something stopped her. The joke was true in her case. The marital lovemaking she'd remembered so nostalgically was a high days and holidays occurrence. Their sex life had tapered off before Smith, before Helena.

We ruined our marriage without any help from other people.

'The last time we did it . . .' Ignoring Sarah's rolled eyes, Jane counted on her fingers. 'Over a month ago.' Jane let out a growl of frustration. 'Jamie was in London for forty-eight hours, some ceremonial bollocks at his regiment's HQ. He slipped away and met me at a hotel.'

That was the day Sarah ran into Tom at the car wash. The day she'd snapped his olive branch in two. 'I've been thinking back through our conversations and with hindsight it all seems obvious. The truth almost came out so many times, but each time we just managed to skate over it. When I used to comment on how much you loved Tom—'

'And I'd say yes, sure, but I want to kill him some days! That sounded like a typical married couple.'

'Exactly. I'd mention "your husband" meaning Tom—'

'And I'd assume you meant Jamie.' Jane shook her head at the absurdity of it. 'So many near misses. If we'd sorted this out earlier you and Tom could be doing the do right this minute.'

'I don't understand why you never said anything about Jamie being a soldier.'

'I truly thought I had, Sarah. We made friends so fast that I obviously skipped a few basic facts. I feel like I've known you all my life.'

'Me too,' smiled Sarah. *At least I came out of this debacle with one Royce to call my own.* 'We have a lot of catching up to do. Is Jamie in any danger?'

'Not in Cyprus,' laughed Jane. She glossed over his tours of Afghanistan – 'Let's just say I didn't sleep' – and explained that he'd be out for good in January. 'I'm literally counting the days. There are one hundred and twenty-seven. You'll be back at St Chad's by then.' Jane was carefully off-hand.

She wants me to earn more, to remortgage, and stay put. The women needed each other. Sarah warmed herself at that little bonfire, but couldn't visualise herself among the children. 'Did Tom mention my lunge at the carnival?'

'Haven't seen him. He stayed at Camilla's last night.' Jane cast around for ketchup. 'First time.'

'I drove him into her bed. I'm a sexual sheepdog.'

'They're going steady, to use a hideous phrase of my mother's.' Jane sighed, watching Sarah quizzically. 'I could say something if you like. Tell him how you feel.'

The idea appalled and thrilled Sarah. 'No. Yes. Is that a good idea?'

'Tom's private about his love life. I don't know, Jane. He does his own thing. It might do more harm than good.'

Sarah absolved her. 'You're right. Leave it.'

'I'm astonished Tom tried to kiss you that night. He's usually too proud to wade in if he's not getting the signals. He must have really, really liked you. When I said that Camilla was barking up the wrong tree, I meant he was stuck on *you*. That's why I faked a migraine in the bar, so he'd have a chance to reel you in with the old Royce charm.'

'You faked—?'

'Jesus, Sarah, you can be very slow on the uptake.'

'I humiliated him.'

'He'll get over it.' Jane seemed to see Tom as a child still, the robust brother she'd grown up with. 'What's *really* the deal with you and Leo? This U-turn feels a bit sudden.'

Sarah used to liken her love for Leo to a tap, insisting that she couldn't just turn it off because he'd walked out; now the tap had dribbled dry of its own accord. 'It seems like it happened overnight, but just like it takes a while to fall in love and then *bam*, it's taken me a while to fall out of love.'

'And we're at the *bam* stage?'

'Yeah.' The tea was cold; Sarah motioned for a top-up. 'I've been nursing a fantasy. The Leo I loved is mostly my own needs projected. It's not his fault.' She waved away Jane's spirited protest. 'No, really. Leo's the victim this time around. I've been telling him – not in so many words, but with my behaviour – that I'm madly in love with him, that I want him back; I want *us* back, when really it was just blind panic. After the divorce and Smith's so-called death, I wanted to crawl back to the familiar, the way you want to crawl back to bed when you have flu. I hoped everything would be fine if we revived the marriage. But there's no mystery why the marriage failed, is there?'

'Leo couldn't keep his wotsit in his pants. That story about coming on to Smith when he thought she was dying . . . the man has a problem.'

'I didn't suspect, so what does that tell you about the communication in our marriage? There was so much wrong. He didn't just dislike my job, Jane, he didn't *respect* it. He thinks social workers are sissies.'

'When really they're soldiers on the front line.'

'We rarely had sex. I was tired. Or he was drunk. All that cooperation I claimed to miss so much? We couldn't even decide on a paint colour! Leo forced decisions on me, and I made allowances. I was cruising along, in love with this fictional hero I'd created, one who was faithful, who wanted to make a forever home with me, have a family. I never pushed for any of those things. Now I look back and think, hang on! *Why* was our flat unfinished? *Why* did we never talk about a baby?'

'Sarah, you're crying.' Jane leaned over and wiped Sarah's cheeks with her fingers. 'I wish I could do something.'

'You do plenty.' Sarah sniffed, resetting her emotional thermostat.

'You might not like what I did this morning . . . but it's for your own good.'

Sarah quailed. 'Go on.'

'Look, this financial adviser guy is going to think you're playing a late April fool's joke when you tell him what you earn and that you want to double your mortgage.'

'Maybe he'll—'

'Sarah, this is my profession. Trust me. You need a Plan B or Leo will have all the power and you'll have to move out.' Jane dipped her head to look at Sarah's lowered eyes. 'Don't hide! If you can face the zombie of Southwold you can face this. That's better,' she said as Sarah smiled wanly. 'Plan B is either you go back to being a child psychologist, thereby earning more and having a decent shot at upping your mortgage . . .'

'Nope,' said Sarah, short and far from sweet.

'Right then. You can't or won't leave Mavis, so we're on to Plan C. I've had a little chat with a contact of mine. An estate agent. Shush!' ordered Jane as Sarah opened her mouth. 'Hear me out. This guy's a local. Very select clientele, all filthy rich, not generally looking for a home, but for properties to add to their portfolios. They snap up lots of little gems, period flats in good postcodes. When I told him of a fabulous small flat at the top of my house that wasn't even on the market yet, his eyes lit up. He has the perfect prospective buyer, apparently. Looking for a property to rent out. No names, all very hush-hush. Your flat would suit him down to the ground.'

'It suits *me* down to the ground,' said Sarah sulkily, drawing a face in some spilled sugar.

'My contact is very interested. *Very.* I told him there was a proviso. That the buyer would have to allow the vendor – that's you, by the way, bug-a-lugs – to stay on as a tenant.'

Sarah sat up at this curveball. 'But I can't afford the fancy rents landlords expect.' In Merrion Road, unless you were on benefits like Lisa or a lifelong resident like Mavis, rents were higher than the average mortgage repayment.

'We talked about that. If you're willing to discount the asking price, then perhaps we can negotiate a discount in the rent.'

Sarah appreciated that 'we'.

'You'd be able to stay at number twenty-four, look after Mavis, get pissed with me, *and* have a few pennies left at the end of the week.' Jane sat back, pleased with her scheme.

Sarah tried to like it, tried to see the positives, but couldn't shake the thought that renting again after gaining a toehold on the property ladder would feel like going backwards.

She chewed her lip; a habit she'd had as a child that was making a comeback. That ladder was slippery, but as a single woman with no family support she needed to try and keep her grip on it.

Jane said into Sarah's silence, 'Leo's going to be on your back when you kick him to the kerb. You need to be prepared.'

'I know ...' Sarah felt an urge to defend Leo; old habits

die hard. 'He's been patient, you know. It's over a year since we split up.'

'You mean it's over a year since he waltzed off with that sex-bot! I wouldn't call it patient, I'd call it guilt. Leo's been having his cake and eating it: current wifey in his bed, sexy ex on the floor above. Just watch – he'll start piling on the pressure.'

Sarah had never shared Helena's sly story about needing Flat A for a nursery. Old suspicions flared up, clogging up Sarah's mind. *I need to finally divorce properly from Leo.* The flat was all that connected them. It was a big step. *But hey, I'm getting used to those.* 'OK. Let's do it.'

'I'm glad you said that.' Jane wiped her brow with an exaggerated gesture. 'I've booked a viewing for next Thursday.' She squinted at the bill, ignoring the expression on Sarah's face and changing the subject. 'If I were you I'd communicate with Leo through lawyers. Wash him right out of your hair.' She ferreted for change in her purse. 'He's a—'

'Leo's everything you're about to say and more,' Sarah sighed. 'But we were happy once. I need to tell him to his face that our whatever-it-is is over.' Sarah still couldn't bring herself to call it an affair. 'It'll be a relief not to feel guilty about Helena any more.'

'She didn't feel guilty about you!' Jane was outraged, but calmed down to add, 'Which makes you the nicer person. So you win, I suppose.'

'I don't think anybody wins,' said Sarah.

*

There was a premonition of autumn in the garden, like a rumour whispered in Sarah's ear.

When Una saw Tom at Mikey's house, she sped up. Sarah relinquished the child's hand and hung back.

Ethereal and fair with pearly skin, Camilla was at Tom's side, her head on his shoulder.

As if somebody's glued her ear to his jacket, thought Sarah sarcastically, wishing somebody would glue *her* ear to Tom's jacket.

'Una!' said Tom. 'I was just about to introduce Cam to Mikey, although we shouldn't really get him out because he's nocturnal and it's dayti— oh, OK.'

All self-respecting six-year-olds are indifferent to rules. Una reached in for the snoozing hedgehog and embraced Mikey as if they'd been parted for years. With a grin, she presented him to Camilla, who seemed unsure of hedgehog etiquette. Mikey's nose lifted in her direction, his one good eye shining.

Taking a step back, Camilla said, 'Ooh, um, hi.'

Una pressed Mikey on her, but Camilla backpedalled frantically, almost losing her footing. 'Urgh, no, they're full of fleas!'

'That's a myth,' said Tom and Sarah, both of them startled by the echo, looking at each other.

'What's she doing here?' Camilla demanded of Tom, looking upwards as if the sight of Sarah might damage her eyes.

'Living, Cam. She lives here.' Tom nodded at Sarah. 'Hi.' He was polite.

'Hello.' Sarah was also polite.

'Una and I are off to the corner shop,' said Sarah, keen to get away.

Una's disgruntled displeasure lasted only as long as it took to promise her a Curly Wurly. The child looked over her shoulder as they walked back to the house and shuddered.

Sarah looked and she shuddered too. Not with disgust – she'd seen grown-ups kiss before – but with longing.

Chapter Nineteen

ƆONFUƆIUS FAKEAWAY
Notting Hill, W11

This calendar is FREE to valued customers!
Tuesday 6th September, 2016

A FALL INTO A DITCH MAKES YOU WISER

Sarah was serious about many things. Loyalty. Truthfulness. Peanut butter ice cream. Friendship was serious. Family, with its power to heal and harm, was deadly serious.

Love was top of the pile. It touched everything, and changed everything it touched.

Love didn't have to be of the romantic variety; love fuelled Sarah's devotion to what was left of Mavis's future. It was the driving force behind her feelings for Jane, her tenderness towards Una, even her ambivalent interactions with Lisa.

Love left its fingerprints all over her father's memory; it rose off the page each time she re-read his letter to remind herself that she was good enough, that there was beauty everywhere.

Love was at the bottom of her mother's rage.

Love wasn't pink for Sarah. No harps. No cherubs. Love was monumental, and unchanging. That's why she'd found it so hard to disengage from Leo, even when they had nothing left.

The way Sarah felt about Tom was elemental, part of the natural world. She and Tom – Sarah felt nervous pairing them in her mind – were chiselled in stone. Hard but magnificent. Durable. Constant.

Leo was persistent; Tom was invisible. One cornered Sarah on the stairs at all hours of the day and night; the other spent most of his time out of number twenty-four altogether.

Sarah supposed Tom was at Camilla's as she dodged Leo, avoiding the inevitable conversation. She fobbed him off, backing away as she told him about the viewing booked for the flat.

'Yes, but, *darling* ...' Leo's eyes had tried desperately to communicate. 'There's other stuff to sort out.'

'Is there?' Sarah had looked innocent as she made her escape. A handwritten note landed on her doormat. Dashed off, shakily written, it wasn't signed.

Dearest S
   I can't stop thinking about you. Are you still mad at me? Sod the flat, darling. Do what you like with it. Just confess to me that you want me like I want you. Please, please let's be alone together.
   Destroy this obvs!!!!!

Sarah read its paltry lines over again, marvelling that she'd been satisfied with such morsels. Cocksure Leo thought he still had the upper hand.

Pushing her hair back into a ponytail, Sarah surveyed herself in the mirror that now hung on her bedroom wall. A mirror attached to a wall at the correct height still felt novel. The revamped flat was a constant revelation; like the homely secretary who takes off her specs, it had revealed its true, lovely self.

There was still some way to go. As Sarah flicked off the lights and left, she heard the ancient plumbing hiss. *A job for whoever buys the place,* she thought, trying to be glad to hand over such a tedious project, but deep down she was possessive even of the worn-out water pipes.

'As it's September,' said Mavis, ushering Sarah in, 'I made something hearty. Hope you like shepherd's pie.'

Peck got there first. 'Stupid! Stupid!'

'Watch it,' murmured Sarah as she passed the cage. 'Or it'll be cockatoo pie next week.'

Mavis had tethered her wiry hair into a bun; Sarah was touched by this evidence of 'making an effort'. She was on good form, with none of the crankiness or lack of focus or physical instability that Gan at St Chad's had warned of.

The weekend had been a low point. Mavis had skulked behind the chain on her door, refusing invitations to come out, muttering that she needed to be alone. 'Let me be!' she'd snapped, her face congealed into sourness. Sarah had stood outside for a few minutes, debating with herself – was this, she wondered, the beginning of the end? She'd noticed Mavis's wild hair and dressing gown buttoned up all wrong.

No dressing gown today; Mavis was as presentable as she could ever be, and humming contentedly as she manhandled the pie out of the oven.

Over dessert of apple crumble – the nearest thing to a cuddle a cook can provide – Peck bounced on his perch, inviting them and the rest of the world to get stuffed, put a sock in it, stick it up their bum, et cetera.

'He's getting worse,' sighed Mavis.

And so are you. The 'bad' days would, at some point, outweigh the 'good'. 'Maybe the RSPCA can rehome him.'

'Peck and I are a pair. Some promises one has to keep.' With counterfeit innocence, Mavis said, 'Tom and his young lady knocked on my door earlier.'

Sarah had decided that her need for Tom, even though it permeated every cell of her body, down to the split ends of her hair, wouldn't cripple her. Instead, she welcomed it as a sign of life returning to her extremities. She closed her eyes, the slight nausea she'd woken up with that morning returning, telling a story all of its own. Massaging her tum, she willed the discomfort to recede.

'She's in love, poor what's-her-name.' Mavis had loyally contrived to forget Camilla's name.

Or is it the motor neurone disease?

'Tom, however,' said Mavis, 'is showing no signs whatsoever of being in love.'

'You're biased, Mavis.'

'There's a click, rightness, when people find each other. Tom and his girlfriend are well suited, but it's not special.' Mavis patted crumbs from her sleeve. 'Nothing to give *you* sleepless nights, at any rate.'

'I've missed that boat, Mavis.'

'Tom isn't a boat.' Mavis leaned on her knuckles and rose. 'Coffee, yes?'

'Please.' Sarah closed in on herself as the gentle noises of coffee preparation wafted from the hellhole kitchenette. Her inner thoughts were repetitive again, just like they used to be when she was still smarting from the divorce.

The thought process was circular and went like this: yes, it was good that Tom wasn't married. But it was bad that she'd treated him like a low-down hound. It was very bad that he was in a relationship with a woman who was nuts about him. It was very, very bad indeed that Tom seemed to be keen on the woman.

And so on. And on and on and on.

There was no way to step out of this loop. Sarah had already tried the magical kiss that solves everything in Disney cartoons. It had ruined what was left of her dignity and driven Tom deeper into his new lover's arms.

A suspicion niggled at Sarah, that if she squared her shoulders and really went for it, she might wrestle Tom back from Camilla. *But I don't want to be that person.* Sarah longed for clarity, for purity. If Tom really wanted her, he'd make it happen. Adultery hadn't worked out for Sarah before, and she was reluctant to try it again.

Leaning back on her chair, she noticed a black shape lolling in a corner. 'I'll take out the rubbish for you.'

'That's kind,' called Mavis.

The bin bag tore on the front step, vomiting trash over Sarah's feet. A dainty heel appeared just as she bent to gingerly pick up sopping kitchen roll and fossilised teabags.

Camilla gave a tiny shriek. 'Careful, Tom, careful!' she said over her shoulder, as if the eggshells and potato peelings constituted grave danger.

'Sorry, sorry,' muttered Sarah.

'Let me help.' Tom's boots joined Camilla's kitten heels. He bent down, his hair almost brushing Sarah's face, to round up a recalcitrant box that had escaped.

Shivering at the almost-touch, Sarah took the small package from him. Shut out from the couple's nice ordinary happiness, she kept her head down and said, 'Have a great evening.'

The stars hung low over the house, and the growl of traffic on Kensington Park Road hinted at things to do, people to see. *Here I am,* thought Sarah, *picking up rubbish.*

The smell of coffee met her in the basement. 'Just the way you like it.' Mavis pushed the small cup towards her; like all its comrades it didn't have a matching saucer.

Sarah took her seat slowly, her eyes fixed on her hostess. 'Mavis, I know.'

Peck wheezed, and rattled the bars of his cage.

Still as a waxwork, Mavis said nothing.

'I *know*,' repeated Sarah. 'It's going to be . . .' It would be crass to tell a dying woman that everything would be 'OK'. 'We'll get through it.'

'How do you know?' Mavis challenged her. 'I've been so careful.'

'It's nothing to be ashamed of.'

'I beg to differ,' said Mavis under her breath.

Sarah tossed the cardboard packet Tom had handed her onto the table. 'Rilutek, Mavis. *Your* Rilutek. It helps with the symptoms of your motor neurone disease. You can't just throw these tablets away. You *must* take them.'

Mavis reached for the box, turned it over in her hands.

'From now on,' said Sarah, 'I'll take care of you.' It was a huge promise, but it was easy to make. 'Just like you took care of your sister.'

Mavis put down the tablets. She tapped them once with her finger. 'These aren't mine.'

Sarah was gentle. 'Your name's on them.' She pointed to the printed sticker. 'See? Mavis Bennison, twenty-four Merrion Road.'

'Mavis Bennison was my sister.'

'You're confused,' said Sarah. '*You're* Mavis.'

'I'm not in the least confused, dear. I do not suffer from motor neurone disease. I am not Mavis. I set foot in this house for the first time eight months ago. I'm Zelda Bennison.'

The hairs on Sarah's arms lifted. 'This is a delusion, Mavis. Let's sit quietly until you feel better.'

'Here I am, confessing at last, and you don't believe me?' The woman with two names stood up. 'Mavis, my sister,

301

is dead. I know, because I killed her.' She fetched a bottle of whisky from a shelf and set it down on the table. 'We're going to need this.'

The shot of whisky rattled Sarah's sinuses. 'You really think you're Zelda?' she said eventually.

'I know I'm Zelda!' Whoever she was, she was exasperated. 'Why not let me talk, dear, and see what you think when I'm finished. Deal?'

The Mavis Situation had distorted completely. *Perhaps it's now the Zelda Situation.* 'I'm listening.'

'There's the "why" of it, and then there's the "how". I'll start with the "why".'

Another sip of whisky for them both. They regarded each other with carefully composed faces. Suddenly, the old lady opposite Sarah had become a stranger. Either she was Mavis and she was in an unreachable land of make-believe, or she was Zelda and she was a murderer.

I don't know what to call her.

The woman Sarah knew as Mavis took a deep breath, as if she stood on a diving board. 'It's not common knowledge that Mavis and I were twins. We were never dressed alike, even as children. Similar in every physical regard, we were polar opposites in personality. As if the gods played a trick on us.'

Their parents' glacial indifference, she said, might have pushed the little girls together, but the Bennison girls were never close. 'Mavis was born angry. I tried. I would have loved a confidante. But she rejected me. And all of us.'

Mavis duelled with nannies and pinched her twin black and blue. 'Hard to believe when you only knew Mavis in her bleak years, but as a child she was full of energy. All of it negative, unfortunately. If there was nobody around to torment, Mavis raged at the mirror. The luxuriously appointed family home was a bed of nails. 'Mother and Dad led their own lives. We had the status of expensive pets. Granny lived with us. Well, she was in the same house, but locked away, a source of shame as she descended into what my parents called madness, but would now be diagnosed as frontotemporal dementia. She was shown no kindness. Mavis and I spent our childhoods plotting our escapes. From our parents, from the memory of poor Granny.' The woman closed her eyes. 'From each other.'

The whisky glowed like plutonium in Sarah's stomach.

'I left home the moment I could.' This woman who claimed to be Zelda gave a first-person version of the biography Sarah knew from the back covers of the Chief Inspector Shackleton novels. 'I had no qualifications. How I got a job at Faber and Faber publishing I'm not sure, but they took a chance on me and I started at the bottom, once I'd learned to type. Badly.'

This is taking a toll, thought Sarah, listening to the voice dry out and watching the hands writhe together. Whoever she was – Sarah could only think of her as Mavis – she didn't seem confused. She was purposeful. Sure of her facts. It was as if a genie trapped in a bottle had finally escaped; the 'confession' had a momentum of its own.

Sedated by the Scotch, Sarah allowed her mind to open just a crack. To take the tale seriously. She listened for a bum note, anything that jarred. 'You married your boss, didn't you?'

'He wasn't my immediate boss.' Charles Mulqueeny was her mentor, said Zelda or Mavis or whoever the hell she was. They fell in love neatly, elegantly: 'it felt *right*'. Then came the meteoric success of the first book. Literary fame. A high-minded, well-connected life. 'I was happy and – silly, silly me – I took that happiness for granted.'

A thought embedded itself in Sarah's brain. Like a pearl growing inside an oyster, it grew, gained lustre. *What if*, she thought, *what if this is all true?* Sarah knew the woman opposite to be kind and tough and useful. She studied the eyes. And they told her.

'You're not Mavis,' she interrupted. The twins' bodies were identical, even their striking blue eyes were the same shape and colour. But the expression in their eyes was entirely different. Their souls weren't twinned; nobody can clone a soul. This woman hadn't transformed into a warm and loving person. She hadn't been rehabilitated. She'd always been that way. 'You're Zelda Bennison, and you're my friend.'

Zelda put her hands to her lips as if praying. She couldn't speak for a few seconds. 'Thank you,' she managed, eventually. 'It's hard denying who you really are.'

Another whisky. A warm silence. Sarah encouraged her to go on. *I need to hear this and she needs to say it.*

'While I got on with my life, Mavis embedded herself into the fabric of this house like a tick. Ignoring the world.' And above all, resenting her sister's success.

Like a scientific experiment into the effects of lifestyle on health, Mavis had embraced all that was bad for her, while Zelda sought out only what was wholesome. 'She neglected herself,' Zelda said of her sibling, 'as if she was a worthless toy. All her stories about my neglect of Mother and Dad, and indeed of *her*, were tosh. She ran away from our family home in the middle of the night, not long after I married Charles. This would be, let me see, more than fifty years ago. I tracked her down.' Zelda looked about her at the squat walls, sweating with damp. 'To number twenty-four Merrion Road.'

There was no welcome. Outside, London was swinging through the sixties, but Mavis, her face sour, hair scraped back, looked 'as if she'd bypassed youth altogether and landed in miserable middle age. She wouldn't let me past the front step. When Mavis left the family behind it wasn't a plea for attention; she genuinely wanted rid of us.'

As Sarah listened to Zelda, she had to remind herself that Mavis was dead. How she came to be that way would possibly test the limits of friendship. *Just as Zelda said it would.*

'I sent Christmas cards and birthday cards, invited her to my home. I kept visiting, even when Mavis stopped answering the door. I used to steal around the side of the house and tap at that window. The only answer I ever got was Peck screeching at me to go away.' On the last of those doleful visits, Mavis came out to tell Zelda she was moving away. 'Despite her lifestyle,' Zelda gave a weary look about her, 'Mavis was a wealthy woman and could live as she pleased. Our parents quite rightly left her everything.'

That was the most gracious response Sarah had ever heard to being left out of a will. 'But Mavis didn't move out, did she?'

'The promised change of address card never arrived. I assumed she'd moved on and I'd lost her. Mavis bamboozled me so I'd leave her alone.'

'Tell me about your first husband.'

'We were friends. We travelled. We worked. We would have welcomed children, but . . .' Zelda brought her shoulders up to her ears. 'Charles and I were in love from the day we met until he died.' Zelda shook her head. 'No, that's wrong. We're still in love, Sarah. Some bonds are unbreakable.' After his death, she kept calm and carried on. 'I didn't have you, my tame psychologist, to diagnose the shaking and the crying and the fracturing thoughts as a nervous breakdown. Then I saw light at the end of the tunnel.'

The light turned out to be a speeding train by the name of Ramon Kaur. 'His beauty blinded me. His desire proved I hadn't, after all, toppled into the grave alongside Charles.' The lust was fake; the ink was barely dry on the marriage licence before Ramon was using Zelda's credit card as a magic carpet to travel the world in luxury.

Sarah recalled the widower's waxed eyebrows at the funeral. 'Why didn't you leave Ramon?'

'Vanity, maybe. Certainly shame. I slunk away from my friends into a half-life, a place of shadows.' Now Zelda could see where she'd gone awry. 'All the missteps, all the wrong turns are obvious in retrospect.'

'Amen to that.' Sarah poured more whisky.

'Like a fool, I expected my second marriage to ease the pain of losing Charles. But I miss Charles in the marrow of my bones. It hurts, physically hurts.'

I want to love like that. Leo had never inspired such depth of feeling. Sarah knew a man who could, but he was locked into a different section of life's Venn diagram.

Zelda attended literary events, was snapped alongside the great and the good, but went home to a deserted townhouse each night. 'My publisher was waiting for another manuscript but I could barely compose a shopping list. My house felt unstable, as if the paintings might fall off the walls and the new kitchen might explode. No love, no writing, no family to lean back on.'

'Oh, Mavis. I mean Zelda.' Sarah pulled in her chin, appalled at herself.

'I get it wrong myself,' said Zelda charitably.

'At the funeral . . . *your* funeral, one of your friends, a tall lady, flamboyant hat . . .'

'That was Miriam,' smiled Zelda.

'She wished she'd been with you at the end. She didn't give up on you. There was real grief by that grave, Zelda.'

Sarah sensed Zelda parking the feelings, to return to them later. 'Shall we take a walk? The whisky and the confession are having quite an effect on me.'

For the first time since summer began, they needed to wear jackets. They turned left at the gate, towards the main drag. Sarah had almost vetoed the idea of a walk as too tiring, before remembering that Zelda didn't have motor neurone disease. She hoped the night air would help to clear her head, put the jigsaw together in the proper order.

'Last year, out of the blue, Mavis wrote to me, via my agent.' Zelda kept a careful distance between herself and Sarah as they walked. 'The letter was brief. Basically "I'm sick, come visit".' Zelda, surprised and 'slightly embittered' that Mavis was still at the same address, found her sister greatly altered. 'She was so grey. I don't just mean her hair. She was transparent, a wraith surviving on malice.'

'I recognised you that night.' Sarah recalled leaning over the bannister when Mavis came upstairs to deliver the letter that Smith had returned. That tranquil face was the one before Sarah now. *It seems so obvious.*

Sarah had misread another person close to her.

They were at the corner of Holland Park Avenue, the street lights bleaching the cars that flew past. Zelda recalled being permitted at last into the musty labyrinth of Flat E. 'Mavis said she was sorry about Charles's death. She said it brusquely, of course; Mavis never mastered tenderness. She said, "That new husband of yours looks like a good-for-nothing."' Zelda stopped. They were outside a framer's studio but she was evidently in her own past. 'I didn't defend Ramon. There was no point lying to Mavis. I felt something I hadn't felt for years, the uncanny communication that flows between twins.' She blinked, her mouth turned down. 'Whether they like it or not. Mavis knew all about Ramon and, in a flash, I knew all about her.'

The cord between them had glittered darkly, like coal.

'She was ill,' said Sarah.

'She was, as she put it, going the way of Granny. She said, "Mother was right: I do take after her." She wasn't in the least bit sorry for herself. Even though we both remembered Granny naked and sobbing.'

'Frontotemporal dementia.'

Zelda nodded. 'Apparently Mavis's doctor wouldn't be drawn on how long she could expect to live. He said it might be ten years, it could be two. Mavis knocked everything off his desk and shouted, "Thanks for nothing."'

'Good old Mavis,' said Sarah, nostalgic for her awfulness. They trawled on, past a chip shop and its vinegary bouquet.

'Mother's assertion that Mavis took after Granny affected Mavis like a curse. She'd spent her life waiting for the dementia to pounce, until suddenly ... gotcha!' Zelda pulled her thin coat around her; an ancient cloth number of Mavis's, it was greasy with age. 'She was almost gleeful about it. I put my foot down. Told her she was coming home with me. That I'd look after her, that there'd be no shame, no struggle, no lack of love.'

'Zelda,' said Sarah, still wary of the name. 'That was the speech I prepared for you.'

Zelda stopped and looked at Sarah's face. 'Thank you,' she said simply, and Sarah felt as if the sun had elbowed the moon out of the way for a moment.

'Mavis was sarcastic about my offer. Said she could imagine how Ramon would react to having a "mad old trout" in the house. And then came the killer punch. She was suffering with motor neurone disease.'

'As well?' Sarah reeled.

'Apparently it often comes along for the ride with dementia. Mavis painted a grim picture for me. She said, "The MND is weakening my limbs. My muscles will waste away. I already have trouble swallowing." It had many symptoms in common with frontotemporal dementia. Or, as Mavis put it, she'd have a double helping of uncontrollable screaming and carrying-on. Eventually, she could anticipate paralysis and not being able to catch her breath.'

'Jesus.' Sarah shivered.

'I tried to tell her about a dear friend of mine who lives with MND, confined to a cumbersome bed but amongst his family. I used rather flowery language, I'm afraid. Something like it didn't have to be a dark descent, that we could light lamps along the way.'

'That's beautiful,' said Sarah.

'Mavis just laughed. Her whole life had been a dark descent, she said. I felt powerless in the face of her cynicism but

I insisted we put a plan in place. That's when she told me she already had one.'

'Go on.'

'Mavis seemed proud that her MND was fast-moving. She'd already spent a day lying on the floor, apparently. I asked why she hadn't called out to her neighbours for help and she said, "Them? Don't be stupid. All those trashy books you write, but you don't have the first idea about real people." She made a point of telling me, very proudly, that she'd never read a single book of mine. Then she showed me her arsenal of medication. She said . . . she said, "These keep me alive, and they can help me die."'

'Suicide,' said Sarah.

'She was brisk, excited, as if we were discussing a holiday. She wanted to take control, she said. She wanted to "go". Mavis assured me she wasn't depressed, just opting out of a life that had never held much charm for her and could only get worse. She'd worked out that an overdose of Rilutek – the tablets you found – plus an overdose of the SSRI she took for her mood instability would do the trick, as she put it. Given her condition, it would look accidental.'

'What did you say to all this?'

'I fought dirty. Mavis was a devout Christian, despite her ungodly behaviour. I told her that she couldn't destroy the life her God had given her.'

The pause lengthened as they reached Pembridge Gardens. 'But *you* could,' said Sarah.

'Precisely. Mavis summoned me to help her die.'

'Not kill her, Zelda.' Sarah saw the vital difference.

Zelda ignored the interjection. 'She was blunt. If I wouldn't help, she'd pay somebody to do it. My sister was smug, as if she'd won, as if I'd already agreed. But I couldn't countenance it. Then she began to talk to me about *my* life, as if she'd been watching me on CCTV. All my unhappiness poured out of a mouth shaped exactly like my own.'

Mavis was a grimy mirror for Zelda, reminding her of the loss of Charles, the writer's block, the PR demands, the failure of her second marriage, the lack of home comforts, the pound signs in Ramon's eyes.

'Only a twin I'd shared a womb with could read me like that. Mavis laid out my life like a threadbare rag.'

'She left out hope,' said Sarah.

'She always did. I just thought "yes, yes, she's so right". She whispered, "Nobody can tell us apart, so why not let Zelda die? When I go, you can carry on as me. Leave all your mess behind and start again."'

'The writer in you felt the lure of the clean page.'

'I wouldn't put it so charmingly: I should have resisted and I didn't. I gave in. I was never at ease with it, but like your friend Smith, it snowballed.'

'It must have felt good to be with Mavis after years of estrangement.'

'You're so kind to make excuses for me, but yes, I felt happy to have my twin back.' Zelda pushed her hand through her hair, exposing her high, dignified brow. 'Shall we head home? I think we've covered the "why". I need to sit down to tackle the "how".'

Indoors again, up in the eaves, Zelda sat back in Tom's chair. 'It was like plotting a novel.' Mavis had told nobody of her illness; the collapses and lapses had – tragically, to Sarah's ears – all happened behind closed doors. 'As for me, I was, and remain, as fit as a flea. My medical history could be written on the back of a stamp. The first step was for Mavis to visit a new GP, purporting to be me.'

'But, Mavis was . . .' Sarah shrugged. 'A mess! No doctor would think she was a famous authoress.'

'We tidied her up. She fitted into my clothes and I wrestled some make-up onto her face. We were twins, when all was said and done.'

The medical aspect of the plan was the most problematical, the most likely to fail. Yet it had gone like clockwork. Mavis, dressed up and perfumed, signed on with a new surgery as Zelda. Awed by his famous new patient, the GP nervously broke the terrible news that she was suffering from both frontotemporal dementia and the early stages of motor neurone disease. Mavis staged a theatrical meltdown in front of him, and from then on the GP gladly visited his celebrity charge at home, noting that her mental state was deteriorating with frightening speed. The real Zelda was impressed by Mavis's acting ability; she was the image of their Granny whenever the doctor called.

'You told nobody at all?'

'The plan could only work if Zelda – if I – died without

her friends – my friends – around. It was cruel of me. I emailed my closest friends, told them I was feeling poorly, that I'd gone to visit my sister and she'd insisted on looking after me. There were responses, puzzled and worried, but after a while I stopped checking my inbox.' She looked at Sarah. 'I was committed, you see. I had to cut the ties, Sarah.'

'Zelda, I'm not judging you.'

'Is that my therapist talking?'

'No, it's your slightly pissed friend talking.'

Zelda smiled. Despite the gravity of her story, she was shedding ballast as she came clean. She looked down at her scruffy tartan dress, out of fashion since before Sarah was born. 'Mavis stayed in, out of sight, as she grew more and more ill. I began to wear her clothes. The tint in my hair grew out and I washed it in washing-up liquid, like she did. I scrubbed my hands until they were as raw and cracked as her poor fingers.' All Zelda's pricey moisturisers were thrown out, and she cleaned her face with soap. 'I aban-doned the house I'd bought with Charles, all my possessions, my jewellery, my books . . .' Zelda put a hand across her eyes. 'Forgive me. Sometimes it hits me.'

'Take a moment.' It was as if a fire had ravaged Zelda's home. *A fire she set herself.* 'You hung on to some of your clothes.' Sarah reminded her of the finery she'd found in the wardrobe.

'I should have got rid of them. They were a clue.'

'I didn't pick up on it.'

'I remonstrated with you for seeing only the best in Leo, but your tendency to find beauty in people meant you didn't suspect me. You really do follow the instructions in your father's letter, and I used that against you.' Zelda sighed, moved on. 'As soon as my make-under was complete, I ventured out in Mavis's hand-me-downs. She took to her bed, gratefully. The effort had taken its toll. The plan was solid, but it required such *nerve*. Just encountering you in the hall was a potential disaster. I didn't need to act much in the beginning; blind fear can turn the most mild-mannered woman into a harpy.'

'What about money?' Sarah's mind was on the practicalities. 'Your will, or Mavis's will, no, hang on, *your* will?'

'It's complicated, isn't it? Mavis's strategy was straightforward. I took over her bank account, remembering to sign my name with an M instead of a Z. Our wills remained exactly as they were. When I die, Mavis's fortune will go to a cat charity.'

'She hated cats!'

'I know. My will left half of everything to Ramon, with various other bequests. It's odd to think of my friends wearing my jewellery while I'm still alive. Sometimes I think the ramifications of what we did will drive me insane.'

'Why don't we pause there?' Sarah was exhausted just listening. 'Let's get some sleep and you can tell me the rest tomorrow.'

Grateful, Zelda allowed Sarah to walk her to her front door. She asked her to wait there a moment, as Peck flung his water bowl about and told Sarah what he thought of her.

'Peck knows.' Zelda reappeared with a stack of paper held together with a heavy-duty elastic band. 'He's the only one who saw through me.'

'Silly cow,' said Peck.

'He misses Mavis,' said Zelda.

'What is this?' Sarah turned the bundle over in her hands.

'It's a present,' said Zelda. 'From me to you. The real me to the real you.'

Chapter Twenty

In the small hours, Notting Hill belonged to Sarah.

A cafetière (her second) cooling on a low table, Sarah lifted her eyes from the page and stood up from the embrace of Tom's chair. Wandering with a yawn to the kitchen, she gazed out over her empire of jagged roof shapes and pot-bellied chimneys. Here and there a slab of light showed, as houses woke up.

Almost dawn.

The manuscript on her lap had refused to let Sarah go to bed. *Our Meeting Place was Midnight* was the fortieth novel by Zelda Bennison.

'Take this. Tell me what you think,' Zelda had said, stunning Sarah with the responsibility. 'I gave up writing, but writing wouldn't give *me* up.'

At first, Zelda told her, the book had come to life slowly. A scribbled character sketch on the back of a gas bill. A line about the sun hitting the grass in number twenty-four's garden. Then the story ambushed her, and she'd typed compulsively on the laptop she'd smuggled into the house among discounted onions in Mavis's string shopping bag.

There was a simple dedication.

For my friend
Sarah Lynch

Our Meeting Place was Midnight was a cathedral of a book. Romantic, mysterious, a complete departure from Chief Inspector Shackleton. Sarah imagined banging on Jane's door and handing her a warm-from-the-oven Zelda Bennison.

I'm a book club with a membership of one.

Nobody else would ever read Zelda's prose about life's wrong turnings, about how tricky it is to reverse down a one-way street. Zelda's peculiar life after death had inspired her; her writer's block had given way to manic industry.

Death and rebirth was the theme. Appropriate for a night-long reading. Appropriate, too, for Sarah's long coma. She'd thought that only Leo's kiss could awaken her, but no. Tom's lips had revived her. *Tom made me realise I can love.*

But being loved? That was more tricky.

Morning asserted itself. A cat stretched on next door's shed. Plastic sheeting fluttered on a half-built conservatory further down the road.

The revelations of the night before didn't seem so extraordinary now: Zelda was the same person whatever she called herself. She was Sarah's buddy, and her confidante. What *was* extraordinary was how blithely Sarah had accepted a totally different woman in Mavis's place

And I call myself a people person. It was just as well Sarah hadn't given into Keeley's pleas and gone back to working with children.

Sarah had never had a proper conversation with the original Mavis. Keen to get away from the negativity, the cynicism, the – if she was honest – walking talking avatar of sexless old age, Sarah always had one foot out the door when they met. As if Mavis was Medusa, Sarah had never looked her in the eye.

The only resemblance between the sisters was physical. No matter how she tried, Zelda had been unable to disguise her vivacity and her wit and her enthusiasm for her fellow man. The irritable outbursts were results of the unique stress Zelda was under.

The anxiety about Mavis's/Zelda's health had lifted cleanly away, but Sarah knew her friend would need help with adjusting to the new half-life she'd fashioned for herself. *I made the right decision, digging my heels in and staying at number twenty-four.*

It wasn't that Mavis felt like family; Sarah's own family ties had proved feeble. Perhaps her gut certainty was a pale version of the Bennison twins' bond. Asking somebody to help you die is a test of solidarity.

Is there anybody I could ask?

Sarah's treacherous subconscious put forward a name.

Smith.

Jane would talk her out of it; and perhaps she'd be right to do so. It was a one-of-a-kind decision that can't be imagined. Smith, though, was the sort of twisted broken soul who would simply agree. *Smith understands pain.*

Since the Southwold trip, Sarah had been unable to look back on Smith with equanimity. She mistrusted all the small delights she remembered, wondering if Smith had ever meant any of it.

Now, Sarah could accept that, yes, Smith had been her friend at one time. Her supporter. Her conspirator. Before that impetuous lie which Sarah understood with her head but hated with her heart.

There had been understanding. Kindness had flowed in both directions. *Smith could tell by looking at my face exactly what kind of day I'd had.*

The soft spillage of Sarah's tummy groused. Her mouth a thin line, she rode the wave of nausea; it was familiar by now, she knew how to deal with it.

Funny how women carry around the makings of life as casually as we carry a tray of tea things.

Our Meeting Place was Midnight, with its riffs on birth and rebirth, its insistence that nothing is wasted, resonated with Sarah. Over-caffeinated, dizzy from lack of sleep, she drew a whimsical line from herself to all living things. At peace but powerful, she felt something shift and change inside her.

As if she'd conjured him up, Tom was down in the garden. Head down, one hand on his hip, his long strong legs smoothly muscled, he was a classical statue.

Although Michelangelo's David doesn't wear boxers from Gap.

Something had drawn Tom outside, his hair still tousled from the pillow, a sweatshirt thrown on inside out.

Later, Sarah would blame the dreamlike texture of the dawn. A crack between night and day, it was a moment out of time when the unsayable could be said. Emboldened, she leapt up.

When she approached him in the mauve fog, Tom seemed more real than he had from the window.

He's sad. Sarah tugged her cardigan around herself, bare feet squeaking on the dew.

'Look,' said Tom.

The shapes on the ground looked like torn snatches of fabric, but they were Mikey. Something had torn him apart.

'I promised Una he'd be OK.'

Sarah blinked and the magic dissolved, leaving just the cold birth of another day.

'Come inside.' Sarah tugged at Tom's arm, the feel of him sending a tremor through her even in these conditions. 'I'll . . . clear up out here.'

'Nah.' Tom shook his head. 'I'll look after him.' He stared down at what used to be Mikey. 'Poor little sod.'

'You're freezing, Tom. Back to bed with you.' Sarah wanted to save him from the sadness, to protect him.

'Camilla's up there. I don't want to, you know, talk.'

Thank God I didn't declare myself. Sarah had narrowly avoided yet another embarrassment.

Tom looked at her, his face raw. 'Why do things have to end?'

'Because they do.' Sarah hoped it didn't sound like a cop-out. It was a brutal fact; things ended, like the blazing summer they'd just lived through, like Mikey's modest life, but if nothing ended there'd be no beginnings. Sarah didn't say that in case she sounded like her Confucius calendar. Her insides contracted, as if a hand firmly clutched her there, and she gasped.

'You OK?' Tom seemed to fully notice her.

'I'm fine.' Tom's dawn crisis wasn't just about Mikey. 'Good things end, but so do bad things. After all these years waiting for a real acting job, you're going to be famous, Tom.'

When he flinched, Sarah carried on, following her instincts. 'You'll live up to the hype. You're good at what you do. I can sense you're scared of fame, but it doesn't always destroy. You're strong, Tom. Don't run away from the very thing you've been praying for.'

Tom stared. Sarah thought how lovely his face looked when he was sad. He said, 'You really *see* people.'

'I really see *you*.'

His face drifted closer, his mouth driving the rest of him towards Sarah's lips. This moment felt right and just; as if it *must* happen.

The slap of feet on grass brought them back from the brink.

Racing over the lawn, much-washed nightie flapping, Una threw herself to her knees. The sound she made – or *didn't* make – was horrible: a hoarse zero.

Tom squatted beside her, turning her little face to his chest. 'Don't, sweetheart. Don't look.'

Brought to her senses, Sarah ran to the shed, riffling the shelves for something to scoop Mikey up with. She glanced up and saw Camilla, wide awake at a window; Una had saved the innocent woman from collateral damage.

I only just handed in my notice as the Other Woman. Sarah had no desire to be anybody's contingency plan. She needed something – someone – of her own.

Startled from her bed, Lisa came out and held her daughter, whose tears welled up from some bottomless source.

'Why didn't I clear it up the moment I saw it?' Tom, grim, took the dustpan from Sarah. 'Instead of standing about like a fool.'

'Nothing foolish about grief.' Sarah unrolled a bin liner and tore it off with a snap. 'I don't want to put Mikey in one of these but . . .'

'I know.' Tom coaxed gory body parts onto the dustpan. 'What else can we do?'

Summoned, Graham turned up. Sarah detected bemusement at such fuss over a hedgehog, but he made the right noises.

As Tom was tying up the bin bag, he stopped and said, 'You know what? Mikey deserves a funeral.'

All adults remember the sombre goldfish/budgie/mouse burials of their childhoods. Jane and Zelda emerged readily when asked to be mourners. Sarah locked eyes meaningfully with Zelda as they stood around the bin bag, hoping to convey that she wouldn't slip, wouldn't call her by her real name. Zelda was twitchy, and Sarah recognised this as the nervousness she and Jane had mistaken first for irritability and later for illness, when really the woman lived in fear.

Leo and Helena weren't invited.

'We need a coffin . . .' Sarah looked about her.

'Will this do?' Camilla, in an over-sized shirt that was evidently Tom's, approached them, holding out a cardboard box. 'It's from a gorgeous clutch bag Tom bought me,' she explained. 'You all right, babes?' Camilla took Tom's hand and he nodded.

The service was brief. There's only so much even the most sympathetic preacher can find to say about a hedgehog. 'He was loved,' said Tom in a gruff voice, as the Whistles box was lowered into the hole Graham had dug.

'Aww!' said Camilla. 'Poor Mickey.'

'*Mikey!*' Jane was curt.

As damp earth was heaped over Mikey's remains, the little crowd were at a loss. 'Why not come up to mine for breakfast?' said Sarah recklessly, wondering how she'd stretch a few eggs to feed them all.

'Wasn't it sweet?' Camilla said as the residents trundled upstairs, hushed and thinking of mortality. 'Hey,' she nudged Sarah. 'You still shagging your ex?' She recoiled from the shock on Sarah's face. 'Shit. Is it like a secret?'

'It *was*.'

'I'm such a big mouth. Ignore me.' Reaching the flat, Camilla volunteered to scramble the eggs Sarah fetched from the fridge. 'You have a nice little sit-down,' she said, as if Sarah was Mikey's widow.

The little crowd perked up at the life-affirming prospect of food. Sarah looked around for Zelda, but she'd slipped away. For her, this was the morning after a momentous night before.

'We don't have to stop loving Mikey.' Sarah cupped Una's wan little moon of a face in her hands. 'People and animals die, but love *can't* die.'

'We'll get you another hedgehog.' Graham was trying his best. There was a sea change in him, and Lisa too; the faint resentment that coloured all their exchanges with Sarah was kept at bay. She read the subtitles; they were ready to help their daughter.

I have to be ready to let them. It was fundamentally, wildly unprofessional to feel possessive of a patient; it was also natural. A therapist has to tap into their heart at the same time as rigidly ring-fencing it; Una had breached Sarah's defences without even trying.

With Jane as sous chef, Camilla did a fine job on the egg-scrambling-for-the-masses front. So fine a job that the ungenerous might deduce she was showing a certain man what a catch she was. Sarah turned away from her own pettiness and sat in the pink armchair – ironically now a sanctuary – slightly apart from Una and her parents, to give them some space.

Tom, lurking, reached for the manuscript on the coffee table.

'No!' Sarah shook her head, and he approached her, a mug in his hand. 'Sorry. That's private.'

Tom sat on the arm of the chair. He was very close. Which shouldn't have mattered, but mattered a lot. 'You'd better have a sesh with Una later. She's going to need you.'

'I think she has all she needs.' They watched Lisa and Graham, hunched over Una as if she was a hothouse plant. 'I'll wait a couple of days.'

'I'll miss Mikey.' Tom went into a reverie. 'Him and his silly one-eyed face. When I was Una's age my uncle died. The finality of it was like a maths problem. I approached it from every angle but I couldn't make any sense of it.' He sighed. 'Still can't.'

'Loss,' said Sarah, hating the word. 'It doesn't have to be death, though.' She thought of Leo, the man she'd lost; not the bully one floor below but the lover she'd married. She thought of her mother: alive, healthy, utterly lost to her. 'Take my mum. We haven't spoken in, ooh, five years.'

'What the hell happened?' Tom shook himself. 'Ignore that. None of my business.'

'I can tell you if you like.' Sarah wanted to be Tom's business. 'Mum and Dad should never have had a second date, never mind a baby. He left when I was a little older than Una.'

'Did you feel abandoned?' asked Tom.

'Of course. Dad did his best. It wasn't about me, he said. I'd always be number one with him. Mum revealed some home truths I was too young to hear. Apparently my perfect dad had had affairs.'

Tom pulled an *ouch* face.

'Yeah, I know. She said he was sneaky. Like me.'

'Were you? Sneaky, I mean.'

'No more than the next kid. Mum punished Dad by keeping me away from him. Not all the time. She'd cancel at the last moment, ask for me to come home earlier, that kind of thing. So he could never be sure of seeing me.' *And I could never be sure of seeing him.*

'Nobody behaves well when they're hurt, do they?'

'Well, no.' Sarah wasn't accustomed to her mother having an advocate. In the courtroom in her head it was just her and Mum, engaged in an endless slanging match. 'Mum blamed me.'

'For . . . ?'

'Everything!' Sarah laughed at how irrational that sounded. 'She said I ruined her life.' She found herself telling him about her own muteness, about the holiday with her father that had ended her silence.

The intensity of Tom's concentration encouraged her. His eyes never left her, and he made the right noises as she talked. They'd come a long way; there were few people Sarah trusted with this story. *Tom seems to have forgiven the name-calling, and the kiss in front of his girlfriend.*

327

'So, the reason you were able to talk again was because of the lack of pressure from your dad?'

'Exactly.' It was nice to be understood, and even nicer when the person doing the understanding was somebody whose clothes you wanted to tear off. 'Dad was a natural parent. Showing love without losing authority came easily to him. Mum ... she struggled. The responsibility was too much for her.' Sarah understood her mother. Forgiveness, however, was trickier. 'When we came back from Spain, Mum was pleased, obviously, that I was talking again but she was sullen that the breakthrough had happened with Dad. Mum wouldn't let him see me after that. She made excuse after excuse.' She produced the note out of her pocket. 'So he wrote to me.'

'You still have it.' Tom's strong face moved into soft focus, leaving Sarah wondering how he did that. The note was flimsy in his hand. He read it aloud.

'If I can't see you then I have to write to you! I have no news, no nothing except some advice which you must take to heart. Promise? Be yourself, because, my sweet Sarah, you are more than good enough. And always find the beauty in everybody, because that's the magic formula to make everything A-OK.'

Sarah said, 'It arrived the day after he died.'

Tom stared.

'Heart attack. Out of the blue.' Sarah pressed her lips together.

'You poor little kid.' Tom's voice was feather-light but sympathetic.

'I didn't know that the holiday would be the last time I'd ever see him. But I have his note.' Sarah waved it and smiled, as best she could.

'It's the exact opposite of your mum's manifesto.'

Sarah exhaled loudly, causing Lisa and Graham's heads to swivel. 'They think I'm a bit too teary for a dead hedgehog.'

'Not any old hedgehog,' said Tom. 'Did you decide to stop talking to your mum, or was it a row or ...?'

'It was Leo. Mum came for supper every week, to our old flat over by Queensway. Leo had to put up with me clenching like a mussel shell before she arrived, then listen to her poking holes in me all through the meal, and then try to sleep as I tossed and turned beside him, going over it all in my head. One evening Mum went too far. I can't even remember what she said, just more of the usual, and Leo stood up and told her what he thought of her.'

'And what did he think of her?' Tom stroked his chin.

'That she had no right to intrude on our marriage, that she made me unhappy, that I was a different person when she was around. True, every word of it. Mum got into a strop and spouted her usual melodramatic nonsense – "I'll never set foot in this house again" blah blah blah – and Leo said "Good" and off she went.' Sarah's energy petered out. She rarely talked or even thought about that night. 'And that was that. I send a card at Christmas and birthdays, but nothing ever comes back.' *She could be dead.* The thought scorched Sarah.

'So, let me get this right ... you're estranged from your mother because Leo said so?'

'No, no, it wasn't like that.'

'Wasn't it? Maybe I've got Leo all wrong, but he doesn't seem the philanthropic sort. Sounds like *he* couldn't stand having your mum around.'

'He saw the toll it took on me. Leo did it for me.'

'If you say so.' Tom was dubious. Silent for a while, he dipped his head and said, rapidly, quietly, 'It wouldn't have worked, you know.' He was eye to eye with Sarah; this close, his eyes were tigerish. 'You and me.'

We're talking about it at last. 'I shouldn't have called you names, Tom.'

'That doesn't matter. You thought I deserved them. But it would have been a disaster, wouldn't it?' He held her gaze. 'You and me.'

'Yes, yes, a disaster,' said Sarah, because she had to. Because it was the right thing to say. Her voice sank to a whisper. 'But do you ever wonder what if?'

'Eggs!' said Camilla, thrusting a plate of yellow gloop between them.

Tom's efforts not to look guilty made him look guilty as hell. He followed Camilla back to the kitchen, saying over his shoulder, 'Sarah, seriously, you should call your mum.'

He didn't answer my question.

*

Keeley pulled a face. 'You're twenty minutes late because of a hedgehog funeral? It's original, I'll give you that.' She turned back to her computer screen. 'I'm interviewing somebody for reception next week, Sarah. Nice guy, great references, experienced.' She tapped a key here, a key there. 'This is where you fall to the ground and beg me for your old job back, by the way.'

Sarah left the office noiselessly.

*

The flat was cleaner than it had ever been. The estate agent, Richard, had impressed on Sarah just how lucky she was for his client to even cast his pampered eyes over her home.

'If he likes it he'll snap it up. Just like that. Are you ready to talk money straight away?'

'I, um, God, well, yes, I suppose.'

She had strict instructions to stay out of the way. 'My client's a very private person.' With a last neurotic glance at the pink chair, the sideboard, the new curtains, Sarah bolted down to Jane's flat. Tom was diplomatically out; Sarah was glad and disappointed. She was becoming adept at handling opposing emotions at the same time.

'Maybe the client's famous,' said Jane.

'Will you help me with the negotiations?'

'Duh,' said Jane. 'Have you seen Mavis since Mikey's send-off?' She sounded worried. Despite her mixed feelings for the old woman, Jane kept an eye on her health. 'The old bat's been very quiet.'

'She's fine,' said Sarah. The secret of Mavis's real identity chewed at her, just like the gnawing pain in her stomach which refused to go away. She cocked her head at a noise out in the hall. 'That's the estate agent!'

Jane opened her front door just a crack and she and Sarah jostled to peep out at the balding estate agent and his tall companion.

'Dark glasses?' scoffed Jane. 'At night? Poser.'

There was mumbled conversation at the foot of the stairs, the client looking around him at the communal hall. Sarah was torn between wanting him to be impressed and hoping he was horrified by the noticeboard and the scuffed floor. He could save her, this man she could only see in odd angles through the slit of door. But in saving her, he'd also take away the only security she had left.

Chapter Twenty-One

They were squealing like children at a funfair.

Jane said, 'You're sure? *Sure* sure?'

'Call me Mrs McSure. I couldn't be surer.'

They squealed again. They were thrilled but there was fear there, as well.

'This is a champagne moment!' said Jane.

A bottle stood in Sarah's fridge, glamorous among the cheddar and Lurpak, waiting for a special occasion. *Leo gave me this.* Sarah had hoped the special occasion would be Leo's return, once and for all. The Gods of Irony were busy today. 'Is champagne appropriate? I mean, under the circs?'

'One glass can't hurt!'

The bubbles leapt in the crystal flutes that had been a wedding present from the staff at St Chad's; Leo had let Sarah keep them when they divided their worldly goods because they were 'only factory-made'.

Jane put down her glass. 'Is this the right time, though? Doing it alone . . .'

'It's never the right time,' said Sarah. 'Which means it's *always* the right time.'

Support was pledged, and accepted, and cried over a little.

When Jane left, Sarah poured the rest of the champagne down the sink as Leo's loud mangling of an operatic aria in the shower seeped up through the floorboards. Sarah grasped the nettle and called him as soon as the singing stopped.

'Darling!' Leo's voice was hot in her ear. 'At last. You've been laying low and, oh God, I've missed you. Helena's being an absolute cow and I—'

'Leo!' Sarah shushed him. Oily Richard had rung her at the clinic to burble that he was 'very, very confident' that his client was about to make an offer. 'We need to talk.'

'Never good when a woman says that. Now?'

'Can you give me an hour?'

'Excellent. She Who Must Be Obeyed will be having her toes polished or her chakra spray painted or something. See you in one hour, delicious girl.'

*

The delicious girl had an appointment at the organic farm cafe with two friends. Both Zelda and Mavis sat opposite

Sarah in a booth. The venue, she'd thought, would suit Zelda, but she regretted her decision. Although Zelda Bennison was a woman of the world, she was dressed as Mavis Bennison, and therefore looked as out of place as a snail on a Rolls Royce.

'I see now why you fainted at the carnival,' said Sarah. 'You're frightened of being outed as, well, *yourself.*'

'I fainted because I saw my agent in the crowd.' Zelda nodded at Sarah's surprise. 'Yes. I used to speak to her once or twice a day. We even went on trips together after Charles died.'

'Did she see you?'

'No. Mavis and I ...' Zelda put her hand to her mouth and leaned over the table, whispering, 'My sister and I relied on the fact that nobody looks twice at a dishevelled old woman.' Zelda fell quiet until the waitress finished setting down their drinks. 'If people believe that an author has died they don't expect to see her large as life on the street, therefore they *don't* see her.'

Unasked, Zelda spoke about the night that Mavis died.

Of the hours before the death, she said little, just that the tablets were counted out and then counted again. There were enough to do the job, but not enough to cause suspicion. 'It had to look like accidental suicide by a confused old lady. When, in fact, Mavis was calm, and in total control.'

Zelda recalled asking one last time, was she sure? 'Mavis gave me a *stinker* of a look.' Zelda skimmed over the convulsions and the pain, limiting herself to the loaded observation that when the final coma descended, it was a blessing. Dreamily, Zelda recalled, 'I clambered onto the bed beside her. As if we were six again, and frightened of a thunderstorm. I lay beside her. Her breath grew laboured. And I realised something. Mavis didn't want me with her to appease God. I was there because my sister needed me. Mavis wanted to be held while she slipped away.'

'And after that, *you* were Mavis.'

'Her life tightened around me like a corset. I was grieving for Mavis, in shock at what I'd done, and full of regret. I was a walking dead woman, Sarah.' She stopped and put her head to one side. 'Until I met you.'

'Why did you tell me? You could have carried on indefinitely with the pretence.'

'Good question.' When Zelda pursed her lips and narrowed her eyes it amazed Sarah that this sharp, clever creature had ever passed as Mavis. 'I told you partly because you're my friend, and I've hurt too many friends with this deceit. Partly because I knew you'd understand. Partly because I'm turning into Mavis.' Zelda's mouth turned down. 'The poverty of her horizons, the lack of intimacy, the lack of comfort ... bitterness has grown over me like moss. I'm losing my attachment to the world. Then you told me about your mutism as a child, and how you trusted your father enough to speak. Well, I trust *you*, so I spoke.'

There was a silver poignancy to that moment in the farm shop cafe. Sarah felt connected to Zelda, to her father, to all the strugglers and triers. 'I'm glad you did.'

'I'm amazed nobody guessed. I slipped up so many times.'

'But even then we didn't suspect. You didn't recognise Lisa in the corner shop and she told everybody you'd snubbed her, which was classic Mavis behaviour.'

'I didn't recognise her. I barely saw Lisa before my sister passed away.'

'Did you know that Mavis and Lisa were adversaries?'

'Mavis taught me all about her neighbours.'

'I'm getting a mental image of a schoolroom with Mavis as the teacher.'

'It was rather like that.'

'What did she tell you about me?'

'Are you sure you want to hear?'

Not now you've said that! 'Yes, I think.'

'Mavis told me you were, and I quote, "a fancy-pants doctor who wasn't clever enough to work with adults, and too thick to notice that your husband was bonking the tart in Flat B". End of quote. She was scathing about Smith.'

'She was right!'

'No, my sister was never right. She had the opposite of rose-tinted glasses.'

'Coal-tinted?'

'She saw only the bad in everybody. Whereas you, thanks to your father's advice, see the good.' Zelda sat up, pushing back her kapok hair. The cheekbones beneath her lacklustre skin jutted out like chic knives, her nose faultlessly drawn. A flash of Zelda's glamour shimmered and was gone.

'I misread your slip-ups as symptoms,' said Sarah. 'Not

recognising Lisa. When you asked if I had a husband. Thinking Smith was a man. They all added up to dementia as far as I was concerned.'

'Do you realise you hold my life in your hands?' Zelda looked impatient when Sarah laughed and told her not to be so dramatic. 'The stakes are high, Sarah. Why else would I be so anxious to keep my identity hidden? If you choose to tell the authorities, I'll be arrested. Not just for assisted suicide, but for the fraud of pretending to be Mavis. I'm a criminal twice over. If anybody were to spot me – my agent, even Ramon – we'd be talking in a prison visiting room, not this chichi cafe.'

'It would never come to that. The police would understand.'

'Hardly. I broke the law. I'd be infamous as the writer who faked her own death.'

'Keep your voice down.' Zelda's fear was infectious. Their corner booth felt exposed. *This is how Zelda feels every time she steps out of number twenty-four.*

'I have such a yearning to be free of my secret. To raise my voice right now and tell everybody in this cafe.'

'Don't, though,' said Sarah.

'I feel unclean. I want to live honestly again, without looking behind me, without *pretending*.'

'You'd pay a very high price for that honesty.' It would be all over Twitter in a millisecond.

'Mavis had a right to make decisions about her own life. Shouldn't I be able to talk about that?'

'Yes, you *should* be able to, but . . .'

Outside, September had turned sulky.

'Don't expect too much from Leo when you talk with him,' said Zelda, as they both peered sceptically at the sky.

'I'm not expecting anything,' said Sarah. 'I'll bring him up to date on the flat. As for the personal stuff . . . it's me who has to explain myself. I led him up the garden path.'

'Nonsense. He used you when you were vulnerable.'

'There *were* feelings involved, Zelda.' Only the two people inside a relationship know the truth. Only they know the texture of it, the warp and the weft. She changed the subject. To Tom. This was a subject she'd never tire of, even though he'd told her, in plain English, that they'd dodged a heart-shaped bullet. 'Tell me again how badly suited Tom and Camilla are!'

'I could be wrong. Age doesn't guarantee wisdom, as I proved by marrying a gold-digger in my seventies.'

'At least Ramon's handsome.'

'Yes, the sex was good.' Zelda rolled her eyes at Sarah's expression. 'I haven't healed over, dear. Surely we all deserve a romp in the hay? Come on. Let's get you home. The sooner you anaesthetise old Leo the Lion the better.'

He was bang on time.

'So, darling, we need to talk? What about? Global warming?' Leo fluttered his eyelashes, mock contrite. 'Sorry. We're being terribly, terribly serious, are we?'

'Yes we are, Leo. And it's about time.'

'Oh I do love it when you go all dominatrix.' Leo sat in Tom's chair and looked about the room with an expression of humorous disapproval. 'Not sure about this refurbishment, darling. Bit modern.'

'It doesn't matter what you think of it.' Sarah's tongue was unshackled. Not having to please Leo, to placate his toddler ego, was liberating. 'I love it and that's the main thing.'

Leo looked at her appraisingly. Again he didn't seem to like what he saw.

Again, Sarah didn't care. 'First things first. It looks like we may have an offer on the flat.'

Leo sat forward, frowning. 'But, how? We haven't even put it on the market.'

'Jane worked her magic. She knows the property market much better than I do.' Sarah enjoyed adding, 'Or you, for that matter.' She let him pout and asked, 'Aren't you pleased?'

'Well, I should be, but it means you'll be moving out, darling.'

Sarah marvelled at the woman she had so recently been, a woman who would have picked that comment apart and hoped against hope that it meant he loved her. 'Actually, I'll be staying put. ' Sarah outlined Jane's manoeuvre. Leo's face remained set. 'It'll mean a reduction in the price, but I'll take the hit and make sure you're not out of pocket.'

Leo seemed distracted, as if turning something over in his mind. He was a hard man to surprise, but Sarah had managed to do just that. 'You're a clever little cat, aren't you?' he said.

The comment took her back to their marriage, when he had often used that light, double-edged tone, flattering and belittling her at the same time. It had always shut her up back then; it was how Leo alerted her to the fact that she'd displeased him, crossed one of the invisible lines that all lovers draw between them.

Perhaps Leo felt he'd gagged her when she went to the window and looked down at Merrion Road, but in fact Sarah was hiding a devilish smile. She felt electricity pour through her body. Sarah could have lifted a car, or punched through a wall. *Or finally chuck out the useless feelings I have left for this faithless man.*

A figure stood at the gate, looking up. Sarah recognised him by the set of his shoulders and the cut of his coat. 'That's odd. The guy who's buying the flat is coming up to the front door.' Sarah tutted. 'He should have called first.'

They both waited for the doorbell.

'Ignore him, darling,' said Leo into the silence. 'Don't grab at the first offer that comes along. Let me take over. I always looked after the money side of things, remember?'

'Ssh.' Sarah ignored that, and its implication that she shouldn't worry her pretty little head. A minute ticked by. The bell didn't ring and the man didn't retrace his steps. 'Odd,' said Sarah.

'Look, darling, forget him. We don't have long.'

'We never do.'

'Are you going to waste time sulking?'

'I don't sulk.' Sarah wondered how she'd put up with this

jibber-jabber for so long. 'Leo,' she began. 'This has been nice, but—'

'Nice? More than nice, darling.' Leo frowned, insulted.

'It's been less than nice, too.' Sarah folded her arms and looked down at him. 'At times I've been desolate.'

'But Sarah,' said Leo, his voice cajoling, 'all I think about is when I can rush up here to see you. We shouldn't argue. Not us. Not after we … well, darling, you know what we did.'

'That afternoon in the Old Church shouldn't have happened.'

'Why ever not?'

He seems genuinely puzzled, thought Sarah, as he went on.

'How can you and I making love be wrong, Sarah?'

'It wasn't making love.' Sarah had 20/20 vision now; the rosy post-coital glow was doused forever. 'It was opportunistic nookie, nothing more. Sex between us is wrong because you're married, but not to me.'

'Who is this hard woman? Where's my lovely Sarah gone?'

'She's not your anything any more, Leo. This relationship—'

'Ooh.' Wincing, Leo interrupted. 'Is relationship the right word, darling?'

'What word would you use?' Sarah narrowed her eyes, genuinely interested. Here was the nub of it; Leo wanted to both own and disown her. He wanted her to be a docile, flexible doll he could take out of the cupboard whenever the fancy took him.

'Words. Who cares about words?'

'Me,' said Sarah, putting her hand up with a grin she knew would irritate him. 'I care very much.' That tingling feeling made her taller. Sarah towered above Leo, like a sovereign staring down at a serf.

'All I know is that I want you, Sarah, like I've wanted you since I first clapped eyes on you.' He beamed at her. 'Remember? The first time we made love? In your awful flat-share.'

Sarah did remember. It was a warmly tinted home movie in her mind that nothing, not even Leo's transparent playing for time, could spoil. *But it's history.* 'Nostalgia, Leo, shouldn't be used to seduce. I don't want to turn back the clock any more.' There was no point beating about the bush; better to pull the plaster off in one go. 'Leo, we were in love once. Proper red-hot love.'

'Don't I know it!' Leo wasn't on the same page. He was on an X-rated page. 'Let's get back there, now!' He stood up and lunged at Sarah, only to tumble against the sideboard when she sidestepped him.

'Leo, I said we need to *talk*.'

Rubbing his knee, Leo said, 'Can't we talk while we do it? This dawdling is juvenile. I mean, we both know why you asked me up here.'

'Leo, stop making this just about sex. Like you, I wanted more from this.' She saw Leo frown at that, as if it was news to him, and her blood began to simmer. 'I've been kidding myself we're moving forwards, but really we're going backwards. Can you see that?'

343

'See what?' Leo glanced at his watch.

'Somewhere you have to be?'

'Of course not.' Leo reclined on the chair, hands behind his head, to illustrate how very, very relaxed he was. His foot jiggled at warp speed. 'Talk, darling. If that's what you want, talk.'

As if talking is the fee men pay for access to women's erogenous zones. Sarah looked at Leo and saw a man who seemed smaller than she remembered. And that chic shabbiness? *Just shabby.* 'Tell me, Leo. What do you want from me? From this?' Now that Sarah was no longer duping herself she knew the answer, but she needed to hear it from his own lips.

'Me? What do *I* want? But it was you who summoned *moi*, darling.' Leo was cagey. Happy, still, but cagey. Like the time when Sarah found a hotel receipt and he'd had to invent an explanation that didn't involve Helena or suspenders.

'I don't mean today, Leo.' Despite the fire within her, Sarah was cool. 'I mean, what have you really wanted from all our snatched meetings?'

Leo wiggled in the chair, possibly unaware that his stalling was obvious. 'What do any of us want, Sarah?'

'That's not an answer.' As he pretended to think, Sarah circled him and said, 'I've been living in the past, Leo. The past's a dead end. Everything that could happen there *has* happened.'

'I ... suppose.' Leo was watchful, giving nothing away until he knew where this was going.

'Seeing Smith again was a bit like time travel,' said Sarah.

'I'm still giggling about Smith's resurrection.' Sarah had always loved Leo's ability to see humour in the grimmest situation, but now it seemed shallow, as if he never cared enough to engage his emotions.

Sarah savoured what she was about to say as if it was a fine wine she could already taste on her tongue. 'In case you're wondering, she told me about what you did.'

'What did I do?' Leo practically fluttered his eyelashes.

'You made a pass at her. It really is time you looked outside number twenty-four for your conquests, Leo.'

'Darling, you're taking the word of a *sensational* liar? I wouldn't go near your bonkers mate. Alive or dead.'

'I think you'd snog a corpse if there was nobody else around.' Sarah didn't give him time to take offence; she was soaring now, a phoenix leaving the ashes of her marriage far below her. 'You haven't answered my question, Leo. What do you want from me?' She urged him silently, *Say it, Leo, say it!* Would he have the courage to name it at last? To say he'd been after some no-strings fun, that he'd demoted her from love of his life to bit on the side.

'You're painting me into a corner. I never made any promises, darling. You knew the score.'

Stripped of filters, Leo was unappealing. 'Still not an answer.' Sarah had learned to pick up Mikey without pricking herself; she could surely handle Leo.

'Where did this harsh sourpuss come from?' cooed Leo as if Sarah was a recalcitrant pet. 'OK,' he sighed, throwing up his hands when Sarah stared him down. 'What do I want? I want *you*. Right now. Right here.'

'But I don't want you.' It felt good to say it aloud. Sarah felt purged, as if she'd completed one of Helena's beloved detoxes.

'You do want me, darling. You do. Don't you?' Words wreak more havoc than bombs. Leo's face sagged into a blankness that made him look twice his age. 'Is this about bloody Tom?'

'No. And yes. I do want Tom, but I cocked that up. He's not relevant here.' Even as she said that, Sarah reconsidered. *Realising I could desire Tom gave me the confidence to put Leo in the rear-view mirror.*

'Come here, Sarah, please.' Leo stood and held out his arms. The rudiments of sincerity seemed to be grouping on his face. 'You're my best chum, darling.'

'Chums don't sleep with each other.'

'This isn't like you.' Leo looked her up and down, as if bodysnatchers had replaced his easy-going ex with a bolshie substitute. Something struck him. 'You're not planning to . . . it'd be heartless to tell Helena, you know.'

'At last you mention her!' Sarah would have liked to do a movie villain laugh. 'You're so cavalier with the women who love you. As if we're buses. As if there'll be another one along in a minute.'

'This is all getting heated. Let's calm down. I'll just . . .' He gestured at the bathroom and went in.

Sarah leaned against the door. 'Leo, as I'm not moving out

we need some new guidelines.' She was in charge at last. It was time to lay down the law for this regime change. 'This flat won't belong to you any more. You can't visit when you feel like it.' She turned her head. 'Are you listening? This is my home.'

'Home' implied a great deal more than floor plans and mod cons. Sarah hadn't chosen the people in number twenty-four. They were random. They were family. The word crept into her heart. Filled it.

She jumped as the door was wrenched open.

'Now I see why you wanted to *talk*.' Leo was seething. 'All those stupid questions! I'm warning you, Sarah, be very careful about your next move.' Shoving past her like a bull, he was gone.

Alone, puzzled by Leo's transformation, Sarah scanned the bathroom for clues.

Picking up the small wand on the side of the bath, the two lines in its window defiantly pink; Sarah closed her eyes briefly at her own foolishness, and dropped it into the squeaky pedal bin.

You weren't meant to see that, Leo.

The front door slammed shut. Sarah slipped across to the sitting-room window in time to see her prospective buyer hurry down the path, coat flapping.

Chapter Twenty-Two

Zelda was adamant. 'You look like death warmed up, dear.' *Dee-ah*. Sarah was packed off to bed in the middle of the afternoon. 'It's the weekend. You need to be better for work on Monday.'

Despite her protests, Sarah relished Zelda moving about the bedroom, tucking her in, pulling the curtains, giving her permission to fall apart if only for an hour. Zelda had been quiet, more contained than usual that morning. It was only when she registered Sarah's pallor that she swung into action.

Sarah burrowed into the mattress. Healing sleep was on its way.

Zelda regarded her appraisingly from the doorway, only a

slice of her visible in the enforced twilight. 'Sarah, I might need your help later.'

'You got it,' mumbled Sarah.

'I warn you, dear, I'll be asking a lot of you.'

'You're scaring me.' Sarah twisted around in the bed-clothes, hair in her face, eyes bleary.

'Next week's going to be a big week,' said Zelda. 'For now, sleep off the tummy ache and sleep off Leo. You've been in a trance since you spoke to him yesterday.'

Sarah turned to the wall, her eyes closing gratefully.

All divorces are nasty, but Sarah had prolonged the pain of her split from Leo by refusing to let go. Perhaps she'd been doomed to replay the scenes from when the Lynches flew apart.

She couldn't cast her father as Leo, but Sarah identified with her mother. Watching a man you love leave is hard. Tom's advice, impartial and level-headed, didn't sound so extraordinary now. *Should I call her?*

Sleeping during the day sometimes made Sarah rise up with a mouth like the bottom of Peck's cage, but the nap restored her, sending her down to fetch Una with a clear head.

Graham was babysitting. He handed over Una with good grace, zero sarcasm and even a hint of respect.

Taking Una outside for what might be their last outdoor session – the sky was a uniform greige – Sarah began her patter, chatting aimlessly. The little girl was still locked in, alone. Sarah held her hand a little tighter and Una squeezed back.

Reliable, but none the less sexy for it, Tom awaited them in the garden. He wasn't industrious today; he stood with his hands in his pockets, looking into the middle distance.

'Oh,' said Sarah. 'Your hair.'

'It's for the role.' Tom put a self-conscious hand to where his exuberant hair used to live. What was left was bright blond, smarmed down and tucked behind his ears. '*Vile Bodies* is set in the thirties, hence ...' He pointed at his short back and sides. 'It's awful, isn't it?'

'No. It's nice.' *And a bit awful.*

Una stared, frowning ferociously. Clearly she didn't approve.

'My ears get cold,' said Tom with a pout.

I love you. For a second Sarah panicked that she'd said it out loud. It was so clear in her head, like a bell tolling. I. Love. You.

Una kept up her death stare.

Sarah said, 'It'll grow back.' *I can't love him, not literally?* It was a big concept, love; but when it appeared, solid and confident, it couldn't be ignored. Sarah had been wrong about much, especially lately, but her love for Tom had become clear-cut.

'Now you're just patronising me.' Tom tried to mess up his hair. 'It's too short to even move,' he said despairingly.

'Hi folks!' Camilla, cheerful in a determined way, strode up the steps. Her arms were folded and Sarah imagined her fingers twitching as she acknowledged Sarah with a *Seriously? You again?* look on her face. 'Hi, Tommykins.' She kissed him, showily, on the lips.

'Hi, babe.' Tom's eyes met Sarah's awkwardly as Camilla disengaged.

'Oh look!' Camilla pointed. 'That little hedgehog looks like poor Mickey.'

'*Mikey*,' said Sarah and Tom mechanically.

A one-eyed ghost strutted out of the sunflowers, paws high, nose twitching. Mikey headed for his house but Una intercepted him, lifting him off his feet to silently, intensely commune with the hedgehog, nose to nose.

Sarah held her breath. *This could be the moment for Una!*

But Una said nothing. Tom said enough for all of them. He whooped, calling out to the house that Mikey was alive. 'Come on!' he yelled at his sister when she appeared at the window, and soon Jane was there, and Zelda, with Lisa and Graham hurrying out.

From the terrace Leo looked down, caught Sarah's eye and turned to go back inside.

'I noticed him first,' Camilla was telling whoever would listen.

'So we gave the wrong hedgehog a state funeral?' laughed Jane.

'Where's he been?' asked Zelda.

'Off sowing his wild oats,' said Tom. 'Whatever. He's home now.' He picked up Una and whirled her round, Mikey secure in her arms. His look to Sarah asked for permission and she granted it. 'Are you glad,' he asked Una deliberately, 'that Mikey's come back?'

Una looked into Tom's eyes. 'I hate your hair,' she said.

Chapter Twenty-Three

It was Leo's turn to suggest they talk. His turn to sound a touch desperate. Sarah's response to his text was a simple, 'You know where I am.'

Leaving the door ajar, Sarah thought of Una. She'd thought of little else since the day before, even when so much was hustling for her attention. *She came back to us.*

Sarah would never forget how that voice sounded; the one Una had lost and found. It was delicate, a little squeaky. But strong.

The door of Flat B opened and closed. Sarah patted her hair, cleared her throat. Leo would say more or less what she expected him to. It would all be disappointing, some of it hurtful, but she was beyond his reach.

'Hi darling.' Leo appeared, his face brick-red, like a ruined cherub.

Not offering her cheek for a kiss, Sarah avoided the damp rose of his lips. 'So. You want to talk.'

'Yes, I do, if that's OK.' Sarah had anticipated aggression, but Leo was misty-eyed, softly spoken, nothing like the bully who'd barged out of her flat forty-eight hours ago. 'Sarah, I want to make things up to you.'

'I don't need you to do that. I don't *need* you, Leo.'

'Come on, darling. Face facts. You need me more than ever.'

Bighead. 'I might have felt like that a while ago, but it was wrong of me to act on it. Things are different now. When the flat's sold and I hand you the cheque for your half, that really will be that.' That prospect had terrified her once; now it calmed her down.

'This mess is all my fault. I've been so damn *wrong* about everything.'

Sarah's daydreams were coming true too late. Leo's finger hovered over the button that would return everything to 'normal', and Tom was all she could think of.

Tom was what love looked like.

A hunger for him swamped Sarah. She would duel Camilla if necessary. Anything, *anything*, just to be able to tear off his clothes or count his eyelashes or argue with him. They say a dying person's life flashes in front of their eyes; Sarah's potential life with Tom flashed in front of hers. 'Leo, we don't need another scene.'

'Poor darling. Drama isn't good for you when ... you know.' Leo gestured at Sarah's torso, as if it was a vague but important area it was best not to dwell on. 'I'm not going anywhere.' Leo was firm but doting, like a grandma who knows best. 'This gets sorted out today.'

'It *is* sorted.' *Why the sudden fervour to talk everything over?* 'Leo, you're free. You don't owe me a thing.'

'No, no, no! You and me, we're Burton and Taylor.'

'They ended up divorced.' Sarah raised an eyebrow. 'Twice.'

'How did we think we could live so close to each other and not break the rules? We're dynamite.'

'Are we?' Sarah remembered the sexless bed they'd shared towards the end of their marriage.

'We shouldn't disagree, not now. My prime concern, darling Sarah, is *you*. It always has been. These last few weeks have been fun, haven't they?'

'Not really.'

'Now now.' Leo waggled a finger. 'You liked it, too. Secret sex is the best sort.'

'Speak for yourself, Leo. The secrecy made me miserable.' What a poor return on a long-term investment; Sarah's ex-husband knew so little about her. One thing was clear: Leo had been in it for the danger. *Not for me. Never for me.* Without the fairy dust of Sarah's obsession all was tacky and worthless.

'You loved it, you minx.'

'No, Leo, I loved *you*.'

'Now, hang on, darling!' Leo laid his hands on Sarah's shoulders, talking urgently. 'Did we ever mention love? Did I ever once mention a future? Did I? You can't accuse me of that, Sarah.'

Pushing away his hands, Sarah snapped, 'Nobody's accusing you of anything, but it's nice to know you edited your pillow talk so I couldn't *accuse* you of being in love.'

Leo's arms had multiplied; octopus-like, his tentacles battled to hold her closer as Sarah battled to pull away. 'I have nothing but respect for you, remember that.'

Sarah extricated herself and rubbed her upper arm where he'd grabbed it.

'Sarah, darling, it's you I'm thinking of when I say get rid of it.'

'It?' The noise of Notting Hill was stilled. The only sound was Leo's voice.

'The baby. Him. Her.' Leo grimaced. 'I misspoke, darling. Jesus, I'm an idiot. Sorry. It's not an it.'

Sarah turned away. She'd thought Leo couldn't drag them any lower, but he'd found a hidden basement level.

'Get real, Sarah. What could we offer a baby? It's for the best.' Leo's sugary concern subsided into the self-pity it really was. 'Surely you don't expect me to be involved with this child? We had sex once, for crying out loud!' As Sarah kept her back to him, Leo collected himself. 'I'm told it's just a tiny procedure. All over in minutes.' He raised his voice, agitated. 'Are you going to let one mistake ruin both our lives?'

Another voice, husky, querulous, called Leo's name from the front door, left open in his haste.

Sarah spun around and Leo hissed, 'I'll pay for the termination!' just before Helena appeared.

'Is my hus— ah, there you are!' Helena clattered to Leo's side and locked her arm through his. 'Has he told you, Sarah?' Helena swatted Leo, a playful gesture that almost toppled her overwrought husband. 'You might as well be the first to know. We've waited three months before sharing this.' She pulled her shoulders to her ears, her smile a watermelon slice. 'I'm pregnant!'

Leo's eyes, two hysterical dots in a purple face, pleaded with Sarah.

'Isn't it wonderful?' Helena emoted enough for all three of them. 'Poor old Leo's been so good. I've felt so ill. No sexy time for poor Daddy!' She chucked Leo's cheek and he looked as if he might vomit.

A penny dropped. In fact, pennies fell like rain around Sarah. *So that's why you came sniffing around.* The champagne cork that had popped before they visited back in June was to celebrate this news. Then they'd come up to see her, hugging their secret, and Leo had offered Sarah his 'help'.

Helena waggled her finger at Sarah. 'You're a naughty girl, Sarah.'

'I am?'

'Going behind my back like that.'

Sarah swayed a little.

Helena laughed. 'Finding a buyer for this flat without

telling us. Ah well,' she sighed prettily. 'Our little plot has fallen apart. If we can't buy your place we'll just have to turn the spare room into a nursery.'

Sarah couldn't look at Leo. *It was all true.* Sarah's stomach lurched.

'You can be aunty!' Helena's joy made her generous.

Sarah found and held Leo's gaze. 'I'm so happy for you both. Funnily enough, yours isn't the only baby on the way at number twenty-four.'

Leo put his fist in his mouth.

'Jane's pregnant too,' said Sarah.

Helena attempted the right noises, evidently miffed at sharing the spotlight.

'It wasn't planned,' said Sarah. 'Totally out of the blue.' She turned to Leo. 'Jane even did a second test up here, just to be sure.'

Leo looked as if he might never speak again. He moved only when Helena tugged his arm and said, 'Come on, *Daddy*. Let's go and check out buggies.' She told Sarah that she wanted the model used by the Duchess of Cambridge.

'What else?' smiled Sarah.

'May I use your loo? I spend half my life in there at the moment!' As Helena swanned off, precious passenger on board, Sarah let out a short *Oof*.

'Period pains,' she explained, when Leo frowned. 'Just period pains.'

He looked as if he might collapse with relief.

'Leo,' whispered Sarah. 'Do you love Helena?'

He nodded, still wild-eyed.

'Then be good to her.'

He nodded. 'I'm sorry,' he said.

'I know,' said Sarah.

An invitation from Zelda to 'pop downstairs' softened the hard edges of Sunday evening. 'I've got a call to make,' said Sarah. 'Then I'll be right down.'

Scrolling through her contacts, Sarah's thumb paused over 'Mum'.

While married to Leo, Sarah had twisted her own arm to believe his motives for banishing her mother. There was no need to pretend any longer; *Leo excommunicated Mum to make his already easy life even easier.* Tom was right.

Sarah paced as a phone rang in some distant room, and stiffened when it was answered. 'Mum. It's me.'

'Sarah. Hello.' The tone was artfully casual. 'I was napping. You woke me.'

The lack of a welcome, or at least some surprise, threw Sarah.

What did I expect?

'How are you, Mum? I've been thinking about you.'

I can turn this around.

A snort, then, 'I'm fine.' After a moment, her mother upgraded this to, 'I'm brilliant. Everything's come up roses at last.'

'That's good.' Sarah had dreaded an illness, something irreversible. Pretending that her mother had asked the same question, she said, 'I'm well, Mum. In good shape. Nothing's fallen off. Yet.'

'You have my genes.'

'Leo and me, we broke up. We're divorced, Mum.'

'Can't say I'm surprised.'

Choosing to ignore that, choosing to build, choosing to keep chasing that sliver of beauty her father insisted on, Sarah said, 'I'm getting over it. You know how it is, Mum. No need to tell you that divorce takes some getting used to.'

'Hmm.'

Oh God.

That small noise took Sarah back to when she'd lived in fear of her mother's 'Hmm', never able to translate it. 'In a way, the divorce helped me understand how you felt when I was a child.'

There was no reply.

'What I mean is . . .' Sarah's self-possession wavered. 'You went through hell but I was too young to see it. Now I know how tough it is. I wasn't sympathetic, but I am now, Mum. I really am.'

'About time. I remarried. Did you know?'

How would I know if you didn't tell me?

'Remarried?'

'Don't sound so shocked. Your father didn't want me but there are plenty of men who do, Sarah. And before you make a fuss about not being invited, it was a tiny ceremony. Just me, John and the boys.'

'Boys?'

'I'm stepmother to three of the most wonderful young men you could hope to meet. A real credit to John. Maybe if you'd been a boy, things would have turned out differently.'

'Well, I'd have a willy for a start.'

'Everything's a joke to you, isn't it?'

When I'm as nervous as this, yes.

'I'm glad you're happy, Mum.'

'Never. Been. Happier.' Sarah's mother underlined each word with a snap of her veneers. 'I'm a step-grandmother, too. The little ones adore me. They prefer me to their real granny. Second time lucky, after that disaster of a marriage to your father.'

'Dad wasn't so bad, Mum.'

'You always did take his side. I barely think of him now. Perhaps you'll make a better second marriage, Sarah.'

'Perhaps.'

'Are you crying?'

'No. I'm just . . .'

'See? Two minutes talking to you and I'm upset.'

'Mum, I—'

'I get all the blame, when . . . I'm sorry to tell you this, Sarah, but that precious father of yours never wanted you. He wouldn't say it to your face, but he said it to me.'

Sarah sat down. She felt as if a train had hurtled past her face. 'You don't mean that.'

'Don't I? Before we got married your dad said, loud and clear, "no babies". I begged. I cried. But no. The man was a tyrant. He didn't want a child, even if it meant robbing me of my chance to be a mother.'

'Hang on, if he said that *before* you got married . . .' began Sarah.

'I played along at first. Any normal chap would change his mind. Not that brute. So I took matters into my own hands. He had no idea I'd stopped taking the pill. I fooled him, Sarah. I won that round!'

Brand new, freshly minted in the vault of family secrets, the story of her own conception dazed Sarah. 'You tricked Dad into having a baby?'

'Everybody does it.' Her mother was brisk. 'I never hear a "thank you" from you for that!'

'So that's what you meant when you said I ruined everything.' Sarah had taken the accusation personally; it had cost her her voice. 'All these years I've assumed I was some sort of demon child, so unlovable that I chased Dad away.'

'Are you still blaming me for everything? When all I did was give birth to you, feed you, wash you, clothe you?' Sarah's mother sucked on a cigarette, the sound a rasping punctuation to a conversation that had gone the way of all their mother/daughter conversations: into the mud.

Sarah kept the phone to her ear, listening to her mother's breathing.

Her father was two people. To Sarah's mother, he was the womaniser who'd left her. To Sarah, he was a disappointed man who'd been duped into fatherhood, but had never blamed the child. The marriage had collapsed – and no wonder! – but after he left he shouldered his responsibilities with love and thoughtfulness. 'Mum, Dad *did* want me.' She heard another vicious drag on a cigarette, and clasped her phone hard. 'Please don't say that ever again.' The continuing silence conveyed brittle, damaged feelings. 'I'm sorry,' said Sarah, who was an old hand at apologising to her mother, even when – especially when – she'd done nothing wrong. 'Can we start again? I didn't call to make things worse.'

'You expect too much of me, Sarah.'

'I only want to talk.'

You're my mum! Act like a mum!

'Talk about what? About how you stood by as your shit of a husband threw me onto the street?'

'I'm sorry, Mum. I should've—'

'You're not sorry. You're just like your father. You do exactly as you please and sod the rest of us. I've put all this in a box, Sarah.'

'All what? Me?'

'You. Your father. All that nonsense.'

'*Nonsense*, Mum?'

'Don't jump down my throat!'

'I'm not, honestly. I just want—'

'What about what *I* want, Sarah?'

'Do you want . . . me?'

'Is that why you called? To badger me?'

'What if we meet for a coffee and take it from there?'

'John'll be back any minute. I can't spend all evening

arguing with you, missy. See? See what you do to me? Now I'll be jittery for hours.'

'Sorry.'

'That's easy to say.'

It's not. Sorry is powerful, enormous.

'I mean it,' said Sarah, to thin air as the phone went down at the other end.

Immediately, Sarah threw herself into vigorous mental gymnastics, trying to bend the short phone conversation into something less than disastrous.

Until she gave up. Just gave up and admitted that her remnant of flesh-and-blood family was not in working order. She'd tried, and she'd try again.

But for now, I won't think about it.

Trailing down to Flat E, Sarah met Tom. He was leaping up the stairs, three at a time, full of the energy she lacked.

'I've got another part,' he said, amazed. 'A bloody *movie*.'

Sarah congratulated him. 'First Mikey, now this,' she said. 'What a weekend.'

'I'll go and tell the little feller.' Tom looked down at his feet. 'I just said I'd go and tell a hedgehog about my film role, didn't I?'

'I'm afraid you did,' smiled Sarah, wanting to touch him. 'But let's draw a veil over it. Does this mean you won't be doing voice-overs any more?'

'Possibly. *Vile Bodies* is opening doors for me before I've even filmed it.'

'Don't go all starry on us.'

'I promise.' Tom winked, and Sarah's beleaguered ovaries executed a perfect forward roll. 'I keep my promises. Just ask Mikey.' About to walk away, he said, 'Hey, have you rung your mum yet?'

'Are you a mind reader?'

Tom listened and sighed and winced. 'I should have kept my nose out. Camilla told me off for interfering.'

It was reasonable for Tom to discuss Sarah with his girl-friend – presumably he'd had to explain why they were so deep in conversation at Mikey's funeral – but it wasn't reasonable for Sarah to be so dismayed about it. Despite having refused to take delivery of Tom when he was offered, Sarah stubbornly wished she could keep a tiny part of him for herself.

Tut tut! Selfish! Her conscience had recent history on its side regarding the health risks of intruding on other people's relationships.

Proficient at multitasking, Sarah discussed one topic while thinking about quite another. 'You didn't interfere, you helped,' she said, as she wished she'd returned that first kiss. *Tom and Camilla are kind of a rebound relationship*, she decided, wondering if normal rules applied in that case.

'Sarah?' Tom was waiting for an answer.

I'm not that good at multitasking after all. 'Sorry, what?'

'I asked how you feel about your mum now.'

'I feel, well, I *don't* feel. I'm a bit numb. With Mum you expect the unexpected, but that was brusque even by her standards. It's hard to say this about a parent, Tom, but she's toxic. Yes, Leo went too far by cutting her off, and yes, his motives were narcissistic, but it's probably best for me to have some distance from my mother.'

'Not sure if I believe that stuff about the step-family adoring her.'

'They probably string garlic around the babies' necks to keep her away.'

'The lines of communication are open. That's *something*.'

'It's a big something.' Sarah respected Tom's willingness to leap feet first into muddy emotional waters. 'I'm trying to be philosophical about it but, Jesus, not being invited to your own mother's wedding is hard to swallow.'

'As you get older – and that's what we're doing, isn't it, like it or not? – you see your parents as people. My mum and dad have nothing in common. Nada. They barely speak, but they soldier on, in their so-called "good" marriage. Jane and I got out as soon as we could. I used to bang on about them whenever I got drunk, blame them for all my shortcomings, but, you know, they're just two people, making mistakes, figuring it out, getting it royally wrong.'

Sarah thought of her parents' wedding photograph. Flares. A moustache. A snow-white minidress. Both of them smiling so broadly their faces were blurred. She'd had to ask, as a child, 'Who's that lady?'; her mother had been transfigured by happiness. 'Yeah, they're just ordinary people, God help them.' She smiled. 'I'm glad I called her, and you were the catalyst for that, so thanks, Tom.'

Accepting the gratitude graciously, Tom neither downplayed nor exaggerated the part he'd played. 'I suppose . . .

I'd better . . .' He took a step around her, climbing a couple of steps.

This reluctance of Tom to take his leave of her was something Sarah had noticed before. She tried not to construct a hope around it.

On his way upstairs, Tom called over his shoulder, 'Remind me to give you my new address.'

'New address?' said Sarah idiotically, some kindly section of her brain refusing to process his statement.

'I've had an offer accepted on a two-bedder in Chiswick.' Tom elucidated when Sarah looked gormless. 'I can't stick around here much longer. Jane's spare room will be a nursery soon, and Jamie's coming home earlier 'cos of the baby.'

'Chiswick,' repeated Sarah, as if he'd said 'Antarctica'.

'It's not that far. No need for a passport when I visit.'

'You'll visit?' Sarah sounded more nakedly hopeful than she meant to.

'Yeah, well, my new little niece or nephew will be here,' said Tom. He hesitated. 'And my sister.' He hesitated again. 'And you.'

'And me,' said Sarah, as the shadowy stairway claimed him.

Down in the basement, Zelda was supercharged, as if fitted with new batteries. 'In! In!' she said, ushering Sarah past Peck. 'There's a lot to do, Sarah.'

'Is there?' laughed Sarah.

'Yes.' Zelda closed her eyes, centring herself, then opened them again. They blazed. 'I'm turning myself in.'

Chapter Twenty-Four

ᄎONᄃUᄃIUᔕ FᄀKEᔕWᄀᕽ
Notting Hill, W11

This calendar is FREE to valued customers!
Monday 12th September, 2016

**AN INVISIBLE THREAD CONNECTS THOSE
WHO ARE DESTINED TO MEET; IT MAY
TANGLE BUT IT CAN NEVER BREAK**

Keeley slammed the iron drawer of the filing cabinet with her hip. 'Seems like every time you walk into this office you're asking for time off.'

'That's not fair,' said Sarah. 'This is important.'

'So important you can't tell me about it?'

'I made a promise.' Sarah would take the afternoon off if it meant leaving St Chad's forever.

Perhaps Keeley smelled her determination because she relented. 'I guess I can spare you. You wouldn't want to be here this afternoon anyway.' She hesitated, pursed her lips, lined up the papers on her desk. 'I've got somebody coming in to discuss joining the team. As a senior psychologist.'

They're replacing me. 'Oh,' said Sarah stupidly.

'I don't want to do this,' said Keeley. She spoke slowly, carefully, each word heavy with meaning. 'It breaks my heart to lose you, Sarah. I've relied on you. You've inspired me. I miss you. But the children come first and we're not operating at full strength. I hope you understand.'

She did. 'I do.' She hated it, but Sarah understood. 'Can I . . .' She gestured behind her at the door.

Keeley deflated, as if she'd expected something more. 'Yeah. Go on.'

Sarah walked briskly down the corridor, arms swinging, heels clicking, putting distance between herself and the pain.

'Excuse me.' A woman, mid-thirties, in a raincoat and jeans, stood in the middle of reception. 'I'm not sure . . . I'm . . . this is Albie.'

In front of the woman, leaning back on her and clutching a cloth rabbit, Albie was no more than six. He had straight shiny hair and his mouth was tightly closed, as if he was keeping something explosive behind it. Albie was a small, cute, frightened pressure cooker.

Sarah exhaled. The tears made her eyes glisten, but they didn't fall. Her unhappiness and uncertainty underwent a transformation; they became clear, cool resolve. She saw herself and Albie and his anxious mother as if they were suspended in amber. It was obvious. This woman needed information. This boy needed guidance. They both needed muscular love, the sort that moves mountains as if they were sandcastles. They needed her.

And by God I need them.

'Come this way,' she said. Sarah felt tall and strong; she felt like herself. 'I'll find Albie's notes and we'll sit down somewhere quiet where we can have a chat. Is that OK with you, Albie?'

Albie shrugged. He had a birthmark just above his eyebrow. He was special, this kid, just like every other child that came through St Chad's doors.

The other receptionist, cradling a mug in her hands, slowed down as she walked towards the desk. 'Um . . .' she said.

'You'll be all right on your own for an hour, won't you?' Sarah smiled at the surprised nod. 'I'll be with Albie.'

Keeley looked up as they passed her door. Her face was impassive as Sarah said, 'I'm taking Albie's case, boss. Could you look out his file?'

'You do love messing me about,' said Keeley. Her eyes glistened too.

The susurration of conversation, like a theatre audience before curtain-up, could be heard all the way down in Zelda's flat.

'Sounds like Tom did as you asked,' Zelda's voice rasped with nerves.

When Sarah had asked him to assemble all the residents in the hallway at one thirty because Mavis had an announcement to make, Tom had agreed but added, 'Mavis? An announcement? The mind boggles.'

Sarah's own mind boggled as she stood back and surveyed

her friend. 'You'll do,' she said, then, urgently, 'You can back out, Zelda. We can do this another time. Something so important should be managed, planned—'

'You've made your feelings clear, dear. You think this is too hasty. But it's time. There'll never be a *right* time, will there? It will always mean chaos.' Zelda picked up a handbag. 'Sarah, I need this. You of all people should understand how the human mind works. I can't keep lying. I have to put right the wrong I did to my friends.'

'I know, but—'

Zelda interrupted again. She was agitated beneath the surface calm. 'And there's Mavis. I owe it to her to stand up and say I helped her choose her time to die and I'm glad. I'll take the punishment. Perhaps it might start a conversation in the media. Perhaps one day people like my sister won't have to leave the country or risk going to jail if they simply can't face their future.'

'All very high-minded,' said Sarah. 'But what about *your* life? You could leave here, go elsewhere, start a better life on your own terms. This doesn't make sense. There's something you're not telling me.'

'Whoever tells anybody everything?'

'Thank you, Confucius.' They both laughed at that, and Sarah accepted she must fold away her qualms. 'OK, if you're ready, we can get the ball rolling.' *The big scary horrible ball that'll crush you.*

Zelda didn't move. 'That suitcase under Mavis's bed,' she said, as if Sarah hadn't spoken. 'Take a look.'

'Now?' Sarah was puzzled. 'Everybody's waiting.'

'It won't take a moment.'

Sarah tugged out the trunk, and threw back the lid. She put her hand to her mouth.

'I found them this morning.'

Every book that Zelda had ever written, all the Inspector Shackleton mysteries, the stand-alone murder tales, even the recipe book for charity, sat neatly stowed in the case. Each copy was well thumbed.

'Mavis read all my books.'

'She was proud of you.'

'I'll never know *that*.' Zelda patted her hair, changed the handbag to her other arm, and managed a valiant smile.

Sarah took Zelda's hands in hers and kissed her on both cheeks. 'I feel like I should say something clever.'

'There's no need to say anything at all. Off you go, Sarah.'

Upstairs, an expectant hush fell on the waiting semicircle as Sarah appeared. Self-conscious, she shook her head apologetically and nipped to Jane's side.

Taking her hand, Jane squeezed Sarah's fingers and said, 'This better be good.' With visible effort, Jane had asked no questions. 'I'm missing *Judge Judy*.'

Beneath the noticeboard Una swayed, leaning back against her father – included in the round-up as an honorary tenant – and sang a tuneless song into Mikey's ear as Lisa looked around, impatient. Helena, her atypical loose jumper the only clue to her condition, leaned on Leo, who seemed ill at ease.

In her efforts to ignore Leo, Sarah found herself looking at Camilla, who gave her a frigid smile and tightened her koala grip around Tom's middle.

At the sound of heels on the stairs, the hubbub muted. Zelda emerged from the gloomy lowlands of the basement to the sun-kissed plateau of the ground floor, to be greeted with perfect silence.

Standing erect, her hands together and her chin high, Zelda let them take her in. Slender as a leaf in a grey silk sheath, her hair a perfect, gauzy helmet, Zelda was magnificent. Buffed, polished, perfect, she shone like a goddess.

'My name,' she said, certain and mellifluous, 'is Zelda Bennison.'

Jane let out a strange sound. Tom's head whipped round to Sarah. Murmured questions were stifled by the speech Sarah had helped Zelda memorise.

'I have a confession to make, and an apology.'

Sarah watched the others as they listened to Zelda's story, less believable than her most far-fetched fiction. There was anger – Graham's face was stony – and there was sheer enjoyment – Camilla's mouth hung delightedly open throughout. Mostly there was concentration. Jane dug her nails into Sarah's palm as Zelda talked about helping Mavis die. *'What a woman,'* she whispered.

'I've been living in your house under false pretences, moving amongst you as an impostor. So thoroughly have I inhabited my sister's life that I took care to be unfriendly and offensive. At times my mask dropped.' Zelda inclined her head towards Sarah, who staggered when Jane nudged her. 'It was difficult to stay aloof. Number twenty-four is full of goodness and love and, yes, the usual sprinkling of treachery, but it's *alive* and I want to take part in life again. Because of that, now that I've confessed my deception, I need to apologise to you all.'

'No need,' said Tom.

'Too sodding right you should apologise,' said Graham.

'I'm sorry from the bottom of my battered heart for lying about my sister's death, and about my identity. I stand before you now as myself, but in a few moments I'll leave number twenty-four to keep an appointment at West End Central police station. There I'll make a full confession of both my crimes. It's the inevitable finale to a very misguided plan. I've broken the law and I've lied to people who deserve better. Furthermore, I want to declare my role in my sister's death. I want to stand up for Mavis's right to orchestrate her own ending. Given my previous high-profile career, we should expect media interest. I can't allow you to suffer the consequences of a media storm, so if my lawyer secures bail, I'll stay at a hotel until my trial.'

That wasn't discussed! Sarah felt as if something had wrenched adrift in her chest.

Zelda cleared her throat and held her Birkin bag in front of her like a shield. 'I'll go now, if my good friend Sarah is ready?'

Wiping her eyes with the back of her hand, her good friend stepped forward.

'Good luck,' said Jane, her face white. She was the only one who spoke.

Sarah and Zelda left the house's sheltering roof, and walked together into the future.

Eight hours later, Sarah sat in a taxi that crawled through streets washed with sordid street-lamp orange. Her head against the window, she closed her eyes.

The innards of the police station had felt oddly familiar; TV cop dramas got it mostly right. Everywhere really did look hygienic, commonplace, like an insurance company HQ. What the television couldn't convey was the dread that crawled over Sarah when an officer led Zelda into a room where she wasn't allowed to follow.

There was power lodged in the plastic seating, in the carpet tiles, in the terrible coffee from a moody machine: the power to keep Zelda away from Sarah.

Zelda had been swallowed up by the police station, and Sarah spent hours in a waiting area she now knew better than her own flat. All was respectful politeness, but questions went half answered and Sarah got nowhere with her efforts to discover what the hell was going on.

Zelda's lawyer, a formidable woman in sober suiting, emerged now and then to speed-smoke a cigarette and advise Sarah to go home.

'How's she holding up?'

'Bennison's a tough old bird.'

When Sarah wasn't deafened by the white noise of her

anxiety about Zelda, she allowed herself to be anxious about Tom. About somebody else's boyfriend, a man who was soon to move out; Chiswick wasn't far as the crow flies, but it would take Tom out of her daily orbit. He would recede. He would forget her.

The lawyer had stormed back from a cigarette break, throwing open double doors and shouting over her shoulder, 'So much for police discretion!' Outside the building stood a Sky News camera crew, alongside a couple of opportunistic paparazzi unwrapping sticks of gum. 'This place leaks like a sieve.'

Twitter took up the baton. Zelda's publishers were forced to comment that they had no comment. When Sarah searched the hashtag #ZeldaLives she found an array of WTF? and LOL! There was a lot of love, much scorn: the usual hot mess, in fact, so she switched off her phone and shut it all out.

The tough old bird didn't look tough when she emerged, head down, to face the reporters' shouted questions. Zelda's image was all over news websites, but the real thing bore little resemblance to the soft-focus PR portrait.

Perhaps it was underhand to exploit Zelda's fatigue, but Sarah had directed the taxi driver to number twenty-four. 'There's *no way* you're going to a hotel room tonight.'

'But the press . . .'

'But nothing.'

'Tomorrow, then.' Zelda closed her eyes as they stopped at a traffic light. 'I'll move out tomorrow.'

'I'll help,' said Sarah. 'But for tonight I want you under the same roof as me.'

Like a zombie, Zelda answered Sarah's questions in a monotone. 'I'm on bail until the court cases. They'll try me separately, once for the assisted suicide, once for the fraud. It'll take months to get to trial. Yes, dear, of course a jail term is possible.'

It was happening. The storm Sarah had dreaded the moment Zelda announced her decision to come clean. After only a day, Zelda looked battered by the winds she'd conjured up; *how will she deal with months and months of this?*

Sarah suddenly thought of Albie. And little Nadia who was now in a foster home. And of herself, only recently woken up after a long coma. *She'll get through this and I'll help.* When one person falters, another helps them up. It's the commerce of love. 'I admire you, Zelda.' Sarah had to stop hopelessly wishing that Zelda hadn't confessed. It was time to accept. Time to be useful.

'I'm not the martyr you think I am, Sarah.' Zelda had shrunk; her likeness to Mavis was startling, despite the stylish wrappings.

'Don't argue with me,' smiled Sarah. 'It takes guts to do what you just—'

'Guts,' agreed Zelda. 'Or blackmail. I had a visitor on Friday evening.'

Here was the missing piece. Sarah had known there was more to Zelda's sudden resolve. 'Who?'

Zelda's laughter was cracked, dark. 'The mystery fat cat who wants to buy your flat.'

Sarah remembered seeing the man approach the house. 'So he rang your bell and not mine? But why?'

'Because I'm his wife, dear.' As Zelda rubbed her right temple, she told Sarah of Ramon's sudden appearance, all in black, devastatingly handsome, seething with anger. 'I opened the door and he said, "Hello, Zelda."' She shuddered. 'He'd spotted me when he came to view the flat, and returned to see if his eyes were playing tricks. As you can imagine, he was sure some stranger would open the door, that he'd been seeing things. But no. There I was, rooted to the spot.'

Ramon had pushed past her.

'Peck let him have it. Both barrels.' Ramon was full of questions, but each time she tried to answer he roared another one. Or an insult. 'It took quite a while to iron it all out. His fury kept dying down then flaring up. He was every bit as furious when he left as he was when I opened the door. I think he'll go to his grave loathing me.'

'No, no,' said Sarah soothingly. 'People can surprise you. He might come round.'

'Ramon has no surprises left,' said Zelda grimly. 'He told me how the papers approached him after my death, digging for dirt, for some sexual titbit about the age gap. He's been "loyal", he said, but now he sees no need to be loyal any longer. I apologised over and over again. I begged. Whatever dignity I had is now lying on the floor of Mavis's sitting room. He wants revenge.'

'Bastard.'

'I deserve his anger.' Zelda silenced Sarah with one raised forefinger. 'I *do*. Not that I respect him. Far from it. Ramon had no wish to discuss or negotiate; he simply wants to destroy me. He was flying to New York at the weekend – another property purchase with the money I left him – and he took great joy in telling me that as soon as he got back he'd have lunch with a tabloid editor. He said, "He'll demolish you, Zelda." Those were his words. So, you see, Sarah, I'm not a heroine. I'm doing what little I can to keep some control over the situation. At least this way it's on my terms.'

'What a pig.'

'Yes, true. But all Ramon did was give me the final push to do what I knew was right. It does feel better in a way. But in another way . . .' Zelda's silence was deep, a foggy crystal ball of the months to come. 'In another way I feel as if I'm already in prison.'

'Your friends will come forward.' Sarah needed to believe this.

'Who can say? I don't expect them to. I don't deserve it.'

'Stop telling me what you do and don't deserve.' Sarah was stern. 'We'll be the judges of that. For tonight you deserve an early night and tomorrow . . . we'll see.'

'My last night in Merrion Road,' said Zelda. 'And all I want to do is sleep.'

The cab slowed. With a lurching heart, Sarah saw a scrum of all-weather jackets by the gate. 'They got here ahead of us,' she whispered. 'Here goes.' She put her hand under Zelda's elbow. 'Best Louboutin forward.'

'Over here, Zelda!' 'What's it like being dead, Zelda?' 'Do you have a comment for Ramon, Zelda?' Camera flashes punctuated the jeering questions as Sarah cleared a path with an outstretched arm.

'Stay at the gate or I'll call the police,' she said as butchly as she could, wondering if the police would care. Ahead of them, the house was dark, as if the residents had been evacuated. The timer on the hall lights purred as Sarah and Zelda picked their way down to the basement.

Zelda slumped against the wall as Sarah pickpocketed the keys from her bag. 'Thank heavens nobody's about. I couldn't look them in the face.'

'Can you hear something?' Sarah put her ear to the door, wondering wildly if reporters could have broken in. Warily, she went in first.

Welcoming them with a shrill 'Mad cow!' Peck bobbed and wiggled, unfurling his crescent of feathers. Gentle scuffling sounds came from the sitting room.

'Wait here. Just in case.' Sarah pushed at the door.

After the dreary streets, the room was glittering and warm. Candles burned on the table, which was laid with a red cloth and gilt-edged plates that Sarah recognised as Jane's. The owner of the plates sprang up from Mavis's lumpy sofa.

'At last!' Jane passed Sarah and reached greedily for Zelda. 'Come in. You must be starving. Don't be angry but we

379

tidied up a bit and we laid a fire and I hope you like hotpot because it's all I can cook.'

Allowing herself to be led to the table, watching Jane pour out a large goblet of blood-coloured wine, Zelda was silent.

Not so Una, who wriggled from her mother's lap and said, 'Can I taste the wine? Can I look in your handbag? You smell nice.'

'You're all here,' said Zelda, amazed.

And they were. Even Graham had thawed out and sat on a hard chair, arms folded like a benign grandpa. Leo, careful not to catch Sarah's eye, sat on the arm of a chair taken up by his wife, who was dressed for a ball but who was, crucially, *there*.

'Was it horrible in jail?' asked Una, leaning against Zelda as Jane urged, 'Eat! Eat!'

'Would you sign one of your books for me?' Helena was unusually deferential to number twenty-four's home-grown celebrity.

The basement flat came into its own, all its faults rebranded as virtues. It was cosy not dark; it felt safe not subterranean. 'We're not staying long,' said Jane, pulling Sarah to her like a Siamese twin. 'We just wanted to welcome Zelda home, see how she is.'

Through a doorway, Sarah saw the lamplit bedroom. The bed was made with new sheets and a fluffy duvet. The threadbare rug was replaced with a sheepskin Sarah recognised from Jane's flat. 'You're a marvel,' she whispered.

Jane peered at Sarah, and seemed not to like what she

saw. 'Christ, have you eaten? You look terrible.' She kissed her cheek. 'Fancy keeping this to yourself. Let us help from now on, yeah?'

'I'm not sure Zelda wants help. She's very proud.' Sarah saw that Zelda had managed only a couple of mouthfuls. Leo had refilled her glass; she drained it as she answered their questions, still looking dazed, still evidently not quite trusting the evidence of her eyes. Mikey snuffled around the table, knocking into the pepper grinder.

'There's been vile stuff on social media,' said Jane. 'We need to protect her.' She dropped her voice. 'What are the odds of her going to jail? Some blogger wrote something about the establishment making an example of her.'

'Ask me tomorrow.' Sarah was inclined to pessimism after her long day languishing under strip lighting.

'We won't let it happen,' growled Jane.

The doorbell rang. Ignored, it rang again, until it was a constant buzz, some unseen and very rude finger pressing against it. 'Right.' Jane slammed down her glass and rolled up her sleeves. 'Somebody needs a lesson in manners.'

'I hope those paps are ready for her,' laughed Sarah as Jane marched upstairs.

'*Never* annoy a pregnant woman,' said Graham, with the air of a war veteran.

'Tom,' said Helena. 'Go after her! You can't let a woman face those monsters.'

'Tom, dear,' said Zelda, her spirit revived, 'stay put unless you want a black eye from your sister.'

Sarah had to look at him then. Just outside the pool of light thrown by the candles and the lamps, Tom's eyes were bright in the gloom, and they were fixed on Sarah until she saw him, and they flicked away.

Raised voices came from outside. Hoarse protests. High-pitched name-calling. Jane returned, her cheeks flushed; Peck twerked a salute. 'If those bastards want to get to you,' she told Zelda, 'they'll have to get through me first.'

'You're a wonder, Jane.' The application of food, wine and a stole made of love around her shoulders had worked wonders on Zelda's energy levels. 'I can't believe you're all here. It's so unexpected.' She tapered off, as if she couldn't do justice to her emotions.

Number twenty-four had found its feet. Zelda's honesty – or maybe her plight – had won them over. A year ago the same people had ignored Smith's misfortune. *Perhaps they sensed it was a lie.*

Sarah wondered if the added ingredient was Jane; she was a natural leader, always on the side of inclusion and generosity. *A benign dictator.* That didn't cover it; the residents of number twenty-four had been through a lot. Keeley was right; hardship doesn't always cause callouses. It can soften, too. Number twenty-four now found it easier to be kind.

'This wasn't my idea.' Jane routed Helena, who'd already posted four selfies with the woman of the hour. 'Tom organised it. We just did as we were told.'

Sarah had kept away from Tom, like a dieter who doesn't

trust herself at the Pick 'n' Mix counter. Now that everybody looked his way, Zelda raising her glass, it was safe for Sarah to study him.

Graham, drunk and garrulous, slapped Tom on the back, and Helena murmured something about him being a dish. The dish stared back at Sarah and jerked his head towards the kitchen as he left the room.

She hesitated. It was only a second or two but Sarah felt a couple of lifetimes go by. She looked at Jane, who was head to head with Zelda. She looked at Leo, who was staring at the ceiling, probably because Sarah couldn't possibly be up there. She looked down at Una, who waved one of Mikey's paws at her.

And then she followed Tom, because she could see her route to the kitchen laid out in glowing footprints. She had to do it. Her life had narrowed to this moment in this shabby flat with this man, as if the house in her heart had always kept a room ready for him.

The kitchenette was not itself. Some brave soul had polished the windows and scoured the tiles and laundered the curtains.

First things first. 'Where's Camilla?'

'Gone home. Gone for good. Just gone.' Tom was breathless, like a student about to take a career-defining exam.

'Were you kind?'

'Of course. She guessed. She's always known.'

'What has she always known?' Sarah moved a little closer. For now, she enjoyed the fact that they weren't touching.

'She guessed that it's you, Sarah. That it's always been you.' Tom smiled, as if this fact relaxed him with its obviousness.

Sarah closed her eyes. He was good. He was kind. At this distance he was insanely sexy. 'Tom, are you too good to be true?'

He grabbed her, and Sarah felt his mouth press against her forehead.

'Is this it?' whispered Tom against her fringe. 'Can we finally let it bloody well happen?'

Sarah tilted her head. They kissed, with the old-lady milk jugs and doilies and oven gloves as witnesses.

'Thank you,' said Sarah.

'For the party?' asked Tom.

Their diction was slurred by the kissing.

'For giving me a chance.'

'Shut up,' he laughed. It was hard to laugh and kiss; things got messy. 'What else could I do, you crazy woman?'

'I think I love you, Tom.' Sarah gulped. *It's too soon!* She pulled away. 'Sorry, Tom. I'm exhausted, and now this, it's got me all . . .'

'I love you too,' said Tom. 'Even when you didn't love me back, when you were making cow eyes at Leo. When you told me I was evil and dangerous. I loved you then.' He held her face in his hands, the better to look into her eyes. 'It's like when orphan chimps are imprinted on whatever they see first, even if it's an old tyre or something. They love that tyre and they want to be with it.'

'I'm your old tyre?'

'You really are.'

'Tom, we don't have to go this fast.' Sarah couldn't be flippant. She'd lost so much. Whether this was love or something very like it, she wanted to insulate it, keep it safe.

'I know we don't have to go fast. Which is precisely why I want to. Your dad was right. About you. About a lot of things.'

'How'd you mean?' Sarah leaned against him, savouring the way he didn't sway. Even the smarmed peroxide hair was acceptable. *It'll grow out.* And Sarah would get to see it. Their future was unfolding, like a flower, in that very moment.

'When he said you're perfect the way you are. That you're good enough.'

'He was talking about you, too.' She was soppy. Super soppy. Tom was a drug.

'You're sure?'

'About you? Yup.'

'About Leo. About not needing a father figure. Because I don't think I'm up to that role.'

Sarah heard the tremor in his voice. She fixed her eyes on him, soppy no longer. 'I don't need a father figure, Tom. I have a perfectly good father. He just happens to be dead. He's still with me. Up here.' She tapped her head. 'In here.' She laid her hand on her chest.

A fluttering bird folded its wings inside Sarah. A peace descended. She gave up struggling against her mother's accusations and accepted that, yes, she was just like her dad. *And that's fine.* He hadn't been a hero and he hadn't been a cad; he'd been himself.

'Hey. Where have you gone?' Tom lifted her chin with his finger. Their mouths were so close that their breath mingled.

'Nowhere. I'm back.' Sarah squeezed him. He felt just as bulky and warm as her fantasies had led her to believe. 'We've wasted so much time.'

'Time officially starts ... *now.*' Tom marked the moment with a kiss. 'No regrets, OK?'

Sarah, who believed that the best strategy for coping with life was to keep dreams small and hopes modest, leaned against Tom's chest, lost in a dream so vast she could wander its halls forever.

'Speech!' shouted somebody from the sitting room.

Emerging sheepishly to a good-natured burst of knowing applause, Sarah and Tom saw Zelda on her feet. She'd combed her hair, put her face to rights and was a *grande dame* once more.

'Even though I earn my living writing,' she began, looking around her, lingering on each face, 'I can't find the words to thank you for tonight. This is more than just food and drink. It's a rebirth.' She found Sarah and said, in her direction, 'I've felt trapped in this house. I've longed to get away. We all of us feel that way sometimes.'

Sarah nodded, her head on Tom's shoulder.

Zelda winked. It was unexpected from such an

aristocratic individual. 'But my chains aren't chains at all. They're ribbons. I could break them easily, but I find I don't want to. If you'll have me, I would love to stay on at number twenty-four.'

'Of course we'll have you!' shouted Jane over the cheers.

'Don't worry, Zelda,' said Una. 'Me and Mikey will visit you in prison.'

Chapter Twenty-Five

℃ONFU℃IU⑤ FᴀKEᴀWᴀY
Notting Hill, W11

UNDER NEW MANAGEMENT
Thursday 24th August, 2017

A LITTLE FRAGRANCE CLINGS
TO THE HAND THAT GIVES ROSES

Notting Hill prepares for carnival every year with the same gusto, the same combination of practicality and *joie de vivre*. Draped with bunting, number twenty-four fitted right in, but the flourishes were nothing to do with the carnival.

'Is this too much glitter?' Sarah held up a sign that said 'Congratulations!' She and Una had collaborated and she regretted giving the child a free hand.

'There's no such thing as too much glitter.' Jane was folding a stack of paper napkins at Sarah's kitchen table, hampered a little by the baby strapped to her front in a jersey sling. Now four months old, Ben had arrived early, with maximum stress and drama, but had been forgiven everything just for being Ben. Sarah reached out to take one of his waxy little fingers; he looked enough like his

Uncle Tom to make her want to laugh and cry at the same time.

You're all I've got of him, she thought, lapsing into melodrama. The baby gazed steadily back, already an old soul in his Petit Bateau onesie.

'Sarah, take him while I make a call.'

Bundled into Sarah's arms, Ben was just as happy there as he was with his mother, who turned her back to say, 'Hi is that *Newsnight*?' The saying goes that it takes a village to raise a child; it took a house to rear this one. The camaraderie triggered by Zelda's arrest one year ago still held strong; the residents were a team.

Of sorts; Jane and Graham would never see eye to eye on *anything*, and Sarah hated to be left alone with Leo, but Una roamed from flat to flat like a free-range hen and they all pulled together when necessary, such as Zelda needing practical support with her court case or Ben needing a babysitter.

'Let's sit down while your mummy makes her big important phone call.' Sarah's flat had changed shape. The layout had altered, but the air of mild apocalypse had returned, with different holes in different walls.

It's defying my attempts to finish it.

Sarah had entertained daydreams of herself and Tom on matching ladders, splashing paint about and breaking off to make boisterous love on the floor. Things rarely work out the way we imagine; which is why Sarah's mind hopped like a nervous bird looking for a comfortable branch on this momentous day.

What'll I do if Zelda goes to prison?

That, Sarah knew, was selfish; the real victim would be Zelda. Sending her to jail would be like keeping an orchid in a coal hole.

The women relied on each other. The void left by Sarah's mother was partly filled by Zelda; Sarah wasn't sure what deficiency she helped ease in the older woman's life but she knew that Zelda needed her, and it was nice to be needed.

Una barged in. 'Mummy sent me.' She made a beeline for Ben.

Mummy often sent her; Lisa's new romance was a fragile entity, not helped by Una's non-stop yammering.

One day, maybe, Sarah would disclose to Lisa that the landlord who'd rewired, replumbed, and redecorated Flat D was her nearest neighbour. Mavis had enjoyed listening to Lisa's complaints about the damp and the disintegrating carpet, while never revealing that she herself was the good-for-nothing landlord. Zelda had anonymously brought the property up to scratch.

'Let's plait your hair, Una.'

'Yes!' Una clapped. 'Zelda likes my plaits, doesn't she?'

'She sure does.' Sarah had noticed this compulsion to end each statement with a question mark. *To ensure she's answered.* The silence was over, but its aftermath would last a lifetime. Nobody knew that better than Sarah. She thought about Albie and hoped his day was going OK. He was having the first supervised contact with his father round about now; the child had high hopes, but the father was slippery. *I'll ring his mum later.* Later . . . when she knew Zelda's fate.

'Will the judge let Zelda go?' asked Una.

'We hope so.' With Ben slumped like a warm doughnut on her lap, Sarah braided Una's hair. Against everybody's wishes, Zelda had gone alone to the last day of her trial, and number twenty-four was on a news lockdown; they would hear the verdict from Zelda's own lips.

Or from her lawyer, if Zelda was given a custodial sentence. Sarah shied from that image, like a pony refusing a gate.

A male voice said, 'Don't get your hopes up, ladies,' and Jamie stepped through a massive puncture in the wall. 'I keep warning you. Prepare yourselves.'

'I say this with love,' said Jane, setting down her phone. 'But shut up, darling.' She was holding herself together with hope and party planning.

Zelda was number twenty-four's pet, mascot, and queen rolled into one. Super-fan Jane had appointed herself guard dog. She curated the website committed to telling Zelda's side of the story, and fielded the myriad interview requests for the novelist turned *cause célèbre*. '*Newsnight* want to talk to Zelda after the verdict.'

'If she's set free,' said Jamie, who saw everything in black and white. The untidiness of civilian life baffled him; he was the only estate agent Sarah knew of who could take out a terrorist with an L85A2 5.56mm rifle. Jane's advance publicity had led Sarah to expect a superhero: witty; handsome;

stunning. In the flesh Jamie was forgettable; until, that is, you realised what a talent he had for loving.

Jamie loved Jane with every inch of his ordinary body, and now he loved his son that way, too. There was plenty left over for his wife's friends, so Sarah and Zelda were invited into ordinary old Jamie's extraordinary heart. Sarah felt safe with him in the house, especially when she was looking around her decimated flat and missing Tom.

Success has its price. There was nothing 9–5 about Tom's new career. When he waved goodbye to Sarah he could be gone for a week, a month, or longer. Right now, making a movie with two of his heroes, Tom was far away in all senses of the word; Venezuela might as well be a different planet. Mobile phone coverage was, as you might expect, patchy in the Amazon. Sarah dreamed some nights that they had a long, cosy phone chat and would wake up disappointed that it was all in her imagination.

'We all know that Zelda's judge is infamously hard-line on fraud cases.' Jamie filched a tartlet from a tray. Sarah had seen the long list of chores assigned to Jamie; they all involved moving cutesy items – jam jars full of flowers/ fairy lights/tissue paper pompoms – from the house to the garden. He'd been up and down the stairs countless times; he'd muttered that he'd rather do an army assault course. 'We must face facts.'

'We mustn't,' said Jane. 'Facts can get lost.' She swept up Ben, kissing the top of Una's head as she did so. 'Zelda got off last time. On the assisted suicide charge.'

'No, love, she didn't *get off.* The CPS decided it wasn't in the public interest to prosecute.' Jamie clocked the baby's gurn. 'Uh-oh. That's his poo face.'

'So it is.' Sarah held Ben out to Jamie. Jamie folded his arms. The stand-off stretched until Jamie said, with sarcasm as heavy as his son's nappy, 'Oh. OK. I'll change him, shall I?'

'Try and change him for a baby who doesn't poo his own weight every couple of hours,' said Jane, handing him over.

'This waiting is horrible.' Sarah primped the bow at the end of Una's plait; the child was fussy. And vocal. 'I should be in court with Zelda.'

'You heard her. She was adamant.' Jane looked out at the garden below them. 'Helena's setting the table all wrong.'

'Let her.' If Zelda didn't come home, the table settings wouldn't matter. A year ago, Sarah had been jubilant when Zelda announced her decision to stay on at number twenty-four. A few weeks later, Tom had pulled out of buying the flat in Chiswick, and said he was staying, too. He'd bought out Leo and moved into the attic with Sarah. Now he was absent more than he was at home.

The basement had been remodelled in its owner's image. Workmen had crawled over it like ants, transforming it in weeks, putting Sarah's never-ending refurbishment to shame. Now Flat E was a five-star oasis of seagrass flooring, hand-blocked wallpaper, and serious artwork.

One detail didn't change. The chipped, wobbly table where Mavis had eaten her lonely meal, stood in the midst of the glamour. 'It has a story to tell,' Zelda had said, stroking its pockmarked surface. 'This is where my sister and I made our plans. And where I served you our weekly meal, Sarah.' The table would remain as all around it changed. 'To remind me of my incredible second chance.'

Many times Zelda had told Sarah she was calm at the prospect of a prison sentence. It was, she said, 'a risk I had to run'.

There was support from the wider world. People warmed to her courage, her vulnerability, her eloquence. Many old friends had forgiven Zelda and turned up, eager to help; others stayed away and wrote damning articles. Ramon was especially prolific: not a week passed without his photogenic features above a few paragraphs of astringent newsprint.

Zelda had leaned on Sarah throughout the separate investigations of both Mavis's suicide and the resulting identity fraud; the publication of *Our Meeting Place was Midnight*; and the emergence of saviours and foes. Their friendship had ripened, as Sarah, in her turn, leaned on Zelda on the days when missing Tom got too much for her.

Days like today. Sarah willed her phone to ring, or her computer to chirrup, but there was only echoing silence. Her man was deep in a jungle; mercifully, he was only pretending to be a soldier, but the big-budget movie kept them apart as surely as a war.

Sarah followed Jane down the stairs, their arms full of party doodahs. Una plodded carefully ahead, placing both feet on each step, carrying her own contribution of misshapen jam tarts, some garnished with cat hair. 'Did you call the publishers about pre-orders, Jane?'

'They're through the roof!' Zelda's new semi-autobiographical novel, *The Basement*, was due for release after the bank holiday. All profits would go to a frontotemporal dementia charity, proving, perhaps, that even the darkest of clouds have a silver lining.

It was all hands on deck as the table was tweaked, and lanterns were fixed to trees, and buckets were filled with ice. Not as ardent as the previous summer, August did its best, but a storm lay in wait at the fringes of the day; Sarah saw how Jane ignored the brief insistent blasts of cautionary cold. The other residents were in a defiant, this-*is*-fun mood. Over-laughing at pale jokes, over-praising the home-made food, number twenty-four staved off the moment of truth. Graham hoisted Una onto his shoulders as Lisa placed a sleepy Mikey on a cushion of leaves. Leo handed out wine. Helena shadowed Jane around the table, reinstating each change she made. A jug of sunflowers, slightly droopy, took centre stage.

Off to one side, Jamie was lost in Ben, their noses close, when his head jerked back. 'D'you hear that?' he called out.

A toot-toot, bold in the still afternoon, turned all heads towards the house. Police had cordoned off Merrion Road; supposedly for the carnival preparations, but actually to keep paparazzi away from the gate. Some loyal and well-placed chum of Zelda's had the power to do this.

'Keep calm.' Jamie switched to officer mode. 'It could be a neighbour coming through, so let's just take it slowly.'

Nobody took the slightest bit of notice. A stampede coursed through the house.

A black cab was at the kerb. Sarah pounded to the gate. Ready for the worst, she stood impassively as the others caught up, bracing herself to see Zelda's lawyer. The back door of the cab opened, and out stepped Tom.

'But you're in Venezuela!' accused Sarah.

Smart in a dark suit, Tom held out his hand to assist Zelda as she quit the cab with the elegance of a debutante.

Deafened by the cheers – even the policemen and paps at the end of the road joined in – Sarah's sudden tears blinded her. A group hug enveloped Zelda and carried her through the house, and into the garden, where music boomed, corks popped and Leo yelled, 'I told you so!'

'You're free!' Sarah hugged Zelda, hard, as if checking she was real.

'Suspended sentence,' said Zelda. 'They really listened.'

'I can't take it in. You're here. You're *here!*'

'Shush now.' Zelda dabbed at Sarah's eyes with a handkerchief. 'You're the strong one, remember? You're the girl who saved my life.'

'You did the same for me,' sniffled Sarah.

'I think,' said Zelda, playful again after a year of stress, 'that was somebody else's doing.'

'In here.' Tom dragged Sarah into the shed. It was dark, and musty-smelling – the pong of life in all its dark and dirty glory. He put his lips to Sarah's and she fell upwards, if such a thing is possible, into the kiss.

Surfacing, they clung to each other.

'You're in Venezuela,' said Sarah. 'With no internet and crap-at-best phone coverage.'

'I'm right here.' Tom kissed her nose, daintily this time, as if she was poorly. 'And I'm staying.'

'The shoot doesn't wrap for another month.'

'I quit.'

'You can't do that! They'll sue you. They'll say things like you'll never work in this town again.'

'They've already said it, but who cares? Leave it to the lawyers.' Tom's smile created dimples deep enough to paddle in.

'Wait, wait, wait.' Sarah untangled herself from the cat's cradle of his embrace. 'You can't give it up for me.' She'd tried so hard to keep her loneliness to herself. Knowing Tom was fulfilling his most cherished fantasy, she'd kept the sighing to a bare minimum. *But he knew.* Anybody who loved Sarah the way Tom did would know.

'I'm giving it up for us. I'd rather be here.'

'We said we'd take the long view. We'd make it work. You're an actor, Tom.' Sometimes Sarah forgot her husband was famous. Then she'd spot his face three feet high on a bus. There was the Tom Royce who massaged her feet during *Downton* re-runs, and there was the Tom Royce who fought duels and kissed celebrated beauties and had a cameo in the most vulgar, witless, Hollywood buddy movie Sarah had ever seen.

Sarah had been born in the moment she and Tom got

together. Before that she'd been a floating dust mote; her histrionics over Leo seemed comic when she compared him to Tom. It wasn't that Tom was 'better' than Leo – although he was – it was more that Tom was hers and she was Tom's.

Life had rolled out like a red carpet. Sarah relaxed into her career and into her friendships. She'd found the sweet spot in a cold bed; Sarah was doing the work she was born to do, alongside the man she was born to love.

There'd been a wedding. A party not unlike this one, with Sarah and Tom in new clothes. Zelda made a speech; Keeley heckled; Jane filled out her maid-of-honour frock with the outlines of soon-to-be-born Ben. They'd retired at dawn for legal, rather sleepy, married sex in a new bed in Flat A.

Something had happened between that fresh spring day and this high point of summer, and now the flat was chaotic with a second set of building works and Tom was never there.

'It's like the army,' Jamie had commented when shown the filming schedules. On his agent's advice, Tom had accepted back-to-back roles in two major projects; after years of fantasising about success, he was loath to say 'no' to opportunity.

'I'll pop home when I'm not needed on set,' he'd promised.

Jane had scoffed. 'Pop home from Venezuela?'

The small print was implacable. Before the four months in Venezuela, there'd been a month in upstate New York, pretending to be an English stockbroker who'd murdered his mistress.

Zelda, who'd read the script and guessed the ending,

counselled caution about coming home for the odd week-end. 'You'll be jet-lagged and distracted.'

As so often, Zelda was right. Tom's sporadic forty-eight hour stopovers had been disastrous. He snoozed; she woke him with a shove; he felt bad; she felt bad; he fell asleep over the dinner she'd made; he woke up at midnight just as she nodded off. Sarah had longed for Tom to say he was quitting and coming home, but now here he was, saying exactly that, and she was devastated.

'Absolutely not.' Sarah screwed up her face. 'We can't be that couple. The idiots who can't be apart. We should be able to do this, Tom. I can't scupper your career just because I get lonely at nights. I'll get a cat. I'll move Mikey in. I won't let you abandon your dream for me.'

'You're the dream, stupid.' Tom held her tight. 'Listen. I've proved I can do this movie star lark. And I've proved I don't like it. Whereas *you* ...' He smiled, the long slow smile that spoke straight to the red-hot centre of Sarah. 'You I like. You I love. Living here is the dream.' He folded her against his chest. 'It's not that you miss me, Sarah. That's only half the story. I miss *you*.'

'I could come with you.' Sarah's voice was muffled by his chest, a small price to pay for being up close to such a nice slab of flesh.

'Come on, Sarah, you *are* your work. You need St Chad's, and St Chad's needs you. You can't do it just anywhere. It's only actors who are nomads. You're the sensible one, remember?'

'I don't want to tie you down, Tom.' Sarah knew that resentment was a ticking time bomb in the foundation of the most solid relationships. 'I'll deal with it. It'll get easier.' She only half believed that. Being this close to Tom filled up her senses, unleashed a lust that was part sexual, part emotional, all irresistible. Tom was her holy grail. He was her cream tea, her hot bath, her rodeo ride. 'I'm greedy for you, Tom. That's all.'

'That's *all*?' laughed Tom. 'I've waited my whole life for somebody to be greedy about me. Let's give in! Let's do what we want to do.' Tom cleared a spot on a wooden box, and perched on the edge of it. 'Sit.' He patted his thighs.

Obediently, Sarah sat. Thousands of *Vile Bodies* fans would swap places with her if they could. She remembered, with a pang, Camilla's brave, wan face at the wedding. Perhaps he was right and they should make the most of each other.

'I'm not giving up this shoot for you, OK?' Tom was grave. 'I'm giving it up for me, and for us. I don't enjoy it. There.' Tom shrugged. 'I've said it.' His head lolled back and he let out a deep growl.

Sarah listened as Tom let it all out. How he'd tried to tell his agent that the high-profile films were sapping the life out of him. 'I want to do some Stoppard, some Feydeau, but I've been offered a fart-joke comedy that'll make millions on its opening weekend.'

'Hang on.' Sarah got comfortable on the bouncy castle of

her husband's lap. 'Does this mean we have to stop laughing at fart jokes?'

'Not at all,' said Tom earnestly. 'Fart jokes are still very much on the agenda. But please don't make me act in movies that rely on them.' The last couple of weeks had been hard on Tom. He described insomniac nights in an opulent tree house wishing he were back in their attic love nest.

Sarah leaned against Tom, liking the idea that their yearning hearts had met somewhere in the middle of the vast space between them. Now those hearts were close again and the sadness fell away.

'Two days ago something clicked. Me and Sarah, I thought, we don't need the big bucks. I can definitely get by without being interviewed by *Hello!* magazine. If success means getting what you really want, I already have it. Only problem was, what I really wanted was 5,000 miles away.'

'Me!'

'Yes, you. I was straight with my director and my co-stars, some of whom were great, one of whom tried to kill me with her shoe. It took a day to get to London.' Tom grimaced. 'We'll be in a legal mess for a while, but hey, this house is used to that, isn't it? The stakes won't be so high this time. I already have another job.'

'Loving me?' said Sarah, hopefully.

'No, well, I mean, *yes*, obviously.' Tom laughed at Sarah's half-serious outrage. 'But apart from that, I've been asked to do a new play in the West End. Of London,' he clarified, as she continued to look confused. 'A commitment of six months, but I've said I'll stay on if it's a hit.' He tightened his grip around her. 'Work will be a Tube ride away. I'll come home every night.'

'Ooh.' Sarah savoured that thought. It was cold champagne after weeks of room-temperature water. 'What's the play?'

'You can read it later. Funny. Moving. Gritty. Incredible cast.'

'You sound excited.'

'I am.'

Tom hadn't sounded excited about Venezuela; he'd sounded incredulous, gobsmacked, as if he'd wanted to ask if they were sure they had the right guy.

'So, Mr Royce, you're home for good.'

'Yes, Mrs Royce, I am.' Tom squeezed her until she gasped. 'Let's finally finish off our flat, OK?'

'You're a one-off, Tom Royce.' Tom had seen through fame, rejected it, and taken back his destiny. 'Suspended and sentence,' said Sarah, as they rejoined the party, 'aren't interesting words in their own right, but if you put them together you come up with my new favourite phrase.'

'It's rather a relief,' said Zelda, with the cut-glass understatement her readers relished. 'Can you conceive my astonishment, Sarah, when this gorgeous chap appeared in the courtroom?'

'I went straight there from the airport. I assumed it was the most likely place to find my wife, but Zelda was on her own.'

'And regretting my martyrdom. I needed my darling Sarah after all.' Zelda bowed her head at the vehement 'See!' from her left. 'Poor me, I had to make do with a movie star. He's made of strong stuff, your Tom. Finding his eye during those ghastly proceedings helped.'

'Was Ramon there?'

'No. Ramon was absent and that's for the best.' Ramon was in the throes of divorcing his dead wife; Zelda contested nothing, had given him all the money and property he thought he'd inherited, but Ramon hankered after blood. Zelda's tone of voice made it clear that the subject was closed. 'I feel like getting drunk.'

'You hussy,' said Tom. 'Me too.' He raised his fist. 'To the booze!'

Well ahead of them in this mission, Jane was performing a hybrid conga/tango of her own devising, alongside Helena, whose heels sank in the grass as she swayed. 'Dance with me, bro!' she ordered, strong-arming Tom away from the ladies.

Depositing Zelda on a chair, Sarah went in search of wine. She found Una's parents hovering by the array of drinks.

Despite having married his 'other woman', Graham struggled to hide his jealousy of Lisa's new boyfriend, a man he referred to as 'the toy boy' because he was two months younger than Lisa.

'Is Una all right?' asked Lisa over the rim of a plastic tumbler.

'She's dancing with Mikey.' Sarah accepted the way they deferred to her as a nanny figure when they felt like it. The couple weren't wildly likeable, with their petty grievances and their fondness for a scrap, but they were part of number twenty-four, and had to be embraced.

'Did I tell you?' Lisa grasped Sarah's arm. 'About my rent? It's gone *down*. Rents never go down, do they?'

'Well, yours has,' said Sarah.

'I feel secure,' said Lisa, 'for the first time in years.'

'Is that a dig at me?' Graham wanted to know, as he and Lisa wandered away, taking their endless rolling squabble to another part of the garden. Their departure revealed Leo, helping himself to Merlot.

Spotting Sarah, he became furtive, as if the Merlot was contraband. Neither of them spoke as Sarah browsed the bottles, until eventually Leo said, 'So. Well. You must be relieved. About Zelda.'

'I can't quite take it in, to be honest.' Sarah and Leo never spoke. Sarah had cauterised the wound when she'd finally lopped him off.

'You're very close, you and Zelda. I guess she makes up for your mum not being around.'

'My mum *is* around. We speak once a month. At least, I call her and she endures me.'

Now that Sarah had finally accepted her mother's theory that she was 'just like' her father, she was proud to share qualities with her dad. Bitterness evaporated as happiness wormed its way in. Sarah had ditched the perspective of a child and saw her parents as fellow adults. Her father had saved his own life – what little of it was left – by separating from her mother. He'd never relinquished his duties towards Sarah; it would have been so easy to belittle her mum, but instead he'd shored up the mother/daughter relationship.

His counsel that she see the beauty in everybody had been his last gift. Even though the beauty in her mother was hard to find, Sarah did her best to seek it out. She owed it to her father.

'Zelda's no substitute,' she told Leo. 'Zelda's my friend.'

They stood, glasses in hand, their backs to the buffet table, like awkward wedding guests reaching for small talk.

'I see Tom's home,' said Leo, nodding at where Tom danced with his sister, approximately in time to the music.

'Yeah,' said Sarah. There was a pause long enough for her to wonder at the distance that can exist between two people who were once each other's all in all. 'How is she, Leo? Really?'

'Not good.' Leo looked at his sex-bomb wife, hips swinging, arms in the air, waterfall of hair covering her face. 'I want to try again, but . . . Christ, you of all people, you don't want to hear this, Sarah.'

'I do.' Sarah inched closer.

'It's nine months since she, since, you know.' Leo and Helena had lost their daughter before she'd finished growing inside her mother. Leo was thinner these days, less of a dandy, his flamboyance dimmed. He, too, moved closer. 'Some days we're on the same page and we talk. Laugh even.

405

Other days she's flat and I can't reach her. Then she'll rally, but me? I'm down all of a sudden.'

'You're still together. That says a lot.' The couple's staying power had astonished Sarah. Other, sturdier, pairings collapsed under this sort of tragedy but Leo and Helena soldiered on. She'd assumed their bond was based on status and lust and tangible things.

The green-eyed monster messed with my head.

Love was what held the Harrisons together; nothing else is that durable. 'She's the one for you, Leo.' As he glanced sharply at her, checking for sarcasm, Sarah said, 'I once thought you only liked the beginnings of love, when everything's new and shiny. You proved me wrong. And I'm glad.'

Leo sank the rest of his glass. 'My wife's a hell of a woman. But she's frightened of trying for another baby.' He looked down at his body. 'And I'm not getting any younger.'

'Who is?' A year ago this conversation would have burned off the top layer of Sarah's skin. Now she could comfort Leo. 'When the time's right, it'll happen. Or not. Just love her, Leo, and be kind. And don't . . .' She raised her eyebrows.

'God, no, I wouldn't, not now. Those days are gone.' Leo sighed. 'I couldn't cheat on Helena.'

It was an open goal, but Sarah didn't add 'again'. 'The trip will help. Exotic destinations. Odd food. New faces.'

'That's the idea. Costing me a bloody fortune.'

Sarah rolled her eyes; Leo hadn't changed completely.

Jamie, who wouldn't know a strained atmosphere if it smacked him on the bottom, joined them with Ben in the crook of his beefy arm. 'So, Leo, mate, when are you off on this round-the-world adventure?'

'Tomorrow.' Leo stared hard at the baby.

'The new people in your flat seem friendly enough. Hope you screwed them on the price.' Jamie laughed and Ben stirred and Leo looked away, as if blinded by the baby's reality.

'They're idiots,' said Leo. 'They're going to change the layout, even though it was conceived by a famous interior designer.' He turned to Sarah. 'Aren't you? Why not buy a bigger flat with your husband's Hollywood cash instead of knocking together two floors in this old pile?'

After looking half-heartedly at properties Jane showed them with stainless-steel kitchens, marble bathrooms, and utility rooms you could swing a lion in, Sarah had said, in a little girl voice she only ever used around Tom, 'I don't want to leave number twenty-four.'

She was cemented in place, part of the structure. So long as Zelda was in the basement, Sarah couldn't leave. It was duty, yes, but not only that; the house was full of love, stuffed with it, love leaking through its seams.

'Think about it,' she'd said to Tom, trying to convince him. 'Two floors beneath us Jane has our nephew in her tummy. On the floor below *that,* Una's chatting up a storm and Lisa relies on us all far more than she'd ever admit. And across the landing from those two is Zelda. She'll need us when the dust settles. And I need her, in a thousand ways I can't describe.' She'd been exultant, not wheedling, when she'd declared, 'We belong here!'

Tom had agreed that it was good to belong, and they'd made an offer Leo couldn't refuse.

Now, in the garden, Sarah said to Leo, 'Thanks for leaving that oh-so witty chandelier.' She and Tom had been touched, even though it would look out of place in the bright, cheerful new duplex they had planned. Sarah had stipulated 'No antiques'.

When Jamie wandered away, showing off Ben to his eager fans, Leo said, 'I'm sorry. About everything.'

'Shut up,' smiled Sarah. 'It's over. We both learned a lot.' She pulled a wry face. 'It wasn't our finest hour.'

'But we did have some. Fine hours, I mean.'

'We did OK,' agreed Sarah.

'Le-*o*!' Helena was done with dancing.

'Time to go,' said Leo.

They didn't embrace, but their goodbye was shot through with kindness.

'There you are! At last!' Zelda was saying, rising from her chair, crossing the grass to greet somebody.

But we're all here, thought Sarah, tucking a flower from one of the posies on the table into her hair. The dusk was trying to gain a foothold, but high summer doesn't give up that easily and the garden was still bright.

A woman was being introduced to the others, her back to Sarah. It didn't make sense. Yet there she was.

Sarah reached her just as Tom shook Smith's hand.

'What are you doing here?' Unvarnished, it sounded unfriendly.

'Zelda invited me. I can go. If you want.'

Zelda took the young woman's arm. 'You've only just arrived, dear.' *Dee-ah*. 'Do try the jam tarts. They're . . . interesting.' Steering Smith away, she sent Sarah an unmistakable message with the merest incline of her head. 'Manners!'

Sarah read Tom like a book. 'You knew about this and you never said a word!'

'Zelda told me on the way back from court.' Tom smiled. 'Even though she'd just had the biggest news of her life, she wanted to talk about *you*.'

'Tell.' Sarah prodded him. He was taller but she was meaner. '*Tell*, Tom.'

'Zelda tracked her down, and they began to email each other. Don't ask me what about. I'm just rehashing what Zelda told me. Then Zelda suggested she might like to come to this bash.'

Zelda, you sly old puss, thought Sarah. She strode over to Smith.

Zelda backed away into the gathering dusk.

'Am I welcome?' Smith was tamed, with hair that was just brown, and an outfit that was just an outfit.

'Even if you weren't, you were invited by the guest of honour, so . . .' Sarah frowned. 'If Jane hadn't spotted you in Suffolk, would you ever have reappeared?'

'I couldn't.' Smith popped her sunglasses back on, TV-sized shades that hid her eyes and robbed her face of nuance. 'I was dead, remember.'

'Did you *want* to get in touch?' Sarah laid her heart bare;

life was too short – or was it too long? – not to be frank. 'I missed you so much. Every day.'

'Don't, Sarah. I'm a bitch. I can't undo all the shit I unleashed. I'm bad, like I said. And you're not. Standing near you helps me feel a bit less dark. But it probably makes you feel like strangling me.'

There'd been a reason why Sarah had told Smith – and not Leo – about her childhood mutism. She'd known she'd be understood, not judged or turned into an anecdote. *Smith didn't try to fix me.* She'd just given of herself, stood beside her. *She shared the burden and that was all I needed.*

Forgiveness, like abs and glutes, responds well if regularly exercised. Sarah had tried hard to understand Smith, but hadn't been able to make that leap. In the end it hadn't been necessary; instead she accepted her, with all her glaring imperfections. 'I still miss you, actually.'

'Well, no need to miss me any more! I'm here. If you'll have me.'

That was the cue for a speech, but Sarah said only, 'You'd better behave, lady.' This was a day of grand emotions and big gestures. It was a day to be generous, and to believe. She reached over and removed the sunglasses, laying bare Smith's worried features. 'There's only one rule. No faking your own death.'

'I promise.' Smith was meek but Sarah sensed her chutzpah waiting in the wings. 'I won't let you down.'

'Don't put it like that,' grimaced Sarah. 'There's nothing to live up to. I just want you as my mate, Smith.'

Tom, keeping a respectful distance, gave up pretending not to listen. Cupping his hands around his mouth, he hollered, 'This is where you hug each other!'

They did as they were told. And it was good.

The party dwindled, as even the best parties must. Lisa and Graham took their argument indoors, tailed by Una, who was singing very loudly. Mikey took off into the shrubbery to do whatever it is that one-eyed hedgehogs do all night. The lights went off in Leo and Helena's flat for the last time.

Smith was smashed, fast asleep in a deckchair. Jane had been invalided indoors by Jamie, a living testament to the folly of mixing vodka and quiche.

On a bench, in a row, sat Sarah, Zelda and Tom, passing around the snoozing Ben like a bag of sweets.

'I really should feed poor Peck,' said Zelda.

'Jamie fed him. And yes, before you ask, it was a mix of his favourite pellets and some organic banana cut to the right size.' Peck's quarters had been upgraded along with his mistress's; his cage was a white ironwork extravaganza, customised with a swing and a mirror and real branches for him to stand on and pontificate. 'That bird lives like a sultan.'

'Mavis adored him.' Zelda exhaled sleepily, like a kitten. It was a sad sound, for a poignant night. 'Peck was the only thing she truly loved. So he's a monument to her, and he'll always have a home with me.'

'They live to seventy years old, you know.'

'I'll leave him to somebody who'll appreciate him.'

'You mean me, don't you?' sighed Sarah.

Tom, who had beak-shaped scars on his forearms, said, 'Doesn't the constant abuse get you down?'

'I've learned to tune him out,' said Zelda. 'He's not as witty as Ramon.' She paused before saying, 'But he's cheaper.' She felt Sarah draw breath and she pre-empted her by saying, 'No ranting about Ramon tonight, dear.'

'He was a bad, bad husband,' said Sarah. 'Unlike Charles.' Sarah felt as if she knew the man. 'Or Tom,' she added, a little late. 'And Jamie.'

'Jamie,' said Zelda, 'is the most uxorious man I've ever encountered.'

'You and your ten-dollar words,' said Tom. 'What does uxorious mean?'

'It means excessively fond of your wife, excessively submissive to her,' said Zelda, enjoying Tom's sardonic agreement. 'Not only does Jamie allow Jane to boss him around, he *enjoys* it.'

'He's so gentle with her.' Women notice how their friends' menfolk treat them. Sarah had derived great pleasure watching Jamie guide Jane away from the dregs of the booze and suggest, mildly, that no, there wasn't time for one more dance.

'Blokes love being bossed,' said Tom. 'I can't imagine marrying a woman who expected me to make all the decisions.'

'I'll remind you of that,' said Sarah, 'next time we come to blows in Homebase.'

Since Ben arrived, Sarah had noticed the frayed edges of

Jane's certainty. Jane had prepared for motherhood, armed to the teeth with muslin squares and nursing bras and a push-chair sanctioned by *Which?* magazine but it was testing her.

'Why won't he sleep?' she wailed in the middle of the night. 'Why won't he take my milk?' she mewled in the middle of the day. Ben was hell-bent on proving he wasn't just any old baby; each day he starred in storylines of his own devising that weren't to be found in the manuals.

To Sarah, Jane could admit she wasn't up to the job, that Ben's chubby fingers found every chink in her armour. 'I can't do it,' she sobbed.

Jane believed she kept these fears from Jamie, but Sarah knew better. Jamie propped his wife up in small ways that Jane didn't notice. Sarah knew this, because she did the same. Without a word being said, she and Jamie were partners not in crime, but devotion. When Jane rediscovered her equilibrium, they'd stand down, but not before.

Taking the baby, Zelda bounced him a little. 'I thought Jamie might finally put his foot down when it came to naming this little fellow.'

'Jamie wanted to call him after his granddad.'

'Instead,' sighed Zelda, addressing the child, 'you were named after me, Bennison.' She yawned, unable to smother it as both hands were around her namesake. 'Sorry. How rude of me.'

'Zelda, you can sleep for a month after what you've been through.' Sarah took the baby, enjoying the dense weight of him.

'There's so much clearing up to do ...' Zelda looked about her helplessly.

'Leave that to us,' said Tom.

'To bed!' ordered Sarah. Relief overwhelmed her again. The storm had passed them by. *Zelda is safe.* 'What are you going to do tomorrow?'

'Write, as usual,' said Zelda. She seemed to catch Sarah's drift. 'It's really over, isn't it? That demon at my shoulder is gone.' Zelda closed her eyes, breathing in the smell of the night-blooming jasmine she'd planted, and Bennison's nappy. 'Home sweet home,' she said, and took the baby indoors.

'Alone at last,' said Tom theatrically, scooching up.

Their shoulders touched. Sarah sank into his side. He was solid and warm. There was no need to desperately make the most of him, because he was back for good, not a few snatched hours.

Tom reached out and tussled with a rose bush, managing to steal one of its big, flaky blossoms for his wife. 'For you,' he said. A little fragrance clung to his hand.

'*What* a day,' she said.

'What a life,' said Tom. 'What a house.'

The house accepted the compliment graciously. Protective, welcoming, bulky against the night sky, number twenty-four was no prison. Sarah saw the beauty in it.

It was her home.

Acknowledgements

I know a lot more about child psychologists than I did a year ago, thanks to Alison Stewart. Thank you for your calm wisdom and patience. And wine. And crisps.

This book had many midwives, all of them fussing and clucking and wanting the best for it. Thank you so much Sara-Jade Virtue, Clare Hey and Jo Dickinson, three of Simon & Schuster's finest humans. Thank you for your dedication, your energy, your cleverness, your diplomacy and your company.

Thank you Zelda and Mavis for lending me your names, and for being the most stupid spaniels I've ever met. Your snoring and your pleas for food get me through the writing day.

Finally, thank you Matthew for being my husband (never an easy job) and thank you Niamh for being my daughter, and sorry for all the *meh* dinners you endured right before deadline.

No, actually, *this* is the final thank you – to everybody who reads this book. You're the reason I do it.

If you loved reading

Turn the page for Chapter One of

Available now in paperback and eBook

The crumpled invitation had somehow survived thirty-five years and numerous house moves, its words still legible, though faded:

Kate tucked it into the corner of the dressing table mirror as she leaned in, eyeing her reflection sideways, as if trying to take it unawares. 'Not bad. Not *good*. But not bad. Happy Birthday, me!'

The invitation slipped a little and caught her eye. Kate had shared her fifth birthday party with Princess Diana's wedding day. She was ambushed by peachy nostalgia: the whole nation had been so in love with Lady Di. She remembered the mums around the TV set, ooh-ing at the new princess's dress.

And then Becca broke my new Action Man. Kate sighed. *Typical.* Her cousin had been unable to comprehend why a girl would want an Action Man, but their classmate Charlie had understood.

Kate conjured him up. Slightly whiffy and very scruffy. The other kids gave Charlie Garland a wide berth because he was different. Kate had overlooked the nits because he was also *good*-different; quiet but not boring, Charlie didn't tease the girls just for being girls.

A sudden noise jerked Kate back to the present. It sounded just like the idiosyncratic yawn of the front door scraping open. She listened hard, but heard only the silence of an empty house, a silence that is actually a gentle soundtrack of ticks and creaks.

Turning back to the mirror, Kate regarded her tired but merry eyes. *This is what forty looks like.* Kate tapped the underside of her chin in case it harboured any ideas about drooping on the threshold of her – gulp – fifth decade. All in all, her reflection didn't look too bad if she left out her contact lenses.

Standing up, Kate paused at a ghost of a noise, more a *swish* than an actual sound. She wondered at her jumpiness. *God knows, I've had enough practice at being alone.* Today, as on every other day, her house curled around her, snug and calm.

And empty. For many, forty was the perfect excuse for a party but Kate had opted out; a lifelong party goer/giver, she'd let the usual suspects know that this milestone would pass with no birthday 'do'.

Reaching into the wardrobe, Kate's hand found the dress immediately. She marvelled again at the weight of it. Pale satin, with the milky sheen of pearls, the dress was cut with a devastating simplicity that echoed more elegant times. Kate could testify to its waist-shrinking, arm-flattering superpowers.

Heavy layers of satin and tulle swooned against Kate as she held the frock against her dressing gown, holding it like a lover. The dress made her feel like Audrey Hepburn. A lumpy Audrey, admittedly, with a few more miles on the clock, but a very happy Audrey all the same. Waltzing dreamily, Kate withstood the urge to reflect and ruminate on this landmark birthday. She wouldn't dwell on the missed chances, the fluffed catches, the absentees she missed so deeply . . .

But sometimes the past pushes in without asking. Suddenly Kate was five again, blowing out the candles on her cake. Charlie had sidled up to her, to stand very close and say 'I like your dress', low and urgently, like a small spy passing on classified information. Kate remembered snapping 'What?' She'd been suspicious of compliments, mistrusting them as much as Becca craved them.

Charlie's hands had gripped his paper plate so hard it trembled. 'I love you,' he'd whispered.

Kate hadn't hesitated; she'd pushed Charlie's face into the iced sponge.

Now, Kate replaced the dress in the wardrobe, where it effortlessly outranked its denim and cotton peers. She stroked it regretfully, as if it was an exotic pet that had to be put down. *Pity I'll never get to wear you.* Kate shut the door on the wonderful confection, its skirt puffing out and resisting. Even if she dyed it or took up the hem, a dress like that could never be anything but a wedding dress, which rendered it quite useless to Kate.

She wheeled at the unmistakable sound of a foot on the stairs. Kate crossed to the door. 'Who's there?' she called, certain now that she was not alone.

BANYAN TREE
~ VABBINFARU ~

WIN A HOLIDAY OF A LIFETIME AT BANYAN TREE VABBINFARU IN THE MALDIVES!

Included in the prize:

- A seven night stay at Banyan Tree Vabbinfaru in a Beachfront Pool villa for two people
- Full board basis, incl. soft drinks, excl. alcohol
- Return transfers from Male to Banyan Tree Vabbinfaru
- Two × return economy flights from London to Male up to a value of £700 per person
- Trip to be taken between 1 November 2017 and 30 April 2018
  Blackout dates include 27 December 2017 – 5 January 2018

To enter the competition visit the website
www.simonandschuster.co.uk

Entrants must be resident in the UK only